THE NINE GODS
OF SAFADDNÉ

Antony Swithin was born in England but now lives in Canada. While still a child, the mysterious Atlantic island of Rockall came to haunt his imagination; and it has done so ever since. Over the years, his concepts of the island have evolved into a whole imaginative tapestry, rich in detail – of its geography, its fauna and flora, and the history of its peoples, so that the island emerges in his writing as a land as real as any to be found in our maps.

The Nine Gods of Safaddné is the fourth volume in a series of novels about Rockall. The first was *Princes of Sandastre*, the second *The Lords of the Stoney Mountains* and the third, *The Winds of the Wastelands*.

THE NINE GODS OF SAFADDNÉ

The Perilous Quest for Lyonesse

BOOK FOUR

Antony Swithin

Fontana
An Imprint of HarperCollinsPublishers

Fontana
An Imprint of HarperCollins*Publishers*
77–85 Fulham Palace Road,
Hammersmith, London W6 8JB

Trade paperback edition 1993

This edition published by Fontana 1993
1 3 5 7 9 8 6 4 2

Copyright © Rockall Enterprises 1993

The Author asserts the moral right to
be identified as the author of this work

ISBN 0 00 617855 3

Set in Ehrhardt

Printed in Great Britain by
HarperCollinsManufacturing Glasgow

TO RONALD AND ROGER,

my long years of friendship with
whom has made them mean
more to me than brothers

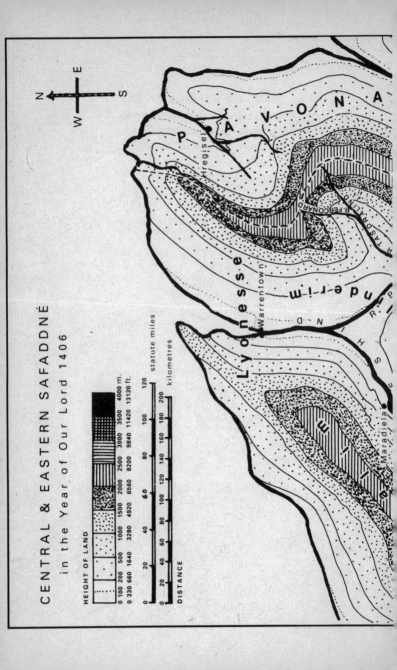

CENTRAL & EASTERN SAFADDNÉ
in the Year of Our Lord 1406

HEIGHT OF LAND

0 100 200 500 1000 1500 2000 2500 3000 3500 4000 m.
0 330 660 1640 3280 4920 6560 8200 9840 11420 13120 ft.

DISTANCE

statute miles
0 20 40 60 80 100 120

kilometres
0 20 40 60 80 100 120 140 160 180 200

PAVONA

Haegisel

Lyonesse

Warrentown

Inderim

RTASDALING

FERRONARD

Maraieia

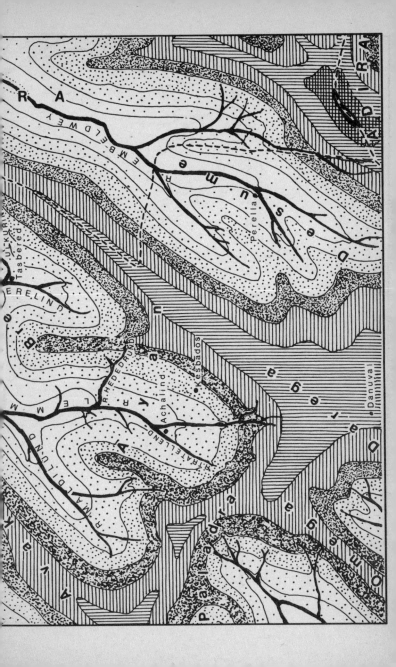

Contents

ILLUSTRATIONS

Prologue

IN SUMMARY OF SIMON BRANTHWAITE'S EARLIER NARRATIVES

The year 1403 brings a calamity to England—the defeat of Henry Hotspur by the King's forces at the Battle of Shrewsbury. Fleeing in the retreating tide of defeat from the King's wrath, Sir William Branthwaite and his eldest son Richard seek refuge by taking ship to Lyonesse, a realm recently founded by knights from England somewhere upon the mysterious Atlantic island of Rockall.

Simon Branthwaite, Sir William's younger son, had been left behind at home when his father and Richard rode away to battle. Spurning the alternative of a peaceful clerical life, he chooses to follow them to Rockall. A chance encounter in Bristol with Avran Estantesec, the youngest son of the ruling Prince of the Rockalese realm of Sandastre, leads to shared adventures and a lasting friendship.

Upon arrival in Sandarro, that realm's capital city, Simon is welcomed by his friend's family and enters into a curious friendship with a small forest animal, a vasian: thus Simon is given the new surname 'Vasianavar'. His wit and his skill with the bow strengthen the rule of the Estantesecs and confirm Simon in their regard. This regard becomes yet stronger when Simon tumbles into love with, and is provisionally betrothed to, Avran's sister Ilven. Though desiring simply to marry her and settle in Sandastre, his own vows cause Simon to leave that land behind and strike northward in quest for Lyonesse. Because of his affection for Simon and his zest for adventure, Avran accompanies him.

During the crossing of the Southern Mountains, Simon falls into the hands of a group of grey-clad riders under the leadership of an Irish mercenary, Dermot Fitzstephen. He escapes them, but without discovering their origin or intentions—a puzzle long to vex the two friends.

After a second escape, from the city of Doriolupata on the mountains' northern edge, and perilous adventures among the nomads of the yellow grasslands, Simon and Avran become part of the company of Vedlen Obiran, a wandering physician and magician from the realm of Reschora in Rockall's Northern Mountains. They traverse the great forests of central Rockall in that company and become involved in further adventures in the Stoney Mountains, an upland region south of Rockall's greatest river, the Aramassa. During these adventures, they gain a high regard for Sir Robert Randwulf, rightful Earl of Odunseth and close friend of Vedlen Obiran. When the two leave the magician's company and travel on northward, Sir Robert's wanderlust causes him to go with them.

They voyage up the Aramassa and then up its tributary the Rimbedreth. While sheltering on its bank from a tempest of wind and rain that has caused the Rimbedreth to rise dangerously, the three travellers are captured by robbers and taken to the ruined city of Kradsunar. With unexpected assistance from Essa, a girl servant of the robbers, they escape from the city, but are pursued. In a skirmish with their pursuers, Simon's skill as archer proves crucial; but he is himself severely injured. An elderly robber, Dan Wyert, is captured after the skirmish and, to elude punishment, elects to become their servant, soon becoming also the trusted friend of them all.

Simon's condition worsens and he is taken to the castle of Arravron to be healed by Dekhemet Arrav, greatest physician of Reschora, a realm in Rockall's Northern Mountains, that is renowned for medicine and magic. Simon's recovery is slow but, in the end, complete.

He and his three friends travel on to Ingelot, the northernmost city of Reschora. There they learn something of the history of the Northern Mountains—once briefly a dominion of a distant southern empire and, for much longer, the feoffdom of the pagan Safaddnese with their pantheon of nine gods. With the coming of Christianity, however, their subject peoples—the Reschorese among them—had thrown off the thralldom of the Safaddnese. In the peace treaty, a frontier was drawn that none should cross. During ensuing centuries, the Reschorese have retained so profound a mystical fear of their former overlords that the frontier never has been crossed.

Simon and his companions learn also that the realm of Lyonesse must lie somewhere beyond the Northern Mountains. The castellan of Ingelot, Toril Evateng, urges them not to travel onward; not to cross that frontier into a realm of darkness and danger. However, when they remain unpersuaded, he does not prevent them from going onward. Instead, he furnishes them with food and with furs to withstand the cold of the coming winter.

Thus equipped, the five cross into what appears a wasteland, with strange forests and seemingly barren mountains. They battle with great winds and encounter strange beasts and they chance upon high towers that have been left locked and forsaken. They become lost. After glimpsing from a mountaintop a city that they believe might be Warrentown, chief and only city of Lyonesse, they descend to it, only to find it deserted. Belatedly Essa realizes they are not in Warrentown but in Sasliith, chief city of Paladra, most sinister of the nine Safaddnese realms. They flee from the wrath of its god Mesnakech and witness, from another mountaintop, the nocturnal reoccupation of that city by a torch-bearing procession whose members, for all they know, may be humans or wraiths.

Though Essa remains enigmatic, they are by then perceiving the strength of her personality and coming to realize that she must be at least of Safaddnese blood. She has found on a forgotten battlefield a golden pendant in the likeness of a *taron*, a seabird of the northern shores, and wears it with pride. This is contrary to the urgings of Avran, who has fallen in love with her without knowing whether his love is reciprocated and who regards the Safaddnese gods as altogether evil. For Essa's part, she shows a particular regard for Robin and has gained the respectful yet profound affection of old Dan Wyert.

Finding a river valley leading toward the northern coast, the travellers strive to descend into it, but chance upon the lair of a *branath*, the great cat of the mountains. The branath attacks them and is slain, but only after gravely injuring Sir Robert. While Simon is seeking in vain for a downward path, Essa finds a solitary branath kitten in the lair and, against her friends' advice, adopts it.

There is no downward path into the valley and they are forced to retreat southward into snow, bearing with them the injured Sir Robert, whose condition is worsening. On Essa's advice, they head reluctantly northeastward, to seek aid for him from the Safaddnese.

In a worsening blizzard, they are rendered incautious by exhaustion and, at last, find themselves surrounded by warriors emerging from the driving snow.

At that point, Simon's narrative resumes.

Chapter One

ACHALIND

Resistance was so evidently hopeless that none of us attempted it. Instead, we each straightened wearily and gazed mutely at the warriors.

The one who confronted me seemed, from his manner rather than any difference in accoutrements, to be their leader. To my surprise, though his axe had so dramatically barred my way, he appeared more curious than hostile.

'*Evyé tavar viré bazan? Evyé darazar viré datsemoi?*'

His tone was not at all peremptory, but rather one of courteous enquiry. Equally to my surprise, though his manner of speech might be unfamiliar, the language in which he spoke was close enough to Reschorese for me to comprehend his meaning. 'Why are you travelling here?' he was asking. 'Have you mistaken your path?'

Before I could frame a reply—I was too exhausted for quick thinking—Essa stepped forward and spoke: '*Tere ehekiyen zakhatinen. Zha navalirlin. Zha melié agharan azhutelan igia galaten padmai.*'

Again I understood well enough, for the words she was using, even if not exactly ones that I knew, were not very different from their Reschorese equivalents. 'These men are strangers,' Essa was saying. 'They have been kind. They have rescued me from captivity among robbers and are bringing me homeward.'

There was a surge among the warriors, suggestive of a surprise quite as great as mine. Indeed, their leader evinced this emotion when he responded: '*Dalu batavinat! Evyé viré letzestre?*' ('That is astonishing! What is your letzestre?')

For answer, Essa merely pointed to the golden taron hanging upon her breast.

At the sight of it, the warriors gave a collective gasp of amazement. Indeed, they seemed awed, their leader quite as much so as his men.

He bowed his head for a moment, then directed at Essa such a cataract of swift sentences that I was quite unable to comprehend what he was saying. Nor did I understand her reply, for it was couched in phrases entirely unfamiliar to me.

What happened next amazed me. The leader set his axe upright in the snow, then brought his hands to his breast and bowed his head over them. After that he made a spreading gesture with both hands and dropped to his knees. At this, each warrior set his weapon upright in the snow, be it axe, spear or broad-bladed sword, before likewise kneeling.

As I looked on in wonderment, the leader began to chant, in sonorous tone, what sounded like a ritual invocation of the Safaddnese gods. I caught the by-now-dreaded names Horulgavar, Daltharimbar, Halrathhantor and Mesnakech and presumed that the other five gods of the Safaddnese nonalogy were also being invoked. At intervals, the other warriors bowed their heads and sang out in chorus: '*Ilai ushazan!*' ('Our praises!').

To be standing upright, our veludain beside us, in the midst of this chanting ring of men, with snow falling steadily upon us, was one of the oddest of experiences. So weary was I that I should have been happy to kneel also, or even to sit, in the snow; yet I felt I should not. Nor did it seem proper to address any word to my companions during this responsory ritual. Instead, we all stood respectfully silent.

His chanting ended, the warrior leader rose to his feet and his men did likewise. Then the leader, inclining his head, offered his clasped hands in welcome to Essa; that gesture, at least, seems to be constant throughout Rockall. When she had smilingly taken them, he made a similar gesture to me, then to Dan and finally to Avran.

After that the other warriors—there were eight of them, completing the *letel* or squad of nine that, as I was to learn, is the basic unit of any Safaddnese fighting force—each greeted us in turn. Robin, of course, was in no condition to be greeted. However, after Essa had uttered some words of explanation of his condition, each of the nine laid a gentle hand on his blanket-enwrapped—and, by now, snow-shrouded—form, in what was clearly intended to be a compassionate extension of their welcome.

Even in the heavily-falling snow I could perceive that the warriors were quite highly excited—more excited than could be accounted

2

for by the mere arrival of strangers, however unusual that event. Why they were so stirred up, I could not conceive.

After this second ceremony, the warrior leader—the *letelar*, as I should have been styling him, had I known that word—urged us, despite the conditions, to mount our veludain. Then he and his men took up their weapons and set off in arrowhead formation, leading us in a direction I thought must be eastward.

Since the warriors' stoutly-booted feet beat down the snow before the veludain, it was easy enough for our beasts to carry us—and a great relief to be riding again. Indeed, I found myself suddenly lighthearted. The long-expected encounter with the Safaddnese was over and, puzzling though it was, we had been neither slain, as I had feared, nor even taken prisoner. Instead, we were being treated as friends—or indeed, as something more than friends.

Suddenly I became aware that Essa was riding beside me. She addressed me quietly, but in a voice that had a strong undercurrent of amusement: 'Well, Simon my friend, did you comprehend what was being said?'

'Only in small part,' I answered honestly. 'I understand that we have been made welcome, but I don't comprehend why.'

'It is the taron, of course. That was indeed a fortunate find! When they asked me from which letzestre I came, I did not know how to respond in a fashion that would satisfy them. Instead, I merely showed it. Well, I could scarcely have done better!'

She laughed outright, that rare laugh which was so very attractive; and, even through the snow, I could see the brightness of her eyes.

'But why?' I demanded impatiently. 'Evidently it impressed them mightily—but for what reason?'

'You recall that I remembered it to be the emblem of one of the three sea-coast letzestrei, but was not sure which? Well, it seems the taron is the symbol of Avakalim. Yet that is not all! The Safaddnese have a legend, as I have now learned, of a lost princess of that realm—a princess who vanished just before the Safaddnese Empire collapsed. Their story tells that she will return at a time of crisis and doubt, to give her people guidance. They believe that I am she!'

Essa laughed again, an enchanting bubble of joyous merriment. However, she had set me wondering.

'Well, *are* you a princess?'

3

'Certainly not!' Essa was scornful. 'Nor am I several hundred years old and miraculously preserved! Do strive to think clearly, Simon, please! As I told you all when we first talked after escaping from Kradsunar, I'm just Essa, no-one special. And yet—well, it must merely be chance, but the name of that lost princess . . . can you guess it, Simon?'

'Of course not!' I answered crossly, still smarting under the whip-lash of her earlier scorn. 'How can I even try to guess, when I know nothing of this people?'

'Nothing at all—even after seeing all the carvings, even after hearing the names of four of the nine gods, even after visiting Sasliith? Come now, Simon; you are more percipient than you pretend! Yet the name of the princess, no, you could not guess that and nor could I, for I had never heard this legend. Her name—why, it was Hiludessa!'

'Hiludessa!' I echoed in astonishment. 'So very close to your own!'

'Yes—strange, is it not? And Simon, I'm afraid you must address me by that name henceforward, at least while we're among these people. So please try to accustom yourself to it!'

'Hiludessa,' I said again, bewildered. 'Princess Hiludessa.'

'That's right, Simon.' She was again amused. 'And now I must drop back to warn Dan and Avran.'

Hiludessa! *Was* this mere chance, I wondered, or were we indeed destined to fulfil a prophecy? I recalled that other prognostication expressed to me by Dekhemet Arrav, the physician and chirurgeon of Arravron who had saved me from death; that Avran and I—and, as I now presumed, our companions—had great tasks to perform. Might our pathless wanderings among the mountains prove to have been, like the sojourns of the Hebrew prophets in the wilderness, a prelude to those tasks, even some sort of preparation for them?

Engrossed in such thoughts, I came close for a while to forgetting my weariness and even the blizzard. Yet it proved a long ride still. Before it ended, I was almost asleep in my saddle; indeed, I did close my eyes at times, opening them again only with effort. Fortunately, Proudhorn's steadiness sustained me and his care ensured that I did not fall forward upon his horns during those brief slumberings.

By chance or through Proudhorn's mental prompting, I became fully awake just before we began a steep and slippery descent into a valley blotted from view by the blizzard. While their leader remained in the van, the other warriors moved back so that two were on either side of each veludu, ready to lend a steadying hand should hooves slip and a rider risk being thrown. However, though odd hoofslips occurred a-plenty, nothing more serious happened and their aid was not required.

Next we found ourselves crossing a broad bridge with low parapets. Ahead, or so it seemed to me through the swirling snow, there was an unbroken rock-face. As we approached it, however, the letelar hollered out some watchword that I did not hear clearly. Immediately two great doors swung inward, revealing a blaze of light within that quite dazzled us.

As our eyes adjusted to this, we perceived that the entrance was blocked by a suspicious line of high-helmeted guards, axes at the ready. In response to their challenge, the letelar addressed to them a gust of words. The guards registered amazement—clearly could I perceive their amazement—and then parted before us, bowing with profound respect.

When we had ridden in and the doors had closed behind us, the guards and our escort formed a ring about us, their suspicions quite swept away by their excitement. Indeed, their eyes seemed avid for each detail of our appearance.

The letelar threw back his hood and stood before us with arms raised. Since my eyes were still somewhat dazzled, I could perceive only that he was tall and lean and seemed unexpectedly young.

'*Vazatié laskatalad, Hiludessa indreletzar igha ghorotelai! Vazatié rad Achalind!*' His tone was ringing and fervent.

The other warriors, and the guards also, echoed the letelar's greeting in chorus, with such verve as to quite startle our poor veludain. Their words were easy enough for me to understand: 'Welcome a thousand times, Princess Hiludessa and companions! Welcome to Achalind!' So Achalind was the place to which we had been brought. Well, the name meant nothing to me.

Essa inclined her head and said in clear tones: '*Aliitreyen daruman, estreveyen zhadis.*' This was evidently a polite reply, but I could only clutch at its meaning. 'Tremendous thanks, people all'? No, that did not sound right; but, whatever she had said, it caused considerable gratification. The soldiers about us—all had by now thrown back their hoods—were beaming.

5

Then there came another surprise for them. The branath kitten had become quite used to travelling on veludu-back, curled up on Essa's lap within the shelter of her cloak and, like many small wild creatures, it was capable of remaining still for a surprising time. So still had it been, indeed, that the Safaddnese soldiers had never noticed it. Roused now by the warmth within the tunnel, it thrust its way out from under her cloak. Bracing itself with fore-paws against the back of Feathertail's neck, it stretched in the fashion of an awakening cat. Then it sat up before Essa, gazing about it.

This incident in no way disconcerted Feathertail, who had become used to her small extra burden and its occasional restlessness. How-ever, the soldiers about us were quite disconcerted. There was a surge backward and cries of '*Zhaiai branzhat!*' and '*Lokassié branzhat!*' ('Look at the branath!' 'See the branath!').

I believe that, as they recovered from their surprise, they might well have pressed closer, in the unthinking fashion of wondering children. However, the letelar rapped out an order in words I did not catch. At this they stepped back, grounding their weapons.

The letelar planted his own axe before him, with hands on shaft and blade, and began haranguing the soldiers in a flow of words too rapid for my comprehension. At intervals he would pause and they would bow their heads, though without any ritual responses this time: otherwise this scene came close to repeating the one we had wit-nessed in the snow.

Now that my eyes were becoming used to the bright light, I could see the soldiers more clearly. Burly men they were, not very tall— the letelar was much the tallest of them—with broad faces and rather pale skin. Their hair, whenever visible beneath their helmets, varied in hue from black to quite a light brown. None were bearded, but several had moustaches; these were sometimes short and bristly, sometimes longer and drooping, but always rather sparse. Since they seemed all to be round-eyed in amazement, I could perceive that the colour of their eyes varied from deep brown to a strange, light amber hue.

On the whole, they surprised me agreeably. The carvings we had seen in corridors and temples had been so impressive that I had expected the Safaddnese to be a formidable race of giants. When I thought back, however, I remembered that only the priests had been tall; the warriors, though gaining apparent height from their helmets, had been quite short and the servants markedly so. Indeed, as I was later to realize, these soldiers were a very representative group of the mountain people. Tallness and slimness are rare, blond hair exceptional and auburn hair, like Avran's, quite unknown. The men grow facial hair sparsely, beards being quite rare, and they go bald early. Nevertheless, they are a strong and resilient people, by no means to be despised.

Since the letelar was continuing his peroration, I had leisure also to take fuller note of our surroundings. The tunnel before us had been excavated into that curious brass-coloured rock that my companions and I had first noticed—oh! so long ago, it seemed!—just before observing our first wind-tree. The rock here must be quite as friable as the piece I had broken between my fingers, for the walls were irregular and a metallic-looking dust had collected in patches at the wall-foot.

In the light of the flaring torches, the walls glistened and seemed to pulse in a fashion I found disconcerting—or was that pulsing just an effect of my extreme weariness? Yes, I was again in danger of falling asleep. With an effort, I brought myself back to wakefulness.

Just then the letelar ended his speech in a flurry of what were evidently orders. The soldiers snapped back to attention. Two of the guards, after setting their axes down against the walls, ran off down the tunnel to bear messages. The other guards then returned to the gate, while the soldiers of our escort grouped themselves anew into arrowhead formation and led us deeper into Achalind.

We rode along for about a furlong before coming to a second guarded gateway. There, however, we were not challenged; its gates were already open and its guards made respectful way for us. I noticed the awe with which they gazed upon Essa and upon the branath kitten crouching so relaxedly before her. Well, if they thought this a legend come true, their awe was understandable enough!

Another furlong of riding past several smaller side-corridors, then we came to a junction of major passages and halted. The letelar bowed respectfully to Essa and they exchanged a series of sentences, none of which I understood. Thereupon Essa turned to us.

'We must dismount here, gentlemen,' she said. 'The letelar—the leader of the soldiers—assures me that our veludain will be well cared for. Sir Robert will be taken to a chamber where a couch is already being prepared for him; a chirurgeon will be summoned to his succour. I wished to go with Sir Robert, but the letelar was shocked and feels unable to permit it. It seems that so elevated a person as I have now become cannot be permitted merely to attend the sick!'

Again she was showing a flash of amusement. I felt this a little dangerous and hoped the letelar would not detect it, for he seemed a very serious young man.

Fortunately Essa continued briskly: 'So, Dan, would you please go with Sir Robert and see that they deal with him properly and tenderly? You will be brought to join us later—or so I am given to understand. My thanks to you.'

As she spoke, I noticed that one of the message-carrying guards was returning towards us down the right-hand corridor. Four serving-men—yes, I recognized their simple leathern garb, from memories of the carvings—were following him, bearing a litter padded with blankets.

Essa dismounted, lifting down the branath kitten and cradling it in her arms. We others dismounted also. The residual snow was brushed carefully from the still-unconscious Robin, after which he was released from his fastenings and taken tenderly from Twistbeam's back, to be placed upon the litter and wrapped in the blankets. In this quiet place, his breathing sounded alarmingly weak and uneven. Then, with Dan in fussing attendance, Robin was borne away down that same corridor by the serving-men.

The veludain, reassured by their mental contact with us that all would be well, allowed our packs to be taken from their saddles and themselves to be conducted away by the rather breathless guard, down the opposite, left-hand corridor. I trusted that our beasts would receive good treatment, for I sensed their extreme weariness.

After that, on the letelar's request, we took off our outerwear— our cloaks, gloves and trews of ameral-fur and our overboots of hasedu-skin. While Essa was slipping off these garments, the branath kitten crouched by her feet. Then it climbed on to her shoulder and perched there, purring hoarsely and loudly. I was surprised, for I had not heard it purr before.

After the furs had been respectfully folded and stowed away, five of the soldiers each picked up a pack and carried it off. We were assured that the packs were being taken to the chambers in which

8

we would sleep; I hoped fervently that the opportunity for sleep might come soon.

So only Avran and I accompanied Essa when, with the letelar in proud charge and his three remaining warriors in attendance, we continued on foot down the principal corridor. Without our furs, the air felt distinctly chill and there were many more side-corridors, each of which seemed to generate its own draught. I shivered and noticed that Avran was shivering also: his injured arm seemed to be troubling him and I was sure he must be even more tired than I. Only Essa appeared warm, serene and unwearied.

What hour was it, anyway? Our struggle with the blizzard had seemed endless and, in this underground place, I found it hard to regain my sense of time. Certainly our midday repast was far behind ... Abruptly I became aware that I was quite ravenously hungry. With that awareness, my desire for sleep receded.

The tunnel we had been following ended in a T-junction with another. As we turned left, we found this new corridor to be very different. It was paved and roofed with blocks of what I thought must be marble, though I had seen that stone only rarely, in churches; not a white marble, this, but one veined irregularly with green. The walls were faced with a bluish stone, into which had been graven complex swirling patterns. These confused the eye and gave a sense of fluidity.

The flaring torches of the first tunnel were gone now. Instead, the illumination was provided by smaller, more closely spaced lights of a type I had not seen hitherto. They were enclosed with bowls of green marble and seemed to consist of a burning wick floating in oil. Within this greenish glow, reflected as it was by the blue walls and echoed by the greenness in floor and ceiling, we seemed to be, not walking, but wading along through the clear water of some river. When we entered the great bowl-shaped chamber in which the corridor ended, it was as if we were swimming into some tranquil lake.

As we went into that chamber, all our eyes were drawn to the immense figure at centre, a figure crusted with silver and illuminated so that it shone like a leaping fish in sunlight. Yet it was not a fish, but a man scaled like a fish and whose trailing robe was divided like a fish's tail—a man whose toes and upraised fingers were webbed and whose outthrust beard was forked—Halrathhantor, god of the rain, the snow and all terrestrial waters; Halrathhantor, god of Ayan! So *that* was the letzestre within which was set this underground city of Achalind!

Because those thoughts were crowding into my tired mind, I was slow to realize that many stone benches were ranged about the periphery of the chamber, forming tiers up its sloping sides. I perceived equally belatedly that those benches were crowded with people — men, women and children, all of them silent and attentive.

Our letelar stopped just beyond the threshold of the chamber, inclined his head and made that by-now-familiar spreading gesture with his hands, a gesture I had come to recognize as a sign of respectful invocation. We stopped also. Then, without a word, he led us forward. We circled to the left round the plinth on which the god's great image was set and, when the letelar did so, again stopped.

Before us was a raised dais on which was set an arc of seats — nine seats, inevitably, and each of them occupied. The three men at right were dressed in the fashion of servants, but not in leather; rather, in some dark, rich fur. The three at left wore the uniforms of soldiers, but with bright gold emblems of rank. Their helmets were set on the floor before them, for one does not remain with covered head in the presence of a god. However, it was the trio at centre who attracted my attention. Tall men they were, much taller than their companions, wearing the imposing robes of Safaddnese priests.

To my surprise, it was not to them that the letelar addressed himself, but to the soldier at the extreme left of the arc.

'*Trasalyé Dakhmen letzahar Ayanai*!' he began. I comprehended those words at least — 'Hail to you, Dakhmen, letzahar of Ayan!' So this burly, grey-moustached person was named Dakhmen and was the ruler, not just of this city of Achalind, but of the whole letzestre!

While I was registering that information, the letelar was continuing to speak, in rolling phrases whose tone made evident his pride and excitement but whose exact meaning eluded me. I presumed, however, that he was describing our meeting in the snow and explaining whom he believed us to be — or, at least, believed Essa to be. As he finished speaking, he inclined his head respectfully, first to the nine men — I presumed they must be the governing council of Ayan — and then to Essa.

At his beckoning gesture, Essa stepped forward. Still with the branath kitten on her shoulder, she stood before the arc of men, returning their gaze levelly and fearlessly. The kitten, however, ceased its purring and made a strange sound, half-mew, half-spit, before falling silent.

There was an interval of quietude while the nine men studied her—a tense interval, it seemed to me. Then the letzahar spoke, not to Essa but to the priest who sat at the centre of the table.

'*Akla dratséyé*, Parudanh? *Terekza dané talumé* Hiludessa *indreletzevren?*'

Though he spoke quietly, his words carried to us clearly. Again I understood. The priest must be called Parudanh, though whether as personal name or as title I could not be sure. 'What do you think?' he was being asked. 'Can this be truly the Princess Hiludessa?'

The priest did not answer directly. Instead, he rose to his feet and stepped down from the dais, his long robe rustling—a sound clearly audible in the silence of the great chamber. Standing immediately before Essa, he looked down upon her from his greater height. She returned his gaze unflinchingly.

The branath kitten tensed, its fur rising on its back and its tail thickening; then, slowly, it relaxed. At that very moment, or so it seemed to me, the priest made up his mind. When he spoke, his voice had a strange, dry resonance, as if he were speaking through a roll of parchment to increase its volume.

'*Asdyesh tamat*,' he announced, '*kre* Hiludessa *indreletzevren*. ('Yes, truly she is the Princess Hiludessa.') As I heard those words, I relaxed also, for I knew that all was again well.

Most solemnly, the priest spread out his arms and raised them to the god. For a moment he stood thus. Then he lowered his arms, bowed his head to Essa and smilingly offered to her the clasped-hand gesture of friendship.

His words had caused an excited bombilation among the watching people, but it had died away quickly enough. Now they rose in unison to their feet to repeat in chorus, again and again: '*Ilai ushazan! Ilai ushazan!*'

As the chamber resonated with their praises, Essa was led up onto the dais, to be welcomed by the other eight members of the council. Avran and I were left to stand at the foot of the great image of the god, our ears ringing from the sounds about us.

By then, my own thoughts were reeling from relief into a sort of bewildered, awed confusion. What did this all mean? Had the prayers of Essa, uttered when she first saw the image of Halrathhantor in that other underground place, been answered after all? In those wearisome meanderings through the mountains, had the god been guiding us, perhaps even guarding us from the dark menace of Mesnakech, to bring us at last to this, surely his principal temple? Might it even be conceivable that Essa, our humble companion from the robber's roost, had indeed been somehow transformed into the long-lost Princess Hiludessa? My Christian training made me reluctant to accept that alien gods might have such powers; yet demons had great power, did they not? Were we, here underground, coming dangerously close to the infernal regions? Might we be in danger of forfeiting our very souls?

A weary mind drifts into such courses; and I was very weary. It was well, perhaps, that Avran was standing beside me. His words, spoken in English, brought me down from these wild flights of speculation to prosaic reality.

'Well, *that* seems all right, Simon friend; yet I hope they won't keep us here much longer. It's time they led us out from this chilly place and found us something to eat!'

Chapter Two

REVELATIONS AT A BREAKFAST

As it chanced, both of Avran's wishes were to be fulfilled. However, before that happened, there were various courtesies to be undergone.

Almost as soon as Avran finished speaking to me, the priest ushered Essa down from the dais. After uttering what sounded like an apology for neglecting her even briefly, he advanced upon Avran and me. His greeting of us, if it lacked the reverence he had shown to Essa, was respectful enough and we were in turn offered his clasped hands in welcome. When I grasped them, I found that the skin of those hands was as rough as shagreen and as cool as a lizard's. Yet I was not repelled.

At that time I did not grasp the names, and even the physiognomy, of the other seven members of the Dakhletzavat of Ayan. Afterward, however, we came to be well acquainted with several of them. Yet, in my telling of this tale, it is necessary to identify only one—Xandor, the *letzumahar*, or leader of the artisan class, of Ayan.

He was a round man with a broad, merry face, whose close-furred black robe had a bloom upon it and gaped to reveal a yellow undershirt, so that he looked like a plum bursting with ripeness and goodness. Among these solemn northern people he seemed as cheery as a ray of sunshine—and was quite as welcome in any company. I took to him from the outset and, when I came to know him more, liked him even better.

During these introductions, our letelar stood smiling beside us, quite evidently proud to be playing so prominent a part in a happening destined to prove so significant in his land's history. When they were done, he conducted us out of the great chamber.

The sounds behind us, as we walked away down the corridor, suggested that some ritual of thanksgiving was beginning. For many reasons, but chiefly because of my extreme exhaustion, I was profoundly relieved that we were spared participation therein.

After leaving the marble-floored precincts of the temple, fortunately we had only a short way further to go. At the second junction of corridors, we turned left and then left again, to enter a small room. In it, a fire was burning cheerfully beneath a flue that disappeared upward into the rock. Beside that fire was a table laden with viands and wines and surrounded by deep, richly upholstered chairs. Two of those chairs were occupied. One of the men I did not recognize; the other was Dan Wyert.

Both men leapt to their feet as we entered, but it was Dan who spoke first. He had been looking anxious, but now he was beaming.

'Why, 'tis a relief indeed to see you, Lady—er, that is, Princess Hiludessa and gentlemen.' Dan coughed embarrassedly at his near error—he was speaking in Reschorese and might easily have been understood by the two Safaddnese—and then went on: 'This other gentleman here seems kindly enough disposed, but we can't talk, y'see. He speaks neither English nor good, plain Reschorese. Pending your coming, he wouldn't let me eat anything, neither. It's been a hungry time here.'

His voice trailed off into wistfulness; and indeed I could sympathize, for we had not seen so fair a repast in many long weeks. There were thick slices of a rich, red meat; a pile of crisply browned legs and drumsticks of some plump little birds; loaves of dark bread; heaps of fruit, some familiar, most unfamiliar, but all enticing; and tall glass flasks of wines of varying hue, from ruby-red to pale yellow. I found myself again ravenous and was hard put to wait while Essa introduced us solemnly to Dan's companion.

He was a spry little creature, by name Kuldu Asbetang. He proved to be steward to the letzelar and responsible for the ample feast that so entranced our hungry eyes. Yet he was desperately apologetic about it, pleading the late hour and short notice as excuses for its shortcomings. He was delighted when Essa praised his efforts and was soon busily serving us.

The letelar would have been happy enough, I am sure, to perform that task. When instead invited to sit at ease and join us in the meal, it was evident that, although highly honoured, he felt distinctly ill at ease.

Though he must have introduced himself when we first met in the blizzard, I had not grasped the letelar's name. It was a pleasantly euphonious one—Taru Taletang. I guessed correctly that the suffix ' –ang', like the Reschorese ' –eng', meant 'man of' and that the first parts of his and the steward's names were place-names. However, as we were to learn, there is an important difference. In Reschora, such surnames are commonplace enough; any farmer, or any farm servant even, might be so styled. In Ayan and the other Safaddnese realms, however, such names are borne only by persons of ancient lineage. They are becoming ever less common with each passing year.

During her meal, Essa managed not only to give titbits of food to the branath kitten but also to maintain a steady conversation with the two Ayanians. Her facility in Safaddnese was quite remarkable, considering that she had grown up in that robber's roost so far from the Safaddnese realms.

I am not sure whether Avran or Dan comprehended anything of what was said. For my part, I was too hungry and too weary to be bothered even to try. The only exchange that I recall was when Essa asked Dan about Sir Robert. It seemed that our poor friend had indeed been examined by a chirurgeon—Dan described him as 'a long, scraggy cove with a beard like you see growing on old cheese'—and his assistants; but with what result, Dan could not tell since he had understood nothing of their comments. He said, however, that they had looked very grave. That meagre information did not cheer me.

By the end of the repast, I was so drowsy that I have only the dimmest memories of an influx of servants, of ceremonial farewells, and of being led back through a confusion of corridors to a chamber in which a sumptuous bed of furs had been prepared for me. I tumbled into that bed and into sleep simultaneously; and I slept deeply and long.

On my first Rockalese awakening, in Sandarro so many months and miles back, I had been greeted by the irrepressibly cheerful Brek and a steaming jug of hot water. My first arousal in Ayan was more decorous, but bleaker. Standing by my bedside was a short, elderly man clad in grey livery, impassive of visage and highly formal in manner. There was water for my ablutions, but it was icily cold. In the ensuing days different servants came and went, but all were alike austere. As for the water they brought, it was never even luke-warm.

However, I was pleased to find that clean clothes had been provided for me. The undershirt, stockings and slops were woven from some sort of grey wool, coarser and with longer staples than that of a sheep; the servant's livery must be made, I thought, of the same stuff. I found it slightly itchy but very warm. Over these I donned a belted garment much like a cote-hardie, though rather fuller in sleeve; this was made from a lighter cloth and had been dyed chestnut-brown. My boots had been cleaned meticulously and returned to me; I wondered what the servants had thought of the throwing-knives concealed in their welts! My belt and shoulder harness, with the other knives, and my sword were lying by my bedside. This pleased me, for it indicated that we were trusted. Indeed, I hesitated before donning my weapons, doubting their necessity. In the end I did so only because I would have felt uneasy leaving them behind.

I contemplated my appearance in the polished-metal reflector on the wall of my chamber and found, to my great pleasure, that my beard had at last grown to quite a respectable length and density. This discovery, and the prospect of a good breakfast, cheered me considerably. When I followed the servant out of the chamber—he had witnessed all my activities without a flicker of expression—I did so with light and brisk step.

This time I watched my route with care, so that I might be able to find my way back to my chamber unguided. Indeed, I had need to observe carefully; this underground city of Achalind was a veritable warren of corridors, in which a rabbit would have been much better at route-finding than I. Yet I did recognize that the chamber to which I was brought was that in which we had dined. The servant waved me inside, then left me without either farewell or perceptible regret.

Avran was there already, eating from a full platter at a table only slightly less amply laden than last night's. His mouth being full, he signalled a greeting to me. The steward in attendance—not Kuldu Asbetang, but a younger, plump-faced man—gave me a bob of the head and a welcoming beam. Soon my own platter was laden and I was as contentedly busy as Avran.

As our hunger abated, we began to chat between mouthfuls—in Reschorese, for we had no particular confidences to exchange—and to speculate where our other companions might be. I had almost cleared my platter before either of them appeared. Then, to my mild surprise, the arrival was not Dan Wyert but Essa, with the branath kitten following at her heels.

At first glance, I thought she was wearing the azure-blue dress which, in memory, I associated with the mountain-top near Ingelot. On second look, however, I realized it was a different garment, even fuller in sleeve and much longer in skirt, that I had not seen before. Her fair hair was swept back and fastened at either side with azure-blue ribbons; her feet were shod in soft brown shoes with buckles of gold; and the golden taron shone upon her breast. On that morning, she appeared a princess indeed.

Both of us sprang to our feet. Avran inclined his head, saying: *'Vazatié, Hiludessa indreletzar Avakalimast'* — 'Greetings, Hiludessa, Princess of Avakalim,' — thus displaying an admirable presence of mind that I could not match. Hastily I echoed his gesture and words.

We remained standing until Essa, having given us a smile of approval and an easy responsive greeting, had seated herself. The kitten curled up by her feet and became instantly still. Then we sat down also.

The steward, quite evidently greatly awed, hastened forward to serve her; but she would take only a goblet of the pale wine, explaining that she had already enjoyed a repast that morning with the letzahar.

Already Avran had finished eating. When I was done also, the steward was ordered, quite courteously but firmly, to take away our platters and leave us. He was most reluctant to go—I am sure he felt it wrong that the princess should be left unattended, even for a moment—but did obediently depart.

As soon as he was gone, Essa began speaking. 'Avran and Simon, we must talk urgently, for I fear we may have few opportunities for private conversation in the days that lie ahead. Last night and this morning, I learned many things that you should know. Even so, there is much else that we all must learn, if we are not to run into trouble. Where, then, shall I begin?'

As she paused, I said: 'Tell us first about Dan and Robin. Where is Dan and how is Robin—is there any change in his condition?'

'As for Dan, he ate early and is with Sir Robert. As for Sir

Robert, well, he seems a little stronger. I have not seen him, but the chirurgeon tells me that his breathing is somewhat easier and more regular. They dosed him with some potion last night: how he was persuaded to swallow it, I cannot guess, but it appears to have done him good.'

To our expressions of gratification, Essa responded: 'Yes, that is good news. I am beginning to hope that we brought him here in time; and Simon'—her glance at me held both triumph and reproof—'I shall remind you that we attained Achalind only by following the flight of the gherek. You did well to accept my advice. Had we followed the course *you* proposed, by now we would all be lying dead and frozen in the snow.'

'Well, that may be so,' I answered somewhat heatedly. 'Yet how could I foresee that the Safaddnese would make us welcome? I believed that, if they discovered us, they would either slay us or, at best, take us prisoner; remember Toril Evateng's warnings! I could not guess the significance of the taron—and how was I to know that you were a princess in disguise?'

She flushed and eyed me angrily. Then, unexpectedly, her expression relaxed and she smiled instead. 'For my part, I have never feared the Safaddnese. As for my being a princess, that has been a surprise to me also!'

Then the smile faded from her face and she continued pensively: 'Yet—well, there are oddities . . . I've learned more of that legend by now; and, do you know, Simon, she disappeared somewhere in the south? The legend does not tell where; only that she was on a journey to one of the southern letzestrei, to Darega or to Omega . . . And her appearance; it seems her hair was as fair as mine and her eyes blue like mine. Then—well, I have always particularly loved the colour azure. Now I find a dress of that tint—this dress—immediately provided for me, here in Achalind this very morning. Moreover, I learn that it is the colour of Avakalim, the hue of the sea in summer sunshine; but, as for me, I have never even seen the sea! And the princess's name, Hiludessa—so very close to mine . . .'

'These are chances,' said Avran bracingly. 'Chances; no more than that. Yet fortunate chances for us, as I will freely confess.'

Essa gazed at him solemnly, and when she spoke again, it was with a strange fervour.

'If these be indeed chances, Avran my friend, then they are

not the only chances that have favoured us. For my part—no, I cannot think them chances, I believe that we have been in the hands of the gods. Rather I should say, of one god in particular—Halrathhantor of Ayan, to whom I prayed by the waters of the underground temple. Did he not defend us from the xakathei—even though he claimed the particular sacrifice of my veludu? Did he not save us from Mesnakech? Has he not, through his servant the gherek, brought us to this, his greatest city and temple? Can you doubt—even you, prince of the south—that his hand has been upon us?'

Her words made me uneasy, for they brought back to mind the concept I had set aside yestereven—that we had been guided in our path, not by mere hazard but by influences more powerful than our own will. I did not savour the idea that Halrathhantor—or any other heathen god of the mountains, for that matter—might have us under his control.

I was sure that Avran's reaction would prove even stronger than mine and would be expressed very forcibly. However, he responded quite mildly.

'Maybe these were not chances, Lady Essa—or Princess Hiludessa, as I must call you now—I do not find it in the least hard to think of you as a princess. Yet—no, I cannot have any faith in your mountain gods. However, here especially where we are guests of a people that do believe in those gods, I shall keep my promise to you. I shall not challenge them directly and indeed I shall strive, little though I might believe in them, to show respect both to your gods and to their other worshippers.'

His earlier words brought a fugitive smile to Essa's lips; but, as he continued, she became again solemn. 'Thank you for that, Avran my friend. Indeed, I think you must exercise great care; and you also, Simon.'

'Oh, yes,' I agreed, hurriedly. 'Yes, indeed.'

'Very well, then. Yet neither of you, I am sure, can perceive even now how very fortunate we have been. To make you understand, I must weave together a diversity of threads of information. Some of these were spun from details that I learned from my father, some from facts that Toril Evateng told us all, and some from information gained last night. They blend to form a tapestry that needs to be described to you. Its picture shows one thing only—the emptiness of the mountains we traversed. An unnatural emptiness indeed, as we all realized.'

As she paused, my own mind slipped back and I recalled those endless-seeming days amid the stillness of the wind-forests and among the stony, mist-veiled uplands. From his expression, I could see that Avran was reaching back in his mind also. Yes, our journey had been strange, most strange.

When Essa resumed speaking, her mind seemed to me to have wandered into unrelated paths of thought.

'You'll recall, gentlemen, that Toril told us of the *tazlantenar*—the "rootless ones", the children taken from conquered tribes by the Safaddnese, to be reared as their servants. At first, as you'll also remember, they were not permitted to rise to any higher rank. However, when the Safaddnese found themselves engaged with enemies on many flanks, the tazlantenar were permitted to serve in their armies and even to gain quite high position.'

As she paused again, no doubt marshalling her thoughts, I broke in impatiently: 'Yes, quite so; I remember all that, and I'm sure that Avran's memory is quite as good as mine. Yet what has it to do with the emptiness of the mountains?'

She glanced at me reprovingly: 'Be not so impatient, Simon! The story is one that you will comprehend only if you keep in mind the events of past times.'

'I'm sorry: please go on.'

'Very well, then; so the tazlantenar gained status. After many years, the child of a Safaddnese father and tazlantil mother came to be considered, not as a mere tazlantil, but as being Safaddnese also. Not in all letzestrei; never in Aracundra or Vasanderim and never, I think, in Paladra; but in most. Yet the tazlantenar themselves have not gained equality anywhere. If a child be born to a tazlantil father and a Safaddnese mother, that has continued to be thought a great shame. In earlier years, both parents and the child were slain. Even in more recent years, even nowadays, the father might well be executed and the mother expelled from her family, she and her child becoming merely tazlantil. Alas! it is a bitter, bitter system.'

As Essa said those last words, she was shaking her head and seemed more deeply moved than I had ever seen her. Avran and I, both quite taken aback at this sudden evidence of emotion from one normally so self-contained, could do little more than utter sounds expressive of sympathy.

After a while, Essa seemed to recover herself, for her ensuing words were uttered quite calmly and firmly.

'Even when the wars had ended, the Safaddnese continued to dwindle; not just the families that were wholly Safaddnese, but also those of mixed Safaddnese and tazlantil stock. Mayhap the burgeoning bleakness of these mountains has been the cause; for indeed, as Toril told us, they are much harsher and more barren now than when the Safaddnese Empire was at its height. Whatever the reason, the mountain people have become ever fewer.'

Essa paused, as if again to marshal her thoughts, then she went on: 'Yet dwindling has not occurred everywhere at the same pace. The people of Ayan and Desume remain quite numerous. So also, paradoxically perhaps, do those of Aracundra and Vasanderim, where Safaddnese and tazlantenar are still so firmly divided. In the other realms, the dwindling has been more severe. In the sea-coast letzestrei of Avakalim and Brelinderim, there are scarcely enough folk left properly to defend those realms, should they be attacked—and I think one *has* been attacked recently, though I have not yet got the tale clear. As for Darega and Omega, their peoples have almost vanished. That was why the valleys have been forsaken, left to be defended only by the wind-trees. The few Omegans and Daregans that yet survive, reside only on the mountaintops.'

'Ah! I understand now,' Avran was nodding his head. 'It is because of this dwindling that we succeeded in traversing the mountains unscathed.'

'No, Avran; that is not the true reason. Yes, it does explain why the valleys were unoccupied and why we saw so few traces of humankind. However, it does not explain why those mountaintop towers were locked and dark, the herds of uvudain—yes, they *were* uvudain, I was right—left untended, and Sasliith empty of its people. That is a different mystery. Can you guess its solution?'

She looked from Avran to me and back again; then, seeing the blankness of our countenances, nodded to herself in satisfaction.

'Nor could I. Yet I, at least, might have guessed. As you learned from Toril Evateng, we Safaddnese—I had better so phrase it, had I not, since I am now princess of a Safaddnese realm?—we Safaddnese believe profoundly in the sacred significance of the number nine.

Nine soldiers in each army squad, each letel; nine councillors to rule each letzestre; and nine letzestrei, each having its own god who, in concert with the other eight gods, rules this whole Earth—or, at very least, these mountains.'

Essa broke off to eye Avran challengingly, for his expression made evident his dissent. Remembering his promise, however, he did not speak; and after a while she continued her discourse.

'Those are facts you have come to know, my friends; but did you know also that, in each realm, there are nine divisions of land, each with its ruler, its high priest and its temple? Did you know that each year is divided into nine periods, four of forty days and five of forty-one days? Each of these periods is dedicated to one of our gods, while the odd day at the year-end of every fifth year is a celebration of all our gods. Above all, did you know that a man's, or a woman's, life is reckoned in periods of nine years, in *letzalei*, and that the whole reckoning of our history is done in letzalei also?'

Avran and I made murmurs that admitted our ignorance and indicated our interest.

'Well then, I have mentioned that we celebrate the *Gazhalkrayet*, the day in the fifth year that all our gods join to rule; but we have greater festivals of celebration. You must understand also that our years begin, not when yours do in deep winter, but at the end of each autumn. That was when, as our histories tell us, Horulgavar first set into the earth the seeds which would lie fallow over the winter and, in the spring, yield the first crops. Each year, that time is celebrated; but it is not always celebrated in the same fashion.

'In an ordinary year, men merely gather to feast and worship at the nearest temple of their own particular god. However, at the *Letzelkrayet*, the nine days that begin each ninth year, all the priests join to celebrate in their land's principal temple and each town and farm sends its representatives to worship there also. Even more important is the *Lakuletzelkrayet*, the period beginning the ninety-ninth year. At that time, all the priests from every letzestre and all the letzaharei travel to the sacred mountain of our greatest god, the Fereyek Gradakhar, the Mount of Storms as others style it, in Aracundra. Returning, the priests hold a second celebration in the principal temple of their letzestre, in which all the people of that letzestre must participate.'

Essa paused and surveyed us sternly, as if to ensure that we were giving her words close attention. Having confirmed this, she continued her discourse.

'The greatest and rarest festival of all among we Safaddnese is the *Dakhletzelkrayet*, the festival beginning each nine hundred and ninety-ninth year. At that time, all our people, whether they be priest or servant, infant child or sere elder, healthy, sick or lame, must travel to the Mount of Storms to celebrate with the gods and await their revelations. Yes, they must leave home, farm or flock, to journey all that long way and worship together. At that most important of our festivals the priests inform us, under divine inspiration, of their prognostications for the fate of the Safaddnese over the next *dakhlet-zel* — the next nine hundred and ninety-nine years. Though we travel to the Fereyek Gradakhar also to give thanks, it is principally to hear those prognostications that our people make that great journey.'

Seeing the dawn of perception in our faces, she smiled.

'Yes, you have guessed it, my friends. As I should have known, this is the year of the Dakhletzelkrayet. That was why the mountains were empty and the towers dark. That was why Sasliith was deserted, save by its god. When from the hillside we saw the Paladrans returning by torchlight, it was from the Mount of Storms that they were coming. On this year, of all years, we have chosen to travel north from Reschora, to cross the frontier that had not been crossed for so long. Chance, gentlemen? I do not think so. No indeed; it was all part of a design—and that design was not ours.'

Chapter Three

LEARNING THE WAYS OF AYAN

Essa sat back, folded her hands in her lap and gazed at us triumphantly. Avran was nodding silently, like the earthenware head of a child's doll set rocking on its wooden shoulders. As for me, I found nothing to say; yet my thoughts were whirling.

Essa was right. There had been far too many chances—chances that had combined to bring Avran Estantesec and me all the way from Sandarro to this strange underground city of Achalind in the one year, and at the only possible time in that year, when we might reach it safely. Had we passed this way earlier, Achalind would have been temporarily uninhabited, as Sasliith had been; had we delayed even a few hours, we would have died in the snow. Moreover, not merely had the two of us been brought here but also Essa herself, Essa of Kradsunar, the pattern of whose life was now so closely interwoven with ours—a servant girl of robbers when we met, but now become a princess.

No, this must be more than mere good fortune. Yet, if it were not chance alone, what was it? Were we indeed being manipulated like chessmen in some game played by the gods of these mountains, as Essa believed? The Christian training received by Avran and me forbade us from accepting that such gods existed, that they could have power in these mountains or anywhere. Steadfast Avran properly refused to credit their reality. For my part, however, I was less settled in mind. I had wondered before, and now I wondered again, whether we had strayed beyond the reach of the long, strong arm of our own God, into realms which lesser but still powerful gods yet held in their malign clutch.

I remembered the physician Dekhemet Arrav, who had saved my life. He was Reschorese and a Christian also, member of a race that had fought long against the Safaddnese and their gods and that had, in the end, won victory. He had predicted that we travellers were to play some great part in the history of this island of Rockall. Well, we had done nothing yet, save to visit some strange places and to survive some terrifying adventures. If we had indeed some special tasks to perform, those tasks lay before us still.

Or might it be that Avran and I had fulfilled our purpose already? Perhaps our only significance had been as escorts, as travellers whose motivation—the quest for Lyonesse and, in that land, for my father and brother—had served to transport Essa from Kradsunar to Achalind? Maybe it was she who was important, and not we!

When that thought surfaced amid the turbulence of my mind, I was initially comforted. I have never craved to be at the centre of the arena of life; I prefer being among the spectators to being out amid the waving banners and sounding trumpets. How nice, if indeed the perils were over for Avran and me and a return to tranquillity was in prospect!

However, on further consideration I found myself becoming rather alarmed. If Avran and I had ceased to be necessary in that divine contest, might not our days of safety be numbered? Might we, as pieces that had lost their importance in whatever game was being played, be simply discarded? Robin, now; his injury had served its purpose, for it had brought us back southward—and alas, it was all too likely that he might soon die. Here in Ayan, Essa had become a powerful figure already and might gain greater powers. We others had been treated kindly so far, but we were of small interest and no particular significance to these Safaddnese folk. Essa might achieve much, but however could Avran and I exert any least influence upon their affairs, let alone upon those of the whole Safaddnese people?

Essa was smiling at me. 'Well, Simon, I have evidently set you thinking, but your thoughts seem not of the happiest. What is troubling you, friend?'

'Well, er, I was just wondering . . .' Hastily I strove to dissemble my anxieties by formulating some reasonable question. 'Here in Ayan—well, Avran and I, we can't even speak the language—speak Safaddnese, that is. Nor can Dan. If you will be separated from us most of the time—well, I don't see how we'll manage; how we'll occupy ourselves, what use we'll be, that sort of thing.'

Now it was Essa's turn to nod, as slowly and rhythmically as Avran had done.

'As so often, Simon, you are properly perceiving a difficulty. That question occurred to me also, whilst I was taking breakfast with the letzahar; so I raised it with him. He was most courteous and helpful. He is arranging for you to receive instruction in this, the most venerable language of these northern realms—for Reschorese, after all, is merely a junior variant, a mere dialect of Safaddnese. Your lessons will begin this morning.'

I expressed my pleasure, but Avran groaned. Though he had not found the task hard—and maybe, indeed, for that very reason—he had not much enjoyed learning Reschorese. Evidently he recoiled at the prospect of having to master yet another tongue.

'Now, Prince Avran,' Essa chided, 'you will need to be able to make your thoughts and desires known, if you are to spend the winter here in Achalind—and that seems to be our destiny. You must strive to learn quickly, you know. Yet of course'—she smiled at him, a smile that was almost a grin—'there will be other things for you to do. The letzahar is arranging that you be shown his city and its ways and, when the weather permits, that you be taken out hunting in the mountains. The Ayanians have their own method of travelling in winter, even over deep snow; you have much to discover.'

Avran brightened at this. However, Essa quickly became solemn again.

'Yet remember also, my friends, that you must be continually on guard. You must never forget that here, at least, I am considered of high rank. I do indeed fear that I shall be involved in duties, secular and religious, that must keep us apart for many hours in the days to come. Though I be no such person, you must learn always to speak, and mayhap even to think, of me as the Princess Hiludessa, for centuries vanished but now miraculously returned. You must be watchful never to contradict that idea of the Ayanians, for our very lives depend upon it.'

Naturally we acquiesced hastily and fervently. Nevertheless, when Essa spoke again, there was a shadow of strain in her expression and an echo of apprehension in her voice.

'Yes, your role-playing may prove arduous, but mine will surely be much more so. The Ayanians accept that I might have forgotten some things during my long confinement and might never have known others; after all, they believe I am from another letzestre, not from Ayan. Yet they expect much of me. They assume I must understand, without instruction, everything that is important to them—not merely as well as, but even more profoundly than they. I must know more of these mountains than they, more of their lives than they, and certainly more of their gods than they.'

Her voice, as she went on, was becoming quite desperate. 'Soon I shall be required to decide questions of state and even, I fear, to predict the future. Yet how can I—how can I? After all, I am merely a girl who grew up among robbers. I have no special perceptions, no deep knowledge, no statecraft. I am quite simply a commonplace person, with commonplace abilities. How may I even attempt so much?'

Avran looked directly at her, his eyes smouldering, and spoke fervently. 'There is nothing commonplace about you. Though mayhap you were not born a princess, you have the character of one—and the beauty. Whatever the challenge, you will not fail to meet it.'

His words wiped the strain from Essa's countenance, as a moist cloth wipes a slate clean. She gave him the sort of smile—tremulous, uncertain, yet pleased—that I had seen only once before on her face, on the mountaintop by Ingelot.

I have often speculated what her next words might have been and what consequences they might have had. However, at that moment we were interrupted. The door of the chamber was opened brusquely. In hastened the chief steward, Kuldu Asbetang, with the younger steward who had served us that morning and three others following apprehensively behind.

Kuldu Asbetang was evidently both angry and embarrassed. He burst into a speech that, though not in words I understood, was clearly an apology for his younger colleague's neglect in leaving us unattended and a condemnation of that neglect.

Essa answered him coolly but firmly. As she spoke the younger steward, who had been looking quite frightened, perked up considerably and even preened himself a little. It was equally clear to me that Essa had reprimanded the chief steward, telling him that his young colleague had been merely obeying her orders and was not to be chastised.

Kuldo Asbetang apologized again, but this time much more humbly. As he set the servants to their task of clearing up, I noticed that his ears were quite red! Nevertheless, our period of privacy was ended; nor was such an opportunity for conversation to recur during many days.

Our first tutor in the Safaddnese language proved to be one of the junior priests. He was quite young, but so gaunt in feature and already so bald that he seemed much older than his years—a fact which, I do not doubt, delighted him, for he was a solemn, staid creature with an especial relish for ritual.

Even during the early lessons, it became evident to us that our new teacher had no clear idea how to set about his task. He was scarcely to be blamed for that: it must, after all, have been many centuries since there had been need to teach the Safaddnese language to any stranger.

Fortunately for him and for us, that task proved unexpectedly easy. As Essa had said, the Safaddnese language is indeed very close to Reschorese, not only in structure but in vocabulary. Yes, there is a certain extra stiffness of phrase, a greater complexity of pronunciation and a fundamental difference in intonation, but that is really all. The greatest problems we encountered were with words which, having only a religious relevance or referring to social observances unknown beyond the mountains, quite simply had no equivalents in Reschorese, Sandastrian or English.

Avran and I might have progressed faster in learning Safaddnese, had our tutor been less set upon following a predetermined path in his lessons. Indeed, his inflexibility caused him problems. Despite Avran's initial unenthusiasm for the task, he learned the language more quickly than did I; and because of this, he took the task less seriously. Soon he was tormenting the priest by alternately displaying a feigned ignorance of basic phrases and a mastery of complex ones. From time to time, moreover, Avran would introduce into a sentence some Sandastrian or English word, uttered straight or mispronounced.

The effect of these deliberate errors was often so hilariously incongruous that it proved hard for me to refrain from chuckling. Indeed, on several occasions I could not avoid bursting into laughter; and the priest, perceiving he was being mocked yet not understanding why or how, was set gobbling with fury.

At that point, Avran would put on a show of innocent surprise. He would apologize so profusely, and in so irrelevant a fashion, that the priest would be left ashamed of his anger and quite unsure whether or not he had been mocked. Perhaps, after all, Avran had merely been making some quite inadvertent error? Yet, if so, why did his other pupil not make such errors? It was altogether very puzzling for the poor young man.

Yet we did learn a great deal during those lessons, not only concerning the language of Ayan but also with regard to its attitudes and the fashion in which it was administered. For example, I came to comprehend better the circumstances and rituals of our initial reception in the great temple chamber in Halrathhantor.

I had been uncertain whether Parudanh was the priest's name or merely his title. It turned out to be the former. As highest of the nine high priests of Ayan and autarch of the greatest of the temples of Halrathhantor, his title was *letzudirar*. The titles of the other high priests (*udirarei*) were, we were to learn, prefixed by diminishing numbers that indicated the progressively lower status of the eight other temples that were their charges.

In my other assumption I had been quite wrong. The letzahar was not named Dakhmen; that was merely an alternative title indicating his rank, for literally it means 'ruler'. I might have guessed this, for the qualifying syllable *dakh-* is prefixed to the titles of kingdoms and kings in southern Rockall and to the name of Sandastre's ruling council, the *Dakhvardavat*. Indeed, the council of nine governing Ayan, like those that govern the other Safaddnese realms, is called the *Dakhletzavat*.

The first name of the letzahar proved to be Soganreth. As to his surname, we never learned it; nor did we learn the surnames of the other members of the Dakhletzavat. There was good reason for this. Under the austere Safaddnese law, when a man is honoured by being appointed udirar or elected to secular membership of the governing council, he is required not only to abandon his family name but also to sever all his family ties.

Yet the rule is not as harsh as it might seem. No such appointment is made until a man has completed his sixth letzal; that is, until he has attained his fifty-fifth year. By that age, he has had ample time to marry and to see his children grow up. Moreover—or so the Safaddnese believe—he has by then attained sufficient wisdom to recognize the virtues of continuity and to consider new issues with the necessary critical detachment. Whether this is so, I do not know.

Certainly, however, it makes for conservatism in government and militates against change.

Women are never appointed to the Dakhletzavat—not through any innate distrust of their sex, be it said, or of their intellectual abilities, but because it is considered that no woman is ever so able as a man to sever family ties. Again, I am not sure that the view is correct; but it is that of the Safaddnese.

As for the former families of the letzahar and the other councillors, they are granted no favours; rather the converse. Sons retain the family name that their father has abandoned, the eldest inheriting all possessions that had been his father's at the moment of election. The family of the letzahar may keep any positions already held, but its members are not thereafter eligible for high appointment; the families of the other councillors are prohibited from holding any position within their father's gift and can rarely expect advancement from the letzahar. These prohibitions all cease upon their father's death or resignation. In the meantime, however, the family gains only the lustre that their father's election gives to its name. To the stern Safaddnese, that seems reward enough.

Upon her husband's preferment, a wife faces an especially hard choice. She may elect to retain her family name and ties, but if so she must say a final goodbye to her husband, receiving only passing and formal recognition from him thereafter and thenceforward living in the home of one of her children (usually the eldest son). Alternatively, a wife may elect to sever her family ties and forfeit her name, in order to remain with her husband. Wives who select the latter alternative are highly honoured. The wife of the letzahar, in particular, gains the title *letzesahar* and is required to perform important ceremonial duties. However, most women who have borne children choose the first option. In the long history of Ayan, there have been few letzesaharin.

Daughters who have married before their father's preferment undergo no change of status, though they will see their parent less often and can expect no public manifestation of his affection. Unmarried daughters forfeit their family name, but gain an honorific title; in particular, a daughter of a letzahar comes to be called *indreletzar*, 'princess'. These also have been few, since most Safaddnese girls marry young; yet the long-vanished Hiludessa of Avakalim was evidently such a one.

I had expected that Dan Wyert would join us for our lessons with the young priest, but not so. Indeed, we saw very little of Dan during those early weeks in Achalind. He spent most of his time either with Essa, whose particular servant the Ayanians had recognized him as being, or in sitting patiently beside the couch upon which lay Sir Robert Randwulf. At first this was simply through sheer anxiety about our friend. Subsequently, however, it was to ensure that Robin, in the early weaknesses of a slow recovery from serious illness, might not inadvertently reveal some dangerous truth about Essa to the attending chirurgeon or his assistants.

For, to our great relief and against my pessimistic prediction, Robin *was* recovering. On the third day after our arrival, as Dan told me, he opened his eyes and gazed about him puzzledly before subsiding into sleep. On the fourth day, after being propped up on cushions and fed some thin gruel from a horn spoon, Robin managed some words of thanks to the servant tending him—or so that servant presumed, for they were uttered in English and Dan chanced not to be present. Perhaps, indeed, it was fortunate Robin was *not* understood!

After learning of that incident, Dan spent the greater part of his time by Robin's side. When Robin was next awake, he was sufficiently himself to ask coherent questions about Essa, Avran and me. Although, on that occasion, he seemed scarcely to comprehend the answers, Dan managed during the ensuing days to inform him—mostly, for reasons of safety and simplicity, in English—of the events that had transpired since the attack of the branath.

Avran and I were early and frequent visitors to Robin's couchside, but Essa, concerned though she was about Robin, wisely did not go to see him until Dan was sure that Robin comprehended the situation—and her deception—thoroughly. Only then might she expect to be welcomed by him in a fashion that the Ayanians would consider proper.

According to Dan's account, her first visit was a moving occasion. Robin was quite sure that Essa had saved his life. He strove, while sitting up, to bow to her from his blankets—only to lose balance and topple sideways to the floor.

Forgetting her dignity in her concern, Essa ran to him, lifted him and hugged him, in the fashion of an affectionate daughter embracing her father. That episode so much impressed Essa's Ayanian attendants—for, by then, she was always escorted—as to elevate Robin greatly in their esteem. He was thereafter known to the Safaddnese as *indreletzahular*, 'Rescuer of the Princess', and treated with the reverence appropriate to a person of high privilege.

After that, Essa made a point of visiting Robin daily, for short periods or long. During those visits she gave him personal instruction, not only in the Safaddnese tongue but also concerning the character and ways of the land and city in which he was living, but had yet to see.

Essa's attentions caused Robin's spirits to rise rapidly, but his physical condition occasioned us continuing concern. The clumsiness that caused his near-fall from the couch was a consequence of the partial paralysis of his left side. He was able to use his right arm well enough and, after a while, to walk a little, but he found difficulty in moving his neck and could not operate his left arm at all. The chirurgeon—'old Cheesy-face,' as Dan called him, with a curious mixture of irreverence and admiring affection—saw to it that Robin received daily rubbings with oil and massages, but these had no apparent effect.

Robin accepted his disablement cheerfully. 'Why, soon I'll be walking well enough,' he would say, 'and I'm fortunate indeed, for my sword-arm is good and I'll be able to wield a weapon again. As for my left side, why, I need only to hang a shield over that!'

Though delighted that our friend was alive and in such good humour, I found myself once again concerned about our future. Lyonesse must surely be quite close now, though I was still not sure in what direction it lay. The journey ought not to be difficult for Avran and me, if ever we were allowed to embark on it. It was likely enough that we might. Yet I doubted whether Robin would be able, crippled as he was, or Essa even permitted to set out upon such a journey. And if Essa stayed, so would Dan; that, at least, was evident. It seemed all too probable that our close group was destined ere long to be sundered.

In the meantime, Robin welcomed our visits and was soon learning Safaddnese quite as rapidly as we. After all, he had already gained an acquaintance with many languages. He told us that Safaddnese was easier than English, Hispanic or Flemish and much, much simpler to speak than the tongue of the Saracens.

Ere many weeks had passed, Robin began occupying idle hours by writing out and translating songs from the many lands he had visited. First of all this would be done into English for me, then into Safaddnese for Essa. He would write his translations out for her in the curious, angular Safaddnese alphabet. Essentially this was similar to the Reschorese alphabet, but it was more difficult because it included characters for syllables, as well as for individual letters. Avran and I never wholly mastered that method of writing, I through incompetence, he through lack of interest.

Yet we were both happy to play these songs while Robin and Essa sang them. Those were merry occasions, Avran blowing on the pommer and I strumming the timbelan that I had had with me, in my saddle-pack, all the long leagues from Arravron. Essa's voice was soft and had a tentative quality, for she had rarely sung; but Avran found it so enchanting, and listened so intently, that sometimes he quite forgot he should be playing until I prodded him!

As for Dan Wyert, how did he fare? That is a question I cannot altogether answer. He received no lessons in Safaddnese and never gained any fluency in that tongue; yet he managed well enough. In the fashion of soldiers, he contrived to memorize enough words and phrases to ensure that his particular needs were met and purposes served.

That was as well for, in the rigid framework of Ayanian society, our paths were divided. We encountered Dan only in Robin's chamber or in the company of Essa; and, during our musical sessions, Dan would always tactfully absent himself. At other times we could not expect to meet him, for Dan was considered of the artisan class and Avran and I, of the class of warriors. In Ayan, outside the temples, those groups do not mingle.

As a consequence of that identification, Avran and I spent much time in military company. We encountered Talu Taletang and members of his letel quite frequently, for their new task was the honourable one of guarding the Princess Hiludessa. However, we spoke little with them, for they considered that conversation accorded ill with their proper duty. Yes, they would attend respectfully to our greetings and comments, but they would respond only formally and briefly; and such talk quickly palls.

Instead, our particular associates were two other members of the warrrior class, both of them *letelarei* but each excused from their regular duties and assigned the task of escorting and instructing us. Consequently, we saw both of them daily—in one case, with pleasure; in the other with mounting reluctance.

Keld Eslingbror proved a welcome enough companion. He was burly and black-haired, with eyebrows that converged over a snub nose and a moustache that arched about his mouth and drooped alongside his chin. In repose his countenance looked rather ferocious. However, he had a trick of twitching his cheeks as he spoke; this caused his moustache-ends to jerk in a fashion both amusing and endearing, making him look like an amiable cat whose whiskers have been teasingly touched.

His task was the congenial one of instructing us in the ways of the city and the duties of its soldiers. He had been selected for this because of his swiftness in limning. Though he spoke only in his own language, quite often we understood his words or gestures, even at the outset. Whenever we did not, he would pull out from his belt-pouch a wad of parchment and a stick of charcoal. Then, with surprising speed and skill, he would produce for us a sketch to make clear his meaning, his moustache twitching delightfully as he drew. Almost always the sketch enabled us to grasp his intent, causing him to beam with pleasure.

In Keld's company we explored the underground labyrinth that was Achalind. It had originated, we learned, as a hiding-place for priests and warriors in the long-gone days of the southern Empire. While seeking temporary refuge in caves beneath the cliffs at the head of a small side-valley, some fugitives had found an underground spring that flowed copiously, winter and summer alike. This was an indication, for the Ayanians, of the blessing of Halrathhantor upon their refuge.

Moreover, they found many other caves at higher levels nearby—abandoned stream passages, perhaps. In one of these, they discovered the very beautiful green marble. This was a rock never seen at surface and one whose markings made it seem a fitting material for the temple of Halrathhantor, upon whose construction the priests were already determined. That temple was made in the largest cave, while those round about—becoming ever bigger as the marble was extracted—were transformed into residences for the priests and people. In the course of time the new temple became the principal centre for the worship of Halrathhantor, god of rains and terrestrial waters; indeed, the very name Achalind means 'chief temple'.

As Achalind's population grew, new passages were cut about, above and below the original caves and quarries, forming a complex in which the Ayanians might stay the year round, should there be need. Indeed, many do so nowadays, even without need—a reason for the paleness of their skins and, quite possibly, for the sparseness of the men's hair and beards also.

The folk of Achalind continue to live in the upper passages, at the level of the temple; but, in summer and winter alike, most of their work is done in the lower levels. It was only after many days that we were taken by Keld Eslingbror to visit those lower passages; and I, for one, found them fascinating.

Here were workshops of many kinds, food stores and armouries. Here also the veludain were kept over the winter and here, during its grimmest months, the hardier uvudain were also brought for safety. It was a pleasure to greet and share affection with our own beasts, thriving now after rest and good fodder; for indeed, there were plentiful stocks of hay and other foodstuffs.

What surprised me most, however, was to find crops being grown there, so deep underground, so far from the benign light of the sun. Strange enough crops they were, to the eyes of Avran and me. There were mushrooms, quite as good as those I had picked in English fields in high summer. There were curiously shaped toadstools, palely yellow and, to my palate, quite without flavour, though the Ayanians relished them. There were other fungi having a shelf-like shape and growing on sloping rock surfaces, altogether much like the bracket fungi one sees on rotting woodland trees—unattractive to look at, yet having the texture and flavour of good mutton when cooked. There were also strange little red toadstools with tops like coifs: when dried and ground, these furnished a spice that, if too strong, positively made one's eyes run!

Most abundantly grown, however, was a greenish plant like a vastly oversized lichen. This could be cooked like spinach, distilled to make a purgative medicament, or dried to form a springy filling for couches and cushions. Even its roots were useful; when soaked in fat and rolled into a rope, they burned slowly with a bright flame, making excellent candles.

I doubted whether the Safaddnese had known these plants before the time of the Empire, suspecting that they had been discovered by starving fugitives—perhaps in these very caves? However, when I asked, it was only to be told reverently: 'These are the gifts of Horulgavar and Halrathhantor,' which may have been properly devout but was not helpful.

Water for the crops was brought along carefully engineered conduits from the underground stream. The plants were fed by the night-soil of Achalind, which made those tunnels somewhat over-odorous. However, the underground farmers of Ayan sniffed this smell with the same pleasure as a Lincolnshire farmer enjoying the odours of ensilage.

The work of the farming is shared. Men of the artisan class prepare the ground and scatter the seed and spores, but it is their womenfolk who look after the growing crops and reap them. This is not because the men disdain such work, but because the Safaddnese believe that, just as women bear and tend children, so also should they tend and harvest crops. Moreover, though men look after the veludain and uvudain at all other times, women are always called in at the time of parturition.

While the robes of the men are most often grey or pale blue, the colours of Halrathhantor, the women wear green, the colour of Radaionesu and of fertility, at least while they are working amid the crops, though they may prefer brighter hues at other times. Physicians and chirurgeons likewise wear green, for Radaionesu is also their god of healing. Later we learned that he is the particular god of Brelinderim.

There is a shrine to Radaionesu in those lower levels. We looked in upon it, Keld reverently, I interestedly and Avran reluctantly. The god's image is of a strange leafy figure, much like the 'green men' who haunt English legend.

Whether in storeroom or workshop or out among the crops, those artisans of Achalind seemed to me preternaturally solemn. In the fields of any English demesne, hard though the work might be, one would always hear loud conversation, ribald comment and much laughter; amid Sandastrian fields, there seems always to be song or the sweet trilling of pipes; but in Achalind, men and women alike spoke only in low voices or not at all. It is as if they were always conscious, and respectful, of the presence of their gods. However, it made me uneasy. Interesting though those lower passages are, after a while I began to feel oppressed in them, like a child forced too long to behave solemnly in church. I was glad to escape back to the upper corridors, where there was bustle and often the sweet song of small caged birds.

Yet, even in those upper corridors, it was hard ever to feel completely relaxed and at ease. Of course, for we who were accustomed to seeing the sky and feeling the wind, a life in the perpetual twilight and still, cool air underground was unnatural and bound to prove irksome; but that was only a small part of our problem. What caused us most unease was that this society never ceased to feel alien to us. The Ayanians are altogether too solemn, too stern; they seem ever oppressed by an awareness that their gods are hovering nearby and watching all that they do. I imagine that there might be the same atmosphere in England, in the monasteries of the sterner religious brotherhoods; but I have never visited such monasteries. Yes, indeed there were Ayanians who were able to laugh and joke, but they were sadly few. Xandor and Keld were the only two whom we encountered. Even among the children one saw few smiles and heard little laughter; their very play was a solemn preparation for an austere adulthood. Though we spent many weeks in Achalind, we never came to feel at home there.

Since Avran and I were classed as warriors, a part of each day had to be spent in martial exercise, in particular with the sword. To my relief, Avran had recovered quickly from his mauling by the branath. Though wielding his weapon stiffly at first, his skill soon won for him considerable praise, whereas my own lack of it was viewed with impatience. Much time was spent also by both of us in wielding the war axe, that favourite Safaddnese weapon. They use principally the heavy pole-axe. Most such weapons have a crescentic blade and a squarish, hammer-head-like pean. Some, however, have a spike-like pean that, I consider, makes them even more formidable; and a very few have flat blades and a hook at the end of the shaft, like the Lochaber axes the Scots wield.

With these weapons also, Avran's skill exceeded mine. However, in addition the Ayanians use throwing axes, much lighter and again with crescentic blades. At first I found these awkward to hurl, because of their ill balance; but after a while I could embed them neatly enough into the logs that served as targets. Avran was never so handy with them as was I, yet he did well enough to make him a formidable adversary in our mock battles.

Like the Sandastrians, the Ayanian warriors despise the bow as being a weapon suited only to the hunting of birds and small animals; unlike them, they showed no interest in it for, though word of the power of the longbow had crossed the mountains, it had been met with unbelief. Nor was I eager to demonstrate its use, for I did not wish to find myself considered too valuable—or too potentially dangerous—to be allowed to depart from Ayan. Consequently our bows were never strung whilst we were in Achalind; and, as had happened in Doriolupata, their staves were taken merely to be staffs.

Fortunately we were not required to take part in drill with the other soldiers, or to listen to the lectures on strategy that the other officers had to endure—for we were treated as letelarei, though never formally awarded that rank. This may have been because our knowledge of Safaddnese was insufficient for comprehension or it may have been a consequence of a lingering distrust of foreigners. We were not sure which, but we did not complain since it afforded us leisure in which to visit Robin.

We were likewise exempted from participation in the religious ceremonies that occupied a part of each soldier's day. The timing of these was at first confusing to us; they seemed to happen at all hours, sometimes even displacing the morning times of martial exercise or the afternoon sessions on strategy. Eventually, however, we came to understand their pattern.

The Safaddnese have no awareness of the Christian convention of dividing the day into twenty-four hours. Instead, they recognize two divisions, day and night, and divide both day and night into nine parts. Each of the nine *letpraien*, or divisions of the day, and each of the nine *letkranen*, or divisions of the night, is consecrated to a particular god of the Safaddnese pantheon. A baby born during that god's letpra or letkra is considered a child of that god and under his protection, consequently owing him especial devotions and tributes. One day of the nine-day Safaddnese week is likewise dedicated to that god; during it, a ritual of prayer and praise is intoned to him during his letpra by priests and people together and during his letkra by the priests only, though the gods' *praduvaien*, or day-children, may, if sufficiently devout, rouse themselves during the night and participate also.

39

The soldiers of Ayan are required only to attend the letpra ritual; but it was long ere we understood why this involvement changed exercise times so confusingly. Our confusion was emphasized by the fact that, as days and nights lengthen or shorten, so the durations of the letpranen and letkranen lengthen or shorten also, since each must be a ninth of the hours of light or darkness—and, underground, one saw neither light nor darkness anyway!

For us, the religious letpra was never a time of leisure. In the first weeks, it was when we met the young priest for our lessons in Safaddnese; and Avran's teasing of him made those sessions amusing enough. However, when our mastery of Safaddnese was considered adequate, that period came to be assigned for lessons of a harder kind, with a very different tutor; and our pleasure in them swiftly ended. For the new tutor was our second warrior associate, the one whom we never came to like—Yanu Hrasang.

As his surname indicated, Yanu was an Ayanian of lofty and ancient lineage. His ancestors had included letzaharei, udirarei and even letzudirarei—rulers, priests and even high priests. His consciousness of rank, and his contempt for us as mere riffraff of foreigners, was evident from the outset. Though relatively young he was as meagre, bleached and bald as an ancient, with a sharply jutting chin and a long upper lip. His contempt was expressed never in words, but in a pursing of lips and flexing of nostrils, as at an unpleasant odour. Yet he was conscientious. He had been assigned not only to instruct us but also, as we soon suspected, to investigate our backgrounds and keep check on our activities—and those duties he intended to carry out, little though he or we might enjoy the experience.

Yanu Hrasang's proclaimed tasks were not merely to enlarge our knowledge of the Safaddnese language, but also to inform us concerning the history and customs of the nine mountain realms. Inevitably this involved instruction in religion, for the worship of their nine gods is integral to all aspects of Safaddnese life. Yanu did not try to convert us to that religion; quite evidently he considered us unworthy of it. Nor was he inquisitive concerning our own beliefs or the realms from which we came. All too clearly, he considered the lands beyond the mountains to be in a condition of squalid savagery, beneath the notice of any Safaddnese gentleman officer!

I have heard men say that lack of curiosity means lack of intelligence; but that is not always true, for Yanu was certainly intelligent—quite alarmingly so, in fact. Moreover, I have to confess that he was an excellent teacher, far better than the priest had been. Yanu had the ability to present facts, and to answer questions, in the simplest and clearest fashion. Indeed we learned much from him, but without ever enjoying the process, for he was as cool to us as any marble slab on a temple wall. The sallies of Avran that had, with our previous tutor, brought me so often to laughter, were tried in vain on Yanu Hrasang. The only response they evoked was that disdainful pursing of his lips, making one feel like some creature that had crawled out from under a rotten log.

Our particular problem was that not only did Yanu teach us during lesson time, but also he haunted us during our evenings. Keld Eslingbror left us at some time after the midday repast, according to the pattern of letpra rituals and his duties. We did not see him afterward, for he had a family to which he returned. However, each day before leaving us, Keld would punctiliously educe from us our plans. We presumed he passed that information on to Yanu Hrasang since, before the time of the evening meal, Yanu would come to wherever we were. If we were with Robin he would not enter, in respect for Robin's eminence; instead, he would wait in icy impatience outside the chamber till we emerged. If we were elsewhere, he would enter immediately and interrupt our activity ruthlessly, whatever it might be, with the command to accompany him to dinner.

During those meals and throughout most evenings, he would continue to instruct us. It was not possible to converse with him, for he had no conversation. It was quite difficult even to converse with the other letelarei while Yanu was present. Though I was sure they viewed him with respect, I was equally sure that most of them disliked him thoroughly, from the tardiness and reluctance with which our corner of the messroom table was filled.

Sometimes, with a rudeness induced by sheer weariness of Yanu, Avran and I conversed in Reschorese or English; but his bleak gaze and silent disapproval meant that this afforded us little release. Indeed, Yanu's presence quite destroyed our enjoyment of our evenings. Only when invited to dine with the letzahar or with Essa—the Princess Hiludessa, I should say, for such meals were extremely formal—were we free of Yanu Hrasang.

All in all, we came to be very tired of him and weary also of confinement in that underground city. We knew there must be mighty winds and blizzards above us—the uvudain were brought underground unusually early that year—and that we could not, with safety, venture outside the caves. Nevertheless, we longed passionately to breathe fresh, cold air again—to be free once more and roaming under the light of the sun, even though it be among barren rocks and snow.

However, Christmas came—to be celebrated quietly and discreetly with Robin and Dan, for Essa could not or would not join us—and the New Year 1405 of our calendar began uncommemorated by us, ere any adventuring forth was even briefly to be permitted.

Chapter Four

A VENTURE TO THE LEMMESHIND

It was Avran who had calculated the date of Christmas for us. The very different Safaddnese calendar had me so confused that I shall be forever uncertain of the dates of most events during our sojourn underground. Yet I think it must have been around the twelfth of January when, at long last, Keld Eslingbror told us we were going on a visit to the surface. This aroused in us the sort of joy that prisoners must feel when a Royal pardon brings unexpected release from the dungeons. Indeed, our glee was so obvious that it set Keld chuckling in sympathetic pleasure.

When our party of soldiers—there were six others apart from Keld and us, making up the customary Safaddnese letel—reached the outer gate of Achalind, we found servants awaiting us with the furs and overboots we would need before venturing outside.

The ameral furs that had been Toril Evateng's gift were greatly admired by the other soldiers. The ameral, though nowhere common, is rarer in the northern than in the southern ranges and few Ayanians, even among the richest, could afford garb as good as ours. The soldiers' garments were made instead from the pelts of uvudain, for the uvudu's dark wool grows longer and turns white in winter, like that of most northern animals. Those pelts are as warm as ameral furs, but they are stiffer and heavier.

After donning our furs and formally exchanging passwords with the guards, we sallied forth through the gates—but only to halt again almost immediately while still under their arch. Two of the soldiers had been carrying bundles of flattish objects, like oversized versions of the kippered herrings one sees hanging on racks in Yorkshire fishing ports. Now these were handed round, two to each person.

As I examined mine, I found they were the huge leaves of some plant unknown to me. Thick, fleshy leaves they had been, but dried in some fashion that had made them leathery and caused their veins to stand out prominently. Into those leaves, thongs of uvudu-hide had been sewn in pairs, one thong of each pair bearing a buckle. I wondered if the leaves served as skates, for the other men were bending to attach them to their boots; but I saw no ice.

Keld was already stooping to aid Avran in putting his pair on. As he straightened he glanced at me, perceived my puzzlement and smiled.

'These are *seslelteven*,' he explained amusedly. 'Leaves of the *sesle-las*—have you not heard of them? They are a great gift of Horulgavar, for they allow us to walk freely on snow. See, now; you attach them like this.'

He bent again and showed me how to fasten two pairs of thongs over the front of my boot, the third and broadest pair about my heel.

'Try attaching the sesleltef to your other boot; yes, good! And now you must step out on to the snow. You'll find it easy enough. Pay heed, though, how you move your feet. As you walk, you must swing your legs a little more to each side than usual; otherwise, one sesleltef will catch on the other and you will tumble. Falling is not hurtful, for the snow is deep and soft, but rising is not so easy; so take care!'

Keld was right; though a little awkward at first, it is not truly difficult to walk in seslelteven. I am sure our clumsiness must have caused the other soldiers great amusement, but they were too courteous to show it—yes, even when Avran trod with his right sesleltef on his left and fell over in a tangle of frantically waving feet! However, Keld soon had him upright again.

After a while, we were moving freely enough over the deep snow that had accumulated during our weeks underground. Our seslelteven made only the shallowest of marks; yet such marks were quite discernible, even in the deep shadow of the valley head. Why, then, were there no tracks, so close to the gates of Achalind? Had no other soldiers, and no citizens, been out during those weeks?

Then I saw what the last two soldiers of our letel were doing, and I understood. They had half-turned and were swinging behind them long-handled devices somewhere between a brush and a light rake. These left the snow surface so smooth again that our passage could not be detected. Nor, looking back, could I discern the gates of Achalind. Now that they had closed behind us, and partly shaded as they were by an overhang, they were indistinguishable from the rock face.

When such precautions were being taken, even after so many years of peace, to keep Achalind concealed from enemies, it was easy to understand how the Safaddnese had succeeded in hiding themselves from the furiously searching soldiers of the Empire.

The side-valley probably contained a stream in summer; I could not tell. If so, then that stream had frozen over and been buried by snowdrifts; maybe we were walking over it. We were in deep shadow and the air was extremely cold, colder indeed than I had ever experienced; however, well wrapped as we were, only our faces felt it.

As I ambled along, swinging my feet outward in the rhythm I had been taught, I noticed a curious dry rustling that had nothing to do with the sound of my seslelteven on the snow. What could it be? Only slowly did I become aware that there came a rustle each time I breathed. Then I realized its cause; the hairs in my nose had frozen and were brushing stiffly together at each indrawn breath!

I told Avran of my discovery and he laughed. 'So that's the cause! I was wondering too. But you know, Simon, when we're back in Sandastre and tell our friends of such experiences, they'll never believe us—they'll consider that we're just romancing!'

I smiled also. Indeed, it was comforting to think of being away from these bleak mountains, back in the warm south and among friends. What if those friends *didn't* believe our stories? What would it matter to me if even Ilven laughed at them, provided I was with her again? Then my smile faded, as I remembered how long it must be before we reached Sandarro, even if all went well—and worse, how unlikely it was that I would ever again encounter my love and clasp her in my arms. Why, oh why had I allowed this endless will-o'-the-wisp quest for Lyonesse to lure me away from her?

At that point, distracted by my thoughts, I missed rhythm and caught one sesleltef against the other. Fortunately Avran was close and, by seizing my elbow, prevented a fall. This near-mishap served me well, for it forced me to concentrate again on just moving over the snow and thus steered my mind out of the dismal channel into which it had been drifting.

Within only a few furlongs, the side-valley ended; it was little more than an axe-notch into the flank of a much greater valley. We paused to look downward and I saw that the rocks immediately below us were sheathed with ice. Yes, there must indeed be a stream here in summer.

In the shadow from which we were emerging, I had not noticed the blue sky overhead. The snow slopes beneath and about us were glaringly white in the light of a sun of whose shining I had been equally unaware. However, when I tried to gaze beyond these slopes, I could see little. Surprisingly on so bright a day, a wall of mist obscured the distant view. It was a strange mist, for it seemed to shimmer and shift, without ever approaching closer to us.

Keld Eslingbror was standing by, so I asked him: 'Is there a river in the valley?'

'Of course there is!' he responded surprisedly. 'Can you not see its steam, rising there and turning into ice crystals in the air? The Lemmeshind does not freeze, even in deep winter.'

The Lemmeshind, I knew, was one of the nine great rivers running from these mountains into the northern sea. Our first tutor had sought to teach us their names by rote; nine principal rivers flowing northward from the mountains, nine eastward, nine southward and nine westward—of course, there had always to be nine! Avran had written down all their names and, I think, memorized them. He was much more interested than I, for he hoped, when back in Sandastre, to prepare a map of this whole island of Rockall. For my part, however, though naturally I remembered those of the two southern rivers, the Aramassa and the Rimbedreth, upon whose waters we had adventured, I had already forgotten most of the other names. Yet I did recall the River Lemmeshind, for had we not been told it was fed partly by the springs of Achalind?

It seemed that we must descend into the valley and evidently that could not be done on seslelteven, for the Ayanians were taking theirs off. Avran and I did likewise, then again followed our comrades' example by attaching together a strap from each and hanging the seslelteven yoke-like about our necks; they were very light.

Keld led us to the left—northward—and started down the slope, picking his way with care over rocks that were steep anyway and rendered more hazardous by snow and ice. Our descent did not take so long as I had expected, but it was difficult enough to make me glad when it was done—and to leave me deterred by the prospect of ascending again.

As soon as the slope eased, Keld put on his seslelteven and we others did likewise. He turned to Avran and me and smiled, the dance of his moustaches adding levity to his grim expression.

'Now, my friends, this is a day for learning. When wearing seslelteven, it is easiest to go down slopes at an angle; but that is slow. If there is need for haste, one may head downward directly. Try it! However, you must take small steps, swinging your legs just enough to ensure that one sesleltef clears the other. Watch me, please, and then follow.'

Indeed, it was not too difficult. I did not like the sensation and felt my toes curling protestingly within my boots; but I reached the bottom of the slope without accident and so did Avran. After that, walking in seslelteven on flat ground seemed supremely easy.

However, now I became aware of a new problem. Our emergence from shadow into sunlight had been sudden and the bright whiteness of the snow was dazzling. After so many weeks in dim underground lights, it was entirely too dazzling for me; I found myself blinking eyes that were smarting and watering.

This problem was soon resolved, for it was one very familiar to the Ayanians. Already strips of brownish cloth, woven from some kind of plant fibre and as light as cheesecloth, were being handed round. One of these strips was tied about my face and over my nose and eyes. I discovered that I could see through it as easily as through the tinted glass of a goblet, though it was strange at first to find that the snowy view had apparently turned yellow. My nose, which had been in danger of becoming frost-bitten and had required intermittent rubbing, soon felt comfortably warm again.

That was well, for we were walking straight into the wall of mist and the air was becoming even colder. It was like no mist that I had ever been in. The frost crystals swirling in the air about us were turned by the sunlight into tiny scintillating jewels, a dance of colour that made that valley seem like a realm of frost fairies. Yet their touch against brow and cheeks was so bitterly keen that I was glad of the cloth strip to filter the ice from my indrawn breath.

Quite abruptly, the flat snow ended at the edge of the river. At that point the ice-crystal mist dissipated a little and we could see out some way. I had expected the river water to be brown and muddy; instead, it was of a curious grey-green hue. Moreover, it did indeed seem to be steaming, like water in a boiling saucepan. Every so often, however, one could see a little raft of ice, its edges upturned like the rims of a cream-pan, being carried along by the current and buffeting against others.

'Is the river water hot, then?' I asked Keld surprisedly. 'If so, why don't those chunks of ice melt more quickly?'

He laughed out loud. 'Hot? Nay, Simon, 'tis cold enough, as you'd find if you dipped your hand in it; and don't try bathing, or you'll congeal! Yet, bitter cold though the water may be, it is warmer than the air above; and so it steams.'

I did not really understand, yet nor did I wish to appear even more foolish; so I posed no further questions. Instead, I looked about me again and noticed other details.

Evidently the river level had dropped in the last while, for there were sheets of ice clinging to the bank—ice that was arched out and downward, leaving a space beneath that small animals might use as a tunnel safe from predators. Not, however, safe from men, for at intervals that ice had been discreetly broken through and traps set within. The reason for our expedition was, I now learned, to check those traps; and, for that purpose, the six other soldiers spread out along the bank. However, Keld did not propose to set us to that task.

'Follow me a distance further,' he ordered. 'Quite close to here, the Tratellend flows into the Lemmeshind. That is a sight you should see.'

The riverside meadows—or rather, marshes, for that is what they would become with the spring melt—had been flat enough so far. Quite soon, however, we found ourselves ascending a broad ridge that swung out eastward from the valley wall. From the extreme irregularity of its surface, it must have contained many boulders. Keld led the way, climbing obliquely, and Avran and I followed carefully in his footsteps.

As he reached the ridge crest, Keld stiffened and made a backward motion of his right hand that urged stillness and silence. Then he moved slowly back to speak quietly to us, his eyes shining with excitement.

'There is a *prasal* just below the ridge—an old male, with a fine horn. I wish I had a spear with me, but no such luck; so I must see whether I can approach him close enough to slay him with a thrown axe. I shall go ahead; follow me to the ridge crest so you can watch the fun, but come no closer!'

The prasal is a goat-like creature, with a single broad horn that curves upward and forward from its head, dividing into a T-shape at its tip. Avran and I had never seen one alive, but we had seen prasal horns often enough. They made excellent drinking cups, for the T-shaped end could readily be shaped to serve as a stand. The letzahar had a matching set of such cups for use by his guests, a set much prized and of great antiquity, for prasalen were by then uncommon in Ayan.

As we followed Keld discreetly to the top of the rise, we saw that the stony ridge was even steeper and rockier on its northern face. Despite the difficulties of traversing such a surface for anyone wearing seslelteven, the skilled Keld was moving quietly and easily downward.

At the ridge foot, just visible before the mist became too opaque, was a sheltered place where a few plant fronds still protruded through the snow. The prasal was feeding on these with tugging bites, snorting as he did so. Though we were quite high above him, we could see he was a massive beast, with a thick, white fleece that trailed below his belly and hid his limbs from view. We could even see the little puffs of white that came at each grumbling breath.

Keld was not far above the prasal now. Our friend's feet were planted firmly on a rock that protruded from the slope; he had drawn his axe out from its sheath and was pivoting for the throw.

He hurled the axe, but then followed disaster! As he threw, the rock on which he was standing came loose from the slope, rolling out and downward. Taken entirely by surprise, Keld tried to leap clear but fell heavily onto a larger rock just below. The displaced boulder bounded away past him to the bottom of the ridge.

Warned by the sound, the prasal raised its head and turned, bringing its great horn up in time to deflect the thrown axe. Even so, the force of the impact knocked the beast over. Briefly we glimpsed a rolling bundle and a flurry of hooves; but then the prasal regained its feet and fled into the mist. As for Keld, he lay still and crumpled on the rock where he had fallen.

Though Avran and I were anxious to reach our friend, we were not adept enough in seslelteven to do so speedily. Indeed it was necessary to be cautious, if there were to be no further casualties on that slope. Hastily we unbuckled our seslelteven and then descended as quickly as we might.

While we were climbing down, we heard Keld groaning and knew that he was alive. However, as we drew closer, we perceived that something was sadly wrong with him. Though he had fallen forward on his face, he was striving vainly even to turn over onto his back.

When we reached Keld, he glanced up at us with a frightened eye. 'My leg,' he gasped. 'My right leg; it won't work! Lift me up, will you, friends?'

I glanced at Avran and saw, by the question in his eyes, that he was thinking as I was—and remembering the training we had received while travelling in the great forests with Vedlen Obiran.

I swallowed, then said firmly: 'Not yet. First, we must discover what is wrong with you.'

Fortunately the rock onto which Keld had fallen had a broad, table-like surface to which little snow had clung. I knelt beside him and began carefully probing with my fingers; I had slipped off my glove. Avran, kneeling beside me, watched concernedly.

Discovering the problem was easy enough. I sat back on my heels and put my glove on again.

'I'm afraid your right hip is dislocated, Keld. Your leg bone has quite come out of its joint.'

He groaned. 'Well, that finishes me. I don't reckon I can be moved without a stretcher and you can't fetch one in time; in this cold I'd be dead long before it came. But then, even if you had one, you'd never get me back to Achalind, with that cliff to be climbed. Turn me over, though. It's no joy, lying here on my stomach in the snow like this. I might as well die looking upward at the blue sky.'

We did as he requested. His forehead was bruised and his cheek cut, but there seemed to be no other serious injuries. After examining him further, I directed another question at Avran.

'You remember that woodcutter, Avran, who'd fallen from the tree? When we visited that steading south of Chancelet?'

'Yes indeed. The wizard set him right, didn't he, and quickly enough? Think you that we might do the same for Keld?'

There was a quick flare of alarm in Keld Eslingbror's eyes and his moustaches twitched indignantly.

'Here, I'll have no southern wizardry! Go away, won't you, and fetch my men to me. I'd rather commend my soul to my own gods, to Horulgavar and Halrathhantor, than be cured by any of your southern magic!'

'This is not magic, Keld; merely bonesetting,' I chided; then hesitated. 'You're stronger than I, Avran—and it needs strength.'

'Yes, but I suspect you remember the method more clearly than do I, Simon—and, as you know, if done wrong it can cause both pain and lasting harm.'

'Very well,' I sighed. 'I'll try. Can you show fortitude for a while, Keld? This will surely hurt, even if all goes well.'

He looked up at me doubtfully; his moustaches were drooping now and his countenance was altogether woebegone. 'Aye, I'll trust you. I suppose it is a question of trust or die; so I'd better, had I not?'

Avran took off Keld's seslelteven and made sure he was lying perfectly flat. Meanwhile I slipped off my right boot and went to stand between Keld's legs. Setting my bare foot on Keld's groin, I crouched over him, thrust my right elbow under his knee and clasped his ankle firmly with my left hand. Then I took a deep breath and levered upward with my elbow, using all the force I could muster.

Nothing happened, save that Keld gave a shuddering groan. Well, I must try again!

This time, as I levered my elbow upward, I tried to use it and my left hand to rotate his leg toward me. There was a sort of dull clunking sound and, simultaneously, a sharp cry of pain from Keld. As I loosened my grasp and stood up between his legs, I realized that sweat was pouring from my brow, despite the day's extreme coldness; also, that my foot was freezing.

'Try it now,' I urged. 'Try your leg now.' And I stepped clear of him, to thrust my foot back into my boot.

Keld was looking up at me, awe on his face. 'It feels good again! There was pain—much pain—but now the pain's gone! Why, I think I might sit up, even.'

'Here, let me help you.' Avran leapt to his aid.

Thus assisted, Keld sat up readily enough and stretched out his right leg, then flexed it.

'Why, 'tis fine—'tis well! I think—yes, I believe I might walk again!' He beamed up at us, his moustaches curving upward to enlarge that smile. 'I'm beholden to you both; I shall not forget this. Here now; help me to my feet, would you?'

While Keld was standing, a little uneasily but delightedly, on the rock, I hastened down to retrieve his axe from the snow, floundering a little since I had not put on my seslelteven again. After that, it needed some steadying from Avran's arm to get Keld back to the ridge-crest, but all three of us got there safely. There Keld insisted that we put on our seslelteven and help him on with his; and it was with evident pride that he led our descent off the ridge to the flat marshland beyond.

The other soldiers had already gathered and were hastening towards us. Three of them bore small fur-bearing beasts that had been caught in the traps; from its pattern of spots, I recognized that one was an ameral.

Keld poured out to his men the story of his fall and gave unduly generous praise to me for what had, after all, been only a simple feat of field surgery. Nevertheless, I must confess to being quite proud of it—and grateful for having learned the method from Vedlen Obiran.

The climb back up to the hanging valley proved quite as difficult as I had feared, but it was managed without further accident. Though he was visibly tiring—as indeed were Avran and I, after so long a first day on seslelteven—Keld climbed well enough. Only when we were again in the shadowy valley that led to Achalind's gates did he suddenly stop and turn worriedly to us.

'My friends to whom I owe so much—really I must apologize! After all, I never *did* show you where the Tratellend joins the Lemme-shind!'

Chapter Five

THE PRIEST AND THE SOLDIER

As it chanced, Avran and I never did see that junction of rivers. Whatever its particular wonders may have been, they remained unknown to us. Yet, in the fortnight or so that followed, we went out several more times on expeditions into the upper world. Indeed, we developed a fair skill at moving over the snow on seslel-teven.

For a while, Keld Eslingbror was not able to accompany such expeditions. Though he had striven successfully to attain Achalind, his leg had been overstrained by the effort. It required a week of resting before he was able again to sally forth.

When Avran and I were leaving the messroom after dinner on the evening of our return, we found a little, tubby, dark-haired woman awaiting us—Keld's wife. She was quite tearfully grateful to us for, as she put it, saving her dear husband, calling down the blessings of Horulgavar and Radaionesu upon us. In parting, she pressed into our hands a flask of wine which, upon later sampling, proved the headiest and most delicious that we had tasted in the northlands. Nor was that to be the only evidence of her gratitude.

Even more pleasing to me, and much more surprising, was an invitation to demonstrate Vedlen Obiran's technique to a group of Ayanian chirurgeons, including Robin's physician, 'Old Cheesy-face' himself. It seemed that particular trick of bonesetting was quite unknown to the Safaddnese. I have often wondered if, in subsequent years, it has saved the lives or the limbs of other men and women. I hope so.

More puzzling was the reaction of our unbeloved tutor, Yanu Hrasang. He made no comment on the affair, though we knew he was aware of it; but it produced a perceptible change in his attitude to Avran and me. Hitherto he had treated us with a sort of cool contempt, like a proud bishop forced by the conventions of his cloth to give charitable attention to the tiresome importunings of peasants. Henceforward he evinced instead a calculating watchfulness, like a chess player considering the ploys of an opponent who, though of lesser skill, might yet surprise him.

On the whole, Avran and I considered this a change for the better.

Our other expeditions were made always in a letel, but under variable leadership and to various destinations. Twice we set out through the main gate as before, though not to return to the Lemmeshind valley. Instead we followed steep paths into the mountains, to spend arduous days on patrol. On the other occasions, we left Achalind by unfamiliar ways, along tunnels that had been excavated as escape routes, should the main gate be stormed or the underground river flood. Halrathhantor's continuing benignity seemed not to be altogether trusted by the Ayanians!

Learning the situations of these tunnels, within the labyrinth of other tunnels that was Achalind, formed part of the training undergone by every letelar. Each tunnel led to an exit on the mountaintops. These exits were so carefully concealed in cliffs or among rock-piles that, without a detailed knowledge of the key indications—apparently natural marks on rock faces or seemingly accidental arrangements of stones—one could never have found them. Nevertheless, every such exit was guarded constantly. The Ayanians, though living well within the borders of the Safaddnese territories, were continually on the watch against invasion.

The weather on those expeditions varied sharply. Our two days of patrol were both under bright skies but in conditions of bitter cold, with biting winds. By their end, despite the exertion and the warmth of our furs, we felt so thoroughly chilled that it needed an evening of quaffing mulled ale to restore our cheer. A third day was equally frigid, but still and sunny, with the white mountaintops and blue sky seeming like devices in argent and azure on a freshly painted shield. Other farings-forth were made under cloud blankets as dully grey as in any English winter, with brief flurries of snow falling from the skies or whipped up by wind gusts from the ground; and on one day, the onset of a blizzard was so sudden that we were fortunate to find our tunnel's entrance again before the snow buried it.

As it chanced, we had been invited to dine that evening with the

54

Princess Hiludessa—for indeed, with the progress of the weeks and the unceasing indications of the dignity she had gained, it was becoming ever harder to think of her simply as our erstwhile companion Essa. It was an important dinner, for it was the first that Robin had been permitted by his physicians to attend—and thus it was a celebration of his recovery.

The evening had, as I realized afterward, been chosen carefully. It was Thursday—for the Safaddnese, the day of Petamedru, god of the moon and stars and of Avakalim. More significantly for Essa's purpose, however, Petamedru was the god of whom the dakhmen Soganreth was praduvai, 'day-child'. In view of the importance of the occasion, she had invited not only the letzahar himself, but also Parudanh, the chief priest, and Xandor, the cheery leader of the artisans. Yet Essa could be confident that all three would leave towards the end of the first letkran of the night, in order properly to celebrate the birth of the dakhmen during the second letkran, that of Petamedru. (The first letkran is devoted to Daltharimbar of the winds and the second to Petamedru, since by then the moon is high and the stars clearly to be seen.)

The branath kitten had, as always, accompanied Essa. I had not seen it for some weeks and was surprised how large it had grown—why, it was at least four times larger, perhaps more, than it had been when rescued from the lair on the cliff. No longer would it ride before Essa on veludu-back; it was much too big. Yet it appeared perfectly tame and, when Essa had seated herself, settled down quietly beside her chair.

Dinner began early and with much ceremony. The chief priest offered blessing and praise to his gods, first, for the rescuing of Hiludessa from captivity by the Indreletzahular—I noted with wry amusement how small a part Avran and I were assumed to have played in it!—and, second, for the Indreletzahular's merciful recovery from serious illness, a recovery for whose completion Parudanh then proceeded to pray. That supplication took some time, during which we others listened with respectful gravity and bowed heads; though, by the movement of Avran's lips, I was sure he was praying instead to our own God. After it, fortunately, the letzahar's address of praise and respect needed only to be brief and Essa's, though especially heartfelt, yet briefer.

Robin's response, also uttered in Safaddnese, was one of profound gratitude to his physicians and to his hosts. He contrived skilfully to avoid making any reference to the intercession of the nine gods, without seeming at all disrespectful to their supposed omnipotence.

After that, we were permitted to eat and everyone relaxed. Xandor's stories of misadventures underground caused us much amusement. Even Parudanh sometimes permitted himself a grave smile: as I was beginning to realize, the letzudirar possessed a sense of humour that warred with the portentous gravity and solemnity demanded by his position. Indeed, I was coming quite to like the high priest.

Prompt to time, the letelar of the dakhmen's escort entered, to remind him respectfully of his need to hasten to the temple. After bidding the Princess not to break up the feast, Soganreth and the letzudirar made their stately departure. The letzumahar Xandor left also, with a shrug and a smile that expressed to us clearly enough how reluctant was his reassumption of the yoke of duty.

When they were gone, Essa urged the stewards to clear the tables of all but our goblets and a carafe of wine. The Ayanians, though not such heavy drinkers as the English, are less moderate in their potations than the Sandastrians, so this was normal enough. The arrival of Dan Wyert reassured the chief steward that there would be someone of lesser status on hand to pour the wine whenever needful. Consequently, he allowed himself to be speeded graciously on his way by Essa; and indeed, he left beamingly.

As soon as we were alone, Essa looked round at us with a smile of relief. Then, unexpectedly, she sighed.

'I am grateful for this hour alone with you, my friends. Believe me, it has taken much contriving; and I must confess I am uncertain when, or even if, I can manage another. Our Ayanian friends are ever entrusting me with greater duties and surrounding me with more elaborate ceremonial. I long to be free, as you are, Simon and Avran, to travel outside and see again the rocks and the sky; yes, even in a blizzard! Well, perhaps that might be contrived soon. However, while we have this respite, there is a great deal for us to discuss.'

Robin looked at her keenly. 'First, I must ask you a question that I have not dared to ask, with other ears listening. Are all the Ayanians satisfied that you are indeed Hiludessa, the lost princess returned again?'

Essa looked at him gravely for a moment before replying. 'Well, I do not believe I've fallen into any grievous errors, though my path has been difficult at times. I was fortunate. On my second day here, I was brought a scroll recording my lineage; my supposed lineage, that is. It contains the names of all the letelarei, letzesaharei and letzudirarei of Avakalim who are considered to be my kin, very clearly set forth, with their dates of birth and death and even a summary of their principal attainments. Happily I had time to study that scroll before any questions on those points were asked; and, believe me, I've kept on studying it, so that now I have it by heart.'

'How chanced it that you received so fortunate a gift?'

She smiled again. 'It was through Xandor; one of his men brought it to me. Xandor is always generous, yet he cannot have known how very valuable that particular present was!'

'So you consider all to be well?'

She hesitated, then frowned. 'Sometimes I think so; at other times, I have doubts. The letzudirar Parudanh; yes, I'm confident that he believes in me. He has been very kind and very patient with what he considers my lapses of memory, when I fail to carry out some ritual correctly or I err in recollecting some chant or invocation. Xandor, of course, is a friend to all of us. As for the dakhmen Soganreth, he accepts the assurance of Parudanh and also treats me kindly.'

As she paused, Robin urged her gently: 'But . . . ?'

Her smile now was wry. 'Yes, I'm afraid there is a "but". The *nuszudirar*, the second priest in rank in this land—do you know him? You do not? Nor you, Avran and Simon? Well, I am not surprised. He is a man to be wary of, for he combines extreme austerity with high ambition. Whenever I have invited him to dine with me, he has found some pretext not to do so—a pretext which apparently displays his extreme piety and selflessness, yet which conceals a straightforward dislike. And not just of me, I suspect, but of all women!'

'Oh, indeed!' observed Robin, raising his eyebrows; and Essa laughed. However, her gravity returned quickly.

'Nevertheless, he does nurse a particular grudge against me. I have learned from Xandor that he desires fervently to supplant Parudanh in the highest office of the worship of Halrathhantor. His difficulty is that, by my seemingly miraculous return, I have given the Ayanians a new reason to respect their present high priest. Thus I am an obstacle in the path of his ambition: and thus he dislikes me—perhaps even hates me.'

'What does he look like, this nuszudirar?' Robin was evidently disturbed by this revelation, as indeed were we all. 'How shall we know him, if we encounter him?'

'Well, of course you could identify him by his robes. Yet, even without them, he is easily recognized. He cannot have seen even forty summers—his preferment has been rapid, but then he is of ancient and honoured family—yet he is quite bald. He is also very lean, with a chin like the prow of a yildrih and with bleak, pale eyes. Though he seems quite to lack any sense of humour, he is very intelligent. Always he is questing for an advantage, for an opportunity to make contemptuous comment on others and to demonstrate his own virtuous superiority.'

Avran winced. 'Ugh! He sounds very like our dear tutor, Yanu Hrasang, of whose company it is a pleasure to be free this evening.'

There was a flicker of amusement in Essa's expression. 'Indeed, very like; for is not the nuszudirar elder brother to your beloved instructor?'

At our startlement, she laughed aloud. 'Yes, the nuszudirar is Zelat Hrasang, brother of Yanu Hrasang. It is the custom, you know, in the great Safaddnese families that, if there be two sons, one becomes a priest and the other a soldier. In that fashion, the family has hopes of attaining honour in one or other sphere, religious or secular. Moreover, since priests are properly more honoured than soldiers, it is most often the eldest son who chooses the temple.'

'How strange!' I commented surprisedly. 'In England, it is the opposite. But then, I suppose we must respect military exploits more than clerkly attainment. Well, what you tell us explains much.'

'It does indeed,' said Avran furiously. 'I thought that Yanu was spying on us and now I'm sure of it. Trying to discover from us, no doubt, something that his elder brother can use against you, my Princess!'

Essa coloured. 'Perhaps, in this land, I may be a princess; yet I am not *your* princess, Prince Avran.'

Yet, though reproving him, she did not sound at all angry with Avran, while Avran seemed not at all disquieted by her reproof.

Hastily Essa went on: 'Until you could speak Safaddnese, my friends, the Hrasangs could not hope to learn much from you. That was why, Avran and Simon, you were permitted another tutor at the outset; Yanu did not want to waste his time. He took the task upon himself only when you reached the point where you might be expected properly to understand his questions—when he could note your responses and store them in his memory, in the hope that they might be used to our detriment. Whenever he sits so silently beside you, be sure he is eagerly awaiting some incautious revelation! Please be careful; please be particularly heedful of all that you say in his presence, so that you let nothing slip that might harm us all.'

While she spoke, I had been reviewing our past conversations with, or in the presence of, Yanu. 'Have we made any blunders yet?' I asked. 'I trust not.'

'Only in one regard. You told Keld Eslingbror that you had travelled with a wizard—a southern wizard. That was unwise.'

Perceiving our dismay, she added gently: 'Yes, Keld is your friend and owes you much, but Yanu Hrasang is his superior—did you not know?—and Zelat Hrasang is his priest. Do not blame Keld. In any event, Simon, you have quite inadvertently made matters worse, for you mentioned to the chirurgeons the name of that magician—Vedlen Obiran. They would recognize it as a Reschorese name; and the Safaddnese remember the Reschorese as their last and greatest enemies.'

'Yes, that was unfortunate,' I agreed rather embarrassedly. 'Yet, when questioned directly, how else could I have answered?'

'I understand well that it has not been easy for any of you,' Essa responded. 'Indeed, matters might have been much worse. On the whole, gentlemen, you have guarded your tongues well during these long weeks.'

Robin was regarding her consideringly. 'I am impressed by what you have learned, Princess; but may I ask how you have learned it all?'

'Through my servants, of course,' she answered rather amusedly. 'They like me and respect me, most fortunately; and they resent the machinations of the Hrasangs and their ilk. Consequently they tell me much, seeking also, I suppose, to gain through their frankness extra blessings from their gods.'

'Well then,' I asked, 'how much have my indiscretions harmed us?'

'Not indiscretions, Simon; merely errors made through inadvertence. With Keld lying injured, you could not be thinking of trivialities; and, when questioned by the chirurgeons, you were equally in difficulty. Yet your answers have provided an opening for the Hrasangs and their supporters. Now, I do not think they will dare to challenge me directly; eventually, mayhap, but not yet. Nor do I think they will attack you, Sir Robert; are you not the Indreletzahular? And, Dan, you are considered my servant; you are safe, for so long as I am safe.'

Dan, hitherto silent, stirred and nodded. She smiled quite fondly at him before continuing.

'However, Avran and Simon, I'm afraid *you* are vulnerable, for the Hrasangs are spreading lying tales about you both. You are being called southern spies, associates of evil magicians outside the rule of Mesnakech. Fortunately your healing of Keld is remembered in your favour. His wife and he are loud in your praise. Consequently, for the moment those falsehoods are not gaining much credence. However, as I say, you must be cautious. You must take heed not to say or do anything further that might give such rumours strength.'

Seeing again the consternation in our expressions, Essa laughed quite merrily. 'Nay, do not be so downcast, my friends. Those may be ill tidings, but I bring you good tidings also. At long last, Simon, I can tell you how to find Lyonesse!'

Chapter Six

A PROBLEM FOR THE PRINCESS

After so many months of pursuing our will-o'-the-wisp quest, this declaration quite took me aback. 'Lyonesse?' I repeated blankly. 'You can tell us how to find Lyonesse?'

Essa was evidently amused. 'Yes, Simon,' she responded with exaggerated patience. 'Lyonesse. You do recall that land for which, as I understand it, we have so long been seeking? The land to which your father went, and your brother also, or so you informed us?'

'Yes, of course, Essa—er, Princess Hiludessa.' I answered in embarrassment. 'I'm sorry that I sound so stupid; my mind was upon other matters. Well, that's excellent! Please do tell us more. Is it close to Ayan?'

'Not close, no; yet nor are we very far from that land of your quest. If you were to follow the Lemmeshind to its emptying into the northern sea, you would reach Lyonesse.'

'So simple as that!' Avran remarked in astonishment. He and Robin were leaning forward excitedly, while Dan, though still sedulously guarding the door, was listening beamingly.

'Yes, in one sense simple; in another, not so very simple. As I understand it, the river flows too swiftly, and through too many rapids, for a voyage by yildrih. Nor can one travel along its banks. At first there are deep forests to the water's edge; afterwards there are marshes and many unbridged tributary torrents. To reach Lyonesse, it is necessary to keep to the mountaintops. However, given guidance and goodwill, the reaching of it should prove perfectly possible.'

'Goodwill?' Robin was surprised. 'Surely those are Safaddnese lands, even if outside Ayan? If the Ayanians vouch for us, why should there be trouble? Or do you believe we might not be permitted to leave Achalind—prevented even from beginning that journey?'

'Will we be permitted to leave, you ask, Sir Robert?' Essa was speaking slowly, as if weighing her words and being unsure she was achieving a proper balance. 'Well, for the moment the snow is too deep and the cold too severe for us to set forth; but later? Yes, I think they will allow me to leave Achalind, even to leave Ayan. Am I not considered a princess of another letzestre, Avakalim? They will be expecting me to return to my realm; but that I must not do. Here, I am accepted; but I fear that, in Avakalim, my deceptions would be swiftly exposed.'

She paused reflectively, then said provokingly: 'The Hrasangs, of course, are eager to be rid of me; they would do much to encourage my departure. When the time comes, we might even consider invoking their aid!'

'Come now, my Princess,' Avran responded reprovingly. 'I trust you are merely jesting! To tell them of our wish to depart—why, that would be perilous indeed! It would quite put us at their mercy.'

This time she took no note of the fashion in which he was addressing her; or, if she did, she made no comment. 'Yes, I was jesting. Yet they are the only ones who wish me gone. Dakhmen Soganreth and high priest Parudanh certainly do not. Indeed, though it is surely the Avakalimins who ought to have been first notified of my supposed return, no word has yet been sent to Avakalim even to report it. That surprises you, does it not? It has surprised me also, but I assure you that it is true.'

Indeed, we were all again astonished; moreover, Robin seemed to be relieved, for he was nodding to himself in satisfaction. However, it was Avran who spoke.

'Does that mean you will never be permitted to leave Ayan? Or might you be expected eventually to travel to Avakalim, whether you will it or no?'

Essa smiled mischievously at him. 'If I were to be sent to Avakalim and Simon was to journey on to Lyonesse, where would *you* choose to go, prince of the south?'

By this question, Avran was entirely disconcerted, as his expression made amusingly evident! Before he could decide how to answer, however, Essa was merciful enough to render a reply unnecessary.

'Yet, as I have said, it is not my wish to go to Avakalim; somehow that must be avoided. Be sure that, if I have my desire, I shall be travelling with you to Lyonesse.'

Avran's relief was so obvious that Essa laughed aloud. Indeed, we others were smiling also—yes, even Dan—for it had long since been perceived by us all how my friend had come to dote on Essa. We knew also that she was not indifferent to him—indeed, her teasing of him showed that. However, I was unsure in what measure his adoration was reciprocated.

Essa was speaking again. 'Unfortunately, I find it harder to answer your other question, Sir Robert. Yes, the lands we would need to traverse are Safaddnese lands; yet I am not confident that we would be welcomed. I wonder also whether, when the time comes, any vouching from the Ayanians would prove of assistance to us. I am being retained here because the letzahar and the letzudirar wish me to solve a problem for them. When I have given my answer, they may well allow me to leave. However, our ability to travel through those lands may depend on how I have resolved that problem.'

Robin was regarding her intently. 'And what is that problem—or is it a secret which must be kept from us?'

'Not from you, my friends. Not from you; though perhaps it might be unwise for you to discuss it with the Ayanians. However, to understand their dilemma, you will require also to comprehend a rather complex political situation; or, mayhap a religious situation, for it is that also. Simon, how much do you know concerning the history of Lyonesse—not the old Lyonesse of Tristan, but the new one of the knights from England?'

I reflected briefly before replying. 'Very little, really. I suppose it must be quite a dozen years since they left England—Sir Arthur Thurlstone, Sir John Warren and their following, off to seek King Arthur's Island of Avallon. I was a very small boy then, but I recall the excitement it aroused. Folk thought them mad, yet admired them; for was not theirs a real quest, such as the knights of romance embarked upon? There ensued a silence of, oh, three years or so. Then back came Sir Arthur, seeking more men and women to help populate the new realm he and Sir John had found for themselves.'

'That must have caused much excitement also,' Avran commented.

'Yes, indeed it did. I was still very young, but I remember Sir Arthur's visit to Holdworth. Quite a small person he is, yet having something of the charm and energy that, men say, the Black Prince had. He impressed me greatly—I thought him a veritable Knight of the Table Round!'

Robin laughed at this and Dan Wyert smiled; but Avran and Essa, to whom the tales of King Arthur were unfamiliar, merely looked puzzled. However, they asked no questions. Instead, Essa enquired: 'Do you remember anything more, Simon?'

'Well, some men from Hallamshire went back with him and some women also, I think. Of course, there were plenty of tales—tales of adventurings so strange that they'd have been quite appropriate to the Round Table knights. I recall little from those stories, but I do remember that there had been some battle that was crucial to the winning of their realm—a battle against great odds, or so the tale ran. Yet mostly folk were puzzled why the new realm was styled, not Avallon, but Lyonesse. I understand *that* now, at least!'

Essa ignored my last comment, instead harking back to my earlier one. 'Yes, there was a battle; and its consequences form the heart of my problem. Would you care to hear the story of that battle?'

Avran was always avid for tales of war. 'Yes, indeed!' he answered; and we others echoed him.

'First I must recall to your minds the present condition of the coastal Safaddnese letzestrei. In Vasanderim, far to the west, there remain people enough; but in Avakalim and Brelinderim, as the years have gone by, there has been a sad dwindling. The frontiers of those two realms march with Ayan, Avakalim to the northwest, Brelinderim to the northeast; indeed, the flow of the Lemmeshind divides those letzestrei. Ultimately that river debouches into a great bay, the only one on the northern coast—or so men tell me—where ships may anchor safe from wind and tempest.'

'Do those letzestrei maintain fleets, then?' Robin was clearly surprised. 'I had not heard of it.'

'No, they do not. We Safaddnese are folk of the mountains, not of the sea. We have no ships and care little about harbours. Unfortunately, close by there dwells a people for whom the sea is as much their home as the land. Toril Evateng called them the Northmen—your name for them also, I think, Simon? By us they are styled the Sea Warriors. They came at first from far away, and consequently they came rarely. Unhappily, long ago they seized from my people the coasts beyond Vasanderim, to make a nearer base for their raiding.'

I was puzzled. 'Do they raid you even yet, then? In our English churches, as I have told you, men still pray to be spared the fury of the Northmen; yet centuries have gone by since last they came upon us.'

'Not so here. The men of Vasanderim are forever fighting the Sea Warriors, in the mountains as well as on the coast. Maybe that is why they remain vigorous, while we other Safaddnese do not; a sword that shines in use might soon rust in the scabbard. For it is true that, during more than a century, the coasts of Avakalim and Brelinderim have been left unscathed; or so I am told.'

Avran was becoming restive. 'Where, then, was the battle?'

She laughed at him. 'You are ever impatient, prince of the south — in this matter, as in others. Yet you must wait a little longer for that tale. Do you remember how Toril spoke of Pavonara?'

'Yes indeed,' I answered. 'Was that not the land of—let's see— the Gadarrans and such of the Seleddens who survived the flooding of ancient Lyonesse?'

'You remember well, Simon. Yes, that is right. Those were the peoples who had been willing servants of the great southern Empire, and whom we drove from our mountains when that Empire fell. Much later, they were joined by some Sachakkans who would not accept your Christian beliefs. Three peoples, all proud and turbulent; and, though long united into one *dakheslevat*, one kingdom, still so quarrelsome that they do well to call their land 'the realm of the drawn sword.' Nor do they confine their battling within their own borders. They have oftentimes invaded other lands, especially the lands to the southward. Also they have suffered much from the Sea Warriors.'

'Why is that?' Avran enquired.

'It is because their coasts are lower and their cities less well concealed than ours. Moreover, their cities are richer and, as such, offer greater temptations to such reivers. In contrast, we Safaddnese have given them many hard buffets and only meagre profits. That is the reason why Avakalim and Brelinderim have been spared, while Pavonara has been so regularly raided. Yet the Pavonarans do not accept this. Instead, they claim that we are spared because we have become allies of the Sea Warriors—that, by our connivance, the bay at Lemmeshind mouth serves as shelter for their ships.'

'How do you know all this—know that they were raided, know

what they think of you?' Robin was again surprised. 'I thought you Safaddnese had no intercourse with lands beyond the frontiers of your letzestrei.'

Essa smiled at him. 'You are remembering Reschora, Sir Robert—and indeed, as you speak, so am I. Yes, it is generally true that we have no contact with neighbouring realms. Yet Pavonara is the exception—and for good reason. The letzestre of Desume occupies and surrounds the upper valley of the great river to the east of the Lemmeshind—the River Embeldwey. Yes of course, you had learned that, Simon and Avran, had you not? But did you learn also that its lower valley was the land of the Seleddens and, as such, forms part of Pavonara?'

We shook our heads.

'Well, you may guess that such a frontier is hard to defend; and, I assure you, it has been much fought over. Yet, for many years now, the Desumeans and the Pavonarans have observed a truce. They have begun to exchange envoys and have even traded. We fear that the Desumeans are falling under Pavonaran influence—to what measure, we are yet unsure. Certainly we learn much from them concerning the Pavonarans and sometimes they have even served as voice for the Pavonarans in our councils. That is indeed part of our problem . . .'

Essa's voice drifted into silence. Then she shook her head, as if to rid herself of discordant thoughts, and continued: 'Very well, then: the Pavonarans believe, or pretend to believe, that Brelinderim and Avakalim have been aiding the Sea Warriors. Twelve years ago, late in the summer, an army of Gadarrans and Seleddens gathered at Hrensedlin and, without warning, crossed the mountains into Brelinderim. Their excuse was that they wished to seize and garrison the bay, to prevent it from being again used as harbour by the Sea Warriors; but, of course, it had never been so used.'

Robin was nodding comprehendingly. 'It is strange how rulers of all lands seem ever to require excuses for indulging their territorial greed. I have often noticed that. Yet you call it an army of Gadarrans and Seleddens; why not style it an army of Pavonarans?'

'Because the King of Pavonara learned nothing of the attack until after it had been launched. So the Desumeans tell us; and they say also that he was exceedingly wroth about it. The attack had been planned by a Gadarran, the Faruzlaf[1] of Hregisel. He rallied to his standard two Seledden leaders, the Faruzlavai of Askevdrayin and Brachang. There were no Sachakkans among the attackers—indeed, no soldiers came from any of the other regions of Pavonara. Even so, the army was much greater than any the Brelinderimins could have raised. Moreover, they were unwary. Hregisel's men had crossed the mountains and were streaming down into the valley of the Lemmeshind before the Brelinderimins even knew they had been invaded.'

'Ah! so that was the battle!' Avran was at last content.

'Yes indeed; and a defence against heavier odds than ought to have been faced, given proper warning. Only a part of the Brelinderimin soldiery had time to rally—those that dwelt closest to the northern sea, a few hundred men at most. The letzahar was a sick man and away ill up-valley; he did not even learn of the invasion till too late. Fortunately his deputy, Talados Esekh, was among the bravest of men; and he had need to be. Yet his warriors were so utterly outnumbered that he must certainly have been defeated, and Brelinderim lost, had not your English knights arrived.'

'What transpired, then? How came it that they fought alongside a people of whose existence they cannot even have been aware?'

'To understand that, Prince Avran, you will need to comprehend the exact situation, as it has been told to me. At the very mouth of the Lemmeshind, a rock ridge strikes across the valley, forming a barrier through which the river flows in turbulence at high tide, more slackly at low water. Immediately upstream from the ridge, there is a marsh. To seaward, there is water at high tide but sands at low tide—sands that should have been dug away, had the Brelinderimins been properly maintaining their defences. For the ridge had been long since fortified on both its sides—so long ago, indeed, that no-one remembers who constructed those fortifications.'

'The men of the Empire, mayhap?' I suggested.

'Mayhap; or the Seleddens of old. Well, to west and east of the river, above and below the ridge, there are meadowlands where hasudain pasture in summer. It was on the eastern meadowlands that battle was first joined. The Brelinderimins were courageous in defence of their land and many an invader was slain for each of them

---

[1] A rank equivalent to a German count or an English or Scottish earl.

that died. Yet Esekh's men were driven back, to make a last stand in the eastern fortress—a fortress whose bastions had been allowed so to crumble that they afforded only a poor protection.'

Robin, the old warrior, shook his head disgustedly.

'Yes, it was neglectful,' Essa answered his unspoken comment. 'But then, the Brelinderimins were becoming ever fewer and had withdrawn their settlements up-valley. On the western shore, the Avakalimins—my people, as I must now regard them—had been quite as heedless of their defences. However, they had the protection of the river from any attacks from Pavonara. Only a rope bridge connects the two fortresses.'

'Ah! So the Brelinderimins had a means of escape.' Avran was listening intently.

'Just so. Yet if they took it, they knew their land would be forever lost. Perhaps Hregisel's army might have let Avakalim alone, for a while anyway; but he would have extended Pavonara's frontiers to the Lemmeshind. That, at least, is certain.'

'Yes, I comprehend that; but tell us of the English knights.'

Essa smiled at Avran. 'Very well; but there is one thing more you must understand. The battle had begun before high tide. When the Brelinderimins retreated to the eastern fortress, it was protected at south and north by the marshes and the sea. However, as the tide fell, the marshes were drained and the seaward sands began to be exposed. The invaders began to close about the Brelinderimins: Esekh was forced to consider a retreat over the bridge to Avakalim. Yet he was reluctant to do so, comprehending fully the consequences.'

'And then the English ships arrived?'

'Yes, then the English ships arrived; two vessels, one under the command of Sir John Warren and the other under Sir Arthur—Sirlstone, is it, Simon? Some difficult name. But the Pavonarans—why, they thought them to be vessels of the Sea Warriors! As the ships sailed in, Hregisel's soldiers waded out into the waters and hurled spears and axes, trying to drive off what they thought were allies attempting to aid Brelinderim. Who else, after all, would come from the sea at such a time?'

'Ah! *Now* I understand!' Avran was chuckling. 'What a blunder!'

'Indeed so. Your English knights saw a combat in progress; they perceived which were the attackers, surely the foreigners, and which the defenders, surely the residents; and, since assailed themselves, they found their allegiance decided for them. Moreover, they had a mighty weapon that the invaders lacked— one you know well, Simon; the longbow. The Seleddens and Gadarrans learned of it late and to their great cost. Under cover of the archers, your knights and their foot-soldiers landed and assailed the invaders with sword and spear; and the Brelinderimins, taking fresh heart, came down upon them also.'

She paused, smiling. 'You might almost guess the rest. The Faruzlaf of Hregisel was slain in single combat by Sir John Warren. An arrow took the life of the Faruzlaf of Askevdrayin and his colleague of Brachang was sorely wounded. With two of their leaders dead and the other seriously injured, the invading army broke and fled. They were so much harried in their retreat that few, I think, survived to cross the mountains back into Pavonara.'

Avran expelled a delighted breath. 'A happy chance and a splendid retribution!' he commented. In different words, we others echoed that sentiment.

'So it was, but it has left a legacy of complications. Talados Esekh realized fully what he owed to your countrymen, Simon. Not only did he make them welcome, but also he convinced the letzahar that Brelinderim would be wise to cede the whole lower eastern bank of the Lemmeshind to those knights. Moreover, the Brelinderimins persuaded the letzahar of Avakalim, my yet unencountered cousin'— Essa made a *moue* at the thought—'to cede to them the west bank also, so that the whole mouth of the Lemmeshind might properly be defended.'

'So that was the origin of the new Lyonesse!' I was fascinated by the story.

'Yes, that was its origin. The English knights have renewed the stone of the fortresses and are in process of extending them to west and east along the rock ridge, to make a new town. Warrentown, they call it; in memory of that knight's slaying of the faruzlaf, I presume. And that is the first element in the problem, though now there is a second and greater.'

'Why should it be a problem?' I did not understand. 'Is it not good that the sea coast be well defended, against Northmen and Pavonarans alike?'

Essa eyed me solemnly. 'Even yet, you do not understand us

Safaddnese, Simon. The people of the other letzestrei thought it shame enough that the Brelinderimins should require help from any outsiders. They consider it quite wrong that Safaddnese lands should have been given to those outsiders by two letzestrei, without the assent of all nine. Yet the situation was accepted, until this latest development.'

'Why, what is that?'

Essa smiled wryly. 'You said, did you not, Simon, that Sir Arthur was a man of both energy and charm? Charming he must be; for he won the heart of Darequel, daughter of Talados Esekh. Before that happened, the old letzahar had died and, most fittingly, Talados Esekh had been elected to his place; consequently, Darequel was indreletzar of Brelinderim. Moreover, not only did her father the letzahar approve that match, but he permitted them to wed in both Safaddnese and Christian fashions.'

Remembering the extreme conservatism of the Safaddnese, I winced; and I saw by their expressions that my companions were sharing my reaction. 'Yes, I can see how that would cause trouble.'

'Nor has that been an end to it. Since that time, Sir Arthur's bride has borne him two sons and a daughter. Many of the other Englishmen have married Brelinderimin girls and some Brelinderimin men have married Englishwomen. Those marriages have been equally fruitful, whereas the purely Brelinderimin lines continue to be unfruitful. Now Talados Esekh is dying and the dakhletzavat has chosen as his successor—no, not a Brelinderimin, but Sir Arthur himself! Moreover, he and his people desire that Brelinderim and Lyonesse should be combined under Sir Arthur's rule, so that it will cease to be a Safaddnese state.'

I drew in my breath and expelled it slowly. After glancing at my friends, I said grimly: 'Now indeed we understand, Princess Hiludessa. And this, you say, is a problem you must yourself resolve?'

She shrugged her shoulders helplessly. 'So it seems. During the Dakhletzelkrayet, there was much dispute over this question. Some thought Brelinderim should be free to decide its own fate; others believed that, if any letzestre were lost, the gods would wreak vengeance not only upon it, but on all we Safaddnese. Argument was bitter and long. When the question could not be resolved either by the letzaharei in council or by the priests, the problem was placed before the Nine who are our gods. Regrettably, no immediate answer was received. Instead, it was foretold that one would come who would serve as judge. The Ayanians, believing as they do that I am a Princess come out of the past, conclude I must be that judge.'

'So what will happen next?'

'There is to be an assembly, to which representatives of all the letzestrei are summoned. No, not at the Mount of Storms, Simon. We have three lesser centres at which we gather to discuss controverted questions, whenever there be need. One is in the west, at Veyzend in Vasanderim; one is in the south, at Danuval in Darega; and the third is in the east, at Kesbados here in Ayan. It is to Kesbados that we must travel, only a *letzental*[1] from now.'

She paused, then spread out her arms imploringly. 'And oh! Sir Robert, Simon, Avran, how *can* I decide? How might I pay proper heed to your relatives and compatriots in Lyonesse, Simon, yet be just also to my Safaddnese kin and honour their trust?'

To our utter astonishment, Essa's voice had risen as she spoke into a wail, causing the branath kitten, who had been sleeping forgotten beneath the table, to stir uneasily and growl in its throat. Now she abandoned herself to despair, crouching over the table and burying her face in her hands.

Avran was entirely taken aback by this; nor did Dan Wyert or I quite know what to do. It was Robin who sought to comfort Essa, going to her and setting his good right arm about her waist. For a while, he allowed her to sob against his shoulder. When he spoke, his words were unexpected.

'Grieve not, Princess. Though I take no heed of your Safaddnese gods, I think the task is one to which you have indeed been appointed. If that be so, then, when the time comes, you will surely find guidance.'

[1] Forty days—the Safaddnese month.

Chapter Seven

LAST DAYS IN ACHALIND

The blizzard that had come so suddenly proved to be the winter's most severe. It raged for the better part of a fortnight, during which time no excursions above ground were even attempted. That was an uncomfortable time, for Avran was perpetually in testy mood and I found little ease with him. My friend seemed to consider that, at the end of the evening with Essa, he had missed something more than the mere opportunity to comfort her; and I was afterwards to wonder whether, perhaps, that might have been so. Moreover, as predicted, there were no further opportunities for private time with the Princess Hiludessa, for Avran or indeed for any of us save Dan Wyert. Even Robin, whom she had been visiting so sedulously, saw her little after that day; we others encountered her not at all.

When Avran and I chanced upon Dan Wyert alone one day, Avran asked him directly whether the Princess was avoiding us. When Dan answered, there was in his eye a gleam of sympathetic amusement.

'Nay, lad, you have no cause for concern. Happen she is keeping her distance, but that is simply for fear certain parties might suspect plottings. It is not for any other cause, be sure of that! And my mistress, she gives herself little enough leisure. She is studying hard into the laws of the nine letzestrei. She spends long hours at the scrolls and in the temple with yond priest Parudanh.'

'Never, I take it, with the nuszudirar?' I asked teasingly. Avran and I had not encountered that gentleman, even yet, but he had been much in our thoughts.

'Him?' Dan grimaced. 'Nay, he's gone off to his temple. It seems he left Achalind the day before the blizzard began. I could hope he were lost in the snow, him and his pryings; but 't would be pointless, for they tell me 'tis no great way to Kesbados.'

73

'To Kesbados? Is his temple in Kesbados, then?' Avran had been shocked out of his personal concerns.

'Aye, did you not know? The second temple to this god of theirs, Halrathhantor, is in that place; and Zelat Hrasang, he's its high priest. I doubt not he'll be preparing a warm welcome for us!'

Our conversation went no further. A trio of soldiers was coming towards us along the corridor; and, in Ayan, it is not considered fitting that one of the artisan class should be seen speaking on terms of equality with warriors. As soon as he saw the soldiers, Dan ducked his head, as if acquiescing to an order, and scurried away.

The exchange served only to add a new complexity to my friend's mood. At one level, Avran was relieved, for he knew now—or, at least, had reason to hope—that he had not offended Essa. However, he had been given fresh cause for apprehension about her future—and, for that matter, about ours. It did not make his company any easier to endure.

As for Robin, he was also too much engaged to spend much time with us; though not on official matters. Instead, with the encouragement of the physician, he was striving to strengthen his body and to develop new skills that might counteract the deficiency resulting from the loss of use of his left arm.

Two days afterward, however, when we eluded our tutor by going to the lower levels to visit our veludain, we did encounter Robin. He was riding Twistbeam along a path between the fungus fields, with Dan on Longshank in close attendance. So intent was Robin that, even though his veludu had alerted him to our presence, he did not immediately respond to our greeting. Instead, it was Dan who spoke first. He was beaming.

'Good morrow to you, my masters. Are you come to see how well Sir Robert is riding? Why, he's masterly! You must witness the ease with which he mounts and dismounts. 'Tis something to wonder at, truly!'

Robin laughed aloud. 'Good morrow indeed, my friends! Dan's words are kind, but he does not pay proper tribute to Twistbeam here. If my veludu were not so patient, I could not manage nearly so well.'

Sensing Robin's approval of him, Twistbeam shook his head in a fashion that caused his five horns to bob up and down. They looked so like tossing feathers in the cap of a foppish youth ackowledging a compliment that Avran and I chuckled.

Robin smiled again in response. 'Aye, and other matters are going well also. I've been pacing myself along the corridors—counting my strides. I find I can walk a full league already and hope soon to do much better. More, I've been trying to wield my sword again. Though my wrist is still weak from so much inaction, I shall hope soon to exchange a few strokes with you, my friends. What say you?'

Avran's response was immediate. 'Why, I'd be delighted!'

'For my part, Robin,' I grinned, 'I find myself somewhat less enthusiastic. I have no doubt that, whether or not your wrist be weak, you can readily outmatch me.'

'Aye, Master Simon, that he could!' Dan was again beaming. 'Weak wrist, forsooth! Why, I've watched him at practice. 'Tis another marvel, I can tell you! He's as adroit as ever he was, mark my words. Give him armour and a shield and I'll not fear for Sir Robert in any battle.'

Dan spoke justly. We watched Robin on veludu-back that day and saw how Twistbeam, at a thought, would sink to his knees so that our friend might dismount and mount, then be up in a trice and away. Both veludu and man seemed as happy as could be. All five veludain were in prime condition after so many weeks of rest and good fodder, but only Twistbeam was contented. The others were restive, eager for fresher air and action.

As for Robin's sword-play, it was equally astonishing. A few days later, I witnessed a wooden-sword combat between Avran and he. Though my Sandastrian friend had the better of it, that was only by the slimmest of margins; I would not have been prepared to wager on the result of their next encounter.

Seeing Robin in action thus, one quite failed to remark the immobility of his left arm and shoulder. His optimistic prediction, made even before he had been allowed to rise from his bed, was proven right; if that arm bore a shield, no opponent would detect Robin's disability. Quite evidently, if we were permitted to go onward to Lyonesse, Robin would be perfectly able to accompany us; and that was a great relief.

The problem of having to endure Yanu Hrasang's company remained, but we contrived to ameliorate it. I had feared that Avran might explode into violent anger when next we met our tutor, but my friend had simmered down by then. This was in part because I had suggested to him a method of counter-attack.

Before each session with Yanu, Avran and I prepared a long list of questions—on Safaddnese law and religion, on military matters, on the names and relationships of persons of consequence in Ayan, on family ceremonial and custom, or on any other topic for which we could discover the least justification in the previous lesson. Always we would allow Yanu to embark upon his teaching in the fashion he had planned. However, at his first pause, Avran or I would begin our set-piece of enquiry. Avran was particularly good at assuming an air of innocent enthusiasm and I did my best to emulate him.

Moreover, we each took along a wad of parchment like that carried by Keld Eslingbror, some shell pens—those used by the Ayanians were much like those of Sandastre, though made from land shells—and a phial of their curious reddish-brown ink. When Yanu answered our questions, we wrote down his replies in sedulous detail. If he spoke too fast—or if we chose to pretend that he did—we would apologetically request a repetition. If he mentioned names or used difficult words, we would ask that they be spelled out.

It was satisfyingly evident that Yanu Hrasang found all this extremely aggravating. More importantly, it prevented him from guiding the conversation in a fashion that might lead to the injudicious disclosures he sought—disclosures that might enable the Hrasangs to undermine the high position and potential power of the Princess, by demonstrating her to be an imposter, an ally of the Reschorese. He remained entirely uninterested in any possible connexions beyond the mountains; I do not think he ever even considered, as Essa had done, that a resurgent Empire of the south might menace the Safaddnese anew.

Irritated and frustrated Yanu might be by our new tactics; yet he could not, in his role as our teacher, fail to respond to our questions, since we were careful always to feign complete seriousness and dedication to learning.

What annoyed Yanu most was that I was writing my notes in English script and Avran in Sandastrian characters, neither of which, of course, could he read. He did attempt, at one stage, to induce us to write instead in the Safaddnese alphabet. However, since I had, and Avran pretended, great difficulty with this, the result was that our note-taking became excruciatingly slow. Consequently, that particular ploy was soon abandoned.

As day followed day, Yanu's patience wore ever thinner, especially since we began bringing our parchment pads to dinner, pausing between mouthfuls to ask questions and note down his answers.

One evening, after I had three times requested that he repeat a difficult word while I wrote it down, Yanu's ice-crust of composure suddenly shattered. He slammed down his goblet so that his wine spilled, gave us a sudden, wild glare and said something bitter under his breath.

Simulating innocence, I asked him to repeat what he had said more loudly, since I was sure it must have been a valuable comment! This was entirely too much for Yanu; without replying, he stormed out of the messroom.

Afterwards, though sometimes favoured at dinner by Keld Eslingbror's welcome company, we were spared that of Yanu Hrasang. Yes, he appeared on time for next day's lesson, making no reference to what had transpired; but that lesson was cut short, for reasons not explained. Thereafter, even during the daytime, we saw progressively less of him. There seemed ever to be fresh causes—religious, military or personal—why he should not be present. When the blizzard was over, Keld Eslingbror—prompted, we were sure, by Yanu—kept discovering new reasons why we should go on forays above ground: to strengthen our skill in seslelteven, to give our veludain exercise in the snow, to learn more concerning the exits from Achalind and the mountain paths, or whatever other excuses he could conceive. Up to the time of our departure from Achalind, our lessons were never formally abandoned; but by then they had become exceedingly infrequent and as brief as Yanu might contrive.

Yet Yanu Hrasang knew he had been vanquished, even if he never admitted defeat and we never claimed victory. That awareness was, I am sure, deeply galling to him. I am sure also that this was what caused his dislike of us to sour into hatred.

As the burden Yanu had imposed on our lives progressively eased, so did Avran's spirits rise. However, both of us remembered Essa's warning and took care always to watch our words. During our latter days in the underground city, the Hrasang party can have gained little satisfaction from whatever conversations were reported to them. Even when believing ourselves alone, we conversed only in whispers, as a precaution against unseen listeners; who knew what hidden recesses those tunnel walls of Achalind contained?

Indeed, we received clear indication that we were being spied on. Twice, on returning to our sleeping chambers, we discovered that our piles of parchment notes had been disturbed. On both occasions, we had been out in the snow all day on mountain traverses; whoever had gone through them would have had ample time to make such copies as they desired.

However, from this also, our undeclared enemies can have gained little joy. Whether they had made any sense of the notes, we could not tell; but, if they did, they can have found nothing that was seditious or even uncomplimentary to the Hrasangs. Allowing for our ineptitudes in translation and for modifications enforced by alphabet differences, our notes were literal transcriptions of Yanu's lessons and answers—evidence to any reader of our dedication as scholars, nothing more. We both hoped gleefully that the Hrasangs' minions had laboured long in decipherment, for we knew that such labours would merely induce frustration!

There came a day when, during one of those rare lessons, Yanu told us that we were shortly to travel to Kesbados. He informed us condescendingly that the letzahar, the letzudirar and the indreletzar would all be participating in a major gathering of the Safaddnese letzestrei and that, for educational reasons, he had recommended we be taken along.

As he broke this news, he was watching us as carefully as a cat watches the bird on which it is ready to pounce. I am sure he was hoping we would reveal, by comment or expression, that we knew of the meeting and had expected an invitation, though not from him. However, he was again to be disappointed; we had learned too well how to school our reactions.

Avran feigned delighted surprise. 'Why, that will be splendid! How very kind of you!'

For my part, I managed to simulate puzzlement. 'I am sorry. I didn't quite understand. Would you say it again, please? Ah, a gathering—and of all the letzestrei? And we are to go? Why, that should be most interesting! In—Kesbados, did you say? In what letzestre is that? Is it in Desume? Oh, in Ayan—I see. Would you spell "Kesbados", please? I must write it down. Is it north of here?'

Yanu's emotional boiling-point had, by then, become much lower. After Avran's unsatisfactory response and my burst of innocent-seeming questions, one could almost see the steam rising.

'Will you travel with us?' Avran asked, as if equally innocent. 'Ah, that will be excellent. Why, you'll be able to tell us all about what we are seeing. Better still, you'll be able to explain fully to us everything that is happening at the meeting!'

This quite took Yanu aback: clearly, these were considerations he had not envisaged. For the very first time, he was confused.

'I—yes, of course, but—well, I fear I may be much occupied. Er— I shall need to spend much time at the temple, with my brother . . .'

'Oh, your brother is a priest?' Avran evinced interest. 'Surely, in view of what you have told us of the high distinctions attained by your family, he must have achieved high status?'

Yanu, perceiving that his ire had led him into indiscretion, had come off the boil faster than any pot removed from the flames. His face rarely showed any emotion, but now he was looking quite sullen. 'My brother is Zelat Hrasang, nuszudirar of Ayan and udirar of Kesbados,' he stated flatly.

'How splendid!' Avran was beaming. 'What an honour for your family!'

For my part, I had my parchment pad out again. 'Nuszudirar— would you spell that? Slowly, please!'

That was another lesson which was cut short! Yet Avran and I made sure we were alone before allowing our merriment to bubble forth. However, there was cause for more than merriment. We were both relieved to know definitely that we would be travelling to Kesbados; that had been by no means certain. Despite Yanu's assertion, we were sure that we did not owe this privilege to his goodwill; instead, we were confident he had claimed the credit merely to test our reactions. By failing to respond as he had hoped, we knew we had passed the test.

Even more had been gained. By goading Yanu into admitting a relationship he wished to conceal, we had circumvented a possible danger—the danger of inadvertently admitting we knew more than we ought. Better still, a path had been opened for future questions.

Next day we were again sent out on sesleltef patrol with Keld Eslingbror. It was a grey day, but not unduly cold; nor was the snow very deep. This surprised us, for there seemed to have been little melting. One of the Ayanian soldiers told us it had blown away, but I found that hard to believe; where would it have gone?

At mid-morning, Avran and I were with Keld in the lead and the other six soldiers were some way behind. Seizing the opportunity, Avran remarked innocently: 'Yanu Hrasang tells us his brother is udirar of Kesbados.'

'Did he tell you that?' Keld's surprise was too great for concealment.

'Yes; and the brother is also nuszudirar of Ayan,' I added. 'Strange, that Yanu himself has not gained a rank higher than letelar.'

'Well, er . . .' Keld was floundering helplessly. 'He has and he hasn't, like. He's—well, he's done better than you'd think, from his rank. He's in charge of enquiring into anything from outside, anything that might harm Ayan . . . It's a difficult task, very responsible.'

'How did he find time to teach us, then?' I asked in seeming surprise. 'I'd have thought he'd be too busy for that.'

'But Simon—Keld—you don't think he believes *we're* a danger to Ayan, do you?' Avran spoke as if in dawning awareness. 'Surely he must know better than that, when we travelled here in the company of the Princess Hiludessa?'

'Never so, Avran!' I spoke as if shocked. 'That *can't* be possible, surely, Keld?'

Keld's moustaches were twitching miserably; he looked as woebegone as a cat soused in water by mischievous boys. He glanced about him, to ensure he could not be overheard by his men, before speaking again.

'Well, yes, masters, I fear that he does. Those Hrasangs, they don't trust anybody. And then, when Yanu learned from me that you'd travelled with that Reschorese wizard—why, that properly put the branath among the uvudain! If I'd thought, I'd never have told him; but, you see, I didn't foresee how he'd take it . . . And you've done so much for me; why, truly I can't believe you'd hurt we Ayanians, or any other Safaddnese for that matter. If you'd meant us harm, you'd have left me to die; that'd have been all too easy . . .'

'Harm you? No, we'd not harm you, any of you.' Avran was very positive. 'But Yanu Hrasang—well, we know he doesn't love us much, but would *he* harm *us*? Or the Princess?'

Poor Keld was deeply upset; again he glanced back at his men before responding. There was a desperate earnestness in his voice.

'Well, you see . . . No, he doesn't like you. I wouldn't trust him too far, were I you. And that brother of his, the priest—he doesn't like Princess Hiludessa. To me, she seems a fine woman and a beautiful; truly regal indeed. But . . . well, her arrival didn't suit the game of that nuszudirar of ours. I'm from Kesbados and he's my priest; and Yanu, he's my superior. He's forever asking questions about you and doesn't often seem contented with my answers. Yet, for my part, I can't say that I like the Hrasangs much. You two, though, you've become my friends. It's not easy.'

'No, I can understand that,' I commented sympathetically; and Avran concurred.

Again Keld looked about him, then he dropped his voice.

'There's something I shouldn't be telling you, but I will. It's something my wife overheard, when she was serving at a dinner and out of sight of the Hrasangs. She told it to me and asked me to pass it to you, for she feels beholden to you—but I've been hesitating . . . That branath the Princess has; the Hrasangs don't like it, maybe because it guards her, maybe for some other reason. They're going to try to get rid of it. The Princess should watch its food, here and in Kesbados. She can trust Taru Taletang; he's loyal to her, and so are his men; but she mustn't trust others. No, I won't say more; I daren't. I've said more than I ought already.'

We tried to thank Keld, but he was turning to call up his soldiers. During the rest of what proved a stiff day in the mountains, he was friendly enough; but he made sure that he was not again alone with us.

Chapter Eight

INCIDENT ON A JOURNEY

In England, when the King elects to travel from one place to another, he is accompanied by a host of courtiers and servitors, both male and female, and is guarded by many knights, archers and spearmen. This is not only to guarantee his comfort and safety, but also to impress his people with his royal dignity.

In Ayan, matters are arranged differently. We set off for Kesbados, according to Avran's reckoning, on Devbalet Tanrim (in English, the 27th of February); but not in a single, massive host. Instead, three quite small groups departed at different times on the morning of that day, through different doors and to travel by different paths. Each group consisted of only nine persons, guarded by a *vekhletel*—three letelei—of warriors, two letelei on veludu-back and the third on foot.

The first group was led by the letzahar Soganreth. Accompanying him were two of his advisers, neither of high rank, and six servants led by his steward, Kuldu Asbetang. They left shortly after the late winter dawn. In the second party, leaving at mid-morning, were letzudirar Parudanh, with two junior priests and, once again, six servants. The third party was headed by letzumahar Xandor. In his charge were the indreletzar Hiludessa and the indreletzahular, Sir Robert Randwulf; and, accompanying them, a further six servants. Taru Taletang and Keld Eslingbror headed the two mounted letelei, Avran and I being numbered among Keld's soldiers; and the letelar of the foot-soldiers was not Yanu Hrasang.

When he noticed this, Avran wondered aloud: 'Why, where is our beloved mentor? Are we, then, to be deprived of his valuable instruction during the journey? I thought it was to be an educational event for us.'

'How disappointing,' I responded, equally straight-faced. 'Why,

I'd hoped to ask Yanu many questions—I've even brought along my pad and pen!'

Keld, standing nearby, was evidently perplexed by our comments. 'Why, did Yanu Hrasang tell you he'd be travelling with us? That was once his intent, but then he changed his mind—oh, four or five days ago it was. By his own request he is travelling with the dakhmen, not as letelar but as an ordinary member of the guard. I wonder he did not mention the change to you—and maybe he might have explained it. 'Tis a choice none of us can understand, and he so very proud.'

Avran and I solemnly indicated a shared puzzlement. Inwardly, however, we were both bubbling with merriment. We, at least, understood why Yanu preferred a minor position in the letzahar's guard to one of command in Xandor's; it was to avoid enduring any questioning from Avran and me!

Ours was the last group to sally forth, in the latest hour of a morning of mild air and turbulent cloud. More snow had fallen since we were last above ground, forming a surface soft and moist enough to be deeply imprinted by the hooves of our veludain. The unfortunate foot-soldiers at rear had to work hard to obliterate our tracks. Indeed, when our exit from Achalind—a remote one, reached by a long, narrow corridor and concealed in a stone-pile—was sufficiently far behind, they were allowed to abandon a task they could not perfectly perform.

No longer did the branath ride before Essa on Feathertail, for it had grown much too big; or rather, I should say 'he', for the branath was a male. He had become as large as one of the collie dogs I had so often seen following at the heels of Pennine shepherds. His upper canine teeth, though still far from fully grown, already formed quite impressive curves of ivory against the brown-flecked whiteness of his lower jaw. Essa had named him Rakhamu; the word was an ancient Safaddnese one, meaning something like 'blessed warrior' or 'crusader', but it had special overtones I came never to comprehend. She had obtained for him a broad leather collar elaborately patterned in silver, to which a chain might be attached at need; but that day he loped along quite freely beside Feathertail.

This spectacle was one that dismayed most of the veludain and, I suspect, made most of our fellow riders almost equally uneasy, too much so for them to comfort their mounts. However, Feathertail and the other four veludain on which we had ridden to Achalind were not at all disquieted, perhaps because we, their riders, were not; no, not even Robin who had suffered so much from that branath's dam. Consequently he chose, and Dan, Avran and I were deputed, to ride alongside the Princess, Dan as servant at need and Avran and I as guard. Xandor, on an especially massive pure-white veludu, rode in the van with Taru and Keld; all the others stayed cautiously behind us, the foot-soldiers last of all and particularly relieved to be far from the branath.

Neither branath nor foot-soldiers needed to travel very fast: the ride was steadily, if not steeply, uphill and, in such conditions of snow, the veludain could only amble.

It was evident—gratifyingly so, to Avran—that Essa was pleased to be again in our company, but it was equally apparent that she was weary from much study and apprehensive as to what might transpire in the coming days. However, Robin's pleasure at being again in the open air stirred her own, while his talk of past court and camp experiences, and Avran's evident adulation, caused her to relax and enjoy herself also.

The distance from Achalind to Kesbados must, I think, be quite a dozen leagues. That is a fair way for a veludu to travel in a day, even if ridden directly, and we were not travelling directly; nor had we started early. When light began to fade at the day's waning, we were still far from Kesbados. Our halt for a repast, even though on a barren hill slope, was more than welcome.

Xandor, the Princess and Robin dined elaborately, seated on cushions and tended by the servants. We mere soldiers—for Avran and I had been temporarily relieved of our duties as the Princess's guards—formed a defensive circle about them and made do with standard soldiers' rations.

It was as the meal was finishing that a sudden hubbub called our attention to what was happening within the ring. Two of the soldiers had seized one of the servants and were hustling him towards Xandor, while Taru Taletang escorted them, his expression grim.

Xandor, setting down the flagon from which he had been quaffing, regarded them sternly. 'Why this commotion? What has this man done?'

'We found him offering food to the branath,' Taru answered.

'Only my men and I are permitted to feed the beast, by the Princess's particular order.' He inclined his head toward Essa.

'Indeed so?' Xandor was evidently rather puzzled. 'What have you to say to that, fellow?'

The servant, a stocky man with a rather flat, owl-like face, strove to smile pacifically. 'Only that I did not know the rule, master Xandor. And—well, I like beasts. I was trying to be kind. That was good, cooked hasedu-meat. It would never have harmed the branath.'

Xandor hesitated. 'Well . . . The offence does not seem to me serious. What think you, Princess?'

Essa glanced at Taru Taletang. 'Has the meat been brought? Good.' Then she turned and eyed the servant sternly. 'Well, my man, if indeed it be such good meat, would you care to eat of it?'

This question quite took him aback. 'Why . . . It has been dropped, it will be no longer clean.'

Essa was inexorable. 'If it has been dropped at all, then it has fallen only into fresh snow. If you be honest, you must eat.'

The servant glanced about him desperately; then, suddenly, he tore himself from the grasp of the soldiers. Groping within his tunic, he produced a broad-bladed kitchen-knife. Its freshly sharpened edges gleamed as, with knife upraised, he hurled himself, not upon the soldiers or Taru, but upon Essa.

The three soldiers were too much taken aback to act swiftly; they had been anticipating a break for freedom, not an attack. Robin's reaction was much speedier. He had been seated upon a cushion and I would not have thought, knowing him to be half-paralysed, that he could have risen so swiftly from the ground. Yet, in a trice, he was standing before the Princess. Ere the servant's knife could impale her, he was himself impaled upon Robin's sword.

There was a surge of excited chatter. A red-faced Taru was alternately cursing his soldiers and condemning himself for inattention. Avran, in contrast quite white, was expressing relief at Essa's escape and disgust at his own failure to protect her; and everyone else seemed to be discovering some comment that demanded to be made.

Only when Xandor raised a protesting hand did silence fall. Even in the fading light I could see that, like Avran, he was extremely pale.

'I am ashamed,' he said bitterly. 'Ashamed that so murderous an attempt could be made on our Princess and her beast; ashamed that you who are supposed to guard her'—his tone was withering, and poor Taru bowed his head in abject self-reproach—'quite failed to do so. That cannot be forgotten.'

Then his tone altered. 'Yet I am comforted also, and deeply relieved; for the attempt did not succeed. For that, the Princess and we must again offer our profoundest thanks to the indreletzahular. Not only has he released her from captivity and brought her safely to Ayan, but also he has shown that he can keep her safe, even when we fail her. We must also avow our thanks to Horulgavar, our divine *galiletelar*, and to the Eight who stand beside him, for this great blessing.'

Xandor paused and contemptuously gestured at the body of the fallen servant. 'You two soldiers could not hold him in life, yet surely you can hold him in death. Remove this carrion from our view! Hide it far from here, in a place where it will never again trouble our eyes! That shall be your expiation; you may then follow us to Kesbados.'

When they had lifted the body and borne it away, Xandor turned again to Taru Taletang. 'As letelar of the Princess's guard, you have shown yourself inept. It is fitting that you should express to the gods our thanksgiving that another has fulfilled your task. Let us do reverence.'

Taru's petitions to the Nine were contrite, fervent and so prolonged that, standing with bowed head in the snow, I came close to congealing into an icicle. While he spoke, with many a spreading gesture and much bowing, the light finally faded; and, when at last we relievedly rode onward, the stars were beginning to peer out from behind the clouds.

Avran and I were again appointed to ride beside the Princess. Both of us expressed our heartfelt relief at her escape, Avran with much self-castigation; but she was swift in silencing him.

'Come now, my friends, it is to you that I owe my life—or, at very least, the life of my branath. Had not Dan brought to me your message of warning, Rakhamu would certainly have been poisoned.'

'Say rather, you owe it to Keld Eslingbror,' I responded. 'Had he not passed on to us his wife's message—and, in doing so, transgressed against the interests of his masters the Hrasangs—we could have told you nothing.'

'Yet that, also, I owe to you, Simon; for were you not the instrument of the gods in saving Keld's life, on that foray to the Lemmes-hind? Indeed, Robin, Simon and Avran, I owe you much, for you have twice saved my life, as well as bringing me from the shadows of Kradsunar to the brightness of this, my own land.'

'Not so bright now, Princess!' Robin gestured at the night sky. 'Yet, for my part, I owe my own life to you. Speak not of indebtedness.'

She laughed shortly. 'Well, if I had cancelled my earlier debt, you have this evening occasioned one anew, Sir Robert. I shall not forget.' Then she sighed: 'However, in the days to come, your kindnesses will not ease my choice.'

After that Essa fell silent. During the remaining hours of our ride to Kesbados, she was as withdrawn from us as if we had been, not riding close by her, but far back in the rearguard. For my part, I also found much to ponder upon.

Chapter Nine

THE CHILL WINDS OF KESBADOS

During our northward wanderings, we had seen fortified towers and had visited, memorably if unenjoyably, the city of Sasliith. We knew, therefore, that the Safaddnese were builders as well as being burrowers underground. However, we had become so used to the subsurface life of Achalind that Avran, Robin and I were all expecting Kesbados to be also a place of caves and tunnels.

Arriving as we did in the dark of a late-winter night and entering through massive gates in what seemed the face of a cliff, we assumed at first that such indeed was this second city of Ayan. When the Princess and Sir Robert had been escorted away to their (presumably) luxurious quarters and we soldiers dismissed to our more austere accommodation, Avran and I continued to believe ourselves below ground. Only next morning did we perceive our mistake.

Yet we were not entirely in error; for, though the houses of Kesbados were built largely from shaped stones and its streets open to the sky, many inner chambers and cellars were hollowed directly into the rock. Stone and rock were exactly matched: moreover, great care had been taken that no obvious roads should lead to the city, while no lights were permitted to be visible from outside. In summer, anyone gazing uphill from the Lemmeshind valley, or looking north-eastward or south-westward across its barren slopes, would have thought this merely a mass of granite topping a ridge—a substantial but lesser outcropping overshadowed by, and not very visible against, the greater peaks behind. In winter, with ridges crowned and hollows concealed by snow, it would have been even harder to distinguish the city. Though not so entirely hidden as Achalind, Kesbados would have proved hard for any invader to discover—and still harder to assault.

On the least visible side—the south-east uphill side, visible only from the peaks beyond—there was a great pool. Whether it had been originally hollowed by natural causes or by the hand of man, I never learned; but certainly its rock wall on the city side had been elaborately carven.

Midmost on the rock wall is a mighty figure of Halrathhantor standing with arms upraised and hands widely open. Out between those open hands there spouts water. This comes in part from some natural fountain, in part from the gatherings of the street-drains of Kesbados; yet, when one looks at that mighty figure, it seems as if Halrathhantor is conjuring the water from the air and casting it down into the pool.

That pool is deep and serves as a moat in summer. Moreover, even in midwinter, the constantly falling water causes its centre to remain unfrozen, while the ice about its margins is too frail to be traversed in safety. Thus the pool serves at once as a fitting place for worship of the water-god and an extra defence for the city.

At either end of the rock face are two other great figures. The more northerly in position is a leaf-shaggy figure that seems half-man, half-tree: Radaionesu, the benign god of fertility and healing, the god of Brelinderim. The more southerly is a figure that was less familiar to us, with a round, flat face whose features are scarcely marked, hair and beard spreading outward into a ring of spikes about that face, and a naked, smooth-skinned torso with urgent phallus—a very manlike body, though both hands and feet are clawed. This is Tera-ushlu, god of the sun and of heat and dryness, god also of Desume.

Radaionesu has hands reaching out invitingly, as if welcoming Halrathhantor and the rain. Tera-ushlu, in contrast, is in defensive posture, as if driven back by the waters that Halrathhantor is producing. Yet somehow Tera-ushlu seems to mock the water-god, as if allowing himself to be defeated for a while, yet knowing he may conquer whenever he wills.

High on the rock wall, in an arc between these greater figures, are carven in smaller dimension the figures of the other six gods; three to the left of Halrathhantor, three to the right. They seem benignly to be overseeing the contest between drought and fertility—

benignly, that is, save Mesnakech, whose toad-like depiction is utterly malign. Between and below are many lesser figures, of priests, soldiers and servants. Some are freshly carved and clearly to be seen, but others are masked by mosses and lichens to which, on that winter day, snow clung.

Avran and I were taken to see the figures by Keld Eslingbror, on the morning after our arrival. We circuited the pool on the outer side, a lengthy enough walk and a bleak one, for the sky was grey and the wind biting. Interested though I was, I would not have been sorry if Keld had been less loquaciously informative. Despite our furs, Avran and I were thoroughly chilled before Keld's enthusiasm permitted us to return to the warmth of the messroom.

Perhaps because I was striving so hard to keep warm, Keld's stories of the city have largely faded from my memory. I remember only that Kesbados is of great ancientry, its foundation amply predating the Empire. It had been the original capital of Ayan, until the priests revealed to the people the greater sanctity of Achalind. Also I recall wondering whether the Ayanians met in worship about the pool: on such a day, remembering as I did the lengthiness of Safaddnese orisons, the very thought made me shiver! However, when I asked Keld, he told me no. Instead, they gathered in a temple within the rock behind the great image of Halrathhantor.

Our midday repast served somewhat to warm us, but the afternoon that followed proved as bleak as the morning had been—and much more effortful. Avran and I, together with two others of Keld's company who were equally unacquainted with Kesbados, were taken by him on a lengthy tour of the city and its fortifications. The city was a place of narrow, steep streets and sharp turns. Perhaps, in summer, those streets might have been busy places, crowded with people and merchants; but, at this season, they served only as chill wind funnels. Our inspection of the fortifications involved many wearisome ascents and descents of winding staircases within the rock, illuminated dimly by light from embrasures or entirely in shadow. For any attacker who succeeded in gaining entry to Kesbados, they would have been a terrifying labyrinth, fraught with the hazards of ambush and pitfall. For Avran and me, however, they proved merely dusty and bewildering. Yet Keld Eslingbror delighted in the complexities of his home city and pointed out each new feature with an ever-bubbling enthusiasm. I was soon shivering and longing for the underground warmth of Achalind; but, since Avran was enduring better and contriving even to simulate interest, I strove to emulate him as far as I might.

After what seemed an eternity of chill and effortful boredom, Keld led us back to the quarters shared by our letel—a long, corridor-like room, in one stone wall of which were nine curtained sleeping-recesses and at whose other side was a trestle lined with stools. He sat on one of these, motioned us others to do likewise, and produced from beneath his tunic a stoppered leather flask. Extracting the stopper, he offered it to me with an understanding smile.

'Have a swig, Simon my friend. You bore the cold well!'

I gazed at him speechlessly, then obediently took a hearty pull at the flask. The liquid seemed to set my throat afire, so that I coughed and spluttered till my eyes ran with tears.

'Why, 'tis evidently warming you!' Keld chuckled. 'Have you not sampled *efredat* before?'

'Yes,' I gasped, 'but never of such potency!'

'Happen not,' he responded in satisfaction. ''Tis some that my grandfather laid down—of the very best. Take another swig; but more cautiously, now!'

So I did and began indeed to feel much warmer. The flask was then passed around. Avran managed to drink without such spluttering, though the efredat did cause him to cough. The two young Safaddnese fared little better than I, arousing Keld to further chuckles. For his part, he took a long swig with such aplomb as to earn my admiration. How could anyone swallow such a fiery brew with such enjoyment and so little effort?

A while later, we all walked over to join the other members of the letel in the messroom for dinner. After we had dined, both Avran and I felt so weary that we excused ourselves early and returned to our quarters. Keld and the other soldiers exhibited greater hardihood, for they remained behind, quaffing the ale of Ayan and exchanging the occasional brief and austere pronouncements that, in that land, pass for warm conversation. Consequently, the chamber was quite empty when we returned to it. Even so, when Avran spoke, it was in a voice sufficiently low pitched as not to carry far.

'How many exits from this city did you notice, Simon?'

'Why, I was not thinking about that . . . The great gate on the valley side and the lesser doors that led out to the northern and southern ends of the pool.'

'All three heavily defended.'

'Yes, all three defended, of course. And—let me see—two ways out by tunnel, though I misdoubt that I could find them again in this warren of passages and streets. Oh, and a couple of places where, at need, a man might descend the rock, given strong nerve and weather less bleak. Yet why should it matter, Avran?'

'Perhaps it does not. However, somehow I feel we may need to leave here in haste. We must remember all those exits, Simon.'

While I spoke, Avran had thrown off his cloak, unfastened his sword-belt and pulled off his boots: it was too chill to contemplate any further disrobing before sleeping. As I sat on a stool and began to take off my own boots, my friend went over to the recess where he had slept, drew back the curtain and grasped the upper blanket, preparatory to climbing in. Then, suddenly, he cried out in fear.

A glance told me the cause. As he pulled back the blanket, Avran had disturbed a grey snake that lay within. It had glided forward onto his arm and, even now, was poising to strike.

My left boot was in my hand and a knife within. Without conscious thought or even aim, I drew the knife from its sheath and threw.

It was not one of my best casts, but it served. The knife twisted in flight, as a well-thrown knife should not; and it was the handle, not the blade, that hit the snake. Yet the force was enough to knock the creature off my friend's arm.

Avran leapt back, snatched up his swordbelt and drew out his sword. Then, in a passion of frantic horror, he slashed at the twisting, hissing thing in the recess, continuing long after it was silent in death.

Breathing heavily, Avran replaced his sword in its sheath. When he turned to me, he was quite white and shivering worse than he had done all day.

'Ugh, how I hate serpents, Simon! It is dead but—friend, would you pull out those blankets and shake them? I doubt if I can sleep in them tonight; I—doubt if I *shall* sleep tonight, after that.'

'Certainly I will; but first, come and sit down.' I put my arm about his shoulder and conducted him to a stool. 'See, Keld has left his flask; take a swig. He will not grudge it you, after such a happening.'

While he obeyed, I fetched out from the recess the blanket with its bloody contents, handling it cautiously from fear of the venom. Next I shook the snake's remains onto the floor and retrieved my knife. Then, very hesitantly, I drew back the curtain to my own sleeping-recess and even more cautiously checked the blankets within, my knife in readiness. They contained nothing untoward.

'No, they would not have planted two snakes,' Avran remarked grimly: after a few swigs at the flask, he had ceased trembling and regained some colour. 'That would be too obvious, would it not?'

'You think it not chance, then?' I sat down on the stool beside him, for my limbs were feeling suddenly weak.

'I am quite sure it was not chance. Yes, I have heard of snakes seeking refuge in warm places; but Simon, mine is the fifth recess in from the door! Would a snake not have entered the first? Remember, it was not here last night: it has not passed from one place to another, for all were occupied.'

I sighed and nodded. 'I cannot argue with that conclusion. Think you that this is the work of the Hrasangs?'

'Not directly, mayhap; but indirectly, yes certainly. Who else is there that hates us enough? But Simon,'—he placed his arm about my shoulder—'once again I am infinitely obliged to you. Twice, now, you have saved me from serpents. A death in battle I do not fear; but death from the bite of such a creature—how horrible!' He shuddered.

'Speak not of obligation. Had you not volunteered so generously to come north as my companion, you would never have been subjected to either peril.'

'Yes, it has been a perilous passage . . . But be silent now; our comrades are returning.'

Neither of us suspected, even for a moment, that Keld Eslingbror might have planted the snake among Avran's blankets; he was not capable of acting so meanly. Had we conceived it, the letelar's astonishment and horror were so obviously unfeigned as to drive away any such suspicion. The dismay of the other soldiers, and the care and trepidation with which they searched their own sleeping recesses, made it hard to suspect any of them of the act. However, one of them must either have placed the snake or, more likely, identified Avran's place to the person that did. No other snakes were found, of course.

After making his own careful check, Keld turned to Avran and me. As he spoke, his tone held an undertone of disgust. 'My good friends, I am appalled by this incident. Well, you will not wish to remain here this night and dream of serpents. Nor must you. Please put on your cloaks and boots, both of you, and bring your weapons. I am going to find you different lodgement.'

We obeyed wonderingly, said farewell to our other comrades and followed Keld out of the chamber. Down a short corridor we went, turned right into another and then left, out through a door into one of Kesbados's windy streets. Keld glanced up and down its bleak emptiness, then paused to address us again.

'Those snakes—*ksasaskevren*, we call them. Yes, occasionally they do stray underground; but also some are kept in the temple for purposes of divination. I shall not speculate how that one came to be where it was. However, you are my friends and I wish you safe from further perils. Henceforth, while in Kesbados you shall lodge with my brother. Until injured in a cliff-fall, he was a *latletelar*'—a commander of nine letelei—'and he is yet accorded much respect in this city. Moreover, though wise enough to conceal the sentiment, he loves not our priest. You will be secure in his house.'

It was a chill, uphill walk to that house, set as it was against one of the highest crags of Kesbados; yet the warmth of our reception was ample compensation. Aflar Eslingbror was a stouter and more grizzled version of his young brother, with the same curious fashion of twitching his moustaches: we liked him from the first and liked also his stout wife and trio of plump daughters. A hot punch made from spiced efredat soon warmed us thoroughly, but caused Avran and me to become so drowsy that we sought our blankets as quickly as manners permitted. Sharing a small room that was just behind the fireplace and delightfully warm, we slept well, quite unhaunted by ill dreams of serpents.

Though the winds seemed never to cease to blow about Kesbados, the ensuing two days were much milder. After an excellent and ample morning repast we rejoined our letel, to be marched forth through the main gate and for some distance down valley. There we served as honour guard for a not very large party—some forty-five persons, if my count was right—which constituted the delegation from Avakalim.

Riding at their head was the letzahar, Perespeth. He was as lean and stiff as a lance. His eyes were deep brown in hue and had a withdrawn quality; he seemed to me one who thought deeply but who had schooled himself to conceal his motivations, even after a decision had been announced. I found him impressive, but disturbing; and I am sure Keld was not at ease with him. However, his letzudirar and letzumahar, both stout and (for Safaddnese) cheerful, appeared to be not at all in awe of their ruler.

Next day—by my reckoning, the second of March; by Avran's, Vekhalet Deva—we were sent southward to meet, and escort to Kesbados, the delegation from Omega. This was a smaller group of only twenty-seven souls—for even men as bleak and silent as they must surely have souls? I did not learn, then or thereafter, clearly to distinguish their leaders; all seemed made from a single spare, grim mould. It was if their dwindling as a people had taken from them all joy. The snarling animal masks the soldiers bore on helmet and breastplate, in tribute to their god Gamvalessdar, seemed more alive than they.

On both days, after returning to Kesbados our letel was swiftly dismissed from duty. Both evenings were spent with Aflar Eslingbror, his wife and daughters. It was overlong since Avran and I had experienced such cheerful domesticity and we enjoyed those hours greatly.

The middle of the month is considered by the Safaddnese an auspicious time to begin new endeavours; and the third of March is the middle of the third division of their nine-month year, the month of Edaénar. On that morning, we received an early and excited summons from Aflar.

'Wake up, wake up! Ye're bidden to attend the assembly of the letzestrei, as guards for the Princess Hiludessa herself, no less! You must make haste to breakfast and be away!'

It was Aflar who guided us to the place of assembly, limping before us down the steep street and plunging unhesitatingly into the complex of alleys. Eventually we reached a doorway where a guard was on duty, great axes at the ready. In a gust of words, Aflar bade us farewell and his god's blessing till our evening reunion, then stumped away.

On each day in the cities of Ayan, the soldiers on duty are given a new password, the uttering of which permits them to enter guarded places. That day's word had been furnished to us by Keld through Aflar. Avran spoke it and we were admitted to a short passage that led to a spiral stairway down into the rock. At the stairhead, as instructed, we awaited the Princess.

The wait was not long. To our pleasure, there arrived not only Essa but also Sir Robert Randwulf and Dan Wyert, escorted by Taru Taletang and his letel of soldiers. The branath was pacing on its chain by Essa's side, gazing about with eyes that glowed green in the dimness. We were greeted briefly and formally, but a swift, warm smile from Essa gave Avran particular gratification. Then Taru dismissed his men and led us down the narrow winding stairs into the chamber of assembly.

This is so strange a place that I find it hard to describe adequately. It is excavated entirely below ground and has the shape of a star with nine rays. At the tip of each ray is a stairway to the surface, such as we had come down. From that point each ray widens and slopes downward, having a passage at either side and stepped seats at the centre. The fewest and broadest seats are at the front and evidently designed for the nobility: farther back, the seats are crowded closer together to accommodate less important beings. All are of stone, but made comfortable by straw-stuffed cushions. I was told that each ray could seat a *lakulet* of delegates—ninety-nine persons, that is. However, not nearly so many were present that day, on this ray or any of the others. Yet plenty of seats were already occupied and more persons were arriving all the time.

At the chamber's centre is a domed space, lit that day by brightly burning torches positioned at each junction of rays. Beneath the dome is set a high throne, also carven in stone but inlaid with an intricate tracery of some red metal, surely not copper, for it glowed crimson in the torches' flicker. That was the first thing to attract my eye, but then I glanced higher and noticed the carven emblems over the arches above each ray of seats—the panpipes and sword of Daltharimbar and Darega, the grotesquely grinning mask that signified Mesnakech and Paladra, and others that I did not recognize or could not properly see. Each ray, then, must be reserved for a particular letzestre; the three seats directly below the emblem must be for its letzahar, letzudirar and letzumahar—the leaders of the three classes of its citizenry, soldiers, priests and artisans.

Indeed, I had been so much engaged in looking about me that I had not noticed Xandor, sitting in the left-hand place at the inmost end of the ray we were descending. At our approach, he rose to greet Essa and Robin with smiling courtesy, ushering them to seats in the second row. Essa took the furthest seat and, as she sat down, loosed the chain from Rakhamu's collar. The branath stretched, bared his great fangs in a yawn that caused persons close by to move back nervously, then crouched down in the fashion of a cat that is at ease but watchful.

After Robin seated himself beside Essa, Taru Taletang retired to join his men, who were sitting in a group several rows back. Responding to an equally courteous gesture from Xandor, Dan, Avran and I took places in the third row.

I was about to sit down when a voice called out: 'Why Simon — Simon Branthwaite! However come you to be here?'

As I turned, I received perhaps the greatest surprise of my entire life. There, hastening beamingly across from one of the other rays of seats, was a massive figure, blond-bearded and clad in a scarlet cote-hardie embroidered in silver with the figures of three badgers.

It was my brother Richard.

Chapter Ten

THE ASSEMBLING OF THE LETZESTREI

Heedless of the watching eyes, I ran to embrace him. After hugging in the delight of reunion, we stepped back to consider one another. What Richard saw seemed to amuse him quite as much as it pleased him.

'Why, little brother, how you've grown! A beard and all—I wonder that I recognized you so readily. Since I beheld you last, you've become a man!' The warmth of his smile quite counteracted any condescension in his words.

'I cannot say the same, Richard,' I responded breathlessly, for it had been a powerful hug. 'You were big enough already; there was not need for more of you. But—well, it's a delight to see you again, whole and handsome!'

Handsome he certainly was—indeed, always had been. While I was fashioned in the small, dark style of my mother and the Watertons, Richard was his father's son and a proper Branthwaite—quite two spans tall, ruddy, blond and blue-eyed.

He gave me a friendly grimace. 'Handsome! Why, I'm about as much so as a sumpter-horse! As for you, brother Simon, I'd think the ladies would rank you a deal more than passable. Has one yet engaged your affections?'

I blushed and avoided answering by asking: 'How came you here, big brother?'

'I'm accompanying the Brelinderimins, by their invitation, to speak for Lyonesse if permitted. But a greater question is—how came *you* here, Simon? Not by ship to Warrentown, certainly, for there has been none from England since ours.'

'No, I came by quite another way; but that is too long a story to tell now. Instead permit me, if you will, to introduce my friends.'

Remembering the courtesies of the Safaddnese, I presented

Xandor first of all. After clasping the clasped hands that Richard properly extended, the letzumahar commented amusedly: 'Brothers, eh! Yet you're as unalike as a hasedu and a veludu!'

'Then I shall not enquire, my lord, which of us you consider most like a hasedu!' Richard responded smilingly; and Xandor chuckled.

Next I said: 'It is my privilege to present the Princess Hiludessa, for a while our travelling companion. Princess, my brother Richard.'

Richard glanced at me in astonishment and at Essa with a reverential surprise; then he bowed deeply before extending to her his clasped hands. As Essa took them, she said: 'It is a pleasure to greet the brother of my friend, a friend to whom I owe very much. May I in turn introduce to you my particular saviour, Sir Robert Randwulf?'

Robin's grasp had the firmness of one welcoming a friend. 'The indreletzar has said that she owes your brother much; so also do I. It is a pleasure to greet you, Richard.'

My brother looked at me surprisedly. 'I am beginning to comprehend that there are many stories to be told to me, Simon.' Then he smiled at Robin: 'You will need to convince me, however, that someone so young has truly been able to aid so doughty a warrior as yourself!'

Robin laughed and might, I think, have answered; but Richard was moving on, to greet Dan Wyert with equal heartiness. Dan was at once embarrassed and much pleased. Since his garb proclaimed him to be of the artisan class, while my brother was so evidently a warrior, Dan had expected to be ignored; but Richard was incapable of such discourtesies.

'Dan was also my travelling companion, Richard; and so, above all, was this redheaded gentleman here—Avran Estantesec, prince of Sandastre and my best of friends. Avran, my brother.'

As his hands clasped those of Richard, Avran said smilingly: 'This is a particular pleasure, Richard Branthwaite.' (He managed our difficult surname unexpectedly well.) 'We have been seeking you so long that I misdoubted we would ever find you.'

'Have you indeed?' responded Richard in renewed startlement. Then he glanced over his shoulder. 'Simon, I must break off this reunion. The letzudirar of Brelinderim is arriving and I must take my place. Moreover, I see that yours of Ayan is approaching. Please excuse me. We must meet later and oh! how we shall talk!'

'How is my father?' I asked hastily.

'Oh, in fine fettle; but I must go.'

Richard departed swiftly to a ray of the chamber at our right. My eyes followed him wistfully, but then I turned away. It was time for me to resume my duties as soldier of Ayan and guard of the Princess, duties for a while forgotten.

Parudanh and an entourage of three priests were already descending toward us. After formal greetings, the high priest took the front centre seat, while the other priests found places directly behind us. Shortly afterward we rose again to pay our respects as the dakhmen Soganreth arrived. He took the right-hand seat before us, while his escort of soldiers and advisers had to be content with places behind the priests.

To my relief and rather to my surprise, Yanu Hrasang was not among the letzahar's company; but then I noticed the priest seated at centre—the place of greatest honour—in the row behind us. Very spare he was and quite bald, with jutting chin and eyes that seemed almost without hue; bleak, unreadable eyes, in a face as pale and emotionless as if carven from marble. Yet his robes were rich . . . Why, that must be Zelat Hrasang, brother of Yanu and nuszudirar of Ayan!

I glanced quickly away, but Avran's eyes had followed mine and so did his recognition. My friend stiffened; he had been smiling, but the smile drained from his face like milk from a toppled pitcher. Then, as I had done, he averted his eyes; yet his expression had become grim.

As more and more representatives of the Safaddnese realms arrived, I strove to determine which ray of the chamber accommodated which letzestre. The arch opposite and to my left was adorned with a chevron on which were superposed three jagged darts. These were meant, I assumed, to represent lightning bolts. Lightning bolts . . . storms . . . oh, of course, the chevron must represent a mountain; Mount of Storms—why, that must signify Aracundra!

The adjacent emblem I could blazon but not recognize—a battle-axe palewise (set upright). Next came the grinning mask that signified Paladra and under it a group of cloaked figures, their visages hidden beneath cowls. As past fears were briefly renewed, I shuddered.

Glancing to the other side, to the right of Aracundra, I had less difficulty in reading the emblems. The panpipes of Darega, with a group of men much akin to the figures we'd seen on wind-temple walls. Next—oh, of course, I should have recognized it immediately!—the taron of Avakalim, with our acquaintances of two days earlier taking their places beneath it. Though the next emblem was strange to my eyes—a flowering bush surmounted by a sword with blade erect—I knew it must mean Brelinderim, for my brother was sitting alone in the second row.

The letzudirar and letzumahar were in their seats; why was the letzahar's place empty? Oh, of course, stupid of me—because he was grievously sick. After all, was not Sir Arthur Thurlstone's succession to that position the subject of dispute here? Richard, then, must be Sir Arthur's representative; that would be why he was sitting alone, though the rows behind him were crowded.

I could not see the emblems above the arches to our immediate right and left; nor could I perceive the grinning animal mask that meant Omega or the emblem of Desume, presumably a sun in glory. It seemed likeliest to me, somehow, that the men of Omega would be to our left and those of Desume to our right. In any event, I could presume by elimination that the upright axe must mean Vasanderim. The men seated in that ray were indeed all massive and grim-visaged, fit products of their long war with the Northmen.

At that moment, there came from somewhere high in the dome a shrill whistle. It was prolonged for several seconds and then died away in a wavering trill. By then everyone was silent and still, waiting.

The trill came again, but now it was louder, throbbing, insistent: moreover, it seemed to come, not from overhead, but from somewhere opposite us. Immediately the men of Aracundra got to their feet. The sound ceased, then resumed to our left: and up rose the men of Vasanderim. Again it ceased, then resumed; but closer, causing the hooded Paladrans silently to rise. Next it was to our immediate left and sounding much louder, causing a shuffling of feet as our neighbours, whoever they were, stood up.

As it sounded loudest and overhead, we rose also—all but Essa, who remained determinedly seated. Was that because she was a princess, was it because she was supposedly of Avakalim, or was it simply because she was a woman? I could not enquire then and never did learn the reason, since subsequent happenings drove the question from my mind till it was too late to ask.

As the trilling whistle sounded again and again, ever farther to our right, the men of the other letzestrei rose in turn. When all nine were on their feet, there came a last, prolonged shrill, this time on a rising note. Then all was silent; though I suspect that most ears were, like mine, still throbbing.

After a moment, Parudanh walked forward with firm, slow dignity; in his palely blue robe, he looked curiously like a heron stalking across a sandbank. The letzudirar took up a stance before the throne and, holding out his arms with hands turned inward, made a gesture of invitation. Then he turned to face us.

At once the other eight letzudirarei came forward. They formed a ring about the High Throne, each facing the men of his own letzestre. All nine high priests raised their arms in invocation and began upon a solemn song, their voices almost as high and throbbing as the whistle had been. Though I did not properly understand its words—indeed, I suspect the language was archaic—I knew this must be a hymn to their nine gods. At intervals the lesser priests would chant a response; and, at set pauses, all the other Safaddnese chorused '*Ilai ushazan!*'

Essa, from her seat before us, joined in the responses; but Avran and I—yes, and even Dan Wyert—remained determinedly silent. Nevertheless, in that great place of assembly, reverberating as it was with the ululating antiphonic chant of the priests and the fervent chorusings of the other worshippers, it was hard not to feel awed.

At last the chant ended. Eight high priests returned to their places. As they seated themselves, so did the rest of us.

Parudanh, however, remained standing before the throne. I knew already how resonant was that strange, dry voice of his. Even so, when he spoke, I was surprised how clearly his words might be heard across that large space.

'Ye that are children of the Nine, hear me! Ye that have been pilgrims and have gathered before Their home, the Fereyek Gradakhar, hear me! Ye that demand answers to hard questions, that require direction in deciding upon new courses, hear me! Let us unite in conclave with quiet heart and open mind, receptive to Their guidance and ready to fulfil Their will.'

He paused and gazed about him challengingly. Instantly there came the response from all about us: '*Stalusor vlesté: khadutor vlesté.*' ('We listen: we receive.')

Parudanh smiled, a twitch of the lips that gave brief prominence to his cheekbones, so spare was he. Then he became solemn.

'All here are aware that we have left behind a *dakhletzel*' (999 years) 'that brought the joy of great triumph, but also the bitterness of defeat and long years of isolation. In this new dakhletzel, that isolation must surely end; but what new paths should we tread? What new links should we forge and what old ones should we sever? What old laws must be cast away and what new laws promulgated? Which peoples must remain our enemies and which peoples shall become our friends? Those were the questions that we, your priests, asked at the Dakhletzelkrayet, when we gathered below the clouds that hide the high seats of the Nine from men's view. Answers gained we none, for the Nine were not yet ready to answer.'

There was utter silence in that great chamber; one might have thought it empty, so completely were all present attent upon Parudanh's words. After allowing that silence to prolong awhile, he resumed his discourse.

'Yet we were told that an answer was being prepared for us — that one appointed by the Nine would come, to bring their response and pronounce their judgement. We were told we would know that person by the signs provided to us; yet we were not informed what those signs would be. Instead we waited, for we knew that They our gods would not long delay in giving us Their message.'

Again he paused; then he declared in tones of utter fervour: 'Children of the Nine, the messenger is come! The signs are given! Out of the past has returned the Lost One, Hiludessa of Avakalim! She has been released from her long captivity by strangers and brought, miraculously unseen, across the mountains, bearing upon her breast the royal emblem of the Avakalimins. Here is our messenger! Hiludessa indreletzar, Hiludessa *dlaluhanzar*' (divine messenger), 'stand forth!'

There had been a mounting susurration of excitement at Parudanh's words. It swelled to a bombination and then, as Essa rose, to a thunderous chant: '*Ilai ushazan! Ilai ushazan! Ilai ushazan!*'

Parudanh stood with head bowed and hands clasped before him till the chant died away. Then he asked ringingly: 'Children of the Nine, are you ready to receive the messenger? Shall we place her in the High Throne, to grant advice and pronounce judgement?'

There was the beginning of a chorus of response. Before it could properly swell, however, a voice rang out from directly behind us — the voice of Zelat Hrasang.

'Do not accept her! This is no messenger from the Nine Gods of Safaddné, but an emissary of our enemies—a spy! She deserves, not elevation to the High Throne, but condemnation as a traitor! Peoples of the mountains, I crave speech!'

Parudanh drew himself up, so evidently outraged that, for a moment, I thought he might reject that audacious plea. Yet then he relaxed somewhat and demanded of the concourse: 'Do you choose to grant speech, Children of the Nine, to Zelat Hrasang, nuszudirar of Ayan?'

There was a murmur of doubt and dissent. For a moment, I hoped the request might be declined. Unfortunately, all too soon voices were answering: 'Yes, hear him; him be heard!'

Zelat Hrasang rose and strutted forth, with the complete confidence of a champion cock facing a smaller, shorter-spurred adversary. In that moment I loathed him passionately, indeed with a depth of passion that my dislike of his brother had never approached; but that was because I feared him, as I had never feared Yanu. Avran, beside me, was sitting tensely, hand on swordhilt.

Zelat stationed himself directly before we Ayanians and began speaking. His expression did not change, but in his voice was all the purring pleasure of a cat that contemplates an entrapped and helpless victim.

'This supposed princess, this messenger; shall we examine her claims? Look at her; does she seem to you a survival of the past, a person who has seen three *lakuletzelei* (periods of 99 years) 'go by? Does she not seem young, immature even? Do you discern any royalty in her? For my part, I do not. I see no princess; I see only a commoner!'

Zelat paused and stared challengingly about the great chamber; but there came no response, no repudiation. With a shake of the head that expressed his arrogant self-confidence, he continued his speech.

'So she was rescued from captivity, eh? But from whose captivity? And who are her associates? Four men who have travelled, they say, from distant lands. One comes, he claims, from an *eslevat*[1] called Sandastre; another, he claims, from a *dakhmenat*[2] called England; and the others, they claim, from *dakhmenatar* called Odunseth and

[1] principality
[2] kingdom

Herador. Have you heard ever of such realms? No, of course not; those realms do not exist!

'Yet there are matters of which we *can* be assured. That they have come from Reschora—Reschora, the land that has been our greatest enemy! That they have travelled with one Vedlen Obiran who, they admit freely, is a great wizard of that land. Does this suggest they are messengers of the gods? No, of course it does not. Does it suggest they are spies, sent to discover our ways and undermine our defences? Yes, most certainly it does!'

Zelat's earliest words had been received coolly, with many disapproving mutters; but now he had his audience's entire attention. I knew he must be revelling in every cadence of this carefully prepared tirade. As he resumed speaking, his voice expressed utter derision; yet his face, that carven-seeming face, altered expression not at all.

'That *miraculous* crossing of the mountains; miraculous nonsense! Why, were not the mountains empty? Were we not all far away at the Dakhletzelkrayet? Did that woman and these men not choose the time for this espionage with great care? Did they not know well that our towns, our fortifications, would be for once undefended and open to their eyes? What better time might spies have chosen—and what safer?'

'But the golden taron of Avakalim?' Parudanh was furiously angry now. 'In your fabricating an accusation, how do you account for that, Zelat Hrasang?'

The nuszudirar was contemptuously dismissive. 'Pah! A clumsy forgery—a device fabricated to enable these spies to enter our most secret cities, which otherwise they might not have penetrated. Children of the Nine, reject this supposed princess, this imposter! Set her not on the High Throne, but cast her down—and cast down also those who have travelled with her! Give them what they deserve—death! Death to them! Death!'

He had leapt forward and was pointing contemptuously at Essa. Still his facial expression had not changed, but now his eyes were glistening with the delight of cruelty and his tongue flicking out beads of saliva.

Yet Zelat had been foolish, for he had forgotten Rakhamu. Perceiving that his mistress was threatened, the branath had tensed. The extra menace of the nuszudirar's close approach was too much for the animal. Without even a warning growl, he leapt.

Zelat Hrasang's cry of 'Death!' merged into a shriek of terror. The nuszudirar swung about, throwing up his arms; but he was entirely too late. With jaws widely open, Rakhamu was upon him. Zelat Hrasang was thrown forward to the ground; but already he had been slain, the branath's great, curving fangs driven deep into his neck.

There was a turmoil of noise, with everyone on their feet and shouting. I had expected that the Ayanian soldiers would try to kill Rakhamu, but that did not happen. Instead, a white-faced Essa ran forward and, reattaching the chain to his collar, hauled the branath off his victim. It was an action that Rakhamu did not resist, for he had been acting in defence, not seeking prey. Later, when Zelat's corpse was lifted to be taken away, it was discovered that his back was broken. The death he had proclaimed had been his own, and almost instant.

Parudanh watched Essa's action in seeming impassivity. However, as the noise began to die down, he made a silencing gesture. When all was quiet again, he spoke in the passionate tone of complete conviction.

'The Nine have given their answer! The impious, audacious one who sought to challenge their messenger is dead, furnishing them with the sacrifice they sought. Men of Safaddné, here is the Lost Princess returned—Hiludessa of Avakalim! Receive her, Children of the Nine, for she is predestined to be your guide and your judge!'

As I listened to their passionate response: '*Ilai ushazan! Ilai ush-azan!*' I found myself trembling. A danger, a very great danger, was past. Essa had been definitively accepted; surely she must be safe now, and we also?

Chapter Eleven

THE HIGH THRONE

During those choruses of praise, Essa stood before the letzudi-rar of Ayan, her head high and her two hands grasping the branath's chain. As for Rakhamu, he also stood still, gazing about him with a sort of proud puzzlement. When two Ayanian priests came forward to remove his victim's body, the branath gave a low, throaty growl but did not strive to prevent them. However, the growl served to add apprehensive haste to their departure!

Only as the chanting died away did I notice that the letzahar of Avakalim, Perespeth, had risen to his feet. As soon as he might, Parudanh acknowledged him and invited him forward to speak.

'My fellows of Safaddné,' the letzahar began, 'for my part, I am confident that we do indeed see before us the Princess Hiludessa, returned after so long to serve as messenger and judge. However, it is proper that the foul calumnies of he who was slain should be altogether disproven. Princess, may I crave your permission to exam-ine the taron emblem that you wear about your neck?'

Essa inclined her head in acquiescence, then unfastened the pen-dant and handed it to Perespeth. To do this, she had to allow the chain to drop from her grasp, but Rakhamu did not stir. Nor did the letzahar of Avakalim hesitate, despite the recently demonstrated ferocity of the branath, before stepping up to her and receiving the pendant.

Only when he raised it against his breast did I perceive that an identical pendant hung about the letzahar's own neck. With a golden taron cupped in each hand, Perespeth spent several minutes in silent scrutiny—sufficiently long, indeed, to cause me to become again anxious. His words, however, were reassuring.

'He who died claimed that the Princess's taron was a clumsy forgery. Not so! It is a work of great and delicate art, one of a pair fashioned long since by Evenal Tasurlang, greatest of workers in gold. They were made at the time when we Safaddnese had driven the southern invaders from these our mountains, in celebration of that great victory. From that day to this, one taron has served as emblem of we letzaharin. The other adorned the necks of our letzesaharin or indreletzaharin until, with your vanishing, my Princess, it vanished also. Yours differs from mine only in that, having been less often worn, it is in finer condition. My Princess, I am honoured and most deeply moved that I am able to welcome you back to these mountains. Until such time as you deign to return to your own realm, Avakalim will await that return with the pleasure of impatience.'

After inclining his head reverently, Perespeth placed the pendant again about Essa's neck. Then, with another bow, he offered to her his clasped hands in greeting. When she had taken them smilingly, he returned to his place amid a renewed chant of '*Ilai ushazan!*'

Not until Avran had nudged me and pointed did I notice that a second, more sinister figure had risen. From his hood and his position at the front of the ray to our left, I knew this must be the letzudirar of Paladra, the high priest of Mesnakech. For a third time, I felt extreme unease.

After recognition from Parudanh, the high priest moved round the chamber in a sort of slow shuffle until he stood before Essa. She appeared entirely unafraid, but the branath tensed: I saw the fur rising on his back, in the fashion of that of a tomcat confronted by a dog. That caused me a further lurch of the heart; and I could sense that Avran was quite as uneasy as me. Indeed, the whole great chamber was silent and tension general.

The high priest scrutinized Essa for almost as long a time as Perespeth had examined the taron. When he spoke, his tone was soft and sibilant, giving an impression of great age and extreme evil.

'Ah, yes: you are indeed the one whom Mesnakech, mightiest of magicians, sensed in the mountains and summoned to His presence. You came to Sasliith, as any mortal must when a god calls—you, and those who travelled with you. Not willingly did you come, no; yet you came. You entered our city, for were not its gates open for you? You passed inward to the place of the god, so that he might examine you and discover the truth that is of you and in you. When he had considered you, he permitted you to leave his presence. You fled in fear and awe—the fear and awe that all must feel who have suffered the scrutiny of a god.'

That fear and that awe were finding new echoes in my own breast. As the Paladran paused, I glanced at Avran and saw that he too was sweating. His hand was clasping his sword, but not by its hilt. Instead, he was gripping the scabbard just below the swordhilt, in the fashion of a bishop clasping a cross.

Yet, when the hissing voice of the Paladran letzudirar was again to be heard, it brought renewed reassurance.

'Mesnakech has judged you already, Princess Hiludessa. Had he thought you false, you would have been destroyed—aye, and your companions also. Instead, you were released; you were permitted to resume your journey through the mountains and even furnished with food. Your tribute of gold, properly left, was found by us, the people of Paladra and worshippers of Mesnakech, when we returned to our city. Since our god has accepted you, so also must we.'

The hooded head was inclined respectfully, but no hands were extended in greeting—to Essa's great relief, as she confessed to me afterward. She had been even more afraid than Avran and I, yet had contrived not to show her fear. As the priest moved away, the branath relaxed also and began again to gaze about the chamber. For my part, I was left wondering how the priest had known so much about our visit to Sasliith. It is a question that, even now, I cannot answer.

There was no chant of applause this time; only a susurration of whispers. To the Safaddnese, as to us, the Paladrans were a remote and forbidding people. Their god was regarded everywhere with apprehensive awe, but nowhere else was he beloved.

When the Paladran had resumed his place, high priest Parudanh gazed questioningly about the chamber.

'Is there any other that requires to speak? No? Then I shall again welcome our long-sought Princess back to her grateful people and ask her to take the High Throne of Judgement. Join me in that welcome, please, Children of the Nine!'

Parudanh made a formal obeisance and, with a courteous gesture, urged Essa to ascend the throne. As she climbed its steps and, with a sweep of her robe, seated herself, all those in the chamber chanted in thunderous chorus: *'Vazatié laskatalad,* Hiludessa *indreletzar Avaka-limei! Vazatié laskatalad,* Hiludessa *dlaluhanzar reda Safaddnéiei!'* 'The greatest of welcomes, Hiludessa, princess of Avakalim! The greatest of welcomes, Hiludessa, divine messenger to Safaddné!'

During this chant the branath, his chain still coiled loose about his mighty shoulders, settled in a watchful crouch at the foot of the throne steps. As for Parudanh, he returned to his place in the seats before us.

When all was again silent, Essa spoke in a clear voice that evinced neither nervousness nor hesitation. 'People of the mountains, Children of the Nine, we are in conclave here to discover truth and to receive guidance. Let all who speak do so in honesty, seeking for justice, not for gain. Ye Nine who rule over us, grant that I who must judge shall pronounce judgement exactly as You would desire. Grant also that those who are judged shall accept, or shall enact, those judgements with whole heart and entire submission.'

Essa's studies among the parchments had not been vain. She had learned by rote, and now had pronounced, the proper opening phrases for a Safaddnese assembly. Her success was made evident by the approving murmur that her words aroused.

After the briefest of pauses, she resumed speaking: 'As you all know, Aracundra is of all letzestrei the most blessed. It is fitting, therefore, that I invite the dakhmen Etselil to serve as summoner in this assembly, that all arguments may be properly and justly heard.'

The letzahar of Aracundra, a tall and striking figure in a black robe richly broidered with silver, strode forth pridefully to take his place before the throne. I noticed, however, that he kept at a careful distance from Rakhamu!

Before inviting other speeches, Etselil began his own peroration. It proved to be of great length, a recounting of the whole history of the mountain realms since the beginning of memory. His voice was clear and carrying, but very even in tone. Indeed, his words flowed forth as steadily as a mountain torrent—and were quite as likely to overwhelm and carry away the incautious listener into a tide of oblivion.

The Safaddnese appeared to find his address entirely enthralling. For my part, however, I allowed my thoughts to be borne so far away that I recall little of what he said. What would happen now? With Essa safe from criticism in this assembly, safe also (I assumed) from the malign machinations of the Hrasangs, much had been gained; but much else remained uncertain. Might she yet be able to leave Ayan and travel with us, as she had vowed she would, or might the pressure of Safaddnese desires overwhelm her own? Would she find a means of guaranteeing a future for Lyonesse, or would her sense of justice—Safaddnese justice—leave her unable morally to favour and defend that new, frail realm in which my father and brother had found precarious refuge?

Concerning Essa herself, I found myself more than ever puzzled. Surely she could not be a revenant Princess from the past? After all, she had not been in captivity in Kradsunar, as the legend required; instead, she had been a servant of the robbers, certainly not free but equally certainly not in confinement. Surely she must be the child of some fugitive Safaddnese father and an unspecified, perhaps Heradorian mother? Had not Dan Wyert known and, in his fashion, admired her father?

And yet—so much had transpired that was strange. The finding of the taron; was that merely chance? Our visit to Sasliith; was that chance also or, as the priest had claimed, a response to a summons from a god living within his own gross image? Had we, being lost in the mountains, merely happened to reach Achalind or had Halrath-hantor sent the gherek to fetch us here? Was Essa a mere maid, to be saved from drowning by my archery skills and to be beloved by Avran for such reasons as any man loves his woman, or was she somehow different, more than human? Might it be that she *was* the appointed agent of the nine mountain gods? Might she be, if not the lost Hiludessa herself, the *spirit* of Hiludessa given new flesh?

The speech of Etselil lasted fully three hours. Mercifully, when it ended, there was a pause during which food and ale were brought into the chamber by a regiment of servants under the fussy, perspiring direction of Kuldu Asbetang. I would like to have sought Richard, but felt I should not; nor did he seek me.

All too soon, the call came to resume our seats and the proceedings recommenced. I had thought our lesson in history at an end; but no, it had been barely begun. Etselil now summoned the letzahar of Omega—yes, he *did* emerge from the ray to our right; my guess had been correct—to recount how the laws of Safaddné had developed over the centuries, and to explain why. The Omegan's voice had a curious, rough quality, as if his throat were rusty and slowing down his words; nor did it alter much in tone. Though the Ayanians about me were listening with polite concentration, my own thoughts—and, I am sure, those of Avran—again drifted into other channels, though this time I was wondering about Lyonesse and excited by the realization that, having met my brother again after so long, I might hope soon to meet my father again. As for Dan Wyert, he had fallen asleep.

When eventually this second peroration ended, the Omegan dakhmen returned to his place. Even as he did so there came a whistle from high above us, beginning on a low, wavering note and rising to a high shrill. At that sound, all rose—even Dan Wyert, who woke and stood up in a single, convulsive movement. When the whistling ceased, I saw that Essa had descended from her high throne and knew that the day's proceedings must be over.

Her elevation to the High Throne had altered the order of precedence. She was the first to leave the chamber, Rakhamu before her and Robin beside her, with Taru Taletang, Avran, Dan and I following respectfully behind. When we had climbed the winding stairs and reached the doorway, Taru waved back Avran and me, for his letel were waiting outside to conduct Robin and the princess back to their lodging and only Dan was required as attendant.

The short hours of daylight were by then almost ended and, though the sky was cloudless, the wind had become again chill. Avran and I were hesitating in the street when, to our surprise, we saw Aflar Eslingbror approaching. After looking about him to be sure he was not overheard, he addressed me quietly.

'Ye'll be seeking your brother, Simon? Aye, I heard the tidings. Well, as you'll appreciate, it would not be thought fitting for you, a soldier of Ayan as you are, to enter the quarters of the Brelinderimins.'

Perceiving that I was about to protest, he held up his hand to silence me. 'Hold till I finish, my friends! You shall both come back to my house to dine; and there, Simon, your brother will be joining us. My own brother has passed word to yours and will serve as his guide to our house.'

My brief wrath quite swept away, I beamed at Aflar. 'Why, that is most kind—and, I'm sure, most wise. I am again greatly beholden to you.'

While we walked back toward his home with Aflar—slowly, for the lame ex-soldier's pace uphill was not fast—he discussed with us the day's events. News of the death of the nuszudirar had been swift in spreading. Since he had been more feared than loved in Kesbados, it had aroused much excitement but little regret. Moreover it had been so devastating a setback for the Hrasang party that Aflar believed their influence must have been utterly destroyed. Even so, he urged us to be watchful—especially on the Princess's behalf, for he thought Yanu Hrasang might well seek vengeance.

After that warning, Aflar's mind switched into a new channel. He stopped abruptly and turned to me rather worriedly: 'Simon, I shall need to greet your brother. His name—I find it difficult . . . Rykhhard? Rishkhard? Please teach me how to pronounce it properly!'

However, though I strove to do so, the best Aflar could manage was 'Rishhard'—and so my brother was greeted that evening. As may be imagined, our dinner was a joyful time, with Richard and I chattering away in the excitement of reunion and Avran quite content to smile and listen. After eating with us, the Eslingbrors withdrew discreetly into another room. From the gusts of laughter we heard, we were sure that the demise of Zelat Hrasang was occasioning them almost as much joyful relief as our meeting had brought to my brother and me.

Richard was told the whole long story of our journey from Sandastre; but it was evident that, though prepared to be entertained, he was not much interested in our adventures south of the mountains. It was only when I described our bringing to, and escape from, Kradsunar that his interest truly kindled.

In telling this, I felt I should be careful; I did not believe the Eslingbrors were listening but, if they chanced to be, I had no desire to undermine their faith in the Princess Hiludessa. Consequently, though stressing that she had been bound in servitude to 'Lord' Darnay and his robbers, I was careful not to dismiss Essa as a mere servant; nor did I mention Dan's naming of her father. Instead, I permitted it to seem possible that she *was* the lost Princess, implying—though not stating—that we had only learned this much later. From Avran's smile, I knew that he had perceived my stratagem, but knew also that he approved it.

Richard was enthralled by the story of our escape from the robber city, commenting admiringly on Essa's role therein; and he listened with avid attention to my recounting of our subsequent adventures and misadventures. When the long story was told, he sighed and smiled at us rather wistfully.

'Do you know, brother Simon, I have been picturing you all this time as quietly settling to the life of a clerk in some church or monastery? Yes, I know my father's farewell message challenged you;

yet I must confess that, for my part, I conceived you as too cautious—or, mayhap, too wise—to respond to his challenge. Indeed, in my thoughts I've been contrasting the hazards of my own life with the tranquillity of yours. Yet now—why, in comparison with Avran and you, I've scarcely known any perils! Oh yes, there was Shrewsbury field and our flight afterwards; but, since we left England's shores, it has been Father and I who have known tranquillity!'

'Tell me of our father, and of Lyonesse,' I begged. 'I have been wondering about you both for so long.'

'Our father is flourishing. As you know, he was long the friend and adviser of Hotspur. Indeed, had his advice been properly heeded, Henry Bolingbroke would not now be sitting on England's throne—or any other . . . Well, as you may know also, Sir John Warren and Sir Arthur Thurlstone rule jointly in Lyonesse. They were swift in recognizing father's wisdom and he has come to act as their chancellor. However, it is truly Sir John that he serves. Since Sir Arthur took Darequel Esekh to wife, he has spent the greater part of his time upvalley among the Brelinderimins. Yet father remains busy and contented enough. Presently he is charged with the fortifying of Warrentown; and he delights in that task. Were he not so occupied, it is he who would be functioning as our land's spokesman, not I. Only because Sir John and Sir Arthur consider—falsely, in my judgement—that I have inherited father's wisdom, did they choose me as their ambassador. So here I am.'

We all smiled at this; but, for my part, I shared my brother's doubts. Though Richard was a doughty warrior, I could not conceive of him as a skilled negotiator; he was too honest and straightforward. Yet maybe that very honesty might stand him in good stead, when it was so patent. Since he was incapable of guile, he was sure to attract the trust of anyone capable of trusting.

'And the land of Lyonesse itself?'

Richard spoke soberly now. 'It is a good land, where a man might make a good life if left in peace. The Brelinderimins, of course, are our friends; their choosing of Sir Arthur to be dakhmen demonstrated that friendship beyond doubt. As for the Avakalimins, they are our friends also. If these other Safaddnese signify their agreement, then our three realms will fuse and, with their aid, the new Lyonesse can become a strong kingdom.'

'But what if they do not? Can Lyonesse survive without approval from the other letzestrei?' Avran was asking this new question.

Richard sighed. 'Perhaps, if it were let alone. Sadly, that seems hardly probable. The Pavonarans hate us. If they invade again with a mightier army, I question whether we can withstand them, for all father's fortifying of Warrentown. If the other Safaddnese realms should sever their links with Brelinderim and Avakalim, we shall have nowhere to turn for aid. Moreover, though I do not think Ayan or the more distant letzestrei would ever march against us, the Desumeans might. They seem now to be firm allies of the Pavonarans.'

'The decisions of this assembly are crucial, then?'

'Yes indeed. For we of Lyonesse, much rests in the hands of your little rescued Princess. Will it be peace for us, or a tide of blood?'

Chapter Twelve

THE SAFADDNESE IN CONCLAVE

Before the end of that first day in the great chamber in Kesba-dos, it had become clear to me that the deliberations of the Safaddnese would be prolonged. It occurred to me also that, if I were properly to understand what was happening and not drift away into daydreams, I must have something on which to focus my attention. Consequently, when we returned next morning, I brought with me my parchment pad, my pens, and a stoppered phial of ink.

Again the proceedings began with those mysterious whistlings; again the priests went through their ceremony, though following a somewhat different ritual; and again Essa took her place on the High Throne. From that point, our duties as her guards ceased till she should descend from it, so I was able to make notes of what was said. I did this in the Reschorese script; I had not mastered that of Safaddné, while to use the Latin alphabet would have seemed too deliberate an attempt to keep my thoughts secret from those about me.

It was well that I took this precaution to keep awake, for that second day was even duller than the first. Having endured a recounting of the political and military history of the Safaddnese by the letzahar of Aracundra and of their legal system by his compeer of Omega, we had now to be instructed in their religious history!

First the letzudirar of Aracundra spoke devoutly of how the nine gods had made themselves manifest to the faithful over the years. His tone was so reverently hushed as to approach inaudibility, yet his words provoked considerable restlessness among his auditors. It was evident that the worshippers of gods other than Horulgavar were far from gratified by his portrayal of the actions and significance of their own particular deities. Indeed, when the high priest had droned to an end, several other high priests would, I'm sure, have liked to make responsive—and, I doubt not, indignant—comments; but they were not given an opportunity. Instead the letzudirar of Vasanderim was invited to describe how the ritual of Safaddnese worship had evolved. He was a burly man in whose orotund loquacity there seemed little that was controversial. By the time he was into his second hour of discoursing, all desire by others to speak seemed to have ebbed away. Moreover, I'm sure most of the Safaddnese were, like me, praying for him to cease, so that we might partake of our increasingly overdue midday repast. Long before his peroration reached its eventual end, I had given up taking notes; and I was most grateful that dakhmen Etselil immediately declared an adjournment. Probably he too was hungry!

During that adjournment, Essa descended from the High Throne and, for a while, resumed her place beside Robin; but she showed no desire for conversation and he did not force it upon her. When Etselil recalled the meeting and she had to return to her place, I am sure she did so reluctantly.

After that, however, matters became more interesting. Quite to my surprise, Xandor of Ayan was called upon to speak—to my surprise, because I had not expected any letzumahar would be considered of high enough rank to be invited to address so august an assembly. He described how their closed frontiers had forced the Safaddnese to develop a very special economy, relying entirely upon their own crops and beasts for food and endlessly re-using materials and metals which, being from sources outside, they could no longer replace. Xandor made it clear that this was presenting increasing problems. For example, though the Safaddnese were able to mine copper, they had no new sources of tin for bronze-making; they had silver enough, but little gold and almost no *evrakhar*. (That, I presumed, must be their name for the red, glowing metal they valued so highly, a metal called *evragar* in Sandastre but unknown in England.) Most importantly, their supplies of iron were perilously low, so that weapon-making would soon become a serious problem.

Xandor spoke well and, though he avoided jokes, entertainingly. When he ended, Etselil invited comments and received indication that several others of the letzaharai and letzumaharai wished to speak. Each was given only a relatively brief time, but their speeches took up the rest of that day. The dakhmen of Vasanderim spoke feelingly of his people's need for weapons, in order to continue their long struggle with the Sea Warriors. The letzumahar of Darega complained of the problems of maintaining any sort of economy, with a population so small and still dwindling; why, not even their herds and fungus fields could properly be maintained, let alone their defences! The plump letzumahar of Avakalim proved much more cheerful. He wondered about opening trade by sea with England, France or Flanders. To my surprise, this suggestion was received almost with indifference; but, after a little thought, I understood why. Those names meant nothing to most Safaddnese—and what is unknown cannot, of course, be important.

During the Avakalimin's speech, I noticed that Richard was gazing about him rather anxiously. I'm sure he was disheartened by the evident lack of interest among the other letzestrei in foreign trade and I suspect he would have liked to speak in support of that concept; but, of course, he could not do so unless invited and had little chance of receiving such an invitation. However, it was the last speech of the day that upset him most—and worried me also.

This was delivered by the letzumahar of Desume, a smooth-faced, small-eyed man of the sort that, in England, usually finds high place in some guild of merchants, through a combination of glib persuasiveness with submissiveness to superiors and mercilessness to underlings and competitors. With great detail and oh! so convincingly, he described the benefits that had begun to accrue to his realm since they had begun trading with the Pavonarans. What riches it had brought to Desume!—not just in material terms, but also through the new techniques they were learning to use, and the new awareness they were gaining of the World beyond their borders!

All this evoked a murmur of approving comment from several of the rays of watching people. However, to my gratification, it caused dakhmen Etselil of Aracundra increasingly to frown. I could guess his thought—that this opening of borders had been done without sanction from the other letzestrei. When the Desumean letzumahar had resumed his seat, I expected a furious response from the Aracundran letzahar. Instead, the whistles sounded from above, ending that second day.

Richard had warned us, on that first night together, that he dare not risk any repetition of our meeting. However, an invitation to dine with Robin gave us a pleasant enough evening. Xandor was also present; he was in benign and talkative mood and, from his comments, very much out of sympathy with the Desumeans. However, to Avran's disappointment, we saw nothing of Essa till the resumption next morning of our duty as her guards.

That was a day of discussion of the mounting military problems faced by the Safaddnese in maintaining the integrity of their realms. All the letzaharei spoke in succession. The Vasanderimins told proudly of how, despite their lack of weapons, they were keeping the Sea Warriors at bay by land and repelling their attacks by ship. Etselil of Aracundra spoke equally proudly of how his letzestre had likewise been attacked, but had beaten back those attacks—yet, yes, the paucity of weapons was a problem for his people also. The letzahar of Darega complained again of the dwindling of his people: yet he thought their god and their wind-trees would continue to be effective as defence against invaders. (I believed him!) His compeer of Omega, rusty-voiced as before, confessed frankly that, if his own realm were invaded, he would need to seek help from the other Safaddnese. His people were too few to defend it—and the Reschorese, he reminded us, were upon his frontier. Soganreth of Ayan was more optimistic. He and his people had weapons enough and good defences; they could maintain their realm's integrity and even hope to lend aid to their neighbours.

As he stepped down, the letzahar of Paladra drifted forward, as smoothly and soundlessly as a spider-cobweb blown by a wind. Faceless under his hood, he told us, in a voice thin and dry as a spider's might be, that Mesnakech had furnished his land with its own defences. No more than that; he neither specified those defences nor stated whether the Paladrans might be willing to aid their neighbours at need. Yet he returned to his place unexamined.

Six representatives of letzestrei had spoken before midday, then; but not the three that were most significant in the controversies dividing the Safaddnese. Their turn came afterwards.

I had wondered if Richard might speak for Brelinderim, but he did not; and, on reflection, I realized why. Since the union of that realm with Lyonesse had not yet been even discussed, let alone approved, by the other letzestrei, Richard could speak only for Lyonesse—and only upon invitation, since Lyonesse had no status in this assembly.

Instead it was the letzudirar of Brelinderim who was called upon to address us all. He was as lean and tough-looking as a pick-helve, but there was a gleam of humour in his eye as he looked about him and an echo of it in his voice when he spoke. He was called Balahir, 'strong breeze'—a name more appropriate, perhaps, to a priest of Daltharimbar than to one of Radaionesu, but somehow suiting both that voice and his personality.

Balahir began by harking backward to the time when the Brelinderimins had been strong and readily able to defend themselves. He recalled how they and the Avakalimins had repeatedly driven off attacks by the Sea Warriors until, with the reconstruction of the fortress at Lemmeshind mouth, such attacks ceased altogether. However, there had followed a dwindling of both peoples and, with it, their withdrawal into the mountains. During that time, the fortress had been allowed to fall into disrepair, nor had it been properly manned. Indeed, the Brelinderimins had not even been able adequately to guard the mountain passes on their eastern frontier. So inadequate was the guard that the Pavonarans had come unheralded upon them. Radaionesu had inspired their soldiers' hearts with great courage, yet their land would have been overrun had not Edaénar, god of the sea, brought them help at the crucial moment. (This allusion to their particular deity evoked a gratified murmur among the Vasanderimins.) With the help of those sea-borne English warriors, yes indeed, the invaders had been driven out of the realm of Brelinderim; but a second attack, should it come, could not be withstood unaided.

Balahir had been speaking in a steady, controlled flow of words, though with evident passion when he told of the invasion. Now he spread out his hands in a gesture that invited comprehension and sympathy.

'For what we did then, Children of the Nine, we have received much abuse. Yes, we gave our lands at Lemmeshind mouth to our new allies; and yes, we persuaded our neighbours of Avakalim to do likewise. Yet I ask you: what other solution was there to the problem of defending, not just our shores, but our two whole letzestrei? We had striven to do so with too few soldiers, and we had learned how completely we had failed. What else might we have done?'

There was a murmur of comment, but it was hostile rather than sympathetic. Balahir gazed about him, listening intently and recognizing the lack of any positive response to his appeal. When he resumed speaking, all humour had gone from his voice; instead, it evinced a controlled bitterness.

'You people of Ayan, Desume and Vasanderim whose lands lie nearest to ours—yes, you are our close kin and might well have rallied against the Pavonarans. And you of Aracundra, Paladra, Omega, Darega—would you have rallied also? Perhaps; but how swiftly could you have come, any of you? Not in time to aid us. Mayhap, indeed, you might have driven the Pavonarans from our lands; though that is not certain, for they were many and fierce. Yet, if you *had* driven them away, what would that have profited us? You would have been too late. You would have regained only the ruins of Brelinderim and found only the unburied bodies of its people!'

Shaking his head in disgust, the high priest returned to his seat, amid a renewed hum of comment. However, even then, the response to his words was not favourable. I heard an Ayanian soldier behind me mutter: 'Better to die in honour than to live in dishonour.' His words seemed to epitomize the general reaction of the other Safaddnese.

However, there was no immediate adverse speech. Instead, summoner Etselil called forward letzahar Perespeth of Avakalim.

Perespeth wasted no words. 'My good friend, the letzudirar of Brelinderim, has told of the circumstances of his realm. What he said applies in equal measure to Avakalim. So ill, indeed, were we guarding our letzestre that we did not learn of the battle at Lemmeshind mouth till it was over. Our realm is too large, and we are too few, to defend it properly. We required aid; and the people from beyond the sea, the Lyonessans as they must now be styled, have furnished that aid. I trust that you others who are subject of the Nine Gods will comprehend our need and approve our actions— those that we have taken and those that we propose to take. I trust also that the Nine may give their blessings to us, in days to come as in the days that have been.'

Without more ado, Perespeth returned to his seat. He did so amid a hum of protest so loud and sustained that summoner Etselil had to demand silence before calling upon the letzahar of Desume. The fact that, on two successive days, his letzestre had been granted the last word made me uneasy. During the address that followed, my unease waxed mightily.

Ekulag of Desume was a massive man, slab-like in shape, heavy-browed and pouchy-eyed, with a small, pursy mouth between drooping beardless cheeks. Nor did I find agreeable those large, coarse hands, so amply utilized in gestures; that nodding smile, as if assuring the assembly of an obsequious friendliness; or that crooning voice with its consciously charming cadences. From the outset, I thought him one in whom no trust could be reposed—and not just because of my distrust of his letzestre. Yet he spoke lucidly and, I feared, all too beguilingly.

Not for him a short speech, like that of Perespeth. Instead, he began by harking back to the earliest days of Desume; how it had valorously joined the other Safaddnese letzestrei in defeating the Southerners and how, later, it had helped to drive from the mountains their Pavonaran puppets. Yes, at that time the Pavonarans had been the enemies of Safaddné. Moreover, during many subsequent generations the Pavonarans had constantly warred with the Desumeans for control of the valley of the Embeldwey, the Desumeans sometimes driving the Pavonarans back almost to the sea, sometimes being forced to retreat up-valley. Yet his people, the people of Tera-ushlu of the Sun, had been always vigorous and numerous; and so they remained, even today.

That statement aroused a murmur of surprise; evidently it accorded ill with the assessment of the other Safaddnese. Ekulag perceived the doubt he had aroused and hastily modified his statement. Vigorous and numerous the Desumeans were, certainly, in comparison with other letzestrei; but, well, no, not quite so numerous as formerly. Moreover they suffered, as did their Safaddnese neighbours, from a mounting shortage of tin and iron for weapons and of gold and evrakhar for ornament. For the tributes demanded by Tera-ushlu, gold especially was required; for was not gold the metal of the sun?

Happily—Ekulag gave us a brief beam to stress his happiness—the Desumeans had discovered that the Pavonarans were eager for peace and trade. Yes, of course the Pavonarans remained a warrior people; but had they not learned that the Desumeans were formidable warriors also, better as allies than as enemies? Why continue a battle that neither realm might win? Why not instead discover new strength in friendship?

So his letzestre and Pavonara had made peace. Moreover, they had begun to trade, to their mutual benefit; his letzumahar had told us already of those benefits, we had no need to hear of them again. And now—why, to his pleasure he was empowered—yes, empowered by the envoys of the King of Pavonara himself—to offer an extension of that friendship and trade to all nine letzestrei!

This announcement aroused a clamour of comment in eight rays of the chamber; only the Paladrans remained, as always, silent. Nor was that comment favourable; rather, it was indignant. Certainly the Ayanians about us were greatly aroused. Why, the Pavonarans were enemies! They had shown themselves untrustworthy in the past; how had they changed? Rather, they must be toying cat-like with their Desumean dupes, ready to pounce at will!

Ekulag waited for the hubbub to die down, hands on broad hips and that obsequious smile on face. He looked like a merchant who, though not relishing a customer's insults, is too avid for profit to allow his annoyance any expression.

When summoner Etselil's exhortations had again brought silence to the chamber, Ekulag proceeded with his speech. Yes of course, he quite understood that his brothers of the other letzestrei must still distrust the Pavonarans. Why, one had only to remember the history of these mountains to sympathize with that distrust! However, he assured us that the Pavonarans of ancient days were a very different people from those of today. Had not their descendants been vigorous in combating that foreign religion of three-gods-in-one, when it had gained so many adherents? Were not both Pavonarans and Safaddnese equally steadfast in adhering to older faiths—not the same faith, admittedly, but comparable faiths—faiths that had grown in these mountains, not arrived from outside? If the time had come when Safaddné should end its isolation, would it not be better to find friendship with neighbours who retained their ancient beliefs, rather than with foreigners of a different religion or with neighbours whose faith in the mountain gods had lapsed?

These arguments were couched in the tone of a mother chiding a beloved but tiresome child. They provoked another hum of comment, but now there was in it a note of uncertainty. All the Safaddnese knew how the coming of Christianity had strengthened the resolve of their subject peoples to throw off their yoke; few knew enough about the religion of the Pavonarans to comprehend whether or not it was indeed close to their own. If the dakhmen of Desume said it was, well, perhaps he was right; and, yes, it *did* seem better to treat with a realm long known to them than with realms far away and with unfamiliar names—England, France, Flanders, or whatever.

Ekulag waited again, then said: 'And remember, we have enemies at hand—vigorous enemies, not just of Safaddné but of Pavonara also. You have heard them several times mentioned today: the Sea Warriors. If we ally with Pavonara, then we might drive them from our coasts and even, maybe, from these whole mountains. What say you to that, Children of the Nine?'

Balahir of Brelinderim was on his feet before anyone else. 'Yet we face a greater enemy—Pavonara itself! Has not that realm with which you urge friendship sought recently to destroy us?'

Ekulag's clasped hands had moved up to rest on his chest, in the attitude of one whose back is warmed pleasantly by a good fire. He was again beaming. 'Why should they not, my friend, when your own letzestre had so traitorously allied itself with the Sea Warriors? When the Pavonarans perceived this and, seeking to root out that evil, attacked you, did you not receive help from they who are your allies?'

'Not from the Sea Warriors, no!' Balahir was furiously angry. 'When we were so treacherously invaded, our aid came from the sea, yes: but, as you must know, from a very different people—the English!'

Ekulag laughed derisively. 'The Sea Warriors came in their ships from far away; your English came in their ships from far away. What is the difference, to us of Safaddné? And have I not heard that this realm you mention, this England, was long ago settled by those same Sea Warriors? Do they not still hold much of it under sway?'

That argument quite disconcerted me, for of course Ekulag was right. Why, the whole northeast of England, and much of the Midlands also, had indeed been settled by the Northmen and had long been called the Danelaw! To the Safaddnese, there could be little cause for differentiating between Englishmen and Northmen. How had Ekulag learned so dangerous a fact? Who had schooled him in this speech?

Fortunately, Balahir did not know enough to perceive that argument's strength. 'The English are not of the same breed as the Sea Warriors,' he responded contemptuously: he had not sat down, although gestured to do so by summoner Etselil. 'How can you claim such a thing? Why, their language is different, their weapons are different, their very ships are different! If you speak thus, you speak in ignorance!'

Ekulag was quite taken aback; his face flushed and that ugly little mouth hung open. Before he could frame any reply, however, Etselil spoke to him and to Balahir.

'This discussion is degenerating into an unmannerly wrangle! It is an offence to the Princess our judge and to all others present here! Resume your seats, both of you! There will be time for further discussion of these matters, and for more orderly questions and answers, in days to come.'

Under his cold eye, the letzahar of Desume slunk back to his seat; but the letzudirar of Brelinderim, though also obeying, sat down quite unapologetically. The whole great chamber fell silent. When Rakhamu stretched and yawned, it seemed an irreverence.

Etselil allowed the silence to extend awhile, then said: 'It is proper, I think, that I should clarify some matters now. Yes, we are at the beginning of a dakhletzel and yes, at such a time we must consider changes to our policies. Yet, peoples of Safaddné, we should be making those changes by common agreement and should act in concert. Regrettably, when we met before the Seat of the Gods, we learned that common consent and common action had been rendered impossible before they were even considered. Already one letzestre, Brelinderim, had ended our tradition of independence by accepting aid from strangers. Moreover, that letzestre and another, Avakalim, had agreed to cede lands—Safaddnese lands—to those strangers!'

To my surprise, Soganreth of Ayan rose to his feet at that point. 'We must recall that there is a precedent for their action. Did not we of Safaddné cede lands to the Mentonese long ago, on promise of their neutrality thenceforward?'

This observation caused a rustle of comment, ending as Etselil responded. 'There is this difference—that our borders with Mentone were thereafter closed. Yet it is certainly a precedent. Indeed, you may feel that, under the stress of invasion and its aftermath, the actions of Brelinderim and Avakalim were justified. That is a question still to be resolved. Furthermore, I understand we are shortly to receive new, and even more extreme, proposals from those letzestrei.'

This produced a renewed hum of excited comment. During it, Soganreth sat down. When the hubbub had died away under Etselil's bleakly searching gaze, he resumed speaking; but now his tone expressed an utter disgust.

'That is not all. Yesterday and today we have learned of another independent action, and one that seems to me altogether inexcusable. During the Dakhletzelkrayet we heard rumours, no more, of trade between a third letzestre, Desume, and our ancient enemies the Pavonarans. This was in itself a breach of our long-held policy of isolation. Now we learn that Desume has not only made peace with Pavonara, without consent from us other Safaddnese, but has even become the *ally* of that Kingdom! I am appalled at such tidings; and I am sure that most of you must be quite as appalled. That action has not the excuse of having been taken under pressure. Indeed, I consider it utterly inexcusable.'

A murmur of affirmative response travelled like a wind about the chamber; but Etselil was again speaking. 'Tomorrow, and in the days that follow, we shall examine those various actions and the fresh proposals that are to be made to us. Under the guidance of our judge, we shall formulate our responses. For today, I think, we have heard enough.'

As if at a signal, there commenced the trill of a whistle high above his head, swelling to a louder note as everyone rose. The day's proceedings were indeed over.

As before, Avran and I fell into procession behind Essa and Robin, seeing them into the charge of Taru Taletang and his letel before being dismissed for the day. Outside in the street, the setting sun was throwing long shadows and a keen wind was blowing. Yet there had been melting of the snow, for the cobbles stood clear of it, even if the cracks between were still white.

Avran gave a sigh and then smiled at me. 'What an afternoon that was! Well, the choice is plain before the Safaddnese; either to trust the Pavonarans, or to support your brother's new realm of Lyonesse. Surely they can discover no third path?'

I laughed. 'Well, it's evident that the letzahar of Aracundra places no trust, either in the Pavonarans or in Desume! Yet I believe the Safaddnese may try to find some compromise, or some alternative. Mayhap they'll choose to trade with the Mentonese instead, or with the merchants of Warringtown:[1] after all, the Mentonese are not

---

[1] A mercantile port on the eastern coast of Rockall

Christians and the men of Warringtown seem to worship only money! Or mayhap they'll decide to open their southern frontiers.'

Avran snorted. 'With the Mentonese, yes, possibly; but with Warringtown? I question whether they've even heard of that city! And do you truly believe the Reschorese would welcome the idea of such trading? Why, even after so many years, they're still quite terrified of the Safaddnese!'

By then we were walking up the steep street. Behind us, it was filling with men leaving the conference; Essa had been the only woman present. Since I did not wish to proclaim my thoughts to any listeners, I lowered my voice when I asked a responsive question.

'Yesterday, Avran, I cherished little hope that Lyonesse would be allowed to survive and grow. Today, I must feel more optimistic. Those Desumeans are most obnoxious, are they not?'

'Yes indeed! I—why, what's the matter, Simon?' For I had hesitated, then stopped.

'Nothing serious. It's merely that I've left my pad of notes behind in the great chamber. I'll run and fetch it—it shouldn't take me long. Why don't you walk on up the street? I'll soon catch up with you.'

'Why, I could come back also . . . Oh, very well!' My friend set off again uphill, while I turned and ran back down.

By then the street had become quite congested. Some delegates and soldiers were hurrying away, but many were moving slowly, deep in discussion, or had coagulated into stationary clots of conversation. Through this tangle of people I threaded my way as swiftly as I might. Soon I was stepping into the shadow that concealed the door to the chamber stairs.

I did not recognize the soldier on duty, a stupid- and surly-looking fellow; but, since the guard might well have changed several times during the day, that did not surprise me. When I spoke the password, he admitted me without hesitation.

I hastened along the short corridor and began going down the winding stairs. I was moving quietly, in part from habit, but largely because I was not sure how this unauthorised after-hours return might be viewed. Not until I was nearing the stair-foot did the sound of voices tell me that I had blundered—that I had entered the wrong door and was descending into the wrong ray of the chamber.

Yet I did not retreat but, instead, paused to listen: for I had recognized the voices as being those of the letzumahar and letzahar of Desume. The letzumahar was talking loudly and excitedly.

'I tell you again, Ekulag, you have been most unwise! You should have revealed our pact with King Rafanesar, and his offer, later in the meeting or not at all! To do so today has merely served to stir up hostility against us!'

'I am fully aware of that hostility; you need not remind me of it.' The letzahar's tone was much less musical, now that he was no longer striving to charm; indeed, he sounded sour. 'I realize equally clearly that not even my own followers are pleased with me. Why else do you think I am lingering here, allowing them to leave before me and waiting for the streets to clear, instead of returning to my room and that good Hradaulian wine? I am not anxious to suffer abuse, be it physical or verbal.'

The letzumahar sighed in exasperation. 'Well then, why *did* you report that matter to the meeting? Much better, by far, if you had spoken only of trade, as did I. *That* went well enough, did it not?'

'So well that I thought I might go further—and went too far, maybe. Aye, indeed I was surprised by their hostility.' Yet, in Ekulag's voice, there was now an undertone of amusement that puzzled me.

'Could you not have predicted it, after all the fuss aroused at the Dakhletzelkrayet by the mere rumour of what we had done?'

Ekulag spoke in dismissive derision. 'A lot of old women they've become, they and their Nine Gods! They're all so accustomed to doing nothing that it upsets them when any letzestre dares to take a novel action! Old women, all of them—yes, even those Aracundrans and Vasanderimins, for all their scrapping with the Sea Warriors! And Nine Gods—faugh! There's only one god that matters—our own God of the Sun, Tera-ushlu. Why, even the Pavonarans worship Him, though they give Him another name. They and we, we'll get along fine, when together we rule the mountains!'

Evidently, from his impatient sigh, the letzumahar was becoming even more exasperated. 'That may be; that may very well be; but why stir up trouble now? Why not keep our own counsel; why not just work against the Avakalimins and Brelinderimins, so that this new realm, this Lyonesse, does not gain sanction from the other letzestrei? Surely that would be our wisest course, Ekulag?'

The dakhmen laughed outright—a triumphant laugh, that of a gambler who is about to throw down the winning piece. 'As to what they approve or disapprove, or what that judge of theirs decides—

that princess from the past, if such she be and not a creation of the priests—what does it matter? All we need to do is to keep them talking. The more problems they see before them, the better—it'll keep 'em going longer!'

The letzumahar was clearly puzzled. 'What might that gain us? It will only waste *our* time as well, surely?'

Ekulag laughed again, an unpleasant laugh that expressed a contemptuous superiority. 'Did I not tell you? No, perhaps not, for I don't always quite trust you, Zhanag! Let me say merely that your commercial instincts are a little, just a little, too well developed for complete trust!'

'What is it, then? What is it that I do not know?'

'That, while all the leaders of the letzestrei are spending their time in talk here, the question is being settled for them! The Pavonaran army is already on the march. In four days' time or less, they'll be across the mountains and into Lyonesse! That new town has its fortifications still unfinished; our Pavonaran friends will crush it like a nut under a hammer!'

'Ah! Now I understand!' The letzumahar sounded both impressed and subdued.

'So you and I, we'll keep 'em talking, won't we?' Ekulag was almost purring. 'Then, before they're done, Lyonesse will be finished and Brelinderim also!'

Zhanag began upon obsequious congratulations, but I did not linger to listen to them. I had heard enough—indeed, too much! I crept back up the stairs, passed the guard and fled away up the street after Avran.

Chapter Thirteen

THE BACK OF THE GOD

'I believe we all comprehend the situation?' Robin looked round the circle of our faces. 'As you must perceive, we are faced with three major tasks and two very serious problems.'

I had not caught up with Avran before reaching the Eslingbrors' dwelling. Both brothers chanced to be there and, on Avran's urging, I had told my story also to them. Though greatly disturbed by my tidings, they would not attempt to approach the Princess Hiludessa, even in so serious a regard; but Keld had felt able, at least, to convey word to the indreletzahular.

Fortunately, that night Robin was not embroiled in any official function. On hint of what I had overheard, he had invited the four of us to his quarters, two sumptuously appointed chambers close to the temple in the southeast quarter of the city. Robin had himself transmitted a message to my brother Richard, such as to bring him there hotfoot. Moreover, since Essa was dining with the three leaders of Vasanderim and Dan Wyert's services were not required, he had also been invited. He was sitting opposite me in the circle, looking as doleful as a drenched cat.

'I am not sure that I *do* understand,' Avran observed carefully. 'Through the happy chance of Simon's going to the wrong place—'

'Not chance!' Keld Eslingbror was positive. 'He was guided by Halrathhantor, who loves not Desume!'

'Well, perhaps not chance.' Avran was not prepared to argue that point at so critical a time. 'Whatever the cause, we have been vouch-safed crucial information—and vouchsafed it just in time. As for our tasks, I see two of them clearly enough, but not the third. First, we must alert the Princess to the menace from Pavonara and, through her, make the other letzestrei aware of the duplicity of those accursed

Desumeans. Second, we must warn Warrentown of its danger.'

'And not only Warrentown, but also our friends, the peoples of Brelinderim and Avakalim!' Brother Richard was leaning forward, concerned certainly but also exhilarated by the prospect of action.

'That first task is easy enough to execute.' Robin spoke calmly. 'Through Dan here, I can transmit word to the indreletzar that will ensure she talks to me before tomorrow's session. However, as to conveying word quickly to the threatened realms—how will you manage that and what word will you convey? Come now, you must perceive the difficulties?'

'For my part—well, not really.' I was puzzled. 'Surely, all we have to do is to send a warning—a warning of the Pavonaran invasion?'

'Yet that is only partial information. To mount an early defence, our friends of Lyonesse will need to be told the quarter from which the attack will come. Yes, we can be sure it will come from the east; but that is all. And no, Simon,'—he was anticipating the apology I was framing—'I do not believe that, had you lingered longer on the stairs, you would have learned anything more. Obviously letzahar Ekulag distrusted his letzumahar—and, I do not doubt, with just cause! He would not have divulged any fuller details of the Pavonarans' plans. But that means we also do not know those details; and there is more than one possible route, is there not, Richard?'

'Those mountains are damnably easy to cross.' Obviously my brother had not thought this out and was now much disturbed. 'Their east and west walls are steep enough, but they're seamed with narrow valleys, each affording a possible ascent or descent. Once you're on top, it's almost as flat as a kitchen bench. The Pavonarans can go where they please and choose among a whole variety of routes down into the Lemmeshind valley.'

'Have you not been on watch?' Keld was shocked. 'I thought that was the task of you Lyonessans!'

Richard flushed. 'So it is; so it is. Yes of course, we do maintain a watch. Yet I wonder how good our watch is, just now? Like the Brelinderimins, we've had this meeting very much in our minds. And, you know, we hadn't expected the Pavonarans to attack again so soon. Worse, like the Brelinderimins, I think we'd come to anticipate an adequate warning from Desume—fools that we were!'

Robin was nodding judicially. 'So matters are as I suspected.

Then our second task must be to discover the direction from which Pavonara will invade—if we may. However, as you said, Avran, our prime task must be to send warning to Warrentown.'

'Well, surely we may do that?' Avran was becoming impatient. 'We need only to leave quickly, travel fast, and trust to be ahead of the Pavonarans!'

'Leave quickly, Avran? How will you manage that?' Robin's tone was bleak. 'The gate of this city is closed from sunset to sunrise and the few other ways out of it are guarded. As you surely know, no password operates during the hours of darkness. Nor do I believe that letzahar Soganreth will permit anyone to depart from Kesbados, without approval from the other letzestrei in conference; this time of decision is too crucial. What think you, Keld?'

'Not a hope of it.' The letelar was positive. 'After the Princess has spoken tomorrow, it might well be permitted. Not until then.'

'But that is disastrous!' Richard was quite appalled. 'Why, we will lose a night and half a day, at very least! Before word can reach Warrentown, the Pavonarans will be across the mountains!'

'Have you no system of beacons, Richard?' I asked.

'There *was* one; we are trying to renew it, but it is not yet fully in operation. The distances are quite great, you know, if the whole border is to be covered.' He shook his head disgustedly. 'The plain truth is that we are like to be taken unawares, just as were the Brelinderimins.'

'A night and half a day!' Dan Wyert seemed to be speaking to himself. 'Nay, that won't do.'

Robin eyed us compassionately. 'Kesbados is a strong fortress, designed to defy attack from without,' he commented. 'Yet, as I learned long since—and to my cost—such fortresses can also be prisons for those within. Keld and Aflar, has either of you any suggestion as to how an escape might be managed? By six or eight persons, let's say? I do not think we dare risk more.'

Keld considered, then shook his head. 'The main gate is impossible. The other exits—remember, I showed them to you, Simon and Avran?—are all difficult and all guarded.'

'Can we not persuade the guards on one of those lesser exits to let us out? Might we not bribe them—or, at worst, fight our way out?' Richard sounded desperate.

'These soldiers are Ayanians, not Desumeans,' Keld responded stiffly. 'We of Ayan cannot be bribed. Moreover, I do not believe any guards would be persuaded to let you out, whatever your argument. If you tried that, you would merely be referred to the dakhmen—and properly so!'

'Then we must fight our way out!'

Robin shook his head decisively. 'No, no, Richard! Consider the consequences. If you succeed, you will forever besmirch the name of your realm in Safaddnese eyes. If you fail, you may bring a greater disaster upon yourselves—imprisonment, even death perhaps. No, that will not do.'

Poor Richard was quite taken aback. He sought for a response, failed to find one and fell unhappily silent.

Avran glanced at me. 'You remember, Simon, how I predicted that we would need to find a way out from Kesbados? You have helped us to escape from other tight places; can you do it now?' But I could only shake my head.

'Simon has done his part by gathering the crucial information.' Robin spoke in my defence. 'It is for we others to solve this problem, if it be soluble. Aflar, you have not spoken. Can you think of any unguarded exit from Kesbados?'

'Well, you know, maybe I can.' The ex-soldier was diffident. 'Though it's a tricky enough way—dangerous, even—and not one by which you might take your beasts. But then, at this season, you'd be better to travel on seslelteven anyway.'

'What are you thinking of, brother?' Keld was surprised.

'Do you recall, Keld, that I was part of the guard when the temple was rebuilt, oh, about a letzal back? When first Zelat Hrasang became nuszudirar and was wanting everything clean and fancy, to show what a splendid fellow he was?'

'Aye, that I do.' Keld snorted in disgust. 'As soon as he'd made his point, he stopped wasting the temple's wealth—or *his* wealth, as he'd see it—on such things.'

'Well, we both know he was only after power. No fervent worshipper of Halrathhantor, he! And now, see what it's brought him to!'

Robin seized the reins of the conversation anew before it ran away from him. 'You were telling us of a possible exit, Aflar?'

'Aye, so I was. Well, there are conduits high in the southeast wall, to carry the water into the hands of our god so that He may cast it into the lake. Those conduits needed to be cleaned and, while the masons were working, we were told to guard them: I couldn't think why at the time, but afterwards I understood. There's a sort of catwalk, high in the wall above the head of Halrathhantor; and there we had to perch. The masons were not so badly off, for they were busy: but for we guards, it was a dizzifying task—and a pretty tedious and cold one also. Yet it seemed to me I was becoming even chillier than was reasonable. So I followed the draught and found a door ajar.'

'A door, so high in the temple wall?' Keld was astonished. 'Whatever is it for?'

'As you might suppose, I wanted to know that myself. So I gave the door a push—it opened easily enough—and peeked out. There's a narrow, deep path, like a sort of gutter, running down from under the upraised arms of Halrathhantor and behind the images of Horulgavar, Edaénar and Petamedru, to the back of Radaionesu; it goes no farther. Well, I closed the door more firmly and soon felt warmer—and rather less bored, with something new to ponder upon. As it chanced, next day I was posted on the other side and found a second door. I didn't strive to open that one, but I don't doubt there's a similar path leading down to behind Tera-ushlu.'

'How extraordinary!'

'As to what they're for: well, no doubt they might serve as watchpoints in time of war, but principally, I think, they're for cleaning. They'd allow men to be lowered on ropes, to scrub the mosses and lichens off the carvings below. It's long since that was done—and it *needs* to be done . . . But, if our artisans could be lowered down on ropes, so might your six or eight persons, Sir Robert.'

'Yet I don't understand, Aflar.' I spoke doubtfully. 'Would we not merely fall into water or, if landing on ice, crash through it into the lake?'

'If you were lowered from the doorway, yes. But you wouldn't be. You'd follow down that gutter till you were behind Radaionesu—I don't reckon you'd risk Tera-ushlu, as things are!—and have a short descent onto ice that should be thick enough to bear your weight. Yours certainly, Simon—you're small enough!' Aflar chuckled.

'Yes, well, that's excellent, Aflar! But can we gain access to the temple at this hour?'

Aflar seemed surprised. 'Why certainly, Sir Robert! Did you not know that our temples, like those throughout Safaddné, are open for worship of the gods at all hours?'

'Oh, of course; stupid of me! Then we must decide now who goes, and make our preparations quickly. Remember, there must be two parties; one to carry warning, the other to seek the Safaddnese. As for carrying warning, I think that task is for you, Richard; for you and one or two of the men of Brelinderim who have come here with you.'

Richard agreed unhesitatingly; he was smiling with relief now.

'As for seeking the Pavonarans, somehow I think that is a task for you, Simon! You are good at gaining information from unexpected sources. And Avran, you will want to go with him? Yes, of course. I wish I might come also; but, with one arm almost useless'—Robin screwed up his face disgustedly—'I cannot even attempt to shin down a rope.'

I broke in swiftly. 'But Sir Robert, your own task is vital. You must talk to the Princess; and, Dan, you'll have to make their conversation possible.'

'Be sure I'll do that, Master Simon!' Dan was now quite perky.

'Very well, then: but you'll want a guide through the mountains, Simon and Avran. Richard, have you some colleague that might travel with them?'

'No need to seek for one, Richard,' Keld broke in. 'I'll go with them myself! Years back, me and some friends, we decided we wanted to walk the shores of the sea; so, along with some other friends from inland Brelinderim, we travelled all the way across those mountains. Why, I've even seen the great black tower of Hregisel, though only from a distance: we weren't foolish enough to go down into Pavonara!'

'That would be splendid, Keld, but—your duties?'

'I'll chance that,' he answered gruffly. 'Simon and Avran here, they're my friends; I owe them my life.'

'But—your wife and children?' I was hesitating, concerned for him and them.

'We're all beholden to you.' Keld was unshakeable. 'If my wife were here, she'd be urging me to go.'

So the decision was made, to be followed by a time of frantic preparation. Since we were anxious that there should not be too many comings and goings from Robin's chambers, only Aflar and Richard left immediately. Aflar would arrange the bringing from his home of our packs and weapons (including our bowstaves), of clothes and a pack for Keld, of rope and six pairs of seslelteven. Richard went to seek his Brelinderimin comrades. He and they would join us in the temple at the end of the night's second letkra—an hour, more or less, before midnight. While we waited, Robin ensured that Avran, Keld and I ate an ample meal and drank enough strong ale to raise our courage without clouding our wits.

Quite soon there came a gentle knock upon the chamber door. Dan Wyert opened it and, since I was close behind him, I glanced out. Three figures were standing beside a covered hand-cart, of the broad-wheeled sort used by Ayanians when moving residence. The figures were Aflar's wife and two elder daughters; the third and smallest daughter I did not notice at first, for she was sitting cheerfully on the cart. Since Ayanians are shy people who prefer to move their possessions by night, I am sure that sight of the cart and its steerers would have convinced any passer-by that he was witnessing such a removal. Instead, however, this cart carried our packs, seslelteven and weapons. These were swiftly unloaded and brought inside. Even more swiftly, Aflar's family departed, the small girl again delightedly riding the cart.

Only after Dan Wyert had inspected the street and pronounced it empty did we three set out. All three of us had packs on backs, swords at left side and seslelteven under one arm; Keld had his axe strapped at his right side. He eyed with puzzlement the bowstaves carried by Avran and me, but did not ask their purpose. We had not donned our furs, though it was bitterly cold, for they would be awkward to climb in.

Rather to my surprise, Robin, after a clasped-handshake with Keld, embraced Avran and me in turn and gave us his blessings in farewell—an unwonted gesture of affection from one normally so undemonstrative. Dan said nothing, but gave each of us a parting hug; I noticed that he seemed, of a sudden, much older and that his eyes were a-brim with tears.

Keld knew the way to the temple well enough to lead us there by the most shadowed ways; the distance was not great. Though watchful, we saw no-one in the street and, indeed, did not spot Richard and his two companions until almost upon them. In the shadow of the temple gate, we were introduced to the two Brelinderimins—to Etvan Samenast and, with somewhat more ceremony, to Marasar Esekh, cousin of the dying letzahar. Both gave us firm handclasps, but it was too dark to see more of either of them than that they were massive men, albeit rather short.

The two temple doors were shut. However, when Keld pressed his hand against a broad copper disc that adorned the right-hand one, it swung open with the soundless ease of a door that, though heavy, has been perfectly hung and well oiled. Within was a short corridor, so dimly lit that I could see only that it was flagged with the same green marble as the temple corridors of Achalind. Down this we walked as quietly and cautiously as we might. Then Keld's hand opened for us a second door into the sanctuary itself.

As we entered it, we found ourselves in a much greater space, with walls soaring up on all sides into darkness. I was conscious of banked benches to right and left, but principally of the immense figure of the god looming directly before us, scaled with silver and having a robe ending in an immense fish-tail—a figure with its back to us, for Halrathhantor forever gazes out upon the lake that his worshippers have created for him.

On moving into the sanctuary, we spread out into an arc, each gazing about cautiously. The light, furnished only by the thin bluish flames of a scatter of candles, was reflected by the silver scales in a bright, shifting pattern that bedazzled the eyes, but elsewhere there were abysses of deep shadow. Only slowly did I become aware, with a clutch of the heart, of the catafalque that stood by the feet of the god and the corpse that lay upon it.

Why it happened to be Avran who went forward first to look upon the body, I cannot say; but so it was. Why he should have set down his bowstave and seslelteven and shrugged off his pack before doing so, again I cannot say; but so he did—and that proved well.

'Friends, 'tis Zelat Hrasang!' he called back wonderingly, his voice unnecessarily loud in that silent place. 'I'd have thought they'd have buried him in haste!'

'Why should not a priest return to his god?'

The voice came from the shadows beyond the catafalque. For a brief moment, I thought it supernatural and felt a shiver of awe. Then I recognized it, as did Avran.

'Well now, if it is not our beloved tutor! What do you here, Yanu Hrasang?' Avran's words were light, but they had an edge of tension.

'Should a brother not mourn for his brother? And what do *you* here, Avran Estantesec, you and your seven fellows? Are you come to worship Halrathhantor, with your packs, weapons and all? You choose a strange hour and a strange garb! Or are you come to mock him that is gone? You are good at mocking, are you not, Prince Avran—if prince indeed you be, in anything other than your imaginings!'

I could see Yanu now, for he had risen to his feet. Those pale eyes of his were gleaming and his voice manifested a rising fury; it had an uneasy quality of shrillness, suggesting an unstable mental balance. The old, cold Yanu was gone indeed! With disquiet I noticed that he had a sword at his hip.

'No, we are not here to mock, Yanu—not to mock you, certainly not to mock your deceased brother.' Avran had detected that tone also and was striving to speak calmingly.

Yanu laughed. I had never known him to laugh before, and this was a terrible laugh, a laugh which ran up the scale into a peal that sent echoes into the dark heights. Then he said: 'Well, Avran of the south, it matters not why you are here. It matters only that you *are* here! Slaying you will set my brother's spirit at ease!'

His drawing of his sword was so sudden, and his attack upon Avran so swift, that my friend came close to being slain on the spot. His avoidance of the sword-thrust was, I think, more instinctive than conscious. Before his own sword was drawn, Avran was again almost slain by the mighty sidewise sweep of Yanu's blade.

However, Avran's sword met Yanu's next thrust; and, during further thrusts and parries, my friend swiftly recovered his fighting skill—as he needs must, to survive the viciousness of the Ayanian's attack. Yet Avran strove also to calm his attacker.

'Why try to kill me, Yanu?' he demanded breathlessly. 'I am not your enemy! I have done you no harm—you, or your brother!'

His immediate answer was another thrust, only just parried; but then Yanu, without ceasing his attack, hissed a reply.

'Southern spy! Associate of that accursed Princess! First I shall slay you, then I shall slay her—yes, and all others who side with her! Twice I have tried and failed; at thrice, I shall succeed!'

So hard, indeed, did he press his attack upon Avran that I thought he might well succeed in his first objective, at least. As for we others, we had our weapons out but dared not try to intercede, so swift was the interplay of the swords of the combatants and so rapid their movement about the temple. Indeed, the blades seemed ever to move faster, imposing a new, swirling pattern of silver upon that formed by the candlelight on Halrathhantor's scaly cloak.

As the minutes went by, Yanu showed no least sign of tiring; rather, his frantic energy appeared continually to increase. He was laughing now at each stroke, and laughing again at each counter-stroke—a gasping, mad laughter that sent trickles of fear down my spine. Avran, grim-faced, countered onslaught after onslaught; but, for his part, he would not attack in return.

Quite abruptly, the combat ended. Yanu broke it off and ran backward, to stand beneath the statue of Halrathhantor. He laughed again, a shrieking laugh that echoed disturbingly in the vaulted roof high above.

'Why, I cannot slay him—I cannot slay him! And he will not slay me—why will he not slay me? You want blood, Zelat my brother—always, indeed, you wanted blood! Well then, you shall have it!'

To our complete horror, he set the point of his sword at his own breast and fell forward upon it. As he did so, he laughed one last time—a laugh that ended in a hideous, choking bubble. At the very feet of Halrathhantor, Yanu Hrasang died, his god's back forever turned to him.

I hope that, through some other god, he has found mercy.

Chapter Fourteen

THE LEAVING OF KESBADOS

'Why, the man must have quite lost his sanity!' Richard spoke in a tone of appalled awe. 'What a terrible happening!'

'Yet it is terrible to set yourself against your god, as did his brother and he.' Keld Eslingbror spoke in measured, judicial tones, but his face was pale; it was evident that we were all, in our various ways, greatly upset by what we had witnessed. 'The vengeance of Halrathhantor is complete!'

'And you're a mighty swordsman, Prince Avran!' Richard's voice now held a note of enthusiastic admiration. 'I've never witnessed such skilled sword-play! Had he picked on me, why, I'd have been lying dead there in his stead.'

'Yes, your skill is indeed great.' Marasar Esekh was speaking. 'Yet I believe also that the protective arm of the god was about you.'

Avran was quite white and shocked. Before replying, he thrust his unsullied sword back into its sheath; and I saw that his hand was shaking.

'If his arm was about me, then I am thankful. Yet . . . Well, I do not wish to linger here. Shall we proceed on our way, gentlemen?'

'You are right, we must not waste time. However, it is proper that we offer our thanksgivings.'

Keld made the by-now-familiar spreading gesture that betokened respect of a god and began upon praises that I neither understood nor recall. The two Brelinderimins dropped to their knees and, with bowed heads, intoned responses, while Richard stood in respectful silence. For my part, I put my arm about my friend's shoulder and he leaned against me, grateful for the support I afforded. I was not surprised to discover that Avran was still shaking. It was a relief to us both that Keld's prayer occupied a full five minutes, giving us some time for recovery from our emotions.

Eventually Keld ceased his devotions and turned briskly about. He bent, shrugged his pack back onto his shoulders and hung his seslelteven about his neck, then led us off into deep shade to the left of the great image. Avran and I were last in line; I made sure that he walked before me, so that I might steady him, if necessary, during the climb that lay ahead.

If one must ascend a ladder to a high place and grope one's way along a narrow ledge unguarded at one side by wall or rail, it may be best to do so in darkness. The narrowness of the rungs and the steepness of the ladder meant that our bowstaves, so helpful in an earlier climb, were merely a nuisance; they left us only one hand free to clutch the uprights. Arduous our climb was, but not frightening, even to one like me with a poor head for heights.

During our traverse of the ledge, the problem was that the darkness was not complete. The flickering candle-glow far beneath tended to draw one's eyes unpleasantly downward. I shuddered at the concept of sitting upon such a ledge for hour upon hour passively on guard, as Aflar Eslingbror must have done, with a full view of the depth below and the need to keep looking down into it.

Fortunately, our traverse was not long. Fortunately also, Keld's exploring hand located the door and found and disengaged its catch with ease. The door's opening admitted an icy breath of air, informing Avran and me of his success before we were otherwise aware of it.

Keld stood beyond the door on the inner side, holding it open; and it was Marasar Esekh who led the way out onto the gutter beyond. Etvan Samenast followed, then Richard; and this time I preceded Avran, since it seemed likely that the path down the gutter might be slippery. As Keld stepped out also, we heard a thud as the door closed behind him.

'How did you contrive to close it?' I asked in a surprised whisper.

He chuckled. 'I looped a cord about the catch, then gave a sharp tug just before letting one end of the cord come free. Worked well, didn't it?'

Fortunately, the snow within the gutter had been too deeply in shade to have begun melting. Had it turned to ice, our careful descent would have become a perilous glissade. The trouble for me was again my awareness of the drop. Though there was only the merest rind of an early March moon in the sky, the stars were bright. The ice-bedecked lake shone palely below, beguiling one's eyes into vertiginous contemplation. As I stumbled along between Avran and Keld, I found that, despite the cold, I was in a sweat of fear.

Quite soon, the great image of Radaionesu was looming tall before us and our descent of the gutter ending. Marasar had found a projection of the god's leafy cloak about which a rope might be fastened, while Etvan had gathered the coil into his two powerful hands. As I joined them, Marasar addressed me quite casually.

'You are indeed the lightest of us, Master Simon. Would you go down first, to try the strength of the ice?'

I swallowed, shivered and was grateful that the darkness hid my shiver. 'Very well,' I croaked.

'Yes, the coldness *does* catch one's throat.' Looking back, I'm sure that Keld, standing behind me, was speaking in innocent sympathy; but, at the time, I felt I was being gently derided.

Marasar, however, was proceeding with explicit instructions. 'Leave your stave and pack here; we'll lower them to you. Good. Now take a loop of the rope and wrap it round your hands: excellent! You must go over right in the corner here, where the path ends — yes, step past me — and back over the edge, here where the fringe of Radaionesu's cloak meets the rock wall. I know you are not afraid' — how wrong he was! — 'but indeed you need not fear, for Radaionesu will protect you, be sure of that!'

His words did not comfort me. Though my recent life had held many other bad moments, few matched for sheer unpleasantness my straddling of the outer wall of the gutter, my lowering of my right leg to find purchase for its foot in the angle between rock and image, and my leaning back to put stress on the rope — a leaning backward into nothingness, with the heart-halting fear that my foot might slip.

Yet the grip of the two Brelinderimins — for Marasar had grasped the rope also — was strong and my foot did not lose its purchase. Carefully and most reluctantly, I lifted my left leg clear of the gutter edge and, leaning further back, stretched down till that foot found a hold; how blessed, in that moment, was the leafiness of the god's cloak! Slowly I moved downward, finding foothold after foothold, till a palely grey glow below told me that I had reached lake level. Yet another reaching down of a foot — the ice felt strong, good! — and in a moment, I was standing upon the lake's solidly frozen margin.

After that, the rope was drawn upward. It returned with a pack attached, which I untied swiftly and set aside on the ice. Five more packs were lowered, plus a bundle of the seslelteven and a curious, long object that proved to be the two bowstaves knotted together. Only after that did Etvan Samenast make a grunting descent. He was followed by Richard, then by Avran and Keld. Finally, while Keld, Etvan and Avran all held the rope taut, Marasar, his hands cloth-wrapped to avoid chafing, slid competently down to join us.

'What a shame we'll need to leave the rope!' I observed. 'It'll make our escape route so obvious tomorrow.'

'Leave it? Not we!' Marasar responded; he was only a little breathless. 'Watch, now!'

He gave the rope a sort of sideways flick and a quick tug. To my utter surprise, it came free and cascaded down upon us: or rather, upon Etvan. Though the falling rope wreathed itself about his shoulders, he merely grinned—I could see the whiteness of his teeth in the moonlight, though his face was in shadow—and allowed Keld to lift it off and coil it up.

We sorted out packs, seslelteven and staves and donned our furs, then set off, keeping to the strong ice at the lake's edge till we reached its northernmost rim. There, under Keld's instruction, we strapped on our seslelteven before venturing onto the snow. Close to the lake, it was so crisp-surfaced that it did not mark. When we reached softer snow, Keld took care to obliterate our tracks, swinging the knotted coil of rope by one loose end. He did it as efficiently as if he had been long practised in the art, yet I found it hard to imagine why he might have learned any skill so esoteric.

Curiously enough, it was only while looking back and watching him that I felt a cold clutch at my stomach, as I realized belatedly how very weakly anchored that rope must have been when I backed down the rock face. Yet, had its loop slipped off the projection, only Marasar would have been in any danger. When we five others descended, there had been strong hands holding the rope. As for Marasar, quite evidently he knew what he was doing. However, fear is rarely logical, least of all when retrospective.

That fear caused me to glance further backward. We were heading upslope now, northeast toward the mountain ridge and away from Kesbados. Behind us, the carving-adorned cliff above the lake, curving inward as it did, was deeply in shadow and the distant figure of

Tera-ushlu merely a shapeless black mass. However, through some freak of moon- and starshine, Radaionesu could be seen clearly, each leaf in his cloak edged by light. His benign, thick-bearded face, like some roughly-shaped oak-bole covered above and about by ivy, seemed to be smiling. I had not noticed that smile before; nor had I noticed that his left arm was raised, as if in greeting or farewell.

Looking back at that great image and remembering it to represent the god of Brelinderim, thus of our friends, I felt strangely comforted and quite cured of fears that were, after all, wholly irrational.

Even on a brightly moonlit night, I do not think that, in our white furs, we would have been visible to watchers on the city wall. So early in the month, with the moon so young and the starlight dimmed by so many clouds, the chance of our being observed was slight indeed. Nevertheless, with guidance from Keld, Marasar Esekh led us on a course designed further to reduce that chance, for it placed us at the exact limit of observation between two guard-points. As we ascended the long slope toward the peak that overlooks Kesbados— the Ferekh Vidukhamar or 'Mount of Watching'—the city became indistinguishable from its rock and the rock itself was eventually lost to view.

After four hours of increasingly effortful trudging up ever-steepening slopes—I was becoming very tired and Avran, after the mighty exertion of that combat, was swaying on his feet in a fashion that was making me rather anxious—we found ourselves approaching the mountain crest. We did not ascend since, as Keld had warned us, there was a tower on its peak from which Ayanian soldiers kept watch toward Pavonara. Instead we turned northward, scrambling awkwardly among snow-capped rocks. At last, in a place concealed on three sides by mighty boulders, we found a refuge and were permitted to rest.

Keld wisely insisted that we eat and drink before sleeping, so food and wine were brought out from our packs. It was a pleasure to have both my brothers—the one by birth, the other by adoption—beside me. However, Richard's first words were startling. He spoke earnestly.

'Why, Simon, how you've changed! The calm manner in which you led us down that rock wall—truly, you impressed me. If it had been me, I'd have been frightened out of my wits! I hate heights: I found it quite alarming enough to be third to climb down, even with two of you waiting below to catch me if I fell. Really, brother, I do admire you!'

Recalling Robin's advice—that one should not hesitate to enjoy undeserved praise, since it is so often not given when merited—I coughed in self-deprecatory fashion. 'Well, you know, it was not very far. And—yes, I suppose I've learned a lot during these last couple of years.'

'Indeed, Simon does very well.' Avran spoke solemnly, judiciously; yet I knew him well enough to detect an undertone of humour in his voice. No, he at least was not fooled; he remembered Alunsward too well![1]

Hastily I introduced a different topic. 'You remember, Avran, when first we saw the great image of Radaionesu? I must be very unobservant: I hadn't noticed that the god's hand was raised, as if he were waving in salute or in farewell.'

Avran eyed me askance. 'But his arm *isn't* raised, Simon! I remember that quite clearly. Why, he has his hands clasped before him!'

'Oh yes, it is!' I was obstinate. 'Why, you should have looked back as we left Kesbados. In the moonlight—or was it the starlight, maybe?—I could see Radaionesu clearly—and *certainly* his arm is raised! In blessing, maybe, since he's smiling? Ask Keld; he'll tell you.' For I had become aware that the Safaddnese were listening intently.

There was an odd note in Keld's voice when he responded. 'Well . . . No, Simon, I have never seen Radaionesu's hand raised in salute; nor have I seen him smile. Yet, for my part, I do not question what you saw.'

Marasar Esekh sounded positively devout. 'It is the highest of privileges, to receive the blessing of Radaionesu. I do not doubt that it bodes well for you—and, I trust, for us all.'

Etvan Samenast spoke heavily. 'Amen to that! Yet, when I looked back—and yes, I *did* look back, Master Simon—I saw only darkness.'

There was little more speech. Quite soon afterwards, while Marasar took watch, we others composed ourselves for sleep. However, I found myself profoundly disturbed. I was sure that I *had* seen the arm of the god raised, and that he had been smiling; yet I could not

[1] See *The Lords of the Stoney Mountains*.

have done so—it was a mere image, a statue carven in stone. And Etvan—why, he had not even seen the god! Had my eyes been deceiving me, after all, or had I been granted some special vision? I recalled how swiftly my fears had subsided, as if I had been comforted. Well, it was all most odd—too odd for a tired brain to grapple with. Progressively my puzzlement succumbed to sleep.

We were not to be granted a long rest. When the hand of Keld shook me firmly into wakefulness, I was deep in dreams and left them most reluctantly.

'Time to be rousing, Simon my friend,' he said gruffly. 'Dawn is upon us. We must eat swiftly and be on our way. Your brother and our two friends from Brelinderim are up and gone already, to make sure their warning is received early enough.'

'What, Richard gone?' The idea jerked me into wakefulness. 'Why are we not going with them, then?'

'Because they and we must take different paths today. This mountain ridge strikes north. They'll follow it for a while, so as to pass the head of the Hededrund River, but then they'll go down into the Lemmeshind valley. Eventually they'll head for Warrentown, I expect: but the alarum should travel there before them. 'Tis a pity you had to lose your brother's company so swiftly, though.'

I was sitting up by then and screwing the sleep out of my eyes. 'Only for a while, I trust. What are our own plans for today, Keld?'

'Why, we must traverse this ridge somewhere out of view of the watchtower, then gain the greater ridge beyond and go seek the Pavonarans. 'Twill be a hard day and a long one, I don't doubt. You'd best eat well, Simon, while you can.'

As Keld roused Avran—an even harder task—I consumed a meal of bread and dried meat; harsh enough fare, but helped down by mouthfuls of good wine. It occurred to me that I had never properly seen our two Brelinderimin comrades of last night; I remembered only their burliness and strength, and the white flash of Etvan's teeth when he grinned. Why, if I met them again, I would not even recognize them unless I heard their voices—how strange!

Yet my thoughts were centred upon Richard. Most certainly I hoped I would see him again, but I could not disguise from myself the fact that we both faced considerable perils. And my father; might I still hope to meet him again? If Warrentown were attacked, then I was sure he would be in the thick of the fighting. After Avran and

I had travelled so far, it would be an ill fate if my father were to be slain ere we met.

Avran had sat up and was stretching to relieve the stiffness of his body. When I asked how he had slept, he answered brusquely: 'Ill and briefly.' It took all Keld's persuasion to make him eat an adequate breakfast. When we set off, Avran's limbs were still so wearily stiff, and his stumbles so frequent, that I feared he might injure himself among the rocks. Twice at least, only the support of his bowstave saved him from a heavy fall.

For indeed, the first hours of that morning were an effortful scramble among the snowy crags and snow-speckled screes of the western flank of the Mount of Watching. The clear sky above and the brightness over the cliffs to our right showed us that this would be a fair day, but that gave us no immediate comfort, since we were in deep shade and bitter cold. Far away to our left, snow-covered mountains gleamed white against the pale blue of the western sky, but the Lemmeshind valley below us was wrapped in gloom.

At length Keld judged we must be beyond view of the watchtower. He found for us a path of sorts; it had been made by animals nimbler than we, but it furnished a practicable ascent. In its last stretch, however, we had to remove our seslelteven and clamber perilously up a face of black rock, our bowstaves again a tiresome burden.

That ascent made, we found ourselves upon a broad saddle where the snow had blown into waves, as if the very sea itself had become white and still. A series of deep slots showed where a herd of veludain had ventured close to the edge, then fled away. So fresh were their tracks that I guessed they had been disturbed by the sight of us climbers, yet they were already gone from view. To the south, the peak of the Mount of Watching could be seen, but it was craggy and I was not able to distinguish the Ayanian watchtower. Away to the north was a second peak on which, Keld told us, the Brelinderimins had a watchtower and beacon; he called it the Ferekh Taslutanar or 'Mount of Answering,' but could not explain that curious name.

The snow ripples were awkward to traverse, their close spacing forcing us either slightly to shorten or considerably to lengthen our strides. However, the snow crust readily bore our weight and scarcely recorded our tracks. So shallow were the impressions we made that they would have been easy to obliterate, but Keld did not trouble to do so. After all, they were unlikely to be seen; there were few travellers at this season and we were beyond the reach of patrols from Kesbados. We passed ere long onto unrippled, virginal snow where our tracks were even more evident, but again Keld was not disturbed by that fact. This better surface meant that we were able to stride along easily and swiftly, thus making a quick crossing of the saddle. Avran was moving quite lithely again and seemed to have recovered his spirits, while the increasing warmth of the sun was cheering us all.

Much too soon, however, we found ourselves again in shade. We were descending, Keld said, toward the great bog at the head of the Berelind River, a tributary of the Lemmeshind and within the realm of Brelinderim. He told us how fortunate we were, for the bog would be deeply frozen and easy to traverse. Within days, the spring melt would be turning it into an impassable morass. Moreover, only a little way further north, the river tumbled down a waterfall into a deep gorge which, since unbridged, was equally intraversable. At any later season, we would have had to make a southward detour of many leagues; but not now.

The traversing of the bog took us till long past noon, but it did indeed prove easy. Several times we crossed streams, but all were deeply frozen; nor were the spikes of marsh grass that stuck up through the snow so closely spaced as to cause any problems for our seslelteven-shod feet.

There were many veludain in that valley. Though they avoided us, they did not move away far and I noted that some, at least, wore collars. Keld said they were Brelinderim beasts, left to subsist on those marsh grasses over the winter. Adequate enough fodder for them it was, as he admitted; but even so, it was evident that he disapproved of such insouciance on the part of the herdsmen. Good Ayanians brought *their* beasts indoors or underground!

On the further side we passed again into sunshine, but only for a while, for the cliffs bounding the higher land—a northward extension of the great Windrench ridge—were soon blocking its waning rays. We did not strive to ascend, or even to approach, those cliffs. Instead we struck northeastward along the easier slopes below.

We were all tiring by then—yes, even hardy Keld. It was a relief when he selected a sheltered place—a declivity at the head of a stream, frozen and snow-drifted over now—for our night's rest. We ate and drank quickly, then sought our sleeping sacks, for we must rise again at dawn. In so remote a situation, Keld saw no need to set a watch; and my slight unease about prowling branaths did not suffice to delay my slumbers.

By noon next day, we were making our toilsome way up a steep gully that provided some sort of a route onto the plateau. The stream in that gully had not frozen, even at this season, so steep was its course and so ample the spring that fed it. The tinkle of the waters was the first sound, other than our own footfalls and speech, that we had heard since leaving Kesbados, for there was still no wind.

Keld led the way in that climb and had much the hardest time, for it was not easy to find firm footholds. Avran and I followed closely in his steps. Our bowstaves proved an asset this time, for they enabled us to brace ourselves against firm rock surfaces while traversing slippery places. We saw many footmarks of veludain and lesser beasts, come to drink from the waters; and in one place, I noticed branath padmarks—old, fortunately. However, the only human footprints were our own.

When the climb had been made and we were buckling on our sesleleven, Keld observed: 'Well, friends, henceforward we must take greater care. Somewhere midway across this moorland lies the frontier of Brelinderim with Pavonara—an unmarked frontier, and often transgressed. We're too far south to be likely to encounter that Pavonaran army, but there may well be guards or patrols; who knows? So I'll ask you both to keep your eyes open, and you may be sure I'll be watchful also.'

The sun was so bright that one could see a fair distance and the moor, now we had gained it, was almost as flat as a riverside meadow. Yet the task Keld had set for us was not easy. The problem was the same as above Sasliith—the great number of rocks; not so much the rock piles and rock ridges, but the many solitary rocks, some large, some small, some snow-covered, some blown free of it, that were scattered everywhere about. A dark boulder can look surprisingly like a watching figure when seen from afar; a snow-covered boulder like a soldier in a veludu-fur surcoat. Moreover, the sun was becoming hotter. Soon I found that I was perspiring, so I shook off my hood, only to pull it back a few minutes later when my ears started to freeze.

Suddenly I became aware of a curious noise—a sort of swooshing sound. Avran was noticing it also; he stopped to gaze about him and so did I. Keld had also halted and was gazing back at us with an amused smile. As for the sound, it ceased when we stopped.

'What was that strange noise, Keld?' Avran asked.

He laughed. 'Listen!' he said, and stepped forward boldly.

Within a moment we heard that curious swoosh again. Avran and I looked at each other puzzledly, then he asked again: 'Tell us now, Keld: what is it?'

'Why, 'tis something one hears often enough when noon is past, the day warming and the snow melting. There's an ice crust on the snow, you know. Well, when we step upon it, our weight causes that crust to settle; and as it settles, it creaks like a badly made wooden floor. But 'tis a sign that we must hasten. All too soon, the crust will be breached and the snow turning sticky.'

Within the hour, Keld's prediction was borne out; and within two hours, our march across the moor had become an ordeal. I was used enough to having my seslelteven sink deeply into snow; that had often happened during excursions from Achalind. Then, however, the snow had been fluffy and light, so that it shook off when I lifted my feet. Not so when the snow was melting! Instead, it clung to the tops of one's seslelteven, like wet soil from a freshly ploughed field. This so weighted one's feet as to necessitate repeated bendings to knock the snow off a lifted sesleltef, with the other settling deeper and the depressing certainty that, at the next forward step, more snow would be adhering to both. We felt too hot in our furs, yet it was too cold to remove them. All in all, we had a sweaty and arduous time of it.

Thus preoccupied with the sheer business of moving, it was hard for us also to remember to keep watch. However, we had no human encounters; and if any beasts saw us, they fled away unseen.

I hoped we might make better progress with the waning of the sun when, I assumed, the snow would begin to freeze again. My hope was not realized, for the snow did not freeze fast enough to reduce the depth to which our feet sank. Instead, matters worsened. The huge leaves on which we were walking were by then water-soaked and freezing, so that the snow clung to them more firmly. I became very weary of knocking snow off seslelteven.

We ended that second day in a concealed, snow-filled hollow in the crest of a rock ridge otherwise bare of snow. Avran and I were quite exhausted and even the more experienced Keld was extremely tired. Yet his choice of a snow-floored resting-place proved deliberate, for he instructed us to set our seslelteven upright in the snow when we took them off, so they might dry overnight.

'But how *can* they dry, when there is no wind?' I asked pettishly. 'Would it not be more sensible to warm them against our bodies, inside our sleeping-sacks?'

Keld pulled a wry face. 'Try it, my friend! Try it! They'll be cold at first, then wet. For my part, I like only warm things with me when I'm sleeping!'

His argument convinced me. No, I did not try it; yet, when I woke at next dawning, my seslelteven proved dry enough.

Again it was Keld who roused us others—and that was fortunate. For my part, I would have slept long past dawn and so, I am sure, would Avran; our weariness was great enough to smother any consciousness of the need for haste. As it was, the three of us devoured a rapid breakfast and were quickly on our way again, to travel as far as we might before noon and a renewal of the melting of the snow.

That proved a wise precaution for, with the rising of the sun, the air warmed faster than yesterday. We crossed many tracks of veludain, all of them coming from the southeast up onto the tableland. Keld told us that they were leaving the Berelind Marshes behind and coming up onto higher ground: sure sign, he said, of a rapid melt. The marsh would soon become too wet for them, while the melting of snow on this higher ground would furnish provender by exposing plants to be browsed upon. It meant also, he observed pointedly, that the going would be very heavy once noon was past.

It lacked still an hour before noon when, gazing ahead, Avran saw something that caused him to stop abruptly.

'Keld! Simon! See over there—yes, just beyond the stone mound —that line in the snow, right across our path. What is it—a road? A low wall?'

'Yes, I see it also,' Keld was speaking. 'Like a road, as you say; yet there is no road here—and, if there were, the snow would have covered it. I know not what it may be. Let us go forward and see— cautiously, now!'

However, Avran was too excited to take heed. He was hastening forward, in the awkward scamper enforced by seslelteven that, if set down incautiously, might catch together and cause a fall.

'Yet it does look like a road!' he called back. 'Not cut to the rock, but beaten into the snow. A broad road . . . No! I see—'tis a trackway—very many tracks!'

By then we were following him so closely that his realization scarcely preceded ours. Indeed, there were an abundance of tracks— impressions of sesleltteven, thousands upon thousands of them, surely made by many hundreds of feet.

Keld looked at Avran and me and shook his head slowly. His expression was grim. 'Well, friends, Sir Robert's idea was good, but it seems we are too late. The Pavonaran army is already across the mountains.'

Chapter Fifteen

Pursuing the Pavonarans

Avran nodded his head in solemn assent and looked quite woebe-gone. For my part, however, I walked closer to the tracks and examined them carefully. What I saw raised my spirits somewhat.

'Yes, they're across the mountains; but they're not far ahead of us—two or three hours, at most. The mass of tracks has beaten a deep enough groove; but see this print here, to one side of the others? The snow crust is scarcely marked. These tracks were made only this very morning!'

Keld bent to examine the sesleltef-print. When he straightened, his expression was lighter. 'Well perceived, Simon! As you say, they are too shallow to have been made before evening yesterday. Like us, the Pavonarans must have risen with the dawn. Well, maybe we might yet give warning! Yet it is astonishing, that they should be crossing so far south. 'Tis a strange route to Warrentown!'

'Where might they be heading, then?'

He considered for a moment before replying, and then spoke doubtfully. 'Into the valley of the Tasdralind, I would suppose. The mountains swing westward about here and two torrents pour southwestward from them, soon to join. The Ferconard is the more northerly and smaller, the Tasdralind the larger and more southerly. Yet I do not see how the Pavonarans could pass down either valley, for there is a great waterfall at the head of each, and then the narrowest and most dangerous of gorges. Moreover, both lie still some leagues north of here ... Ah, but wait now! I have it! There is another valley, very steep-sided, but flat and marshy at the bottom, with no stream draining it. The Ulkurin, men call it—the valley without issue. At this season, the marsh will still be frozen—easy enough travelling. The descent into it would be arduous; but, once in that valley, the Pavonarans could march fast.'

Avran spoke now. 'Yet what might they attain by taking such a path? As you say, it is a strange way by which to attack Lyonesse!'

'It is indeed. I think, instead, that they are attacking Brelinderim. The Tasdralind flows into the Berelind and their two valleys form the very heart of the letzestre, with the finest pasturelands. Moreover, the fortress of Tasbered stands at their junction. In Tasbered, as you'll recall, the Dakhvardavat of Brelinderim meets and its letzahar resides, if he yet lives. Yes, if the Pavonarans take that valley, then they might well destroy Brelinderim.'

I was puzzled. 'But why, then, did that wretched letzahar of Desume speak of *Warrentown* being assaulted?'

Keld laughed—a grim laugh. 'Maybe the Pavonarans misinformed him. It's likely enough that they mistrusted him—and would you blame them? Yet his story of the invasion, at least, was genuine; and that is what matters. We must at first follow the Pavonarans, to be certain of their path. Then, if we can, we must pass them and give warning.'

'Good enough; then we should walk in their tracks, where the snow is beaten down—we'll surely travel more swiftly. Moreover, should any other Pavonarans be following, they'll not notice our seslelteven prints among so many.'

We had not been dawdling earlier that day, but thenceforward we went at as swift a pace as seslelteven permit—little more than a league an hour, yet faster than the Pavonaran soldiers, laden as they must be with weapons and armour, were likely to be travelling. I was grateful that I was becoming accustomed to seslelteven. Had I been required to go so swiftly on the early forays from Achalind, I would have been soon exhausted.

Keld was long pondering in silence before eventually he spoke. 'Had you ever heard, friends, that the Pavonarans used seslelteven? I thought them a special gift of our gods to us Safaddnese, but perhaps I was wrong. Did your people use them, Simon, or yours, Avran?'

'The sesleltas does not grow in Sandastre,' Avran answered, 'and, though we see snow sometimes, it does not spread far beyond the hilltops, nor does it persist long. No, we have no awareness of seslelteven and small need of them.'

'In England, we have snow enough,' I observed ruefully, 'but they were new to me also.'

'I might have guessed your answers.' Keld was grinning. 'I recall now how you both walked on our first day out together—as slowly and carefully as any mother bearing her first child in her womb!'

'Mayhap the Pavonarans didn't have seslelteven either, till just recently,' I speculated. 'Mayhap it formed a part of their dealings with Desume—that they be shown how to make and use seslelteven.'

'Happen it did.' Keld was serious again. 'I recall no tales of winter encounters, in all the long story of our battles with Pavonara. If so, then dakhmen Ekulag will have much to answer for.'

'He has much to answer for already,' Avran observed bitterly. 'All Desume has much to answer for!'

'Nay, friend, be not so bitter against a whole letzestre.' Keld was reproving him. 'Did not Ekulag himself admit that his own people were wroth with him? Was that not why he lingered in the Chamber of Council, Simon?'

'That is what he admitted to that wretched letzumahar of his—that Zharag. Yet I know no other Desumeans; I cannot imagine their attitude.'

'Most Desumeans maintain their faith to the Nine Gods, you may be sure. As to what they'll do, only time will tell.' And Keld spoke no more.

The day was becoming steadily hotter, and already we were hearing the creak of the settling snow-crust—an ominous forewarning of effort to come. The sun was becoming so bright, and the snow so dazzlingly white, that Keld urged us to get out the cloth strips that so conveniently reduce glare. We put them about our eyes. Indeed, they served that purpose; but, on such a day, they made one's forehead so tiresomely hot that I was soon tempted to take mine off again.

Every so often we kept looking forward, hoping to spot that army ahead of us and anxious to see it before being seen. Yet noon passed without any glimpse of them. The snow was becoming stickier, but the weight of the soldiery had so pressed it down that our hastening strides were not much slowed.

Only when we were within a few poles of it did we realize we were nearing the valley head. We realized it not because of any change of slope, but because the tracks swung off abruptly to the left. When we saw the ground beginning to fall away in front of us, we paused. Keld put up his hand to cause Avran and me to stay still, then advanced very cautiously. After a few paces, he bent to detach his seslelteven. Setting them aside, he dropped to his hands and knees and advanced further forward. At his murmured command, Avran and I acted similarly.

I found myself gazing into a great corrie, down a slope that was dizzily steep and quite free of snow. Directly below was a little tarn, frozen now, so that its ice shone in the sun like a burnished shield. Stretching away eastward was a narrow valley, as steep-sided and flat-bottomed as a drainage ditch but vastly more huge.

'Look to your left, friends,' Keld urged quietly. 'See how steps have been cut, down the cliff? Notice that the Pavonarans have even fixed wooden stairs in the steepest places? This invasion has been carefully prepared.'

'Why then, we can follow them down!' Avran was eager.

'And how might that aid us?' Keld was scornful. 'How might we hope to pass the army, unseen? Why, the Pavonarans are still in view; can you not discern them, even from so far? How, then, might they fail to see us?'

For my part, I had not perceived the Pavonarans; but when I looked eastward a second time, I wondered why I had not done so. Yes, there they were; a mass of men on foot moving steadily away from us, the metal of their weapons picked out by pinpoints of light.

Avran drew in his breath, then expelled it slowly. 'Well then, we must stay upon the cliff top, I suppose, and strive to pass them. Which way, though—north or south of the valley?'

'North, certainly.' Keld was quite unhesitating. 'I would like to see more of them, to gauge their numbers and discover who is leading them. If we approached the edge from the south side, we might well be glimpsed against the sun. On the north side, we will not be noticed so readily. Yet we must take care, for the snow overhangs dangerously.'

That was true enough. The valley's steep southern side was crusted at the top with snow, but only meagrely; below was mostly bare rock, with only a little snow clinging here and there. Quite different was the north side. Not only was it plastered with snow from foot to top, but at the top the snow bulged out like a sea-wave arching just before it breaks. In our furs, we would not easily be seen against the snow or even against the northern sky, for it was white with cloud. Keld was right also in that any close approach to the edge was likely to prove perilous.

So we crawled back to retrieve and don our sesleltven. Then, keeping well out of view from below, we made our way round the head of the corrie till we could strike westward again, on a track parallel to the line of the valley.

When we left behind the broad path trampled by the Pavonarans, our passage across the snow became more effortful and, despite our urgency, decidedly slower. This was a cause for serious concern, for it meant that we would not be catching up with, but lagging behind, the invaders.

After gesturing to Avran and me to continue, Keld headed off obliquely to see whether he could find a better surface. Most fortunately, there was a slight ridge above the valley and a dip beyond. Moreover, there was a breeze blowing from the north—not very strong, but enough to counter the melting effect of the sun. Consequently, the snow on the ridge crest still retained its crust. As soon as he discovered this, Keld beckoned us over; and thereafter we made a much swifter passage.

We said little to one another, for each of us knew our objective and each was striving to move swiftly without risking the excessive effort that so quickly causes exhaustion. At one point Keld swung his pack from his shoulder, delved into it and produced a flask. After a quick swig, he passed it to us. I shall never like efredat, but I must confess that my few mouthfuls of that fiery liquid did serve for a while to speed my steps.

When two full hours had passed by and our shadows were lengthening away to our right in the sun's decline, Keld announced suddenly; 'We should be level with them by now. I'd best head for the valley edge and take a peek.'

I had been pondering this and thinking about the dangers of the snow overhang. 'Very well, friend; but, as you said earlier, we must take care. You have that rope in your pack; why not fetch it out and put a loop about your waist? Then Avran and I can both grasp the rope and, if your feet should slip, pull you back out of danger.'

'Aye, that's sensible.'

For a second time, Keld swung the pack from his back; and soon he was stepping southward toward the valley, the rope knotted about waist and shoulders in a fashion that would hold, but not hurt, him under tension. I followed about ten paces behind, with the rope looped about the bowstave and that stave held firmly in my two hands before me; and Avran walked six paces or so behind me as anchorman, the rope tied about his own waist. We were plunging more and more deeply into sun-softened snow with each step; more deeply, indeed, than yesterday, so that we blessed the wind which had kept the crust firm on the ridge.

Keld was advancing steadily but cautiously down an ever-more-perceptible slope. Soon he called back, not too loudly; 'I can begin to see down into the valley. Take it easy, now! Just a few more paces—slowly, slowly. Good! Yes, I can see the Pavonarans; the advance guard is just below.'

Avran and I halted, though it was frustrating not to be sharing that view. 'Are they wearing furs?' I asked. 'They look strangely dark against the snow.'

'Yes, furs; but with surcoats over them—I can see the colours. And some are in chain mail, by its shining. Ah! there is a standard-bearer! Why, 'tis a purple banner—I cannot see the red sword, but that must surely be the standard of the King himself! Yes, for the banner is edged in gold. So this is no mere attack by an over-ambitious earl, but a regular invasion!'

'How many soldiers?' asked Avran, frustrated by seeing nothing of the army.

'I am striving to count. They stretch away down-valley . . . A large army, more than two *dakhletelei*' (about 2,000 men); 'yet not so great a host as I would have expected to be following the King.'

'Are there other earls in his company? Surely; but which?'

'There are other banners, but they are farther down-valley. Ah—now one is coming into view. I cannot see it clearly; let me go further forward.'

We released the rope a little and Keld took one plunging step, another, then a third. At that point came calamity. I heard a groaning sound, such as is made in a wind-gust by a tree that has been almost felled; then suddenly the snow surface before me was cracking open and dropping away.

I flung myself downward, pressing the stave and rope deeply into the snow under my body's whole weight. As I did so, I heard Keld's cry of alarm. The groan of the subsiding snow swelled into a roar as the whole slope collapsed under him. As for Keld, he swung backward, spinning on the rope, till he was somewhere out of view beneath me.

I heard Avran's voice, strangely calm. 'We'll need to haul Keld up. I have you anchored, Simon. Don't try to pull harder; I'll do the pulling. Just crawl backward slowly, bringing the rope with you. We mustn't risk a second snow-slide.'

His evident tranquillity gave me the reassurance I needed. I did exactly as he said, relying at first on Avran's efforts but soon rising and doing some hauling on my own account. After only a few seconds, we were rewarded by the sight of Keld's head and shoulders rising above the new edge of snow. He was breathing gaspingly and there was a blood-dripping cut across his forehead, above the sun-screen strip that covered his eyes. Otherwise, however, Keld was well—well enough indeed, as we drew him up higher, to crawl forward till he was clear of the edge and by my feet.

Setting down the stave that had taken the rope's stress, I raised him up and helped him to walk stumblingly back till we reached Avran and were well out of danger. My friend took a handful of snow and carefully wiped the wound till it was clean and the blood-flow staunched. Only then did Keld speak.

'I was grateful for that rope; thank you, friends. But set me down and take a look into the valley, would you, Avran or Simon?'

'Shall we reverse tasks, Avran?' I suggested. 'I do not think the snow will go again, but Keld can be our anchor. Let's take a look at the Pavonarans.'

Cautiously the two of us turned about and went toward the new, sharp edge where the snow ended. Then we dropped to our knees and peered over.

I have likened the snow on the valley flank to a sea wave just before breaking. Well, now the wave had broken and a huge mass of snow had poured down into the valley. From this altitude, the Pavonarans far below seemed scarcely bigger than ants; and, like ants whose hill has been destroyed, they were milling about in confusion, their path blocked by the new ridge of snow spilled across the narrow valley.

Yet that was only a beginning to their perils. Now we heard a fresh groan of slipping snow. Glancing to our left, we saw a new crack opening across that overhang of snow—a mightier crack, extending rapidly upvalley from the notch caused by Keld's fall. The roar that followed was tremendous, deafening; and a shower of snow particles was flung stingingly into our faces.

As we flinched, we heard a cry of terror from below, soon to be lost in the swelling rumble of that great collapse. When we looked down again, there was no army—just a valley filled from side to side with snow.

Once, when young, I helped another child build sand fortifications, on a beach close by the great castle of Scarborough. The tide had risen swiftly while we were working and suddenly a great surge of surf came upward upon us, obliterating all that we had made in an instant and leaving only a smooth slope of sand. So it was now. In an instant, that valley had been cleansed of the stain of war. Through chance or through the will of the One God or the Nine, the Pavonarans had been utterly destroyed. King and soldiers, bright surcoats and shining weapons—all were gone.

Chapter Sixteen

RAIN ALONG THE BERELIND

'So King Rafanesar sought to seize Brelinderim, did he? I'm not surprised—I'm not surprised. They said he was not pleased when the three earls invaded us, but he'd be even less pleased when they were defeated—those Pavonarans, they cannot stomach any defeat. I knew well that, when we and the Lyonessans stopped that invasion, we were simply ensuring that another would follow, some day, some year. And now Rafanesar is dead and all his pride shown to be vain. Well, well, there are always folk that drop early into the hole leading out of the world, be they kings or be they commoners; but rarely have a king and his whole army fallen together into that hole! The sins of the Pavonarans against the Nine must have been great indeed, for such vengeance to be wrought upon them.'

Dakhmen Talados of Brelinderim was very close to death. His great, gaunt body lay blanket-enwrapped upon a couch in the audience chamber of Tasbered castle—a chamber that was only dimly lit, for the old letzahar had ceased to desire brighter lights. Communicating with him had become like juggling with leaden balls—possible, but very hard work. It had been his castellan Ast Albahar, and not we, who had made him understand what had happened in the Ulkurin; and I do not think Talados truly comprehended the part we had inadvertently played in that affair. As he spoke of it, he was talking more to himself than to his castellan or us. Consequently, when he fell silent, we did not feel we should speak; nor did the chirurgeon and his handmaid, who were watching by their lord's couchside, utter any word.

After a while, Talados spoke again, in ruminative tones: 'A great mercy it was—a great mercy! When word of the invasion came from Kesbados, it told of an attack upon Warrentown—and that seemed likeliest, for must not those Pavonarans have hated the Lyonessans even more than us? For all our battlings, we'd have been destroyed, we Brelinderimins, had not those ships come from England. Just in time, they came; just in time! It was Sir John and Sir Arthur and their men, with their mighty bows, that turned back the Pavonarans at Gles Lemmeshind. Yes, Gles Lemmeshind he called it—'key to the valley'—that old fortress; that was its name when we fought there, so many years ago . . . But now they call it Warrentown; and 'twas to Warrentown that I despatched our young men, when the word came. Had those Pavonarans attacked us here in Tasbered, why, we could not have fought them off, with so few. A great mercy—yes, indeed.'

He fell silent again, but only for a while. When he spoke, it was once more in ruminative vein, but in a tone of puzzlement.

'No, no, I do not understand it; I do not understand why they came this way. It was Warrentown they wanted to destroy—Warrentown . . .'

Once more his voice trailed off into silence and we remained silent also. Then suddenly the old man smiled; I saw the creasing of his cheeks and the upward twitch of his moustache, but the glad lilt in his voice would have sufficed to tell me he must be smiling.

'Yet the news is good—the news is very good! With King Rafanesar gone and his army also, Brelinderim—yes, and Lyonesse—they're safe, safe for a letzal at least, perhaps for longer! The task of defence was mine, but I was past fulfilling it—I could not defend my land a second time. Instead, the Nine have destroyed the Pavonarans in their own way. High praise to Radaionesu! High praise to Halrath-hantor! High praise to the galiiletelar, to great Horulgavar!'

His hosanna to the gods of Brelinderim and Ayan evoked a response of 'Ilai ushazan!' from Keld and the other three Safaddnese beside us. As the old man named the greatest of their gods he sat up, spreading out his arms as if to embrace the whole world; but then, as the responses came, he gave a shuddering gasp and fell back on his couch.

There was an immediate hubbub of concern, during which Keld, Avran and I did our best to efface ourselves. Yet, when chirurgeon Naral Vesang's brief examination of his letzahar had ended, it was to us that he spoke. His expression contained both sadness and joy.

'Dakhmen Talados is gone to the Thrones of the Gods. For his going, I shall long mourn, since he was my beloved friend as well as my ruler. Yet the tidings you brought, guaranteeing to him the safety of his realm, have given him contentment on that long passage away. For that, you deserve our profoundest gratitude.'

'And he died greatly!' The castellan was speaking now. 'Were not the names of the gods upon his lips? Was he not praising them? For that also, you merit our thanks; was it not your news that occasioned those praises?'

We murmured the embarrassed vaguenesses that such tributes evoke and, after proper expressions of regret at the old warrior's death, left the chamber. Yet indeed, there seemed little cause for sadness. Within his realm, as elsewhere in Safaddné, there had long been awareness that Talados's hold on life was slender; and in the eyes of the Safaddnese, no great life could have ended more fittingly. In such circumstances, the Safaddnese discover no occasion to mourn.

Consequently, even shortly afterward when we were entertained to dinner by the castellan, it was not in any atmosphere of gloom; rather, the occasion was one of celebration. The repast provided was excellent in quality, ample in quantity—and welcome, for we had travelled far and arduously. Since witnessing the fall of snow that finished the Pavonarans, we had spent a night and much of a day in wearisome endeavour. We had returned to the frozen snow-crust of the ridge crest and tramped along it for several more hours, keeping parallel to the valley but not daring even to approach it, let alone to try to descend into it, for fear of being caught up in a second slide. Eventually the early darkness of a cloudy night had caused us to seek shelter in the protection of a rock mound. With dawn there came yet another hasty rising and setting forth, followed by a difficult descent down slippery surfaces into the Tasdralind valley and an unpleasant passage through sleet, rain and rapidly melting snow to Tasbered.

No elaborately concealed city, this, but a nine-towered castle set flauntingly upon a high motte. In style it was reminiscent of the smaller defensive works we had discovered deserted in Darega, but of course it was very much greater—too great, indeed, to be properly defended by the residual garrison. The Pavonarans would have taken Tasbered with little trouble—especially if that garrison had been attacked without warning.

Had Avran and I arrived unaccompanied at Tasbered's gates, I am not sure how we might have fared or whether our story would have been believed. Fortunately, Keld Eslingbror was well known there. His presence ensured our immediate admittance, while the tale we told had carried us to the letzahar's couchside on the crest of a wave of excitement. The twin sensations caused by the Pavonaran army's obliteration and the dakhmen's death stimulated so much talk that we could not avoid a late night. It was exhaustedly that we sought our sleeping quarters.

We woke late, to grey skies and steady rain. As on the previous evening, we were invited to share a repast with castellan Ast Albahar. However, now his mood was very different. He was a frail, bald creature, of the worrying sort that casts care away only rarely and with difficulty. Quite evidently, new cares had come upon him that morning—so evidently, indeed, that Keld asked immediately what was wrong. Ast's response was destined quite to stagger us, yet its beginning seemed strangely oblique.

'I am glad that Talados my master died yesterday, in a mood of contentment. Had he lived till today, he would have had smaller cause for joy. You told us, my friends, that you witnessed the destruction of King Rafanesar and his army; nor do I doubt your word. Yet you said also, did you not, Keld my friend, that the army was not a large one for an invasion—not even three dakhletelei?'

A dakhletel consists of 891 soldiers—nine units of 99 men (that is, ninety letelei), so this estimate was correct enough. 'Yes, that is so: though I could not count accurately.' Keld was polite but puzzled.

'Then I can tell you why it was so small, for I have received word this day from down valley. That was but one of two Pavonaran armies! The second and greater of them crossed the mountains far north of here and is even now besieging Warrentown!'

At our thunderstruck expressions, the castellan inclined his head in a grave affirmative. 'So matters stand, I fear, my friends. Dakhmen Talados judged aright that the greatest wrath of the Pavonarans would be directed at Warrentown. That other army, though led only by the Faruzlaf of Hregisel, Kalung Dastenost, must number eight dakhletelei at least.'

'Did our warning reach Warrentown in time?' I asked anxiously.

'Not in time for the Pavonarans' passage of the mountains to be halted; but, yes, in good time to permit the Lyonessans to withdraw within their city's walls. As I understand it, the Pavonarans have invested the eastern part of the city, but they have not yet breached its fortifications. Though the Lyonessans have not been long at their building, they must have wrought well.'

Remembering that my father had been given charge of the fortifying of Warrentown, I felt a surge of pride; but this was quickly subdued by anxiety. How was father faring and where was Richard? Could he have reached Warrentown ahead of the Pavonarans, or must he be still somewhere in the mountains? Wherever he was, I feared for his safety—as I did for my father's.

Keld had another question in mind. 'That army—have you learned anything of its constitution?'

'Yes, something. About thirty-three letelei are riders, while the rest are foot-soldiers—and they did not, it seems, march there in seslelteven. Maybe the Desumeans, or their own Pavonaran craftsmen, furnished only enough seslelteven for the smaller army.'

'Then I trust that, with that army's obliteration, they have lost their whole stock—and the art of manufacture! Yet why, I wonder, did the King choose to lead the smaller army?'

'Mayhap he sought an easier passage by travelling on seslelteven; but I am sure he was also seeking easier conquests. It would seem a graceful act, would it not, for King Rafanesar to allot the greater command to his henchman of Hregisel—and the opportunity for sweet revenge! Yet from the outset, Kalung Dastenost of Hregisel faced the bloodier battle—and might hope only for smaller conquests. He is unlikely, even at worst, to succeed in crossing into Avakalim, for the bridges will surely be breached and the river is much too high at this season. In contrast, two dakhletelei would have been ample enough to take Tasbered. The King bade fair to gain most of Brelinderim and perhaps Ayan also.'

By then the castellan was perceiving our restlessness, that particular restlessness which is produced by apprehension and only to be allayed by action. Though we had scarcely begun to eat, we had each set down our knives and pushed away our platters. Consequently, he brought his musings to a brisk end.

'Well, the King is dead and his army wiped away by the strong hand of the Gods. You will wish to hasten now toward Warrentown, will you not, gentlemen, to help combat that greater army? Yes, of course; and I know you will desire to depart soon.'

Setting aside his own platter, Ast Albahar rose to his feet. Then he surveyed us again, shook his head and sighed. 'Would that I might travel with you, gentlemen—but, alas, my duty keeps me here. However, I can help you, I think, for I can find you veludain to ride. Not our best beasts, for they are all gone to the war already, but beasts that are sturdy enough if not swift. They will be better than seslelteven, in the conditions you will encounter today. Naral Vesang will be riding with you and will serve as your guide.'

He paused, then added chillingly: 'Now that our letzahar is dead, Naral's services are not required here. They will certainly be required at Warrentown!'

We thanked the castellan appropriately and made haste to ready ourselves for departure. I did so with heavy heart, for I had been sure that the war—and our immediate troubles—were over. Nor were my companions in any better spirit. Keld was worrying about the outcome of the battle and its effect on all Safaddné; he appeared pessimistic in both regards. As for Avran, he seemed suddenly weary—quite as weary, indeed, as when leaving Kesbados. Yet all three of us considered it preferable that we ride to battle, rather than stay passively and uselessly in Tasbered. So especially did I, recalling those long, long days of waiting in Holdworth.[1]

Yesterday, despite the sleet and rain, we had made fair progress on our seslelteven, for sloppy snow compresses to firmness under them. However, we had become thoroughly soaked; our boots, in particular, had been unpleasantly waterlogged. Travelling on veluduback in such conditions is only marginally pleasanter, but it is unquestionably faster. We had packed away our ameral furs. Avran and I were wearing the cloaks from Doriolupata, green side outermost— and, in such conditions, no less conspicuous than the yellow side would have been. Keld had borrowed a soldier's cloak from the castle which, since green is the colour of Radaionesu and of Brelinderim, almost matched ours in hue; and so, of course, did the chirurgeon's cloak, since all members of his profession in Safaddné must wear green. In curious consequence, an uninformed observer might have thought we were all wearing the same livery.

Our problem was that, though our cloaks kept off the rain, they

1 See *Princes of Sandastre*

were not warm enough to prevent us from feeling chilled on such a day, whereas our furs would have been too warm. If a proper garb for such weather has been discovered, I have not been fortunate enough to learn of it. On that ride, our physical discomfort and mental unease combined to make us thoroughly glum and mutually uncommunicative. Indeed, the only comment I remember is a brief, grim one from Avran: 'So Ekulag spoke the truth, after all!'

There is a bridge over the Tasdralind close by Tasbered—a narrow bridge, easily defended or breached in case of attack. It arches high over a broad river-channel that, for much of the year, is occupied largely by gravel, with only a few pools or trickles of water; or so we were told. However, when we traversed that bridge, the channel was fast filling with muddy water as the steady rain hastened the snow's melting.

Beyond was a road heading more or less north-westward into the valley of the Berelind. This road followed the fashion of those in Darega, for it hugged the slopefoot well away from the riverbank, thus avoiding marshes and thickets while attaining some measure of concealment from any watchers on the rocky heights above. The snow must have been trodden into flatness by the soldiers hastening toward Warrentown, but that day the road had become a ditch into which rain- and meltwater collected. The veludain splashed along this in a mood quite as miserable as our own. They were indeed sturdy beasts, but they were only minimally willing, in such conditions, to carry riders who were strange to them. Only the chirurgeon's veludu seemed relatively contented.

Had we been attacked by beast or man, our mounts' unresponsiveness might have occasioned problems; but we were not. Instead, we had a dull day of arduous endeavour, with the river valley a channel of dank fog and the heights above us veiled from view in cloud. Naral Vesang's knowledge of our road spared us any doubts in that regard, but also deprived us of the mental exercise of route-finding. Consequently I soon became bored as well as depressed.

I was grateful when, at the day's end, the chirurgeon guided us uphill to a crag-clinging tower. A small garrison of elderly soldiers welcomed us to a bright fireside and furnished us generously with good rations.

Next morning the rain had ceased, though the sky was greyly

overcast. Our garments had dried overnight and we sallied forth in somewhat better spirits. Though the river still hugged itself in mist, the heights above us were only intermittently masked by scarves of cloud and there seemed some hope of sunshine.

Our road climbed steadily toward those heights throughout much of the day, but near eventide it dipped again toward the river; not the Berelind now, but the broader Lemmeshind. By then we had long been among trees; not the dreary wind-trees of which Avran and I had become so weary, but proper trees much like pines or firs, with brown cones clinging to their branches or strewn upon the snow.

Because of the trees and their long shadows, we were tardy in perceiving that our road was joining another and even tardier in becoming aware of the riders approaching us along that other road. On seeing them, Naral Vesang asked us to halt and wait by the wayside; he was immediately sure that these must be friends. While we were waiting the sun broke through, glowing in the saffron haze of a wet winter sunset and causing us to shade our eyes against its welcome brightness.

As the riders came closer, we saw that they were in military array and perceived that they were but the vanguard of a much larger group, albeit one whose size we could not yet gauge. Indeed, I had no eyes for the larger group. Instead, I was gazing with surprise, even with awe, at the three mighty men who rode, helmeted and in chain mail, at the centre of that vanguard.

Could I be mistaken, or was not the one at left Soganreth, letzahar of Ayan? Yes indeed; and at his right the tall Etselil of Aracundra was unmistakable! But who was that yet mightier man beyond him? Oh, of course, it must be the letzahar of Vasanderim, whatever his name was.

With these recognitions there came to us each a sense of joy such as we had not known since hearing of that second army. It was Keld who found first expression for that joy.

'Praise to the Nine!' he carolled. 'Glad am I that I have seen this day! At last, at long last, the letzestrei are riding to battle together!'

Chapter Seventeen

THE RALLYING OF SAFADDNÉ

It is necessary now, if my chronicle is to be complete, that I recount certain happenings which I did not witness. To do so, I must rely upon the recollections of Sir Robert Randwulf; but since I have heard his story at least thrice—once when told to Avran and me, twice more when told to others in our presence—I believe I have it right.

On the morning following our surreptitious overnight departure from Kesbados, the assembly of the Safaddnese began as usual, with the aerial whistlings and the priests' ceremony. When that was done, however, Essa—or rather, the Princess Hiludessa—did not ascend as before to the High Throne. Instead she walked only so far as the foot of the steps, before turning and thrusting out her arms at shoulder height in a gesture that demanded attention. Rakhamu was beside her, but this time the branath did not sink into a crouch. Instead he stood tensely by her, his head moving from side to side and his yellow eyes disquietingly attent.

These departures from precedent were enough to make all present aware that this was to be no ordinary session. So silent was the chamber that, though the Princess did not speak loudly, her voice was everywhere audible.

'My lords and priests, hear me! Harken to me also, all ye other men of Safaddné here present! Today as yesterday, it had been intended that we continue our deliberations into future policy. I had expected again to be calling upon dakhmen Etselil of Aracundra, to serve as our summoner. However, a matter of which I have become cognizant overnight has changed the situation—changed it so profoundly that we cannot proceed with our deliberations. There is no time for them; already, war is come upon us!'

This startling revelation evoked a common intake of breath, then a hubbub of dismayed exclamation and speculation. Essa listened awhile, a grim smile upon her lips, then raised her arms a second time to command silence.

'Such tidings will, I am sure, have shocked most of you; but not all—no, not all! As is well known from our history, there are men who will proffer a gift with one hand and then, when their victim smiles and reaches for it, strike with the dagger hidden in their other hand. Such a one is amongst us. Stand forth, Ekulag of Desume!'

There was a further stir of startlement, quickly stilled, before the letzahar came forward. That he did not want to do so was evident. At first he held back, then emerged with the precipitancy and reluctancy of an otter emptied from a sack into a ringful of hounds. His tongue was flickering uneasily about his pursy lips and his obsequiousness was quite gone; instead he looked about him shiftily, calculatingly. Evidently he was hoping even now to discover some means of evading the peril newly thrust upon him.

At the Desumean's approach, Rakhamu's eyes narrowed to slits and he uttered the faintest of growls—loud enough, however, to turn that calculation to alarm. Yet at first, the Princess addressed Ekulag quietly and courteously enough.

'You told us yesterday, did you not, my lord of Desume, how greatly your letzestre has gained from its friendship with Pavonara? You told us further, did you not, my lord, that King Rafanesar was eager to extend those benefices to us all? That Pavonara was a realm to be admired, even to be trusted; that the old days of its hostility to us of Safaddné were ended forever? No, those were not your exact words; but was that not the burden of your speech to us?'

Ekulag hesitated, sensing the trap that was set for him. Then he replied in a low voice: 'Yes . . . yes, that is so.'

Now Essa's voice became bleak, but with an undertone of bitterest contempt. 'That, then, was the gift being proffered; but you knew also, did you not, dakhmen Ekulag, that the dagger was in readiness? That indeed, King Rafanesar had marshalled his armies already? That, even as we met yesterday, those armies were already crossing the mountains, to invade Brelinderim and destroy Lyonesse?'

Robin had anticipated the springing of the trap upon the Desumean, but was surprised by her words, for he had thought as we had done, in terms of a single army. Indeed, I am sure that Essa was thinking similarly—that her use of the plural was inadvertent. Yet that is what she said; she mentioned armies, not just one army, and she spoke separately of actions against Brelinderim and against Lyonesse. Afterwards, her words were remembered as an exact statement of what was happening. Moreover, since the source of her information was not divulged, the Princess was believed to have been granted insight by the Nine Gods themselves—and gained greatly in reputation thereby.

For the moment, however, all attention was on Ekulag. The Desumean was quite evidently appalled by this public revelation of his stratagems; Essa's disgusted utterance had been as stinging as a whiplash. By the fashion that he cringed before the Princess, his treachery was made apparent to all.

There was a clamour of comment, quickly dying away to silence as all awaited Essa's next pronouncement. When she spoke, she did not again address Ekulag, even to seek any admission of his guilt. There was no need. Instead, she addressed the chamber at large, in a fashion that was scornfully dismissive of him.

'This traitor has sought to trade not merely his own realm, but all the nine letzestrei, for wealth and greater power. You must decide later how to deal with him. At that time you must deal also with his letzumahar Zharag and with any others among the Desumeans who were party to their despicable duplicity. For the moment, we have a more urgent concern—how best to aid the Brelinderimins and Lyonessans.'

High priest Balahir of Brelinderim leapt to his feet, his expression displaying his extreme anxiety. 'May I first implore, my lady, that warning be sent forthwith to my people?'

The Princess smiled at him. 'Be at ease, letzudirar Balahir. Word has been sent already. Yestere'en, my messengers left this city, charged to carry warnings to Tasbered and to Warrentown.'

Balahir expressed relieved thanks and sank back into his seat. Among the Ayanians, however, there was extreme puzzlement. How might messengers have departed, when the gates of Kesbados had not been opened? It savoured of the miraculous; and as a miracle it came afterwards to be regarded.

Essa was again speaking. 'Yet mere warning is not enough, I fear. If left unaided, neither Brelinderim nor Lyonesse can withstand the might of Pavonara. You have been engaged in disputation about those realms, ye of Safaddné. What is your judgement now? Will you leave them to endure the harshnesses or plead for the mercies of King Rafanesar's soldiers, or will you instead lend them your aid? People of the Nine Gods, what is your desire?'

Even before that last challenge was uttered, voices were already crying out: 'Yes! Yes! Aid! Death to the Pavonarans! To arms!' Soon the whole chamber was ringing with such shouts.

As the commotion died down, the Princess—never had she more deserved that title!—addressed the Safaddnese once more. 'That the Brelinderimins here present will wish to hasten to their countrymen's aid, I do not doubt. That my people of Avakalim will do likewise, again I cannot doubt. What of Ayan?'

'Our swords will be drawn against the Pavonarans, now as so often before.' Dakhmen Soganreth spoke without hesitation.

'What of you others, whose letzestrei lie farther away? What of Aracundra, Vasanderim, Omega and Darega? What of Paladra?'

Etselil of Aracundra spoke first. 'My sword will certainly be unsheathed in this war. As you say, my people are far away; but all of us here present will march against Pavonara, be sure of that!'

'We of Vasanderim march with you!' The massive letzahar of that realm—Vazatlel was his name, as I learned later—seemed delighted at the prospect of combat.

The letzaharei of Omega and Darega echoed his words, though with somewhat less fervour. Then its hooded chief priest rose to speak for Paladra, his soft sibilances causing shivers of unease among his listeners.

'So you will each hasten to war, you letzaharei, with your soldiers of Safaddné? And yes, this is a just war. Yet we of Paladra, we shall not ride beside you. We see no need. The Nine Gods will ensure that those Pavonaran armies are destroyed, without aid from our axes or swords. Indeed, we of Sasliith, we have brought with us no weapons. Why should we do so, when Mesnakech has assured us that we will need them not?'

He paused, then spoke again; not contemptuously, but dismissively. 'Yet, you people of the other letzestrei; yes, perhaps you should ride—perhaps, indeed, you must ride. But what of Desume? Will the Desumeans ride with you, or must you fight against them also?'

After casting that problem before the assembly, he returned silently to his seat. As for his fellow Paladrans, they sat as still and quiet as if they were not human beings, but mere cloaked and hooded effigies of wood—or straw.

Essa spoke softly now, echoing the letzudirar's question. 'Yes, what of you other Desumeans? Are you all now to be considered allies of the Pavonarans and enemies of we other peoples of Safaddné? Have you now forsaken the other Eight Gods, worshipping only Tera-ushlu of the Sun?'

This question provoked immediate cries of 'No! No!' from that ray of the chamber. After a brief consultation it was the Desumean high priest, Daliat, who rose to speak for his fellows. He was a small man, bald and by nature habitually reclusive, yet now his eyes were aflame with righteous anger.

'My lords letzaharei, my brother letzudirarei, and all you, my fellow Safaddnese, permit me to speak for Desume! Not all of us have been easy at the growth of that friendship with Pavonara. Some of us have been greatly disturbed by its rapid waxing and doubtful of its wisdom. Now we see clearly how we have been betrayed by our secular leaders; and, be assured, we are utterly horrified! For my part, I can assure you that the evil growth will be excised swiftly. I can assure you also that there will be Desumeans, many Desumeans, marching with you against Pavonara!'

There was a tumult of approval of his words. To Ekulag however, exposed as he was to the view of all at the centre of the chamber and enduring the branath's unswervingly hostile gaze, that tumult must have clearly spelled his fate. He had been standing with head bowed; now he dropped to a half-crouch and seemed to shrink into himself, as a snail shrinks within its shell at extreme danger. Yet he was as evidently doomed as any snail held in the beak of a song-thrush.

The princess continued to ignore him. It was only later that two of his fellow Desumeans came to remove him from the chamber, as his fellow conspirator, Zharag, had already been removed. Their end is likely to have been swift, for the Safaddnese do not waste time on traitors. We never learned the exact manner of it, nor did we ask. For Robin, as for Avran and me, it was enough that their power and they were gone.

Instead, Essa spoke to the other Desumeans. 'These tidings are good indeed! You people of Desume will be our welcome companions in the march against Pavonara. Yet you must act swiftly within your own realm, to ensure that there be no further treachery against Safaddné. To that task I charge you, letzudirar Daliat; and I charge you also to select a war leader, to serve till a new and worthier letzahar be appointed.'

Then at last, the Princess turned and ascended the steps, to seat herself upon the High Throne. As she recognized, it was appropriate and necessary that the last words of the assembly should be spoken from that place.

'People of Safaddné, hear me! At this time, through the great mercy of the Nine who Rule, we of Safaddné are drawn together in common cause once more. Ended are our years of drifting asunder. Our task now is to smash the armies of Pavonara. Be sure that, in that task, we shall receive aid; already the letzudirar of Paladra, serving as mouthpiece for the Nine, has voiced to you that assurance. And remember—in this battle, the Lyonessans are our allies. Before, they were the allies of Brelinderim and Avakalim only; now they are the allies of us all. They are to be regarded, and their lives and interests valued, even as if they were Safaddnese.'

She paused, surveying the chamber from that loftier height. Then, in a voice more resonant than ever hitherto, she cried out triumphantly: 'I proclaim war—or rather, the renewal of war! Of old, we of Safaddné have fought Pavonara not once, but many times; now we are called again to battle! As our leader in war I appoint, in the name of the Nine, Etselil, letzahar of Aracundra!'

There came a thunder of applause. As it died down, the Princess continued her speech. 'It is not for me to counsel you, dakhmen Etselil, in the conduct of your campaign, but I know that you will ride directly to the aid of our threatened friends in Brelinderim and Lyonesse. No doubt all letzestrei, save one only, will ride with you, east of the Lemmeshind. My path is different, as I now see it. I shall ride with dakhmen Perespeth west of the Lemmeshind, to aid him in rallying our own realm of Avakalim. We shall join you in battle at Warrentown!'

Again there came a clamorous signification of approval. Only when it had quite faded away did Essa speak one last time. Her voice no longer sounded exultant, but merely weary. 'I call on letzudirar Parudanh to end this assembly with prayer. With that call I complete my duty here, for the message of the Gods is delivered.'

At the concluding of Parudanh's prayer, the whistles from above sounded in louder chorus than ever before; but Essa seemed not to hear them. Long after most persons had left the chamber, she remained sitting on the High Throne. Only when Sir Robert went to fetch her did she descend from it, to take his arm wordlessly. Thus linked together they left the assembly chamber, never again to return to it.

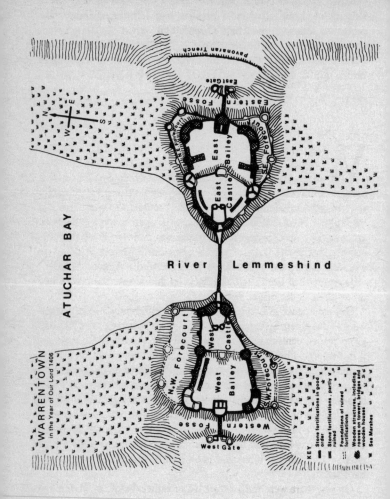

River Lemmeshind

ATUCHAR BAY

WARRENTOWN
in the Year of Our Lord 1406

Pavonarian Trench

East Gate

Eastern Fosse

N.E. Forecourt

S.E. Forecourt

East
Castle
Bailey

East
Castle

West
Castle

N.W. Forecourt

S.W. Forecourt

West
Bailey

Western Fosse

West Gate

KEY

Stone fortifications in good order

Stone fortifications, partly ruined

Foundations of ruined fortifications

Wooden structures, including rooves on towers, bridges and wooden houses

Sea Marshes

Chapter Eighteen

THE HEIGHTS ABOVE WARRENTOWN

When I was younger I had, like all boys, often imagined battles, with myself in the heart of the combat. Those had been brave imaginings, of valorous deeds performed with unmatchable skill amid soldiers who, though themselves engaged, yet had time to admire and applaud my actions. Sometimes those battles had been formal affairs, fought on open meadows between armies drawn up in proper array; sometimes they had involved perilous scalings of the walls of castles or cities. (The role of defender was, of course, too unheroic to be conceived!) Always, however, engagement had been swift and decisive; and always the battles had taken place under bright skies.

Our experience in Lyonesse proved very different. Certainly, when we met dakhmen Etselil and the Safaddnese vanguard, the sun had given benign benison to that joyful encounter. All too soon, however, it had retreated behind bastions of cloud. Even nine days later, these continued to conceal it from our vision. Instead of enjoying warmth, we had endured sudden wind gusts that flung sleet or chill rain into our faces, then faded away into uncertain draughts that tugged tiresomely at the skirts of sodden cloaks and surcoats. Our clothes were given no chance to dry and we were never warm. The ground underfoot was beslimed by surface melting, but frozen only a little deeper. One slipped often and knew that, if one fell, it would be a hard fall.

Oh yes, there were walls before us; or rather, below us. Avran and I were on watch on the saddle of a ridge—the ridge of which Essa had told us in Achalind, the great mound of rocks and clay that strikes from east to west across the valley of the Lemmeshind and almost prevents that river's debouchment into Atuchar Bay (or Xel Atukhar, as the Safaddnese style it). Whenever the sleet and rain sufficiently relented so to permit, we could glimpse the grey towers of Warrentown, built astride the river just where it was at its narrowest. Yet we could not approach those walls, for between them and us were the Pavonarans.

Thus, after travelling so far and through so many perils, I was within half a league of my father; but, with armed men massed between us, I had not seen him. Indeed I could not be sure, even now, that I would ever again do so.

As for a swift engagement; yes, there had seemed a hope of one, but it had come to nothing. When our army had come down from the heights, we had chanced upon a rearguard left to defend the upper ridge. Unfortunately, those Pavonarans had seen us even before we saw them and had perceived we were more numerous than they. Unheroically but wisely, they had mounted their beasts and fled. Nor, despite our advantage of riding downslope, could we catch them. Though we urged our veludain to greatest speed, they had distanced on us and rejoined unscathed the main Pavonaran force, massed in siege about the city.

Yet those fleeing Pavonarans had left me with a memory of astonishment. They had not, like us, been mounted on veludain. They evaded us because they had been riding much speedier and more remarkable beasts. The Safaddnese called those beasts *quetelain*, but during the pursuit I had seen them properly. I had noticed their tossing manes and noticed also the single horn spiralling outward from their foreheads, above and exactly between their eyes. In heraldry classes during childhood I had learned of such beasts; I had even delightedly handled one of those horns, in a London alchemist's shop to which my father had taken me while questing for a potion against some pestilence. Quetelain, forsooth: those were unicorns!

Yet such unicorns! In the art of heralds, the unicorn is depicted sometimes as white, with horns and hooves of argent, or more often as wholly argent. A grey unicorn might have seemed well enough to me: but these beasts, why, from hoof to horn-tip they were as black as sea-coal!

As they bore their riders away, those quetelain—those unicorns—had moved exactly like horses. Yet, when I had leisure to inspect the prints left in the snow and mud by their feet, I was again surprised. These did not show a single hoof, like that of a horse: instead, each foot bore two hooves, like those of a stag—or, for that matter, of a rafenu, a hasedu or a veludu. Yes, the arrangement of quetelu foot-prints was different from theirs; but no more different than are, say, the tracks of a red deer from those of a roedeer.

However, when I came to reflect upon the matter afterward, I wondered at my own astonishment. After all, no heraldic artist ever troubles to depict in detail the *hooves* of a unicorn! So a quetelu was simply a unicorn, and that was that. Why should I have become so excited at seeing a beast well known to English travellers, when I had encountered in Rockall so many creatures that were quite unknown?

This diminution of my excitement came the faster, because it was not shared. Keld Eslingbror and the other Safaddnese could give me little information about quetelain and were evidently not much interested. Yes, a quetelu could run fast enough downhill or upon level ground, but it was not nearly so swift as a veludu when running uphill and not nearly so sturdy: they could not understand why the Pavonarans favoured such unsatisfactory mounts, especially in the mountains. Moreover, I was told that the hides of quetelain made only an inferior leather and that even their meat made poor eating. However, when I enquired further, it proved to be long since any men of Safaddné had either handled unicorn leather or sampled unicorn steaks!

When I asked where the quetelain came from, the answers were vague. Somewhere over in the Black Lands, they thought—the lands that lay beyond the Pavonaran Mountains. Those were lands to which no Safaddnese had ever gone—or, if they had gone as prisoners, from which they had never returned. Black Lands: black unicorns. That was logical enough; why speculate further?

Even Avran could not comprehend my excitement. Well, yes, maybe those creatures *were* what we English called unicorns, but what was so remarkable about that? Was not a unicorn just another beast—like a sevdru or rafenu, but less amply equipped with horns? For his part, he'd have been much more excited to see a sevdru again. It would make him feel closer to home!

Indeed, my usually cheerful friend was in low spirits; in part because of the weather, in part because of Essa. He had not liked leaving her behind in Kesbados. Then, when we met the Safaddnese, he had been sure she must be riding with them. His spirits had risen in consequence, only to slump when he learned that she was not—

that, though earlier averring she would never do so, she had elected after all to travel to Avakalim. It was a decision that utterly bewildered Avran and left him profoundly disturbed.

I was quite as puzzled, but much less concerned. Since Robin was with Essa, I was sure she would be adequately safeguarded—especially since, by now, she must be somewhere west of the Lemmeshind and safely away from the Pavonarans. Mayhap that was why she had gone to Avakalim; it seemed sensible enough. I advanced my idea to Avran, but it would not do for him.

'Simon, she said she would never go there! Yet she has gone! I don't believe it can have been to preserve her own life—Essa would not be afraid of any Pavonarans. No, if she's broken her word to us, there must be some other reason.' After that, Avran withdrew into a silence of doleful meditation.

For my part I was more cheerful, because I had received news of my brother. He and his two companions, Marasar Esekh and Etvan Samenast, had duly carried word of the invasion to the small Ayanian fortresses and Brelinderimin farms of the upper Lemmeshind valley, whence it had been spread by beacon and swift messenger to the people dwelling downstream. The two Brelinderimins had paused to rally the soldiers of their letzestre, but Richard had borrowed a swift veludu and ridden on toward Warrentown. I could be reasonably certain that he had reached that city before the Pavonaran siege closed about it.

So my father and brother must be together again, somewhere within those grey walls. That was a comfort since, even if Warrentown's eastern section be attacked and taken, they might yet withdraw across the Lemmeshind bridge to safety. Yet it was not of entire comfort to me. If the eastern castle was indeed stormed, it would surely not be yielded without a vigorous defence. It was possible that my father might be persuaded not to take part in such a defence, but far from probable. Almost certainly he would be in the thick of the combat, fighting shoulder to shoulder with Richard.

Though we could see Warrentown's walls and towers below us, that would not have enabled Avran and me properly to understand its system of fortifications. Fortunately, at Keld's urging, one of the Brelinderimins had taken trouble to explain them to us. Under his direction I sketched out the plan of the town on the parchment roll which, through habit gained in Achalind, I still carried. I shall attach that plan to this account, but shall explain it in words also, since many folk—yes, even many soldiers—seem never to comprehend such limnings.

As Essa had told us, twin castles had been built, one west and the other east of the river, to defend and to dominate the lower Lemmeshind valley. The fortifying may have been begun in times beyond memory, even before the southerners strove to take the mountains into their dominion. However, though that attempt failed, it was they—or rather, the slaves whip-driven to that task—who had given form to the fortifications. As its mightiest, Gles Lemmeshind must have been impressive indeed; and, though it had crumbled and been rebuilt several times over, I suspect the design had changed little over the years.

The two castles were essentially alike in concept but different in detail, since the ridge west of the river was broader and somewhat less high. Across each ridge a deep fosse had been dug from north to south, to prevent any direct onslaught on the castle. Each fosse was crossed by a narrow bridge that might be raised or destroyed at need; moreover, each bridge had a fortified gate on its outer side, where guards might be stationed to examine strangers before allowing them across. The rubble from the digging of the fosses had been heaped to form two mottes on which had been constructed the inner citadels, the castles proper. These were girded with towers and curtain walls and linked by the narrow bridge that spanned the Lemmeshind. I shall call those inner citadels the West and the East Castle.

Before and below them, taking in the greater part of the ridge between citadel and fosse, were the West and East Baileys. There, most of the folk of Gles Lemmeshind must have lived and pastured their beasts during winter. Each bailey was protected by a gatehouse and two massive towers, linked together and to the castle by curtain walls. Nor was that all the protection, for there had also been defensive walls at a somewhat lower level, overlooked by lesser towers and enclosing forecourts that would need to be stormed before the baileys, and their greater towers, could be even approached. In its heyday and when properly defended and provisioned, Gles Lemmeshind might have defied assault indefinitely.

The problem was, of course, that for long there had been insufficient folk to defend, or even to maintain, all those extensive fortifications, so that they had fallen into ruin. Though the Lyonessans and their Brelinderimin and Avakalimin friends had striven mightily, they had not yet restored the twin fortresses to their original strength. Yet they had perceived that the threat to the eastern fortress, from the Pavonarans, was greater than that to the western fortress, where only an assault by the Sea Warriors need be feared. Consequently, though rebuilding had proceeded on both sides, effort had been concentrated on the east side — and that had proved fortunate.

Little had been done with the outermost defences. Both the West and the East Gates remained in semi-ruinous condition. Reconstruction of the external wall and towers of the North-east Forecourt had been in progress, but had not been completed. The other three forecourts had been cleared of trees and bushes, but their walls were wholly ruinous; indeed, the hungry waters of the Lemmeshind had gnawed away much of the South-west Forecourt. Perhaps the North-east Forecourt might be defended for a while; the others certainly could not.

Also still largely in ruins were the inner curtain walls and towers separating the West and East Castles from their baileys. Part of one — the north-east curtain of the East Castle — chanced to have survived in fair condition, yet this would not suffice to halt any onslaught, should enemies enter within the bailey.

Happily, however, the external towers and walls of the castles and baileys had been very largely rebuilt, sufficiently so to make them an unexpectedly formidable obstacle for the Pavonarans. All of the six towers that ringed the East Castle and Bailey had been repaired; five of those surrounding the West Castle and Bailey were finished and the sixth was close to completion. Even the wooden floors and roofs had been restored, using timber rafted down from the Lemmeshind forests. (It was within these towers that Sir John, Sir Arthur and their followers had lived, until wives insisted on pleasanter and more private quarters; indeed, the unmarried men still lived in them.) The curtain walls were also almost finished; the one uncompleted section, on the south-west side of East Castle, was atop a river cliff and appeared safe enough from assault.

Since the two English knights had received the grant of Lyonesse, many of their men had taken Safaddnese brides, while others had brought wives from England. Though some couples had set up households within Warrentown itself — there were, I was told, rows of wattle-and-daub cottages within both baileys—many others had begun tilling the ground or herding beasts on the Lemmeshind meadowlands upriver from the town or on the slopes above the valley. Moreover, some Brelinderimin and Avakalimin families had moved downriver to resettle lands long forsaken.

Had they been left unwarned, many of the east bank families might have been slain or scattered by the Pavonaran invaders: the Pavonarans had identified in advance, and eliminated, the few Lyonessan guard-posts in the mountains that were in their path and that might have given warning. Inadequately garrisoned, Warrentown itself might indeed have been crushed like a nut beneath a hammer, as Ekulag had so gloatingly foretold. Fortunately, our warning had arrived in time. Though many a humble farmstead had been torched by the Pavonarans, the farmers and their families were safe within Warrentown's walls.

Yet they were safe only for a while. The threat to Warrentown, and to the Safaddnese lands, remained formidable. Not only were the Pavonarans well armed and well organized, but also they outnumbered by a wide margin we who opposed them.

Just as the castellan of Tasbered had told us, Kalung Dastenost had over eight thousand soldiers at his command. Moreover, the Desumeans in our company knew the Pavonaran leader by repute and told us that he was a formidable opponent. He had not seen twenty summers when Sir John Warren's sword caused him prematurely to become Faruzlaf of Hregisel, but even at that early age his reputation as a warrior had been high. Since that time, he had risen to become the foremost commander of Pavonara's armies under the King. Moreover, the Dastenost was said to have vowed to destroy Lyonesse utterly, in vengeance for his father, and to have been promised by his King its lands as a personal feoffdom. Though I questioned the authenticity of such rumours—would even Ekulag have known so much?—I did not doubt their essential veracity.

In contrast, the twin castles of Warrentown could be defended by no more than four hundred men; some of these were farmers, not soldiers, and others were children of Lyonesse, scarcely old enough to bear arms. Moreover, Etselil could count only three dakhletelei—less than three thousand men, mostly Ayanians and Brelinderimins—in his present command. He was much too prudent a leader to engage in battle with the Pavonarans against such overwhelming odds, unless the need of the Lyonessans became dire.

Instead, Etselil was waiting for reinforcements; but we were beginning to question the prospect of them. Beyond doubt, dakhmen Perespeth—aided, we presumed, by the Princess Hiludessa—must be engaged in rallying the Avakalimins; but that was no small task, for they were scattered across wide lands. Our comrades estimated that Avakalim might muster two dakhletelei, perhaps even three; but that was all. Moreover, with the waters of the Lemmeshind already so swollen by snow-melt and likely to rise higher, would those soldiers be able to cross them and come to our aid? Yes, the Lemmeshind was bridged, but only here at Warrentown, far downstream, and far upstream at Maradiela. To use either bridge would involve a detour of many, many leagues.

We trusted that, by now, more Ayanians and Brelinderimins, and many more Desumeans, might be on their way to join us; but would the Desumeans indeed rally to Etselil, after the humiliation and overthrow of their own letzahar? Might not many of them prove passive or even hostile, seeing a greater strength and better prospects for themselves in that alliance with Pavonara?

At worst, only a half-dakhletel of Ayanians, and perhaps as many Brelinderimins from the further valleys, might be coming to swell our force. Even with the strongest possible support from the Desumeans, we could hope only for three more dakhletelei—and, without Avakalimin aid, that would still leave us outnumbered.

To make bad prospects worse, the very weather seemed to be conspiring against us. Even here by the sea-coast, the combination of cold, wind and rain had been unpleasant to endure. Up-valley and in the mountains, it had been much more severe. The few messengers who reached us spoke of blizzard upon blizzard within the last five days, heaping fresh snow upon that already lying until it was piled higher than fetlock depth. Moreover, the snow was not forming the sort of crisp, dry surface upon which men in seslelteven can make good speed. Instead, it was continuing to melt rapidly. Streamlets were turning into rivers and low lands into morasses, while the danger of snow-slides was extreme. Everywhere, those messengers reported exhaustedly, the snow was too deep for veluduriding and so stickily wet as to make any passage in seslelteven either laborious and slow or quite impossible.

So my other boyhood imagining, of a combat between armies

drawn up in proper battle order, was also disappointed. Here were
no pikemen or archers massed for an advance against odds; here
were no ranked cavalry on snorting mounts, eager for a brave charge,
or mail-clad knights clamouring to advance their honour in single
combat. Instead I found myself part of an all-too-thin line of soldiers,
clad more for warmth than for war and striving to function merely
as a fence about our enemies. Outnumbered as we were, we could
not hope to make any meaningful assault upon them. Moreover, we
knew well that, should the Pavonarans decide to attack us, we had
little hope of containing them, even with the advantage of being
upslope; our reserves were simply too meagre.

When would those reinforcements arrive? Was there truly any
chance that they would come in time? The messengers could not
even tell us whether that hoped-for second army had set out; and
there had been no news at all from across the Lemmeshind. The
last of the Avakalimin beacons had long since been extinguished by
the rain and sleet.

Even had it been tactically feasible for us to attack the Pavonarans,
such an attack would have been difficult to launch. The Brelinderimins told us that this lower Lemmeshind valley had been once a fair
place, with many fine farms; but then had come the Sea Raiders and
the retreat up-valley. For many years, these lands had been abandoned; and though farming had begun again, it had been almost
confined to the meadows. The lower, gentler slopes were covered
by scrub, the sort of messy, irregular growth that develops all too
swiftly on disused farmlands in gentler climes but must here represent long years of neglect. The scrub served to shield from our
view much of the Pavonaran camp, yet those low slopes and the
riverside meadows and marshes, frozen solid now in winter, remained
a possible, if poor, terrain for fighting.

A much more serious problem was presented by the upper slopes.
These could never have been cleared, for many of the trees were
gnarled, much misshapen by wind, and evidently very ancient: no
doubt those steep woodlands had been reserved as browsing-places
for hasedain and as sources of wood for fires. However, it was long
indeed since beasts had been pastured there or firewood collected.
Boughs had broken off and fallen; trees had died or been blown
over by gales; and leaf-litter had accumulated in hollows, furnishing
rooting-places for lesser plants that had likewise withered and

been overgrown. The resultant tangle was one through which no cavalry could charge, nor foot-soldiers advance in any sort of order. Indeed, it was close to impassable, even for a man on his own.

The only practicable place for a concerted onslaught was this ridge above Warrentown, upon which Avran and I were stationed. Because of the rigours of winter winds, its crest was bare of any vegetation of greater than grass-height: indeed there had been a road here, whose cart-ruts were still to be observed even after many years of desuetude.

Of course, the Pavonarans were perfectly aware that the ridge formed a possible route for an attack upon them. To counter any such risk, they had spent three of the four days since our arrival in hollowing out a defensive trench. This had been dug just east of the great fosse, where the ridge was still narrow. It was not especially deep—the frozen ground must have made for hard digging—but it had been filled with cut branches, among which were set many sharpened stakes. The earth and boulders from the trench had been heaped to form a protective rampart on its further side, from behind which their javelotiers might harass any assailants. (Having never learned the use of longbows, the Pavonarans used javelots—small javelins designed for hurling—as their long-distance offensive weapons.) We could not assault that trench without suffering heavy losses.

Of course, while the trench and the steep woodlands served to make very difficult any attack by us upon the Pavonarans, they rendered it just as difficult for the Pavonarans to attack us! However, our enemies evinced no desire to do so; quite the contrary. Since we had neither launched any immediate attack on first arrival, nor even attempted any interference while the trench was being dug and the rampart constructed, Kalung Dastenost must perceive quite clearly that Etselil's army was considerably weaker than his own. Nor would the Dastenost expect it to be strengthened. Since he did not know that his monarch lay dead under the snows of Ulkurin, he must be imagining that King Rafanesar's army was ravaging Brelinderim. Well then, he must be saying to himself, why not let those Safaddnese roost as they willed on the upper slopes? Had not that defensive work been constructed, we might have proved a nuisance; but we constituted no real threat to his Pavonarans. Kalung's prime concern was with Warrentown and the Lyonessans. With the fortress taken and Lyonesse destroyed, he would have a secure base, and ample leisure, for dealing with any Safaddnese that dared offer him combat!

In retrospect, I believed that Etselil had been unwise when he decided not to attack the Pavonarans immediately. Yes, we were the lesser force, but surely we might have seized the whole ridge and held it? He had made a second error, I felt, in not launching any onslaught while the trench was being dug. Even some harassment of the diggers by his small corps of longbowmen—among whom Avran and I were now numbered, for the true nature of the staffs we had so long carried had been perceived by our Brelinderimin friends—might have served to prevent its construction. However, our commander had chosen to do nothing.

Certain excuses may be advanced for him. The longbow and its powers were unknown in Etselil's letzestre of Aracundra, while he was necessarily ignorant of the particular problems presented by the topography and vegetation about Warrentown. A Brelinderimin commander would, I am sure, have known better and acted more decisively; but the letzahar of Brelinderim was dead and the succession in dispute. In such circumstances, Safaddnese concepts of status and seniority had made Etselil the only possible choice as dakhletzahar of our army; yet I was coming to consider that choice unfortunate. Oh, for some action!

Huddled in our cloaks, Avran and I were sitting high on the southern slope of the ridge. This was a privileged position, for it afforded us some measure of shelter. The wind was blowing that day from the north-west—and blowing with increasing strength, hurling at us a fine, cold rain that stung one's cheeks and seemed likely soon to turn to snow.

Though we were as close to the Pavonaran trench as was safe, this abominable weather meant that we could see only a small distance. The ruined East Gate to Warrentown, now in the hands of our enemies, formed no more than a black outline against the wet, grey mist. The towers of the East Castle beyond the fosse could be glimpsed only dimly and intermittently; and even the nearer bank of the Lemmeshind was wholly invisible. Downslope from us, we could not see beyond the dense thickets; their further limits faded away into vagueness.

'Much good it is, being on watch on a day like this!' Avran grumbled. 'I wish I were rolled up in my sleeping-sack—or back in Sandastre, where the weather is decently warm. And were I in either of those places, I'd be achieving just as much—or as little!—as I am now.'

'I have a flask of efredat, if a swig of that would warm you,' I offered.

'Thank you, Simon my friend, but I'll say no. Yes, it does warm one, but only for a while; and I have no liking for its flavour. But what a cold and futile task this is!'

'Cold, yes,' I answered, 'though we'd be worse on the ridge-top, or on the seaward slope with Keld and his fellows. Yet futile—well, I'm not so sure of that. Do you not sense that something is happening, down in the mist below us?'

Avran gazed at me surprisedly. 'I cannot say that I do; but what makes you think so, my friend? I have seen no lights of torches or fires, nor have I heard any noise of battle.'

'Like you, I've seen no lights today; but that is one reason why I believe something is happening. When we've been here during the last few days and the rain has been driving like this—well, the view has not been good, but we *have* glimpsed the flames of their fires and seen the gleam of their torches. As for sounds—that doesn't seem normal either, and for the same reason. Just think back, Avran; has it not been quieter than usual—too quiet? Yes, I know that mist blankets sound as well as vision; but usually we have heard horncalls and shouts, the scraping noises of metal upon metal and the thud of axes among the scrub down there. Today, I've heard nothing at all—except once, when there was some sort of distant splash, as if something heavy had fallen into the river.'

'Yes, I remember that sound; but the river must be running higher than usual. Mayhap some tree's roots were washed away, so that we heard its fall.'

I was irritated by the absurdity of this response. 'But Avran, there *are* no trees down by the Lemmeshind's marge; you know that! And how about the lack of other sounds? Does that not mean something to you?'

My friend was annoyed. 'How can a lack of sound mean anything? Tell me that!'

'Certainly I'll tell you, though you don't have to believe me! Consider the weather. Is it not worse than at any time since we've been here, and the rain-mist thicker? That makes it ideal for masking the marshalling of forces for a surprise attack! And if such a plan were being launched, would not Kalung Dastenost make very sure that his soldiers dowsed their fires and torches and kept silence?'

Avran was taken aback by this suggestion. 'But . . . Well, how do you explain the splash we heard?'

'I cannot properly explain that; but might not some heavy object have been dropped by accident into the water—a scaling ladder, for instance? Or perhaps some unicorn may have slipped in the mud and fallen with its rider into the river? Yet I would suppose unicorns to be sure-footed creatures, much though our Safaddnese friends decry them.'

However, Avran had harked back to my earlier suggestion and was evidently disquieted. 'Well—I don't know; you may be correct, Simon. About the attack, I mean. What must we do? Should we send Raden here'—he gestured to the soldier attached to us as messenger—'to explain your idea to dakhmen Etselil?'

I hesitated. 'Perhaps not yet. I'd like to have some more definite evidence. After all, we can't send warning to Warrentown; even a beacon would not be seen by the Lyonessans, through this miserable rain. And it is they who are likely to be attacked, not we. No, I think we should wait awhile.'

But Avran was restive now. 'You are right, Simon; it's too quiet and too dark down there. Sometimes you're wiser than I, you know! Yet I don't agree that we should wait. Raden!—here a moment! Please take this message to the dakhletzahar.'

Hastily he outlined to the soldier my deduction and its causes; then Raden sped away into the mist, leaving me prey to very mixed emotions. *Had* that deduction been reasonable, or was I merely crying wolf when no wolf was near? I was not at all sure that I was grateful to Avran for taking the decision out of my hands.

I was permitted to remain in silent doubt for quite a while longer; and then the wisdom of my friend's decision, and the correctness of my own deduction, were simultaneously made apparent. The sharp sound of ikhils, blown at full blast, clove suddenly into the stillness. There followed a clamour of shouts and the noise of clashing weapons. Yes indeed, an attack *was* being launched by the Pavonarans upon Warrentown!

That, at least, was evident; and, from the mounting noises of conflict, it seemed they were attacking from several different quarters. So long as the mist remained dense, we could not properly determine what was happening; but the wind seemed now to be strengthening and the rain slackening. Surely, soon, we would be permitted a glimpse of Warrentown?

Yet, if we were, what might we hope to do? Yes, we must try to aid the Lyonessans, but could we reach them in time to render any effective aid? Indeed, could we reach them at all? We could not penetrate those dense thickets; we could only assault the Pavonaran earthwork and try to overwhelm its defenders, at whatever cost.

Avran and I were on our feet by then, trying to peer through the mist. However, while my friend was excited and eager for the instructions to arrive that would send us into action, I was becoming disheartened and afraid. Here I was, so close to my father and brother, yet so far from them. Was it our destiny to meet again, or was it not more likely that one or all of us would die within the next few hours?

The swirling mist, and the fashion in which its opacity increased or lessened, seemed a reflection of the fears that were clouding my mind. Why had I ventured on this absurd expedition northward, and brought my friend into such dangers? Oh, if only I had stayed in Sandarro with Ilven ...

Chapter Nineteen

WARRENTOWN BESIEGED

No single soldier can ever properly describe a battle in which he has been engaged: he can merely tell of what he himself witnessed, and that can only be a small part of the action. For this next episode in my story, I must report the observations of others and serve merely as a chronicler of events in which I played no part.

The tidings of my brother's movements were correct in essentials but wrong in details. Following our early-morning parting of ways on the mountainside above Kesbados, Marasar Esekh, Etvan Samenast and he had indeed made their swift way down the valley of the Hededrund, crying warning of the invasion to its Ayanian farmers and seeing the beacons lit to speed that warning. However, their own ways had parted before the inflow of the Hededrund into the Lemmeshind was reached.

They were each riding borrowed veludain by then. Marasar had swum his beast across the swollen river, to cross the mountain ridge that rose west of it. He would bear the fell news to the Ayanians who lived south of the Maldilund and their Avakalimin neighbours on its further bank. Etvan had headed north-westward, to rally the Brelinderimins for war. Richard, however, had stayed close to the river. He was determined to carry the news to Warrentown as swiftly as he might. A mere warning by beacon was not enough; the Lyonessans would need to know that aid was on its way, to give them heart in the battle soon to come.

Richard's veludu was one of the swiftest and most enduring of its race, but he had ridden it close to exhaustion. Following tortuous tracks through the dense forests that flank the Lemmeshind — tracks which, fortunately, were already known to him — he had travelled in two long days to the bridge below Maradiela.

That stronghold is the greatest in Avakalim, a coronet of tall towers set upon a high rocky brow above the Lemmeshind; and its bridge is both fortified and strongly guarded. No stranger would have been permitted to cross, but Richard was not a stranger. He was greeted warmly and escorted to the castle by soldiers already a-twitter at the sight of the Brelinderimin beacons. However, though Richard was feasted and harkened to, he could not persuade the Avakalimins to march to war without orders from their letzahar; and such orders had not yet been received.

Fortunately, Richard did find some boatmen willing to take him down the Lemmeshind. From Maradiela to the sea, that river can be travelled by yildrihen, though not by any craft of deeper draught. Indeed, since the Lemmeshind's waters were rising as the snow melted, the passage promised to be easier and swifter than it would become in summer. Even so, there were adventures enough with hidden sandbanks and floating logs. They set forth on the ninth day of March and were more than sixty hours on the river. Richard, no more a waterman than I, was profoundly relieved when they reached Warrentown with craft and bodies whole.

For two days already, warned by the beacons, families had been streaming in from the countryside, bringing their bundled possessions and their beasts to seek safety within Warrentown's walls. Sir Arthur Thurlstone was far away upvalley, but Sir John Warren was in energetic command of the city that had been named for him. He received Richard with great pleasure, both as a friend and as a source of true tidings from Kesbados: for indeed, only rumour had preceded my brother.

Sir John was a short man, but exceedingly muscular from much doughty wielding of weapons. He had the red face of one who goes often abroad in cold weather and, upon return, does not stint of good ale to warm his blood. His short-cropped hair and bristling beard were still more blond than grey, while his blue eyes were bright with enthusiasm—the enthusiasm of the warrior for whom the prospect of battle provides welcome relief from the long tedium of peace. He heard Richard out, then pondered awhile before responding.

'So the Princess is come out of the past, just as the old tales foreboded. Well, I'd heard those tales, but I took little heed of them—as little heed as I paid to my brother knight's belief that his namesake King would some day return at England's need!'

He chuckled richly, then lapsed into solemnity. 'Well, well, it seems I must doubt less and trust more in those stories of the loremasters! And the Princess, you say, still looks young and lovely? Indeed so. Remarkable; remarkable! 'Twill serve to rally the Safaddnese, for sure—and, I trust, to our aid. Yet I doubt not that we'll be seeing the Pavonarans earlier! I had hoped for an advance warning from our guard-posts in the mountains, but no word has come. I fear they have been already overborne.'

'That is ill news,' commented Richard. 'Yet it adds veracity to the tales told by that knave from Desume.'

'So it does; so it does. We of Lyonesse, we are not strong enough to go forth to battle the Pavonarans, as you'll understand, Richard. Instead, we must endure siege. Well, I am taking such precautions as I can. A few wives insisted on staying beside their goodmen in the East Bailey and a few veludain are being kept there, for message-carrying at need. The older womenfolk and most younger ones, the children and the greatest number of our beasts are lodged west of the river, so that they may escape into Avakalim if all goes ill. I cannot leave the West Castle undefended, yet I think it to be under small threat, so I am stationing the greater part of our force here in the East Castle. Would that our force were stronger!'

Richard was concerned. 'What is our strength, then?'

Sir John grimaced. 'With all counted, perhaps four hundred men capable of bearing weapons; I cannot call all of them soldiers. Not enough, Richard; not enough! The Pavonaran army will outnumber us vastly. Still, they'll be outside and we are within good walls—walls that, even now, your father is labouring to make stronger. If aid comes to us speedily, all may be well.'

'I trust so, Sir John. Meantime, what must I do?'

'Well now, your father will be blithe to see you. I think that, for the moment, I shall assign you to his service. Presently he is striving to set the outerworks of the North-east Forecourt into better order; you'll find him there.'

Indeed, Sir William Branthwaite was very pleased to see his elder son again. Moreover, he was both moved and highly delighted to learn that I, his younger son, had accepted his challenge and followed my brother and him to Rockall. At the same time it must have added to my father's anxieties to know that, far from being pent up safely in some monastery as he had supposed, I was so near by and caught up, as were Richard and he, in this turmoil of war.

Richard learned from our father that the picture of the situation limned for him by Sir John, although sombre, was yet somewhat brighter than the reality. The figure of four hundred was optimistic: it had included the men sent out on distant guard, as well as those within the castles, and those guards were not all destined to return. Moreover, in a siege it is the longbowmen who are most valuable, for they can dispatch attackers at speed and from a safe distance; had they not been crucial to victory during the last attack upon Warrentown? Yet now, among four hundred, there were scarcely forty archers of real skill. Perhaps twenty others could use that weapon in a fashion, but they were not to be relied upon.

The captain of the archers, old Ben of Heeley, had been given charge of the butts in the West Bailey. There, he and four other old archers were striving, with many curses, to inculcate their craft into those twenty novices and into some youngsters who had been clamouring to be taught. Sir John had sent to the West Castle his less skilled foot-soldiers—spearmen, axemen and swordsmen—and had placed its garrison under the command of Mark Thistleton, an elderly veteran of many battles. It was not a strong defensive force, but then its skills were not likely to be tried: surely there could be no assault on the west bank?

In the East Castle, under Sir John's direct command, there were thus some two hundred and twenty men, thirty-five of whom were skilled archers. That might be enough, maybe, to fend off any immediate attack; but it would not be sufficient to sustain a defence for long.

The Pavonaran assault came just after noon—and with the suddenness of a hurricane. Kalung Dastenost had planned carefully and executed his plans adroitly: only the unexpected factor of our forewarning saved the Lyonessans from being overwhelmed.

On the day before, Sir John had sent out fresh messengers to those disturbingly silent frontier posts; the messengers had been given the swiftest veludain and urged to take the greatest caution. In addition, a further guard had been placed high on the ridge so that, even if those posts were lost, he should gain early warning of the Pavonarans' approach. Yet no warning came, either from frontier or from ridge.

A heavy mist hugged the mountain flanks that day. The Pavonarans were skilled at silent movement and their unicorns were fleeter than veludain. Moreover, at near quarters, a javelot is quite as deadly as any arrow from a longbow. Whether those guards were slain or taken, the Lyonessans never learned; but certainly they were never again seen.

Being so sure that the attack would come from the ridge, Sir John had set no guards on the riverbank. He was both right and wrong. Pavonaran foot-soldiers had found for themselves quiet paths down into the Lemmeshind valley, both north and south of Warrentown. Avoiding the meadowlands and farms, they had made their stealthy way by night along the scrub-grown slopes to take up positions within half a league of the East Castle. (Indeed, they must have watched the passing of Richard's yildrih, but neither he nor the boatmen had been looking out for enemies; the hazards of the river and the prospect of arrival had engaged their whole attention.) Meantime the unicorn-riders, under the Faruzlaf's command, were massing high on the ridge.

Perhaps a message was somehow passed between the Pavonaran cohorts; perhaps the timing of the attack had been fixed beforehand with precision. Certainly, when the onslaught was launched upon Warrentown, it came at once from three flanks.

Yet, for all its careful timing and its speed, the assault failed. Since the guards on the towers were alert, the onrush from north and south was seen early. Before the unicorn-riders reached the semi-ruinous East Gate, its guards had withdrawn within the castle and the old, long drawbridge had been raised—effortfully and creakingly but successfully. Moreover, there were archers within both forecourts to greet the attackers with a bitter hail of arrows.

The South-east Forecourt had soon to be abandoned, but its defenders were able to retreat unscathed through a tunnel back into the East Bailey; they left many enemy dead behind them. For the Faruzlaf of Hregisel, it must have been a frustrating day. His battle plan had been executed perfectly, but it had not achieved its object.

After his soldiers had vented their ire by burning the riverside farms, Kalung Dastenost settled them in siege about Warrentown. An inner arc of guards was placed around the East Castle, on the riverside meadows and within and about the East Gate. Outer guard-posts, with unicorn-riders for message-carrying, were set further north and south on the meadowlands and higher on the east ridge, to give early alarm of any force seeking to break the siege. Camps were made amid the scrub of the valley bottoms, where the Pavonarans might find both concealment and protection from the weather.

The standard of the Pavonarans is purple and charged with a sword set with blade uppermost; that sword is pommelled and hilted in scarlet, its blade half-scarlet, half-black. (These combinations of hues offend against the rules of English heraldry; but then, the Pavonarans are not even aware of such rules.) The standard of Hregisel is green, charged with a skull in gold—a skull that lacks a lower jaw. To English eyes it is more heraldically acceptable, but it is a grim emblem. Both jacks were soon flying from the unruined tower of the East Gate: since the Faruzlaf had taken up residence there, the latter jack was his personal standard, bordered with gold. However, the Pavonarans sported no colourful surcoats, but instead wore jupons made from uvudu hides. Against the snow, it was never easy to watch their movements and, whenever snow or sleet were brought in by the wind, it became extremely difficult. From the battlements of Warrentown, there was much straining of eyes and little gaining of worthwhile information.

Spirits were high in the twin castles during the first days of the siege. The walls were mostly strong now, thanks to my father's energy, and the stocks of food were adequate. Yes, those Pavonaran flags might be aggressively displayed against the wind, but was not the Lyonessan standard—argent, a lion salient azure (a blue lion, leaping, on a silver field)—also flying, with that of Sir John and of Warrentown beside it? (Sir John's was a canting arms—vair, five conies statant sable; that is, five black rabbits on a field whose patterning suggested a warren.) So long as those two flags flew, there was nothing to fear!

However, from the time of arrival of our Safaddnese army on the heights above, the Lyonessans became more anxious. Why were we not attacking the Pavonarans? Why did we permit them, unassailed, to dig that trench and throw up that rampart on the east ridge, at once protecting themselves and further strengthening their grip on the East Castle? Even the more optimistic defenders of the city, realizing that we must be awaiting reinforcements, were deterred by the prospect of a long enduring of the siege. The more pessimistic began to question the motives of the Safaddnese. Did they truly intend to lend aid, or was the granting of land to the Lyonessans still resented? Might the Safaddnese be merely waiting, allowing the Pavonarans to waste their strength in taking Warrentown before attacking and destroying an army already reduced?

It was hard to sleep at nights, when an onslaught might be launched at any time. Nor could the defenders relax during the day, with rain and sleet veiling views and causing a constant uncertainty about enemy movements. How much easier things might have been, had the weather been clearer! From one midnight to the next, there was no chance to relax, to forget the imminence of danger. As day followed day, the need for unceasing vigilance placed ever greater strains upon nerves already at full stretch.

After the arrival of the Pavonarans, the repairing of the outer walls could not safely continue. My father strove at first to keep his men working, but it proved hard. Had the rebuilding of the curtain wall between the castle and bailey been feasible, they might have laboured with more enthusiasm, for that wall might have aided the defence of Warrentown. Unfortunately, such a task was too large to be attempted during a siege. As for the other repairs—the reconstruction of inner walls of towers and the building of new floors—his men could see small point in such endeavour. Why sweat at such tasks? If Warrentown withstood the siege, there'd be time enough for them. If it were destined to fall, why toil to make it more habitable, merely for the comfort of the Pavonarans?

To such arguments, my father could make little response. Consequently, the work was brought to an end. He went away to the West Castle to aid Mark Thistleton in the training of its unskilled defenders.

With trained soldiers in such short supply, Richard had been already removed by Sir John from those labours. My brother had been made captain of a contingent of soldiers consisting of eighteen men (three archers and fifteen men-at-arms). Since there were Brelinderimins among the defenders, Sir John found it easiest to employ the military terminology familiar to them; thus the unit was called a *devletel* and my brother gained the title *devletelar*.

Richard's was no easy charge. He and his soldiers were on guard duty for two four-hour stretches each day and spent four other hours largely in martial exercises. Since the times of duty and exercising were changed from day to day, it was not easy to snatch enough sleep. Consequently, at nights Richard had to tour his stretch of walls repeatedly, to make sure his men remained wakeful and vigilant.

On the tenth morning of the siege, while Avran and I were watching on the south slope of the ridge beyond the Pavonaran trench, Richard was on watch also—yet seeing even less than we. He and his devletel were manning the tower north-east of the bailey, immediately above the still-defended North-east Forecourt. His soldiers were quite as ill at ease as Avran; indeed, one came close to echoing my friend's words.

'What weather! How can a man keep guard, Master Richard, when he can see nought—nought at all! Why, with the mist this dense, I can't make out even our comrades below, let alone those accursed Pavonarans!'

'I agree it is difficult, Bevis. Yet we are almost at the turning of the tide. Mayhap there will be a wind from the sea, to drive away this murk.'

'Aye, 'tis possible. I trust so, master; because, were I that Kalung Dastenost, I'd not be letting such a chance as this slip by untried! Why, 'tis the thickest day since the year began!'

'Yet I hear nothing, Bevis—nothing to suggest any attack is imminent. Surely they're all snug in their tents, waiting for this weather to pass.'

The old archer—for such he was, a grizzled veteran of campaigns fought long before Sir Arthur Thurlstone, Sir John Warren and their followers sailed to Lyonesse—snorted disgustedly.

'If that be what they're doin', why then, they're a parcel of fools— and that Dastenost the biggest of 'em! I mind when I was in Scotland, following the old Earl of Northumberland—why, in such weather as this, the Douglas and his soldiers would have been on us in a trice, as eager for blood as gazehounds in sight of a stag!'

But Richard was no longer paying attention. Instead, he was leaning forward against the battlement and looking out into the dense mist.

'Do I not hear something after all, Bevis?' he whispered. 'Some sound, down there in the fosse?'

'Happen you do!' The old archer had tensed. 'Aye, surely men are moving there! Gamlin, lad'—he called to one of the two boys attached to the devletel as messengers—'haste away and sound the alarm!'

But it was already too late. Almost as Bevis ceased speaking, there came the chorusing of ikhils that heralded the Pavonaran assault—sharp blasts from below, fainter sounds from somewhere in the distance.

'You're right, Bevis.' Richard was grim. 'They're attacking on several fronts. I trust we may hold them off, but I fear it will prove a stiff struggle. May God grant us aid!'

The archer had already strung his bow and was nocking an arrow. He grinned up at Richard, for he was shorter than my brother. 'Well, d'you see, the Dastenost is not such a fool! As to whether God will aid us, no doubt He's decided already. Meantime we must strive our best. He'll not help any laggards in the fray, be sure of that!'

Yes, Warrentown was under attack; yet, for Richard and Bevis and the others in the tower, it was hard to make out what was happening and impossible, without leaving their station, to intervene. The mist was thick enough on the ridge; about the castle, it was so dense that they could not see even into the North-east Forecourt.

From the sounds of fray, it became quickly evident that the Pavonarans must have entered that Forecourt already. Its loss seemed inevitable. Would its defenders be able to escape back into the bailey? Yes, there was a tunnel; but how many would attain it and how closely would they be pursued? To be so near, yet unable to lend aid or even to know what was happening, was profoundly frustrating and distressing.

'I like this not at all, Bevis,' complained Richard. 'Why . . . ?' But at that point he broke off, for the archer had grasped his wrist and was pointing.

What was that, rising through the mist over to their right, just beyond the point where the tower ended and the wall linking it to the inner gatehouse began—that strange, long upthrusting shape, like a stiff snake with widely flaring, fanged mouth? Up it came, then toppled forward against the wall.

Only belatedly did the two understand what they were seeing—the upper part of a scaling ladder, its uprights ending in rosettes of barbs that might find purchase even on smooth stone. Calling to his men, Richard rushed down onto the wall. Bevis was close at his heels, bow already half-drawn and arrow at string, ready to be loosed at whatever unwise Pavonaran climbed up first.

Yet whatever *was* coming up the ladder? No man, this; but a shape of horror, whiter than the fog, huge-seeming, vaguely man-like but quite faceless!

Richard's indrawn breath was matched by Bevis's gasp, but the old archer was not deterred. He notched and loosed—and yes, the arrow hit home!

The thing seemed to fall back a little at the arrow's impact; but then it resumed its advance. The feathered shaft could be seen standing out from its centre. The arrowhead must be deeply buried into its body, but there was no wound, no blood . . .

Again Bevis loosed; again the arrow struck home and the white thing was briefly pushed back; but again it resumed its advance. It was near the top of the ladder now—a crudely man-like shape, with head rounded and featureless; blunt, fingerless hands upraised as if to seize; and thick, short legs that were balanced not on the rungs, but on the uprights of the ladder!

Two of the men of the devletel were probing at the nearest rosette of barbs with the wedge-point of a crowbar, striving to unbalance the ladder; but they were doing it clumsily, for they were sweating with fear. As for the man-thing—why, it was halting, bracing and, yes, *leaping* forward on to the wall!

Its leap took it through the embrasure between two merlons of the crenellated wall, so that it landed square onto the wall-walk. The men with the crowbar jumped back in terror, but another soldier bravely swung his sword at the thing. His blade sunk into it and wedged, pushing the man-thing sideways; yet it made no sound. With a wail, the soldier clawed at his sword-hilt, then turned and fled.

Yet the thing did not pursue him, nor did it seek to injure the others. Indeed, it was curiously passive.

Only a sound from behind caused Richard to turn his gaze from it. Two Pavonaran soldiers—massive men wearing fur jupons over mail-coats and carrying unsheathed swords—were at the top of the ladder and about to leap onto the wall-walk. As they did, the man-thing settled forward at a strange angle over the inner side of the wall. Richard noticed the long bar protruding from its back, and at last realized what it was—a dummy in the shape of a man! Those two soldiers had pushed it up the ladder before them, to take the arrows that might otherwise have been directed at themselves—and to frighten the Lyonessans.

Well, their stratagem had succeeded. Now there were Pavonarans on the wall, too close to be shot at safely by Bevis—and looking to be formidable warriors! Moreover, they were favoured by the fact that the narrowness of the wall-walk prevented any attack by more than one Lyonessan at a time. Already the first Pavonaran had beaten down a defender, while the second was engaged in brisk sword-play with another of Richard's men.

Richard had been frightened, but now the memory of fear brought anger. Snatching his sword from its scabbard, he leapt at the Pavonaran who had slain the soldier.

His enemy was a bigger man, but he was still breathless from his climb. His eyes were concealed under the umbril of his burgonet, but Richard could glimpse his drawn cheeks and hear his harsh breath. A thrust, blocked barely in time by a parry; a flurry of strokes and counters; then, suddenly, the way was open for a second, mightier thrust from Richard—a thrust that drove through furs and chain-mail beneath. The soldier was avenged!

As the Pavonaran tumbled backward, he fell against a third who had just leapt onto the wall. Richard drew his sword out effortlly, yet he did it before that other Pavonaran had quite fended off his comrade's corpse. As Richard thrust at him, that third man tried to step back, caught his foot on the bottomstone of the embrasure, and fell shrieking from the wall.

The other Pavonaran was still engaged and the fourth had paused on the ladder, made fearful by the third man's fall. In two quick strides, Richard seized the bar at the back of the man-dummy and picked it up. Though it seemed carven in stone, it was remarkably light! He swung it in an arc upward and threw it out through the embrasure.

Over it went, catching the fourth man upon the crest of his burgonet. Wailing in fear, he loosed his hold on the ladder and fell, tumbling the two men behind him so that all three disappeared backward into the mist. From the frantic sounds, others must be in trouble also, somewhere below out of view.

The remaining Pavonaran, distracted by Richard's action, had been beaten to his knees by one of the Lyonessans. As Richard turned about, that surviving enemy succumbed to a swordthrust.

'The crowbar!' Richard cried. 'Quick—we must prise the ladder loose, ere more Pavonarans mount it!'

Freed from the distracting menace of the man-thing and with little weight left on the ladder, the defenders soon dislodged an upright. The ladder twisted and fell away from the wall. The cries from below suggested that its fall must have wrought further havoc among the Pavonarans. However, Richard had no time to think about that, for another of his soldiers was hastening.

'Master Richard, you're needed! The Pavonarans—they're on the wall west of the tower! Come quickly!'

Indeed, the Pavonarans' device had succeeded much better there. The strange shape on that second scaling ladder—another dummy— had caused the defenders to give back in fear; nor had they recovered so swiftly. Six Pavonarans were already on the wall below the North-east Tower, while others were even then mounting the scaling-ladder.

Yet the Lyonessans were fighting back. Their enemies were striving in vain to mount the short stairway from wall-walk to tower; moreover, an archer in the neighbouring tower of the East Castle itself was picking off the men still on the ladder. In fifteen minutes of brisk fighting, the Pavonarans from this second assault were driven back and slain; and, ere long, that second ladder was also sent toppling.

This time the dummy had been left on the wall. Richard examined it curiously. Yes, it did seem to be of stone, yet it was so pale in colour, so full of pores, and so very light! He had seen pieces of a curious material called pumice, brought into England from Flanders or somewhere farther afield and used by clerks to soak up ink from their parchments. Could this be the same stuff? Yet those were always small fragments, and this was so big!

Once again, Richard was given little time to reflect. A boy messenger, face shining with the sweat of extreme haste, came running up to him.

'Master!' he cried. 'Oh, master! Sir John sends word—there's trouble, great trouble! The Pavonarans—they've broken into the East Castle itself!'

'How?' Richard asked blankly.

'Where the wall—where the wall was down!' the boy panted.

'They've floated boats out into the river from the bank and—and then they used ladders—scaling ladders! They've climbed the cliff! They're into the Castle!'

'That's ill news! Thus Sir John—he'll be needing me there?'

'No, not that, that's not the illest news! Sir John, he thinks he might hold them, mayhap even drive them back—he has good strength there. But he requires you elsewhere! He says you're to give Master Bevis the command here, with half your men. Then you're to take the rest and hasten to the West Castle!'

As the boy sought breath after that tumble of words, Richard gazed at him blankly: 'To the West Castle? Why, surely *that's* safe enough?'

'Nay, it's not, it's not! In the mist, the Pavonarans—why, they've ferried a strong force across the Lemmeshind, much stronger than our defence! Master Mark—his men aren't much good; he needs aid if they're to fight 'em off. And all the women and childer are there! They can't get away!'

Chapter Twenty

THE BRIDGE BETWEEN THE TOWERS

Thus the stratagems of Kalung Dastenost were at last revealed. He had indeed planned well. Anticipating confidently that, at this late-winter season, there must come a day of blizzard or thick mist, he had readied his army for an assault on Warrentown whenever that opportunity was offered.

Yes indeed, Avran and I had heard the ring of axes below us. Maybe we had been in part right; maybe some of the wood had been used to make shelters for the Pavonarans; but that had not been its principal employment. There must have been skilled carpenters in the Faruzlaf of Hregisel's train and some watermen also. Most of the wood had gone into the making of the scaling-ladders and other contrivances which, on this day, had brought the Pavonaran attack already so near to overwhelming Warrentown.

Rafts had been constructed upriver, in a place where the current came close in a deep channel to the east bank before swinging away toward the west. They had been launched two or three nights earlier, loaded with soldiers, weapons and scaling-ladders, and sent off with the current. When they neared the west bank, they had been poled to the shore. Under the command of Kalung's deputy, the young Faruzlaf of Brachang, that Pavonaran cohort had made its slow and careful way toward Warrentown, finding concealment not too far away till conditions became right for the attack.

Kalung Dastenost, experienced warrior that he was, must have early perceived the one serious weakness in the defence of the East Castle—the collapsed section of wall on its south-west side. This was above a steep cliff and the river; consequently Sir John Warren—and yes, even my father—had thought that section safe from assault.

Not so! The Dastenost had conceived a method for attack at that weak point. It was one that would work only when weather conditions limited visibility for, in clear conditions, the vigilant guard would have given alarm too soon.

The Pavonarans had constructed three pontoons. Two of these were light and narrow, intended merely to be used as floating bridges. The third, however, was made more massive, to serve as a stable base for scaling-ladders; indeed, an erect wall had been built in mid-vessel, against which those ladders might be braced. A huge post had been sunk into the riverside mud, to which the pontoons would be roped after launching. Until this day of attack, they had been kept hidden ashore under piled plant fronds plastered over with snow; then in the mist, they had been attached together and set afloat, the great one outermost. It was the splash of the launching that Avran and I had heard, but not understood.

One has to respect the Dastenost's planning, but one must respect equally the perfect discipline of his troops. The Pavonarans were, above all things, a military people. From childhood, they were taught not merely to value most highly the martial arts, but to despise all others, as suited only to slaves and subject peoples. That is, in my judgement, a regrettable attitude; though I admire the arts of war, I admire even more those of peace. Yet it does generate the ideal soldiers for such assaults. The Faruzlaf's men had already been in a ring about eastern Warrentown; that ring had closed so silently that the soldiers' movements had not been detected by the mist-blinded, yet still vigilant Lyonessans. When the time came, the assault had been a perfectly concerted one, from all three sides.

For the cohort on the western bank, the difficulties had been greater. The Faruzlaf of Brachang had needed to keep his men well south of the West Castle, for their presence on that bank must not be discovered too early. Only on that morning of mist had his men begun their advance on the castle; and even then, they had not risked climbing the ridge, where any breath of wind might expose them too soon to the eyes of the Lyonessan guards. Instead they had kept to the lower places. Some had silently entered into the ruined South-west Forecourt while others had passed through the western fosse, quietly to infiltrate the even more ruinous North-west Forecourt also. They had performed the manoeuvre perfectly, but they had been somewhat later in taking up position and launching their assault—not surprisingly, when they could neither see nor hear what was happening on the opposite bank.

On our eastern bank, the Pavonaran attack had virtually succeeded. I do not doubt that the Dastenost hoped the attempts at scaling the walls of the East Bailey might work—the man-dummies were a neat device for circumventing the threat of the Lyonessan archers—but those attacks were essentially feints. They were designed to distract the defenders' attention from the principal attack—the attack upon the East Castle itself, from the pontoons. And so they did; the Pavonarans were up the cliff and into the castle before Sir John was even aware of that assault.

Yet in one way, those feints had worked to the disadvantage of the Pavonarans. Though Richard did not know it, the scaling-ladder attack from the South-west Forecourt—a forecourt indefensible and undefended—had been launched ahead of that from the North-west Forecourt, which had needed to be taken by the Pavonarans. The device of the man-dummies had brought the attackers up onto the walls and there had been a bloody enough skirmish before first one, and then a second and a third, scaling-ladder assault had been thrown back. Richard had lost one man; Gerard Turnbull, devletelar of the south-east tower, lost seven.

However, he had learned early, if painfully, the true nature of the man-dummies; and he proved wiser than Richard, for he had thought to send warning of them by runner to Sir John. Sir John, in turn, had transmitted that warning to the commander of the West Castle, Mark Thistleton. As a consequence, the mock-men did not give Mark's men the sort of fright they had caused the East Castle's defenders. Yet they did serve their other purpose; they screened the climbing Pavonarans from arrows and functioned as shields during the first leap onto the walls.

On that western bank, the fortifications had no serious external weakness. The Pavonarans needed to enter both bailey and castle by direct assault. Thus, though repeatedly thrown back, attacks by scaling-ladder were launched again and again. Since the Pavonarans not only heavily outnumbered the Lyonessans but were also better soldiers than most of the defenders, there was a real danger that the attacks might eventually succeed. In the meantime, moreover, they were causing Sir John serious problems, for he was having to send experienced soldiers from the East Castle to lend backbone to the defence of the West. Richard and his men were not the first, but almost the last, to be despatched across the Lemmeshind.

Following Richard were two archers and seven men-at-arms. As ordered, old Bevis had been left behind and seven men-at-arms with him; two of them were wounded and he who would have been the eighth, completing the letel, was dead.

Richard and his men were moving as swiftly as they might. For that reason, they did not descend into the bailey, nor yet into the inner ward of the East Castle. Instead, they followed the walls. They ran swiftly along the wall-walk atop the East Bailey's northern curtain, then climbed the narrow, unparapeted stairway that linked it to the north tower of the East Castle. Its guards could not see them clearly in the dense mist and met them with drawn swords, but the points were lowered swiftly at recognition and the runners were waved past.

It was then that, for the first time, Richard felt a tug of wind at his sleeves—only a brief gust, dying away too fast, but one that caused him to glance speculatively seaward.

'Aye, the tide's just about on the turn.' One of the guards had observed that glance. 'Maybe this thick brume will soon be blown away.'

'Aye, maybe,' my brother responded curtly. He hastened onward, round the tower's outer perimeter—its inner side was too ruinous to be traversed—and down a few steps onto the wall-walk of the curtain beyond, a wall higher than that surrounding the bailey. Below, within the ward, were the snow-covered roofs of the cottages built against the wall. In happier times, the smoke of their chimneys would have been rising to him, but now all fires were out. Somewhere beyond, Sir John's men must be battling the Pavonarans: Richard could hear the clash of swords, but the mist prevented any view of that desperate fight. On the outer side the walls plunged downward into the mist, their footings on the river cliffs hidden from view.

Yet not for long, perhaps! Again Richard felt wind clutching at his sleeves. This time, however, it did not die away, but strengthened. It seemed to be coming straight down the estuary, from due north— very unusually, for most winds that blew on Warrentown came from varying points of the west or east.

Soon the wind was causing the mist to swirl below him, like curds agitated by a horn spoon. It was a dizzifying spectacle; Richard looked away, concentrating on the wall-walk and his haste. Behind him he could hear the hopeful murmurings of his men. How useful it would be, to be able to see clearly what those accursed Pavonarans were doing!

Now Richard and his men were approaching the western tower of the East Castle, an arcuate outerwork of the massive still-roofless keep. (Only on sunny days had Sir Arthur and Sir John been able to hold feast in its great banqueting-hall.) There was a second narrow, parapet-less flight of steps to be mounted. Up Richard went, more than a little breathless now, but still dogged in his determination to be speedy—and almost lost balance, as there came much the strongest wind-gust in many short winter days.

A guard helped him to stumble up through an embrasure between two merlons of this highest tower's battlements, then turned to assist the soldiers who were following. One had come close to falling onto the chimneys below; he was gasping in fear and needed to be steadied up those last steps. Yet Richard was, for once, paying no attention to his men. Instead, he was looking outward.

Yes, the curtain of mist was lifting—or rather, being torn into shreds by the rising wind. Now he could see down the full fall of the cliffs to the river, almost a straight drop, but with just a few ledges where snow still clung to the untidy remains of river-birds' nests. Below, the Lemmeshind's muddy waters were beginning to be agitated by the wind, like wine slopping in a goblet borne by some hurrying page. Richard could not yet see across the Lemmeshind to the West Castle, but at least his eyes could follow the line of the bridge for some distance out over the water.

The long bridge over the Lemmeshind had its origins in two stone bastions, one built out from this western tower of the East Castle, the other from the eastern tower of the West Castle. To cross the bridge, one had first to ascend one of those towers, then walk out on the bastion to its outermost salient. The bridge itself was a perilous sort of structure, designed to be broken readily at need. Essentially it consisted of just four ropes, two at foot level with planks tied crossways between them, two at waist level to form hand-holds for the nervous on calm days and for all on windy days. The nervous were scarcely to be blamed when the bridge was so narrow, so frail and so high—quite eighty feet above the Lemmeshind's waters, even at normal flood-tide.

'Haste now!' Richard snapped at his men—unfairly, since it was he who had been lingering—and led them out through the portal giving onto the bridge bastion. There they were briefly protected from the wind by one of the great stone buttresses that sustained the bridge's ropes. Consequently, when they ventured out onto the bridge itself, the wind's increased force again surprised them.

Richard, again in the lead, staggered and then seized a hand-rope to steady himself. It was stiff and slippery with ice, hard to grasp with gauntleted hands. 'Have a care!' he called to the men still on the bastion. Then he strove to go onward as fast as he might. However, to do so was not easy. Though the planks had not retained ice like the ropes, they were slippery with the moisture of melting.

Still the wind was strengthening—why, it must be approaching gale force already, and how bleakly bitter it was! A gale from the north was surely something unusual for Warrentown; unprecedented, mayhap! The bridge was beginning to jerk sideways, up and down, in a most irregular and alarming fashion, making it harder yet to retain foothold. Yes, the mist was clearing; but Richard could not spare any glances out over the river, or even toward the West Castle. It was becoming all that he could do to watch his footing and haul himself from handhold to handhold, staggering and slipping as the planks under his feet shifted and pitched.

There were cries of dismay behind, but Richard could not turn to see how his soldiers were faring. He found that he was sweating, quite as much from alarm as from effort. How old were these ropes? They did not look fresh. How well, in their present frozen condition, could they withstand such a wind? If one broke . . . but no, he must not think about that; he must think only about getting across.

There was snow in the gale now, tiny hard particles peppering his face like hard pellets from some mischievous child's blowpipe. Yet the snow surely could not last, for the sky was brightening—how strange! Another hand-hold; loose the last and haul yourself forward, Richard; and another. My, how the planks were pitching, how this crazy bridge was swaying!

The loud complaints from behind had ceased. Was it that the roar of the wind was swallowing up the sound? Much likelier that his men no longer had breath to complain!

Well, he was past the bridge's dip now and heaving himself onward and upward. More than halfway, then! No, don't look down; just keep onward! That plank—it's loose. Care! don't step on it! Another haul, then a hand-hold slipped and he came close to falling. His brief pause for breath, though necessary, was not comforting, with the bridge bucketing so. On again . . . Ah! at last, the buttresses were looming ahead—almost across! Only five more steps now! Four; three; two—and Richard stumbled off the planks, to stagger and shiver on the solidity of the stone bastion.

After the drawing of a few welcome breaths of comparatively still air, Richard turned about, to steady the lurching last step of the archer who had been following him. How much worse it must have been, to be encumbered with a longbow on such a crossing! Between them, they helped the other men into the welcome, stable shelter of the bridge's western buttresses. Several were grey with fear and the last, quite a youngster, had to be fetched from the bridge. He had been clinging to the ropes and sobbing, his nerve gone.

When all were gathered, Richard led the way in through the open portal. He was surprised that no guards had come to aid them and even more so that none were in view on the wall-walk beyond. Might they be too heavily engaged with the Pavonarans to be still manning this, perhaps the least endangered of the West Castle's towers? If so, then the situation must be truly serious!

Ah, but there the guards were—all in a cluster, down on the sunken wooden floor of the tower's northernmost section, below wall-walk level. However, their eyes were not for Richard and his much-shaken men. Instead, they were gazing out through the grilles of the two windows that penetrated the tower's wall. Harry Windeck, devletelar in command of this tower, was a close friend of Richard's; but even when Richard called to his friend, he was scarce spared a glance. Instead, he was gestured peremptorily to the nearer window.

'Look seaward, Richard—look seaward!'

Blinking a little at the gale's cold force through the iron grille-bars, Richard duly looked out—and immediately understood the soldiers' lack of interest in his men and he. Their attention was held by an infinitely more dramatic spectacle.

Chapter Twenty-one

A GALE FROM THE SEA

While in Bristol Richard had been told tales of the Severn bore, that great wave produced when the advancing tide is restricted by the estuary's funnel-like narrowing and grows steadily in height as it travels inland, till it becomes an advancing wall of water quite forty feet high. However, he had never seen it; nor, though the Lemmeshind flows out into a bay that is likewise funnel-shaped, had he witnessed any very spectacular tides during all his months in Warrentown. But then, there had never in those months been the coincidence of the onset of a full gale from the north with the rising of the tide.

The wave now advancing upon Warrentown must surely be vastly bigger than any that Bristol had ever seen! It was yet far off and approaching with a silent-seeming smoothness that was deceptive, but Richard had no doubt of its destructive power. With the sky bright behind it and the river dark before it, the wave appeared a thing of shining metal—like an argent line on a shield, separating the azure of the sky from the dull yellowish-brown of the Lemmeshind's waters—or better, like a bright sword-blade swinging sidewise upon Warrentown!

Harry Windeck nudged him. 'Look to your left, Richard.'

Richard did so. This keep-flank tower was so much higher than the others of the West Castle that, now the mist had lifted, the view of the castle from it was quite broad. Indeed, he could see even beyond the farthest tower to the west ridge; it had been blown almost clear of snow and formed a high brown hummock against the whiteness of the distant hills. Looking down, his eyes travelled along the curtain wall as far as the north tower, though the outer wall of the West Bailey was hidden from view; and below, he could gaze into the North-west Forecourt, marged as it was by only the foundations of walls.

That whole Forecourt seemed a-boil with Pavonarans. Two scaling-ladders were set against the wall, with soldiers surging up each to strengthen the hold already gained upon the wall-walk; for the Lyonessans had yielded the wall to them and retreated into the two towers. Arrows were being shot at the attackers from the north tower, but the archers seemed inept; few of those arrows were finding a mark.

'I have men defending the stair to this tower,' Harry remarked quietly. 'The Pavonarans will not enter it; and, you know, they're not yet aware of the great wave.'

Richard looked seaward again, to be astonished by how much that wave seemed to have grown. Why, it must be twice forty feet in height, vastly greater than any Bristol had seen! Moreover, its front was much wider now; its waters must have spilled over to inundate the sea-meadows on either side of the Lemmeshind. It was as if the very ocean itself were rising and advancing upon them!

With a sudden sick feeling, Richard remembered the fate of the earlier Lyonesse. Had Sir Arthur Thurlstone thrown down a gauntlet before God, by choosing that old name for his new realm? Would the new Lyonesse be destroyed by the sea, as the old had been?

One of the watching soldiers was a Brelinderimin; his perception was more optimistic. 'Why, in this hour of our need, Edaénar is summoning the sea to our aid! Blessed be the Nine Names all! *Ilai ushazan! Ilai ushazan!*'

Louder and yet louder howled the gale; closer and closer loomed the great wave. Yet still the Pavonarans were not aware of it, even though the whole marshlands north of Warrentown were being engulfed! In the Forecourt below, the soldiers were still milling around, intent only upon their battle. A third scaling-ladder, one that had earlier fallen, had been repaired and was being again raised. On this wall and probably upon the West Castle's other walls, men were still fighting and still dying. Even as Richard glanced leftward, he saw a Pavonaran stricken by an arrow and toppling from the wall.

Ah! the wave was upon Warrentown! A great wall of water was breaking upon the stones marging the North-west Forecourt and, with a roar, plunging forward. Yet, even through that uprush of surging water, air and sound, Richard could hear a wail of terror. At last, too late, the Pavonarans were aware of the doom come upon them!

Richard saw heads above the water with mouths open, screaming. He saw scaling-ladders crushed with contemptuous ease and left bobbing on the water like freshly-fallen twigs. He felt the shock as the great wave met the solid stone of the tower and saw how the Pavonarans upon the walls were thrown down. Some, the more fortunate, tumbled only onto their knees, but several fell shrieking to their deaths on the snow-hidden stones of the ward within.

Richard found himself praying frantically, wordlessly, for God's mercy, as were other Lyonessans about him. The Brelinderimin was calling upon Edaénar, his own god of the sea and the particular god of Vasanderim, in an awed mixture of congratulation and extreme apprehension.

Yes, indeed there was reason for congratulation—or, at least, for profound gratitude. The strong stones of the two fortresses of Warrentown had withstood the shock of the great wave and survived unscathed. A spray of seawater through the arrowslits, when the wave broke against the walls, was all that had entered into ward or bailey. In contrast, Warrentown's enemies were overwhelmed. Not even the strongest swimmer could survive in such bleakly turbulent waters—and certainly not soldiers in fur and armour! All who had been outside had been drowned. They were sunk beyond view or become mere flotsam amid the tossing waves.

Suddenly Richard and the others within the tower found themselves carolling and hugging one another in frantic joy. Warrentown was spared! Warrentown was saved!

As for the few Pavonarans who had retained footing on the nearby wall-walk, they were stricken with shock—entirely too stricken to withstand the assault soon launched upon them from the east and north towers. A few attempted resistance and were slain. The others—quite a dozen of them—let fall their weapons and spread their arms out horizontally, in the Rockalese gesture of capitulation to a foe. The battle for the northern walls was over.

At the time of onset of the wave, Sir William, our father, was quite as unprepared for it as the Pavonarans. He had been given specific charge by Mark Thistleton of the gate-tower of the West Bailey and overall responsibility for the defence of its whole west wall. Stationed in that tower with him were old Ben of Heeley and three other archers of smaller skill, together with two devletelar of ill-trained men-at-arms, more of them Brelinderimins than Lyonessans and all, from the outset, apprehensive of the defeat they felt to be inevitable — for they had lost confidence from the moment they realized that the Pavonarans had gained the west bank.

Yet they had fought hard and had not fared as badly as expected; or not, at least, so far. This was in part because the curtain walls fronting the western fosse were less easy of access from below than those on the castle's northern and southern sides. Even so, some scaling-ladders had been raised against them and, in attempting to gain a foothold on the west wall, the Pavonarans had slain or wounded several men. However, the arrows of Ben and the other archers had wreaked enough havoc to deny their enemies any lasting lodgement.

Three fresh scaling-ladders had been raised, two on the north and one on the south flank of the gate-tower, and the struggle was at its bitterest when father felt the shock of the wave's impact upon Warrentown. He clutched at the merlon beside him to keep from falling over. Before he had time properly to grasp what was happening, he saw a wall of water surging through the fosse, sweeping ladders, weapons and men to destruction. At one moment, it seemed, the fosse was crowded with Pavonaran soldiers; at the next, it had been washed clean of them.

Swiftly the surge spilled out onto the meadowland south of the castle, to encounter and briefly drive back the waters of the already swollen, and now tide-pent, Lemmeshind. Then the waters merged and became one rising flood. The meadows and scrub were speedily swamped; even the lower, densely wooded slopes marging the valley were soon inundated.

Long before then, the Pavonarans in the South-west Forecourt were crying out in fear and scurrying around frantically. They were even more unfortunate than the wave's earlier victims, for they had time to comprehend the nature of the doom that faced them.

Mark Thistleton, who was in command of the southern defences, afterward gave us an account of what happened. In its way, it was more appalling than events elsewhere, for the Pavonarans' terror utterly destroyed their discipline. Some struggled to mount the scaling-ladders, in such frantic self-seeking that one ladder was overset. Others sought to climb up onto the cliffs below the walls, kicking away the desperately clutching arms of their fellows below; and a few, who had found precarious lodgement on the highest stones of the Forecourt's ruined outerworks, menaced with swords or axes any that sought to displace them.

By then, however, waters were pouring in through the Forecourt's river-devoured eastern end and through the breach in its southern side. A few Pavonarans were dragged by their friends up from the ladders to safety on the curtain wall. All the others, even those who had climbed highest on the cliffs, were caught in the swash of the tide and dragged down to death in its backwash. If any strove to swim clear, none succeeded.

The wave was moving on upriver and dwindling as the undertow of river water deprived it of vigour. Soon the Lemmeshind had so entirely overtopped its banks that, as far as sight extended, its waters formed a great lake filling the lower valley from side to side. Across this crawled the diminishing wave, fading in scale and from view.

The Faruzlaf of Brachang's cohort of Pavonarans, so great a menace to Warrentown so recently, had effectively ceased to exist as a fighting unit. He himself was not accounted for; it was believed he must have been drowned in the fosse when the wave broke upon Warrentown, but no-one was sure. As for the Pavonarans on the southern wall, they soon surrendered.

Yet a substantial component of that cohort remained undestroyed by the rising waters. Why? Because, with the need for concealment past, the Pavonarans had seized the west ridge and raised their monarch's flag over the ruined West Gate. On that ridge the Faruzlaf had stationed his reserve, ready to reinforce the attackers as soon as a strong enough toehold was gained within bailey or castle. Of the three thousand or so Pavonarans who had been ferried across the river, quite eight hundred were still mustered on the ridge—enough to remain a threat to undermanned Warrentown.

Whether they would have striven to renew the assault on the city, I question. Their spirits must have been shattered by the spectacle they had witnessed. It was enough, surely, to demonstrate that the gods were not with them in this war; no, not even their own god of the sun, however he was named. Moreover, they would have perceived soon, even if they did not already comprehend, that they were isolated: they were on the wrong side of the Lemmeshind, without boats or even rafts by which to cross its wide, bleak waters and with no real hope of returning to Pavonara. As it proved, however, they were given no opportunity to make any decision.

My father, though not appointed seneschal of the West Castle, was nevertheless its senior knight. If the Pavonarans were to be persuaded to lay down their arms, it was his task to arrange that capitulation. Yet he was hesitating—and for good reason. Between the Pavonarans and the castle there was now a deep ditch of icily cold, muddy water. It could be traversed only if the drawbridge were lowered; and that could scarcely be risked, when those Pavonarans were still so well armed and so much more numerous than the Lyonessan defenders. No mutual code of signals was available, by which proposals for negotiation might be transmitted. What, then, was to be done?

While my father was pondering this question, suddenly old Ben of Heeley clutched his arm. Like many elderly men, he had excellent long sight. He was gazing up the ridge that rose to the west of the bailey.

'Cast your eye up there, Sir William!' he exclaimed. 'Right high on yon ridge—yes, there! Do I not see riders—many riders?'

Indeed he did. Moreover, they were approaching at high speed—at the charge, for the Pavonarans had been perceived!

As the riders came closer, there was a yell of joy from the defenders. Was that not the banner of Avakalim—azure, bearing a taron in gold with wings elevated and displayed? Assuredly it was—and not just one banner, but many, among them the gold-edged standard of the letzahar himself. Yes, the whole of Avakalim had rallied to the aid of Lyonesse!

The Pavonarans did not panic at this spectacle; nor did they offer to yield or even seek to parley. Instead, under the sharp commands of whatever officer was in charge, they strove to form into lines of defence—spearmen at the fore, javelotiers second in position, and axemen behind.

However, they were not given the opportunity properly to carry out that manoeuvre. In places, some soldiers did find their appointed situation; but elsewhere, the Pavonarans were still milling for position when the charge came upon them.

Some javelots were hurled and some riders were sent tumbling, but the charge broke right into the defensive line. In among the Pavonarans rode the Avakalimins, endeavouring to strike down their unmounted enemies. Yet the Pavonarans were not deterred, for they had experienced such charges before. They yielded ground at the approach of the veludain, then closed back and worried like wolves at their enemies' flanks.

By then, Richard had come to join father. Abruptly he gave an exclamation and gestured.

'See—on the black veludu, the rider with shield at arm and in full suit of chain-mail? I'll swear 'tis Sir Robert—Sir Robert Randwulf, of whom I told you!'

'And on the white veludu, by his side—who is that? Surely 'tis no man, but a woman! Mark how her golden hair streams out beneath her helmet! My, but she must be a spirited creature!'

Richard had tensed. 'Why, it is the Princess—Princess Hiludessa! I trust that all will go well for her. I like not to see any woman in battle—and so beautiful a lady as she ... The letzahar should not have permitted it!'

Father gave him a searching glance. 'If she be a Princess, and one of such ancientry and such power, he'd find it hard to gainsay her! And see now, how the Pavonarans are holding ground ... yet what is happening? Why, they're retreating! To try to hold the West Gate ruins, I'd suppose. Sir Robert and the Princess, they're in the path of that retreat ... they and only three others! They should strive to break through. Do they not perceive that they're in danger of being cut off?'

'Aye, and dakhmen Perespeth—he's no idea what's happening!' Ben of Heeley was equally intent. 'See, he's leading a charge over there, into that mass of Pavonarans over on the south side. You do well to fear for the Princess, Richard my lad! She and the old knight, I fear they're doomed.'

Suddenly Richard became quite frantic. 'Have the drawbridge lowered, father—have the drawbridge lowered! You and I, we can't let them be slain—we must haste to their aid!'

Father glanced at him again, then laughed suddenly. 'So be it! Glad am I that I chose to repair this drawbridge, not the other old creaker! Gather your men—I'll give the order!'

Father's self-congratulation was justified. With the howl of the gale still so loud and the drawbridge's mechanism so recently over-hauled and so well oiled, its lowering was not heard by the Pavonar-ans. Nor was that lowering seen, for none were watching the castle; the eyes of all were on the Avakalimins. So it was that the force Richard had rallied—a strong one, for all were now in high heart and most eager for the fray—was across the fosse and attacking them from the rear before the Pavonarans were even aware of any new danger.

By then, however, two of the five riders had been overborne and slain. Robin, perceiving that he and his companions were becoming isolated, beckoned to them and charged into the thick of the enemy.

Unfortunately, his signal was not perceived by the Princess or by her companion, a small figure on a rather ungainly veludu. Consequently, though Robin made space for them by cutting a considerable swathe with his sword—I am sure no Pavonarans guessed that his left arm was strapped to his shield and useless!—the two did not follow him. Nor, when Robin tried to turn his mount about, could he do so. The press had become too close to allow any such change of direction.

Meantime a knot of Pavonaran warriors had tightened about the other two riders. Even as the Lyonessans charged out through the West Gate, an axe crashed down upon the neck of the big veludu and it fell sideways upon its rider.

However, the attack from behind was a shock that the beleaguered Pavonarans could not withstand. The Lyonessan contingent—it included Brelinderimins and Avakalimins—drove through them like a wedge, Richard leading them straight toward the place where the Princess was striving to fight off her enemies. Yet, even as they approached, the white veludu was also brought down.

Indeed, that rescue attempt came almost too late. When her veludu fell, Essa had leapt from its back to the ground; but she was tripped by a flailing back hoof and fell, losing her sword. As Richard approached, a Pavonaran was grinningly raising his axe, gloating at his chance to slay one of the foremost of his enemies.

Quite how Richard contrived to save the Princess from death, I have never altogether understood. According to Essa, he turned himself into a javelot and hurled himself, swordpoint foremost, at the axeman! Such a tale I cannot quite believe; yet I must confess that his leap succeeded. Richard's blade struck the axe, diverting it from its downward sweep; and he and the axeman fell together in a struggling tangle.

Before either could rise, Essa had scrambled to her feet, seized her sword and driven it into the Pavonaran. Thus it was she, not Richard, that slew her last assailant.

Her last, because by then the Pavonarans were throwing down their weapons and crying for quarter. It was quite time. Of the original eight hundred or so, less than a hundred remained alive and many of those were wounded. The battle on the Lemmeshind's west bank was over.

It was the Princess who helped Richard to his feet. She smiled at him.

'Richard Branthwaite, is it not?' According to my father, who was standing by, she managed our difficult surname astonishingly well that time; but maybe he was not being critical. 'And Sir William? When Sir Robert Randwulf is not around—and, for that matter, even when he is—it is good to have Branthwaites by me! Sir Robert and Simon have each several times saved my life; I owe them both a great debt. And now you gentlemen have put me deeper into obligation—I shall not forget it.'

Richard flushed with embarrassment and pleasure. 'Nay, it is you that saved me; that Pavonaran had me pinned!'

'Only because you came so bravely to my aid. But Dan Wyert—' her smile turned to a frown of anxiety '—he was fighting by me till his beast was brought down. I fear he may have been slain, as were my two Ayanian guards—and he had become dear to me. Let us seek him quickly!'

Poor Taru Taletang and his lieutenant, an Ayanian whose name I never learned, had indeed travelled with Essa over all the miles through Avakalim to Warrentown, only to die while striving vainly to defend her. For all his high birth and high pride, Taru had little good fortune.

Yet Dan Wyert was not dead, though they thought so at first. The body of Remdegel ('Longshank', as we called her) lay half across him and he was drenched in blood—but the blood was that of the slain veludu, not his own.

Even as my father and Richard pulled the dead doe clear of him, Dan opened his eyes and looked up at them. Then, becoming aware of Essa's anxious gaze, he gave what, even through all the blood that caked his face, they recognized as being a beaming smile.

'Why, Mistress—er, Princess Hiludessa—you're safe! Why then, all is well!'

Essa's eyes, as she looked at the old man, were brimming with tears. Even so, her tone was scolding.

'But what about you, Dan Wyert? I warned you not to ride with me into this battle, but you insisted that you should! And now look at you!' She hesitated, then went on: 'And how—how do you feel, Dan?'

'Why, 'tis sad to lose Longshank; she's carried me many a long league. And my leg—well, I reckon 'tis broken again, so I'll have another long spell of hopping around on crutches. But, you know, in myself I'm well enough—and happy enough.'

So indeed he was. His gladness spilled over to the others, and with it came relief from shock and strain. Suddenly the four of them, and the others about them—yes, even there on the battlefield amid the slain—were smiling and chattering with the effervescent joy of children released early from lessons. There were problems to be solved; there were the wounded to be tended; but the cloud of fear had been blown from Warrentown by that fortunate wind from the sea.

Chapter Twenty-two

THE BATTLE OF THE EASTERN RIDGE

Now I must take this chronicle firmly back into my own hand and recount what transpired on the eastern bank of the Lemmeshind. When the ikhils of the attacking Pavonarans had chorused an endorsement of my deduction, Redén the soldier was already running up the east ridge to bear our message to the letzahar of Aracundra. Through that chance, he was the first to report the onslaught upon Warrentown to dakhmen Etselil. However, when Reden came back, he brought us little comfort.

'Master Simon, Master Avran, the dakhmen's orders are: "Stay where you are." When he sees need for action, he'll send you other word. Till then, you must do naught.'

Such a brusque rejoinder seemed a poor response to our initiative; indeed, it seemed more reproof than reward. I was quite taken aback. However, so evident and so entire was Avran's discomfiture that I found myself grinning.

'Well, thank you, Reden. It seems you'll have plenty of time to recover your breath, then, and to continue enjoying the view.'

Perhaps that was not the proper fashion in which to address a soldier under one's command. However, it served us well, for it evoked a responsive smile and a more encouraging further comment.

'Aye, but the dakhmen, he's shifting his reserves down onto the ridge, Master Simon. They'll be ready, if so be that the dakhmen decides to take any action.'

'Ah! that's better news! Thank you again, Reden.' And the soldier returned to his place.

Though even more cheered than I by that further tiding, Avran voiced no comment. Instead he was silent for a while, absent-mindedly scuffing up snow with his booted feet; for snow still cloaked this sheltered southern flank of the ridge.

'Well, what d'you think should be done, Avran my friend?' I asked at last.

'What indeed? The letzahar must surely be pondering the same question and finding no more of a satisfactory answer than I. Here we be, separated from Warrentown by that accursed trench and rampart the Pavonarans were permitted to construct. If we attack it, many of us will surely die; and would it be worth the cost? Mayhap, mayhap not, for in this thrice-accursed mist we can't even gauge what is happening!'

Richard, stationed up on the northeast tower, had found it trying enough to wait in idleness while harking to the sounds of battle below; but the scaling-ladder assault had brought him quick relief in action. For Avran and me, for Keld Eslingbror on the north side and for the other Safaddnese guarding the east ridge, no such relief was forthcoming. Subdued sounds in the mist above and behind us told that the reserves had arrived and were taking up position; we presumed, correctly, that they were being stationed in serried rows across the ridge. From the mist-muffled sounds coming from below and before, we could guess something of the progress of the conflict: twice, indeed, we heard the Lyonessans' triumphant cries as scaling-ladders were thrown down by Gerard Turnbull's soldiers. However, we could not clearly ascertain how the battle was progressing.

Positioned as we were in the shelter of the ridge, we did not feel the early breaths of the wind from the sea that was so to change the course of the battle. Only when the mist began to be moved, surging erratically along the eastern fosse like steam blown from a fitfully boiling kettle, did we become aware of the altered weather. As we watched, the ruined East Gate took on form and clarity, the two Pavonaran flags streaming out stiffly above its one intact tower in the strengthening wind.

Yet our widening view was disheartening, for we began to perceive how strongly the ridge beyond the rampart was manned. Why, it was thick with soldiers! Quite evidently the Faruzlaf of Hregisel was determined to deny to Warrentown any chance of being relieved by the Safaddnese. Surely a whole dakhletel of warriors—spearmen, axemen and javelotiers—must be stationed there, at least; rank upon rank of them there were and all, regrettably, beyond longbow-shot.

Ah! we could see beyond the East Gate now; not into the fosse, for that was hidden from view, but at least along the whole stretch of Warrentown's walls between the southeast tower and the gate-tower. The scaling-ladder assaults had already ceased and all seemed curiously tranquil. Yes, there were Pavonarans in the South-east Forecourt but, since that was indefensible, the spectacle caused us neither surprise nor particular disquiet. Indeed, though the Pavonarans had invested the East Bailey much more closely than before and soldiers and unicorn-riders were massed in the meadows, nowhere could we see any sign of action.

Whatever were the Pavonarans doing? Had they been so decisively driven back that they had given up their assault? In the increasing roar of the wind, we could distinguish no sound of conflict. With the pontoon bridge quite out of view, we had no reason even to suspect the unfortunate truth—that the Pavonarans had climbed cliff and ruined wall and were now battling Sir John's men within the East Castle itself. For us watchers on the east ridge, it was all very puzzling.

Yet the further strengthening of the wind, carrying away the last shreds of mist and giving us our first view across the Lemmeshind, furnished cause for renewed alarm. Avran responded faster than I.

'Look, Simon, look! Across the river! The Pavonarans—they've crossed the Lemmeshind!'

'You're right, Avran,' I groaned. 'And that means the Lyonessans are deeply in trouble! We'd all believed that, even if the East Castle were lost, they'd be able to cross the bridge and escape into Avakalim; but they can't do it now—no, not even the women and children. This is a black day, Avran.'

'And here we are, just watching it all!' my friend fumed. 'Why, I'd sooner risk my neck in the warmth of an attack than just sit here, biting at my frozen fingernails and kicking my heels in this wretched snow!'

Yet, even as despair for my father and brother was clutching at my heart, there came a running soldier, sent by Keld from over the ridge. He brought astonishing tidings.

'Master Avran, Master Simon—there's a wave, a great wave! 'Tis coming straight upriver at us!'

'A great wave?' I was bewildered.

'Aye, from the sea! The sea itself is rising!'

'But that was the fate of the old Lyonesse, to be destroyed by the sea. Surely it can't be happening again?'

The soldier was uncomprehending and uneasy. 'Nay, I know not. The wave, 'tis huge; yet Master Keld thinks it won't overtop this ridge. Even so, he wishes you to be watchful and ready to flee at need!' He ran on his way to bear the message to others.

On the west bank, as we learned later, the Pavonarans were quite unaware of the great wave before it was upon them; even those on the ridge seem not to have glimpsed it. From the east ridge, however, unquestionably they did see it coming; but they saw it too late. We could tell when it was perceived, by the anxious flurry as the news was passed from mouth to mouth. We saw soldiers hurrying into the East Gate and messengers rushing out, to carry warnings to those below in fosse and on riverbank. However, that attempt caused only the forfeiture of those messengers' lives. It was too late for warnings; the wave was already too close.

Before we saw it, we felt the shock as it struck simultaneously against the ridge and eastern Warrentown's fortifications. We heard the doleful cries of the Pavonarans and saw, rising above the line of the fosse, the wave's frothing crest as it surged through. Out it poured, to unite again with the other, greater wave travelling up the Lemmeshind itself. Within seconds, the mighty conjoint swash of waters was inundating the meadowlands below us.

What were those strange wooden objects, tumbling over and over but borne along by the surge as effortlessly as if they had been mere kindling-wood? I did not know; only later did I learn that they were the remains of the pontoons. But ah! my heart ached as I saw the unicorns below us panicking and rearing, before they and their riders were overwhelmed and drowned. I continued to watch, fascinated but horrified, as shelters, supplies and soldiers were hurled down and then taken up by the wave, as it swept southward across meadow and scrub. Its inexorability and sheer destructive power were awesome.

That tossing flotsam in the foaming wake of the wave; why, only moments before it had been an ordered phalanx of armed and armoured men and beasts! Now that phalanx was destroyed, by the wrath of the One God! In that time of terror I cast aside all belief in the power of the Nine, even in these mountains. As Richard had done and as Avran was doing, I found myself praying with frantic fervour, yet more in sheer, appalled fright than in immediate gratitude.

Nor, indeed, was gratitude our next emotion. Rather, it was a sort of amazed incomprehension. Where now was the army, that had seemed so mighty and so threatening? Why, the largest part of it had been washed away! Where were those warriors we had watched during all those long, bleak days? Why, they were gone, submerged under a greyish-brown lake from which Warrentown's twin strongholds rose like turreted islands. Within a few heartbeats, the whole prospect before us had been changed beyond belief.

Slowly I became aware of the babble of comment among our soldiers, yet I did not find my own tongue loosened. Instead, it was Avran who spoke. The thoughts that he uttered were unexpected.

'Simon, do you recall our leaving of Kesbados? How you told us you'd seen that image of Radaionesu with his hand raised, and how the Brelinderimins were sure he'd been giving us his blessing? Well, I didn't quite believe it then; but now! Why, scarce twelve days have gone by since we saw the destruction of one army by a snowslide; and in this hour we've witnessed the destroying of another by a wave from the sea! Surely there *must* be a blessing, a mighty blessing, upon Brelinderim! I find myself altering in mind; I find myself beginning to credit their Nine Gods with power, just as Essa does!'

'The Princess Hiludessa,' I corrected him automatically. 'Yet remember, Avran, that Lyonesse is the particular home of the only believers in our own God in the whole of these northlands. Why should any of the Nine give Warrentown their blessing? And, as for the Pavonarans, this army at least hasn't been wholly destroyed, by any means! Look at them all, down there below us!'

'Aye, but after such devastating losses, surely they'll capitulate?'

'Will they, Avran? I wonder! That Faruzlaf of Hregisel, I'm sure he's still alive; I don't believe he's left his quarters in the East Gate yet. Do you think he'll surrender, with the prospect of returning in ignominy to Pavonara? I doubt it, friend; I doubt it.'

'Yet see how his remaining troops are pent up there, between fosse and trench.' Avran was made not at all happy by my reasoning. 'Why, things are changed about strangely! If the Pavonarans do choose to resist, it will be they who are under siege! And how can they withstand even a brief siege, when all their supplies have been lost to the waters?'

I smiled. 'Indeed it's strange, to see how their own defensive works have been turned, in a moment, into a barrier that holds them in. I think they'll try to break out.'

'We'll know soon. Do you see those men there, carrying the white standard? Dakhmen Etselil must be sending an envoy to urge the Pavonarans to capitulate.'

I remembered, from our time in the Stoney Mountains, that a triangular white flag was the Rockalese symbol of a desire for peaceful parleying. The envoys—there were three of them—walked up to the trench and stopped, shouting their demand for a surrender to the guards on the rampart. We could not hear the terms presented, but we saw runners carrying word of them into the West Gate.

Out from his quarters within came Kalung Dastenost. His great stature and the white crest upon his helmet—I could not distinguish its nature, but had been told it was a half-skull, the grim emblem of his House—identified him beyond doubt. There was a brief further delay, then a swirl of messengers was sent hastening through the throng of Pavonaran soldiers. Not all were going toward the envoys, I noted; some other message must be being passed.

Within moments, a javelot was flung at the envoys. It was not intended to hit them, for it plunged into the snow a full cloth-yard in front of them. Instead, it constituted a derisive rejection of whatever proposal had been made. Then, even as the envoys were turning away, the Pavonarans poured in a yelling wave up over the rampart they had constructed and down into the trench.

Clearly the Pavonarans were seeking to catch the Safaddnese by surprise; however, their own construction defeated them. The ditch was snow-drifted and deep, while its serried array of sharpened stakes, even though pointing away from them, constituted a considerable hazard. The snow-covered branches in which these stakes were embedded formed only a treacherous foundation for booted feet so that, for safety, the stakes had to be plucked out and cast aside. Even when these obstacles were passed, the steep upslope face of the trench had still to be climbed, and an area of open ground traversed, before the Pavonarans came within javelot-hurling distance of their enemies.

It was a valiant attack but supremely foolhardy, especially when the enemy warriors faced an arc of longbowmen; for quite a few Brelinderimins had already learned the art of archery from the

Lyonessans. Avran and I loosed only a fistful of arrows, for we were at the southernmost end of that arc and the Pavonarans were only within distant bowshot; nor can I be sure that either of us slew a single Pavonaran. Yet many Pavonarans did die in the trench, to be trampled underfoot by the next wave of their charging comrades; and many more fell to the archers before the Safaddnese line was reached.

What happened next both disconcerted and dismayed me. Though our friends were doggedly holding position on our side of the ridge, those at the centre were yielding before the Pavonaran attack and retreating away uphill. Surely the Safaddnese must be feeble fighters, if they were being already driven back by so few Pavonarans?

Out over rampart and across trench swarmed more of our enemies, shouting in triumph at this apparent vanquishing, against odds, of their opponents. However, their triumph turned swiftly to consternation. Down the hill upon them was thundering a line of mail-clad warriors mounted on veludain! The Pavonarans had foolishly entered a trap; now the trap had been sprung.

Surely that was Etselil of Aracundra, tall in the middle of the charge upon a mighty veludu; and beside him at right, Soganreth of Ayan, and at left Tazaldhet of Vasanderim? Aye, indeed; and many more notable warriors in line with them, mighty and wrathful!

The alarming spectacle of that fierce line of sharp, lowered horns and sharper, levelled lances was enough to throw the Pavonarans into disarray. Some courageously held place, but most turned to flee. Yet they found they could not. Other soldiers were still hastening out across rampart and trench behind them, at such pace that there was no room to turn about. The result was utter confusion.

Avran and I were shooting high and long, confident that our falling arrows must find some mark in that press of Pavonarans; and the other bowmen were continuing to claim many victims. Yet it was that charge, not our arrows, which finally broke the Pavonarans. The Safaddnese veludury cut into them like a well-wielded scythe into standing corn. Where they had passed, no Pavonarans stood.

By then, the central section of the trench was quite choked with corpses. Across this horrid bridge surged the Safaddnese veludain, some beasts stumbling but no rider losing his seat. Up over the rampart they went, to pass for a while out of our view. For Avran and I were no longer staying at our stations. Along with the other archers and foot-soldiers, we were following that charge. Hastily we scrambled across the bloody chaos of the trench and—in my case, feeling distinctly sick—climbed the rampart after the veludury.

Already the charging Safaddnese had cut a second swathe through the residual Pavonaran lines and were sweeping down upon the East Gate. There, a group of nobles had formed a ring about their Faruzlaf, determined on a last, valiant defence. However, this proved only brief and quite vain. It was Etselil himself who leapt from his veludu and, after a brisk exchange of axe strokes, cut down the Pavonaran leader; nor were the weapons of Soganreth and Tazaldhet idle in that final skirmish.

The slaying of Kalung Dastenost marked the virtual end of the battle. By then, the old drawbridge had been lowered and the Lyonessans had hurried across, eager to recapture the East Gate and participate in this final humbling of their enemies. Soon the last Pavonarans were throwing down their weapons and spreading their arms wide in surrender. Of the dakhletel that had been massed on the ridge scarcely fifty warriors remained alive, and few of those survivors were unwounded. The stubborn pride of their leader had cost the Pavonarans dearly indeed.

Surely that must be Sir John Warren, coming out from the East Gate with sword bloodied and red face radiant? I did not recognize him after so many years—indeed, had I ever met him, even in childhood?—but his surcoat was unmistakable. Gaily he greeted the three Safaddnese dakhletelar, successively clasping the clenched hands of each with beaming fervour, while other Lyonessans ran out to welcome and joyfully embrace the other Safaddnese.

Avran and I were too far away up ridge to be included in that first greeting. However, we joined in the great shout of triumph when we saw the Pavonaran standards fluttering down from the Gate and we cheered heartily when the flags of Lyonesse and Warrentown were hauled up in their stead, in proclamation of victory.

Yet my own greatest joy came in the evening of that day, when I met again my brother Richard and my father. That reunion took place in the East Castle, to which they had returned to participate in the victory celebration.

By then the daylight was fading and the air very chill. Bright fires had been lit within the roofless keep and happily chattering women were busy preparing what promised to be a mighty feast; the austerities of the siege were over. This was only one of several simultaneous celebrations, for the Avakalimins were mostly being entertained in the West Castle and the Safaddnese were relaxing around larger fires in the East Bailey. (Even the Pavonaran prisoners—a meagre two hundred or so—had had their wounds tended by chirurgeon Naral Vesang and his assistants and were being fed, under the eyes of vigilant Avakalimin guards, over in the West Bailey.)

For Richard, his return across the bridge must have evoked unpleasant memories, but it had been easy enough. By then, the gale had subsided to a steady onshore breeze. The bridge was so elevated that it must have suffered only the small impact of the highest wave-crest—enough to knock away a few planks, but not nearly enough to break the ropes. The replacing of the planks was a task readily performed: it had been done long before Richard's second crossing. That was well, for not only the wounded prisoners from the east bank, but also quite a few persons of high distinction—the Dakhletel of Avakalim, Sir Robert Randwulf and the Princess Hiludessa among them—crossed it that evening. (The Princess's old servant, for whom she had shown a degree of concern surprising to the Lyonessans, was by then wrapped in blankets and fast asleep in a fire-warmed upper room in the West Castle.)

Perhaps Avran and I had been justified in disliking dakhmen Etselil's brusque response to our warning; but that evening he treated us with such courtesy and respect that our brief displeasure was quite forgotten. Along with our good friend Keld Eslingbror and certain soldiers who had especially distinguished themselves in the day's battles, we were bidden to dine in honour with the nobles of Lyonesse and Safaddné.

It was while the trestle tables were still being laid that I saw Richard again, descending the winding stair from the bridge tower. I had learned already that my brother had survived the battle unscathed; even so, I was glad and grateful to be able to discover this with my own eyes. With Richard was Robin, stiff after the battle and limping a little, but talking to him very cheerfully; and behind came Essa, solicitously escorted by two men. One was Perespeth of Avakalim. The other I did not at first identify; but then, with a leap of heart, I knew it to be my father. Like Robin, he appeared a little tired and stiff; his hair was more grey now than fair; but he was hale and happy.

I did not cry out to him immediately, for I was content to watch him approach. Indeed, after so long a separation, I was finding trouble in formulating any adequate greeting, so full was my heart of joy and gratitude.

In the flickering light and shadow, father did not notice me until Richard grasped his shoulder and steered him toward me.

'Do you know who this is, father?' Richard was smiling.

'No, I don't believe I . . . why, it is Simon!'

Beamingly my father seized me and hugged me; nor did I stint from hugging him in return, and I know there were tears in both our eyes. Then, without releasing his grip on my arms, father stepped back and considered me searchingly.

'Simon my son, I would not have recognized you! Yet it is only—let me see—not quite two years since we said farewell at the gate of Holdworth. Moreover, I have never limned you in my mind with moustache and beard—mayhap because I envisioned you becoming a clerk or a monk. Well, most greatly do I prefer the actuality to the imagining, Simon! You've become a proper young warrior, and a valiant one indeed, from what Richard, Sir Robert and the Princess have all been telling me!'

As he paused, I was touched to see that the tears were running down his cheeks and there was an unfamiliar, husky note in his speech.

'Simon, son, I've done you many an injustice. I was meaning well always, but they were injustices even so. I did not believe it was in you to become a warrior, so you were never given the training that you merited. Worse, I must confess that, when I wrote my screed for John Stacey to carry to you, I expected never to see you again; whereas Richard here, he was always sure you'd accept the challenge and follow us to Rockall. Aye, his belief in you was stronger than mine—indeed, his faith puts me to shame! Simon, lad, you have never lacked for my love—you know that. Yet I must apologize to you most humbly for wronging you, in deed and thought. I must also pay you the tribute of my profound respect and admiration.'

Avran was standing beside us and beaming at us both. 'You speak generously, Sir William, but also you speak rightly. Your son is valiant indeed, and to me he has proved the very truest of friends.'

Such warm tributes caused my own eyes to brim anew with tears—whether of embarrassment or of pleasure, I am not sure. Certainly that evening of celebration was one that I shall forever cherish in memory. During our long traverse of Rockall, I had wondered often at my own foolhardiness in embarking upon so dangerous a journey. Many times my resolve had faltered and, on two occasions at least, only Avran's steadfastness had shamed me into continuing onward. In the happiness of that reunion and my awareness of my father's pleasure and great pride, I knew that all I had endured had been worth while.

Chapter Twenty-three

THE REWARDS OF BATTLE

Not only we in Warrentown, but even the weather itself, seemed determined to celebrate the victory over the Pavonaran invaders—and this was fitting, since the weather had been so crucial to that victory. Even as the fires in castle and bailey died down and the last revellers retired reluctantly to couch or bedroll, it was becoming perceptibly warmer. The wind from the north had slackened away to nothingness, allowing milder air to come in from southward. The morning dawned beautiful, with a bright sun giving its benison from a blue sky.

The deep snow in the mountains had long since begun to melt, but now its melting was greatly hastened. Streamlets had already grown into swift streams; now they became torrents. The other rivers of eastern Safaddné—the Maldilund, the Trantellend, the Hededrund, the Berelind and the Tasdralind—all rose in spate and, since each contributed a handsome quotient to the Lemmeshind, that river rose most of all. Even as the tempest-driven tide was ebbing, the Lemmeshind was swelling.

This had a very desirable consequence. Instead of being deposited on its banks by the falling tide, the debris of the Pavonaran camp, the wreckage of rafts, pontoons and scaling-ladders, and the corpses of unicorns and men were all swept out to sea. The valley was flushed clean.

Our Lyonessan friends exulted, the farmers in particular. Those fresh, fast-flowing waters must be washing the sea salt from the fields and, when in due course they subsided, they would leave a fresh cover of sediment for the spring grasses and flowers to grow in.

Yet there were some ill consequences also. The bridge over the Lemmeshind at Maradiela was carried away, leaving Warrentown's slender bridge as the only link between Brelinderim and Avakalim until such time as the spate subsided. The old bridge over the Tasdralind by Tasbered proved stouter; for a while it was submerged, but it survived. However, its temporary impassability meant that, for me, Etvan Samenast came never to be more than a voice heard, and a figure dimly seen, during the escape from Kesbados. He and three other Brelinderimins were drowned when trying to ford the Tasdralind above Tasbered. When I heard that, I remembered how, when Etvan had looked back upon Kesbados, he had seen, not his god's upraised hand and smile, but only darkness.

I did again meet Marasar Esekh, but not until several sun-blessed days had passed. During those days, much happened that was memorable.

The morning after the battle was one of recovery from celebration and clearing or patching-up after battle. Some there were who were mourning. Fifty-nine of Warrentown's defenders and eighty soldiers of the relieving forces had been slain in combat. Moreover, a few others were destined to die from their wounds during the days that followed, despite the strivings of Naral Vesang and his assistants.

Among those assistants, Avran and I were for a while numbered. Remembering our training with the wizard, we volunteered our services and, during that first day, did much dressing of wounds and administering of potions.

By the second morning, the worst of the injuries had been treated. Thereafter our aid was not needed, for the womenfolk from the farms were eager for occupation and had taken firm charge of the tending of the wounded. In consequence, Avran and I were able that morning to give our thanks to God in the castle chapel. We found many others on their knees there, offering their own orisons, Sir John Warren, Robin and my father among them.

Upon leaving the chapel, Sir John invited us to take luncheon with him in his private chambers. Afterwards, father invited me to join him on a tour of the fortifications of Warrentown. In part, this was for him a matter of duty, since he wished to ascertain where repairs had now become necessary. Largely, however, I am sure it was because he was so proud—and justly proud—of what he had achieved; he wanted to show me what had been done, so that I might share his pride. Avran was invited to accompany us but father was, I'm sure, far from disappointed when he declined.

Father and I did indeed have a most enjoyable afternoon together.

Yes, we viewed the fortifications and yes, I praised properly his achievements and those of his men; but much of our talk was about other matters. Some of it concerned old times in England—father knew he would never again return to Holdworth, yet a part of his heart had been left forever there—but much of it was about southern Rockall, concerning which, since it would be my future home, he was very curious. When I told him of my provisional betrothal to Princess Ilven of Sandastre, his delight was considerable and tempered only by the fact that he knew he would never meet her.

Avran's afternoon was much less happy. While we were leaving the chapel, with my friend walking beside us, I had asked father where Richard was. I had been told that he was accompanying the Princess Hiludessa on a visit to Dan Wyert, who was still recovering from his injury in that upper chamber in the West Castle. I had noticed that Avran did not seem overjoyed by that information, but the matter passed quickly from my mind.

When I met Avran again that evening, I learned that he had also gone to visit Dan and found him in good spirits; but, by then, Essa and Richard had long since left the old man's couch-side. Dan had not heard their plans, so Avran sought Mark Thistleton, who was still in charge of that castle's garrison, to try to discover the Princess's whereabouts. He learned that she and Richard had borrowed veludain and gone out riding together in the hills of Avakalim.

That tiding thoroughly spoiled Avran's mood, for he had hoped for a few quiet hours in her company, after so long a parting. He returned to the East Castle in a glum mood and, though somewhat cheered by Essa's friendly greeting at dinner that evening, was by no means wholly comforted.

The next morning was one of busy preparation for us all. Thereafter, in bright afternoon sunshine, all the soldiery who had taken part in the defence and relief of Warrentown, save only those on guard duty, were called together in the East Bailey. We assembled in our companies before a dais on which Sir John Warren, Sir Robert Randwulf and the letzahars of Aracundra, Avakalim, Ayan and Vasanderim were seated in a half-circle, with the Princess Hiludessa in the place of highest honour at the centre.

Very colourful that scene was, for the day's warmth had allowed us to put off our sombre furs and instead don brighter military costume. The green surcoats of Brelinderim and the azure of Avakalim formed solid blocks of colour, the latter hue reflected by the blue patterning on white in the vair surcoats of Lyonesse. There was a wedge of purple surcoats—the warriors of Aracundra—and a splash of the scarlet of Vasanderim. We of Ayan—for Avran and I were again mustered with Keld and our other companions of that long winter—felt splendid in surcoats of golden hue, almost as bright as that day's sun itself. All about the fringes of the bailey, and on stairs and wall-walks, were the women and children of Warrentown. They were clad for this occasion in their finest and most colourful garments; and they were as happily clamorous as a building of rooks.

The figures on the dais were the most splendid of all. Sir John Warren, in his elaborate surcoat with the black conies on their field of vair and his black hosen, was perhaps the least colourful. Robin's surcoat was white, charged with three scarlet escallops (cockleshells); I speculated whether this represented the arms of Odunseth or whether it echoed some pilgrimage to the shrine of St James of Compostela. The four letzahars wore the bright colours of their letzestrei, Etselil being especially splendid in purple, with jagged lightning-stroke and chevron tricked out in bright silver. Their burgonets each bore, above the umbril, the device of their letzestre in gold and were chased with silver, while their sword-belts, sword hilts and scabbards were likewise chased with silver, as also were those of Sir John and of Robin. I wondered how Robin had acquired that scabbard, for it was certainly not his own!

Yet the Princess outmatched them all. Very young and very beautiful Essa looked, in that mature company. She was clad in a dress of her favourite azure-blue (appropriately, since that was the tincture of Avakalim), with tight bodice and sleeves and full skirt. About her waist was a belt of gold links, from which was pendant a gold-hilted dagger in a scabbard chased with gold. I had not seen the belt and dagger before, but I knew well the golden taron she wore upon her breast. She seemed very confident, and not a whit out of place, in that assembly. Yet she contrived also to look demure for, in place of a helmet, she wore a white crespine head-dress draped with a veil of white lace.

We had been gathered for a ceremony of awarding of honours. Since Warrentown had borne the brunt of the battle, it was appropriate that the Lyonessans should be honoured first and, naturally, Sir John had that privilege. Beaming and benign he was when, after a brief formal prayer, he called up onto the dais those of his following who had shown especial bravery—and they were many. Several received promotion to the rank of letelar or devletelar, while each was awarded a skilfully embroidered badge depicting the leaping blue lion of Lyonesse. Henceforward those badges would be treasured, to be stitched onto prized garments and worn on special occasions as significations of courage.

To my gratification, brother Richard was one thus honoured, for his carrying of the warning of war to Warrentown and his defence of the northeast tower; though, personally, I felt that it was in leading his men across the bridge, in the full force of that terrible gale, that he had been most sorely tried!

Last of all the Lyonessans to be called forth was my father, and for him Sir John had especial words of praise.

'Sir William Branthwaite, we of Lyonesse have long been aware how great was our good fortune when the actions of a foolish king drove you into exile from England. Your own land's loss was Lyonesse's great gain. We have admired your resolute strength in the defence of our city of Warrentown; but, most of all, we have benefited from your forethought and energy. These enabled you to bring the fortifications of our city into a state sufficient to withstand not only the onslaught of strong and determined enemies, but also the strength of the very sea itself when it rose in rage against their iniquities. That you merit this badge of courage is beyond question'—Sir John smilingly handed a blue lion to father—'yet such a token is not nearly sufficient. You deserve, and shall receive, much greater honour.'

He paused and gazed about him in such portentous fashion that I knew his announcement would prove momentous. Yet, even so, it astonished me.

'Before this assembly I name you, Sir William, as castellan of Warrentown under my governance, from this day henceforward. Furthermore, I proclaim that, if God grant you a longer life than mine, you shall succeed me in the governance of this realm of Lyonesse, ranking second only to its King, and that Richard your son shall be the heir to us both!'

The tumultuous applause evoked by that proclamation showed how highly my father and brother had come to be regarded in this, their land of refuge. I was deeply moved. Richard was standing not far from me: I could see that he was both astounded and profoundly gratified at finding himself elevated on our father's shoulders to such high rank. Why, in a moment he had effectively been made heir-apparent to an earldom!

After that Sir John returned to his seat, for it was the turn of the Safaddnese soldiers who had shown especial courage to be honoured, including those Avakalimins and Brelinderimins who had participated in the defence of Warrentown. Each of the letzahars presented the awards to his own warriors—silver medallions depicting the lightning-bolt of Aracundra, the battleaxe of Vasanderim, the taron of Avakalim or the leaping fish of Ayan—while dakhmen Etselil was privileged also to hand out the flowering-bush emblems to the bravest men of letzahar-less Brelinderim.

After each presentation, there was a solemn invocation of the name of the appropriate god in the Safaddnese pantheon and a chant of '*Ilai ushazan!*' from the watchers. Yet, though the Lyonessans, Avran and I refrained from participating in those chants, the Safaddnese about us seemed not to resent our silence. Might it be that they were learning toleration?

I noted with some resentment that Keld Eslingbror was not among those hailed forth to be honoured by dakhmen Soganreth of Ayan; yet for this, as I was to learn, there was good reason. When Etselil had handed out his last award and sat down, the Princess Hiludessa rose for the first time and addressed us in a clear, carrying voice.

'Many here have been properly honoured, and others there must be among you who deserve honour also, albeit perhaps in lesser measure. If we have not noticed your valour, be sure that your god will have noticed it, and be content! Those other warriors who died in battle are, even now, being brought in glory before the thrones of the Nine. Yet it is fitting that we who live should pay to them our own tributes. Let us do so briefly, in silence.'

Obediently we bowed our heads. We raised them only when Essa spoke again.

'There remain four persons here present who merit the tributes of all Lyonesse and all Safaddné. We have reserved their names till last, that all may give them honour. I call forth, first of all, Keld Eslingbror of Ayan.'

Looking quite amazed, our friend stumbled through the crowd toward the dais. Before he had reached it, the Princess was continuing to speak.

'With particular pleasure, I shall call forth also the three persons who were my companions in a difficult and dangerous journey. The name of Branthwaite has already gained much honour today; yet I must call upon another of that valorous family. Simon, please come forward.'

Thus I had need to follow Keld, equally stumblingly and quite as embarrassed, across the crowded court. As I went, I heard the two other summonses.

'I call forth also Avran Estantesec, indreslef of the faraway realm of Sandastre; and lastly, from my side here, Sir Robert Randwulf of Odunseth, who is also indreletzahular of Safaddné.'

As Avran and I mounted the platform to stand by Keld, Robin levered himself reluctantly up from his seat—his injured left arm was surely not the prime cause of his excessive awkwardness!—and stood beside us. At the Princess's gesture, Sir John and the four letzaharei rose also.

Essa smiled at us warmly, then spoke again. 'To you, Sir Robert, to you, Prince Avran and to you, Simon, I shall forever be indebted for my release from a long captivity.' (Did I detect the briefest of conspiratorial winks as she spoke those words?) 'However, to all here present, the three of you have rendered services quite as great. As all here know, the dual warning that the Pavonarans were invading, without even the honourable courtesy of a declaration of war, and that certain despicable Desumeans were conspiring with them, was sent to me by the Nine Gods.' (That time, I was quite sure she had winked at me!) 'In that time of difficulty, nine persons were chosen to be my confidants and advisers. Sir Robert helped to initiate action within Kesbados, as did my servant Dan Wyert and Keld's worthy brother, Aflar Eslingbror. Prince Avran, Simon Branthwaite and letelar Keld Eslingbror, along with Richard Branthwaite and two Brelinderimins not here present, were sent out as my messengers to Brelinderim, Avakalim and Lyonesse. For those services alone, these men merit our great praise.'

There was a storm of applause and I felt a warmth in my ears that told me I must be blushing. Yet the Princess was not done.

'Few here will know that, when dakhmen Perespeth, Sir Robert and I set forth from Kesbados with only a letel of warriors to rally Avakalim, we were beset in the mountains by a murderous party of disaffected Ayanians and Desumeans. Yet it is so.'

Avran and I stiffened in astonishment at this tiding, while a ripple of surprise and dismay ran through the watching Safaddnese and Lyonessans. So the plots of the Hrasang brothers and Ekulag had borne evil fruit, even after their deaths! But the Princess was continuing to speak.

'During that time of danger, I was fortunate in the valour of my companions, Sir Robert and dakhmen Perespeth in particular. Most of all, however, I was fortunate in that the Nine Gods had given me the blessing, as friend and guard, of a mighty branath. His attack on our assailants threw their veludain into terror; moreover he leapt upon and slew their leader. Then, his appointed task fulfilled, the branath departed into the mountains.'

So *that* was what had happened to Rakhamu! I had not been wondering, for I had assumed that the branath had been left behind either in Kesbados or in some Avakalimin castle. Well, Essa's rescuing of the cub had indeed proved an inspired action.

'As for Keld, Simon and Prince Avran, they also had a special task appointed to them by the Nine. They were sent to a high place, beneath which were passing the evil King Rafanesar of Pavonara and two dakhletelei of his warriors, intent upon plundering Brelinderim and Avakalim. By the actions of these three men in releasing a great fall of snow upon the invaders, the King and all his soldiers were annihilated. What other three, in all our proud history, can claim to have destroyed a whole army? These men deserve our deep gratitude and our highest praise, as also do the Nine who guided them!'

This time the tumult of applause was prolonged, culminating in the familiar ritual chant of '*Ilai ushazan! Ilai ushazan!*' from the Safaddnese majority. When at last it died down, the Princess resumed her address.

'Keld Eslingbror, it is my pleasure to announce to you that, from this day, you are appointed dakhletelar in the army of Ayan and seneschal of Kesbados under your letzahar. Dakhmen Soganreth, may I ask you to confer upon your compatriot these great honours?'

More applause and a brief, highly emotional ceremony, after which a smiling Keld was cheered back to his place among the ranks in the bailey. Then Essa again addressed the three of us, in her ringing tone.

'Since you, my friends, are from realms outside Safaddné, it is less easy for me to grant you appropriate honours. Nevertheless, it is very necessary that your attainments are commemorated. Thus we propose to act in threefold fashion, so that nine honours will be granted this day. Dakhmen Etselil, may I ask you to speak first?'

The tall Aracundran, splendid in purple and argent, stepped forward and made the crossed-hands bow to us that, in Safaddné, proclaims deep respect. Then he spoke out boldly.

'Simon Branthwaite of England, Avran Estantesec of Sandastre and Robert Randwulf of Odunseth, I proclaim you henceforward to be free citizens of all the nine letzestrei of Safaddné, to be received with honour whenever and wherever you may choose to travel in these, the realms of the Nine Gods.'

'And now, dakhmen Soganreth, would you speak?'

The letzahar of Ayan, in his surcoat of gold, broidered in silver with leaping fishes amid wavy lines simulating water, was almost as dazzling to the eye as the sun and his smile almost as bright. I had always liked Soganreth and, when he spoke after granting us the bow of honour, it was a particular delight to perceive how genuine was his pleasure.

'Simon Branthwaite, Avran Estantesec and Robert Randwulf, I welcome you now as fellow Safaddnese. Accordingly, it is possible and pleasurable for me to accord you each the rank of dakhletelar in the armies of Ayan, with the full privileges of that high position.'

High indeed it was! Until the recent preferment of Keld, Ayan's armies had had only five dakhletelarei. Was it mere coincidence, I wondered, that the number was now made nine?

'And lastly, Sir John, would you speak?'

'Indeed I will, and right gladly! Simon Branthwaite, Avran Estantesec and Robert Randwulf, I proclaim you to be henceforward free citizens of Warrentown and of Lyonesse. I further proclaim a renaming in your honour. What has hitherto been styled the West Gate shall henceforth be styled the Randwulf Gate, and what has hitherto been called the East Gate shall become the Estantesec Gate. As for the name of Branthwaite, it is already so greatly honoured in Warrentown that it requires no further, formal commemoration; but, Simon, you may be sure that your valorous actions are rated quite as highly as those of your brother and father!'

As the bailey echoed again with the shouts and chants of the assembled warriors and people, Sir John and the letzahars gave to each of us in turn the clasped-hands greeting of friendship and fellowship. Last of all, and most movingly, we were each embraced by the Princess. As I saw the tears glistening in her eyes and enjoyed the warmth of her smile, I recognized that her embrace was, for me, as great a reward as the honours of the princes.

Chapter Twenty-four

ENDINGS AND BEGINNINGS

The long-awaited Safaddnese 'relief' army arrived around noon on the third day after the battle, while we were recovering from the round of celebrations that the awards ceremony had naturally occasioned. Those Safaddnese had long since encountered messengers carrying tidings of the victory to Tasbered, so they knew already that they were late and were understandably disconsolate. Though Robin, Avran and I felt some initial exasperation at their tardiness, when we learned of their tribulations we could only feel sympathy for them.

That army was led by Daltsaran, letzahar of windy Darega, with the letzahar of Omega as his deputy—appointments that were in proper accord with the rigid Safaddnese hierarchy. However, the army had been assembled, not by them, but by three high priests.

Parudanh of Ayan and Balahir of Brelinderim had gathered together those warriors of their realms who had not immediately heeded their letzahar's call to duty, either because of distance or through being dilatory; and they amounted to a full dakhletel. Yet the greater part of the army came from Desume. Letzudirar Daliat had been true to his pledge and correct in his judgement of his people. Only a few Desumeans—among them, those who had sought unsuccessfully to murder the Princess and the letzahar of Avakalim—remained loyal to the memory of their dishonoured leader, the odious Ekulag, and to the tarnished allure of a Pavonaran alliance. By far the greater number had, in that time of trial, remained faithful to their traditional loyalties and rallied to the defence of Safaddné. Fully three further dakhletelei gathered at Daliat's summons.

The three parts of the army had mustered at the Ferekh Taslutanar, that 'Mount of Answering' which Keld, Avran and I had approached, but not seen, during our first day after leaving Kesbados.

It had seemed a fitting rallying-point, for were not the Safaddnese answering a summons, the summons to defend their mountain homes?

Yet it had proved an ill choice. There had been a few days of relatively fair weather while the army was gathering; but then the weather had turned foul. Blizzard upon blizzard came, piling snow upon wet snow. There was little accommodation in the tower and, though the Safaddnese knew how to make shelters for themselves amid the drifts, they had passed a miserable time till the blizzards ceased. After that they had endured a long march in the vile conditions of deep, but melting snow—conditions under which no march would have been attempted, had the danger to Warrentown been less pressing. With each stream running strong and swift, the Safaddnese had kept to the heights. Even so, enforced detours added many effortful leagues and stretched out their journey over several more days.

Perhaps those Safaddnese felt some pleasure in knowing that Warrentown had been saved; surely they must have known some relief in learning they would not be required to give battle. Nevertheless, the realization that all their exhausting effort had been unnecessary must have been bitter indeed. So should even I have felt, timorous though I be at any prospect of battle. The Lyonessans showed their understanding and sympathy by making Daltsaran's men very welcome.

Yet I found that the other Safaddnese—yes, even generous-hearted Keld Eslingbror—viewed the matter differently. They considered it a proper visitation by Horulgavar, galiiletelar of the Nine Gods, upon his servants—a chastening of the Ayanians and Brelinderimins for their tardiness and, in particular, of the Desumeans for permitting their faith to waver. However, it was believed also that Horulgavar had shown his forgiveness, by withholding greater penalties. Though the army had suffered many privations and some injuries, no single soldier had died during the long march and all, though denied the honours of war, had been spared its dangers. I thought this an over-harsh illation; but then, the Safaddnese are an austere people.

Rather to my surprise, neither Sir Arthur Thurlstone nor Marasar Esekh were with that army. However, on my expressing wonderment, the matter was patiently explained to me by Richard, who had gained a good grasp of Brelinderimin customs and attitudes.

When the ailing Talados had chosen Sir Arthur Thurlstone to be his successor as letzahar, a change in his priorities had been enforced. Had Sir Arthur been letzahar already, he would have been expected to command his people in war and even, if necessary, to sacrifice his life for Brelinderim. However, while he was merely heir to the position, his whole responsibility was to the person of the letzahar — living or dead — and not yet to the other Brelinderimins. Had Talados been able to lead his people to battle, then Sir Arthur would have been required to follow and support him. With Talados dead, it became Sir Arthur's prime duty to travel to Tasbered and ensure that the obsequies were carried out according to the traditional rituals.

Nothing — no, not even the extreme danger to Lyonesse — could, in Safaddnese eyes, exempt Sir Arthur from that duty. Had he failed in it, he could never have hoped to unite Brelinderim and Lyonesse into a single kingdom. Quite the contrary; he would have aroused such antipathy to Warrentown that, if the Pavonarans had been fought off, the Safaddnese would surely have destroyed it. That is a hard attitude to understand; but then, many Safaddnese attitudes are hard for outsiders to comprehend.

For Marasar Esekh also, the news of the death of dakhmen Talados had enforced a revision of priorities. After transmitting the warning of the invasion to his people, he had been hastening north toward Ferekh Taslutanar when the word of his cousin's death had caught up with him. Along with it had come tidings of the destruction of the King of Pavonara and his army. Confident that this ended the Pavonaran threat, Marasar had redirected his steps toward Tasbered to join in the obsequies. By the time that he learned of the second Pavonaran army, it was too late for him to change plans without giving deep offence to the other mourners.

Thus it was that the latest of the parties to arrive at Warrentown was that captained by the new letzahar of Brelinderim. With him came letzudirar Balahir and notable among his other companions was Marasar.

I found that, yes, I did remember Sir Arthur; after all, it was not many years since he had come to Hallamshire while recruiting settlers for Lyonesse. Quite small and dark he was, more or less of my own size, with bright brown eyes under bristling brows and a beard that stuck out from his chin like a ship's prow. Yet, after meeting him, it was not his appearance but his force, his energy and his charm that one remembered. If he were indeed to become a king, it would only seem appropriate, for he had been born princely.

By the time of his arrival, the tardy Safaddnese army had turned about and directed its steps southward. Many Ayanians and Brelinderimins from our own army had gone homeward also, as had most of the Avakalimins. Yet all the letzahars had stayed, for they had need to join in council. Eight of them there were now, for a new letzahar had been chosen by the Desumeans. Only the letzahar of Paladra was missing. That silent man, who had permitted his letzudirar to speak for their letzestre, had long since gone back to chill Sasliith.

The Safaddnese had found the departure of the Paladrans somewhat troubling; or so I was told. However, for my part, I could not mourn their going. Even so long after, our experiences in Sasliith disturbed my dreams.

Sir Arthur's arrival occasioned a third celebration, during which Keld, Avran and I found ourselves assigned places of honour at the highest table, with father and Richard by our side. That had been a merry evening, for the Lyonessans had particular cause for celebration. After all the earlier disputes, the right of the Brelinderimins to choose Sir Arthur as letzahar was no longer being contested by the other Safaddnese. In consequence, there was every prospect that the hoped-for conjoint Kingdom would soon be brought into being.

On the next night, indeed, Sir Arthur was invited to meet as an equal in conclave with the letzaharei over in the West Castle, where most of them were lodged. Keld, Avran and I had been allotted private chambers in the eastern gatehouse, now called the Estantesec Tower, while the Princess was housed in Sir John's chambers in the south-east tower nearby.

For the first time in many days, I found myself at a loss for occupation. With his letzahar otherwise engaged, dakhletelar Keld Eslingbror was in command of the Ayanian contingent and much occupied. Father and Richard, with Sir John Warren and several other leading Lyonessans, were also in conclave, planning the next stages in the refortification of Warrentown—a task in which the Pavonaran prisoners would be required to lend aid.

As for Avran, he was in difficult mood. Though Essa had been perfectly courteous to him during the time since the ceremony in the East Bailey, he had not yet been able to contrive the hours alone with her for which he had been longing. Moreover, she seemed daily ever more immersed in the affairs of Avakalim and Lyonesse; any hopes Avran had cherished that she might elect to go south with us were fast fading. That night he had retired early to his chamber, where I could hear him playing mournful airs on his pommer.

The rap on my chamber's plank door was thus a welcome surprise, for it had promised to be a dull evening. When I opened to him, the Avakalimin soldier who stepped inside was both peremptory and vague.

'You're summoned, dakhletelar. By one of high rank, though I'm not to say by whom. Follow me, please, master. You'll be needing your fur jupon, for it's turned chill.'

I had expected to be led down the winding stairs into the bailey. Instead, I found myself accompanying the soldier up to the tower walk and thence onto the wall, past guards who greeted us with respectful disinterest that told me our passing was expected.

It was only when we were descending the stairs into the south-east tower that I guessed, for the first time, from whom the summons had come. When I had been brought to the chamber, my guess was confirmed; for it was Essa herself who opened the door to me. As for the Avakalimin, he took up station outside.

That evening, Essa was wearing rather plain attire—a short brown dress with full sleeves, over a linen chemise. She had schooled herself to conceal her emotions on most occasions, but was not bothering to do so now. At first glance, I could see that she was troubled in mind; equally I could perceive that my arrival was occasioning her considerable relief.

'Come inside quickly, Simon; I do not want your visit here to be known. The soldier can be trusted; yet, see, Dan Wyert is here also, so that if it *does* become known, there can be no cries of scandal.'

I glanced about me interestedly. The chamber walls were gay with tapestries; there was fresh, clean straw on the floor and a hanging-enshrouded bed set against the further wall. Dan was sitting on a stool, his crutches propped against the wall beside him. His face was pale and a little drawn, so that the lines of age were emphasized, but he greeted me cheerfully enough.

'Here I am again, Master Simon. Like a bad farthing in a merchant's purse, I'm forever appearing when least wished for!'

'Why, it's good to see you, Dan! I'd been trusting to visit you again, but 'tis several days since I've had the opportunity to cross the Lemmeshind. How are matters with you?'

'Passing well, master; passing well. But the Princess, she's much to say to you and little time. Let her talk, if you will, and pay no heed to me. I know her case, but 'tis not for such as me to advise her.'

Dan relapsed into silence, drawing in upon himself as a hedgehog does into a ball when it wishes to retreat from the happenings about it. Nor did Dan speak again during my visit; indeed, we came soon to forget he was there.

Essa gestured to me to sit down on one of two other stools and perched herself upon the third, in the fashion of a bird ready to take flight at the least alarm. The tension of her nerves was indeed patent. When she spoke, it was in a breathless rush.

'Simon, most urgently I require the counsel of a friend—a friend who knows the truth about me. I cannot talk with Avran, through a cause that I suspect you may appreciate. For other reasons—or mayhap, for the same reason—I cannot confide in Sir Robert.' She hesitated, then said: 'Can you aid me? Will you grant me the favour of your advice?'

'Certainly I shall, though I am not sure of its value; I have no great wisdom, as you must be well aware. As for knowing the truth about you—yes, I believe I know much of it, yet there are other matters at which I can only guess.'

She looked at me steadily for a moment, then dropped her eyes. 'What do you know, Simon, and what do you guess?'

'I know that you are not a princess returned from the past—though I must confess you do make a most handsome princess! I know that you grew up in a camp of robbers and that your father was their chirurgeon. If I recall his name rightly—for I have heard it only once—it was Lerenet Falquen.'

I paused reflectively, then went on: 'As to my guesses—well, I am guessing that your father was one of the tazlantenar, one of the "rootless ones" who have served their Safaddnese masters faithfully across so many centuries, without ever quite becoming recognized as Safaddnese. I guess also that your mother was a Safaddnese of pure birth and that, after she and your father had fallen in love, the two of them fled away together, to evade the harsh penalties that the discovery of their love would have occasioned.'

'The execution of the father, the humiliation of the mother, and the exposure of their baby, at birth, on a hillside so that death might take it.' Essa seemed to be reciting a familiar, bleak lesson. 'Yes, those laws are harsh. Your guesses are good so far, Simon. What else do you guess?'

'Only that they must have fled from one of the frontier letzestrei. I cannot be sure which, but I believe it likeliest that they fled from Desume.'

'And why that guess, Simon?' She was evidently startled.

'From the confidence of your comment on the hilltop above Inge-lot, that the frontier between Desume and Adira was closed.'

She smiled. 'You remember well, Simon! You are right in all your guesses and wrong in only one small point. My father's real name was not Falquen: that is only a name that he adopted. Did you not know that, in Reschorese, it means "fugitive"?'

'An appropriate choice.'

'Aye, too appropriate! When my mother died in the bleakness and heat of the Etolen Dunes only five short months after giving me birth, father decided that their own names were best forgotten. Even to you, Simon, I shall not divulge those names. Yet my mother was indeed of most noble birth and my father, being a chirurgeon, had climbed as high in Desume as might any mere tazlantel.'

'It does not surprise me, that you are of distinguished parentage.'

She smiled again. 'I have long known you to be my true friend, Simon. Do you grasp also the reasons why I cannot speak freely to Avran or Sir Robert?'

'Yes, I think so. As for Avran, we your other companions have all long perceived how deeply smitten Avran has been by your beauty and your intelligence. He is a true prince, in character as well as by birth. Without knowing it, I believe he recognizes in you the high qualities of his own kind.'

To my amazement she blushed. 'Thank you again, Simon. Please go on.'

'I think that, after hating him at first, you have come both to like and to respect Avran. I believe it to have been even conceivable, for a while, that you might have responded positively to his love. However, that time is gone past.'

She was staring at me fascinatedly. 'I thought myself skilled in concealing my emotions, Simon; yet you are probing them with the precision of a chirurgeon—or a magician! You disconcert me! What, then, about Sir Robert?'

About this I was more hesitant. 'At first I thought he was regarding you with the concern and affection of a father for his daughter. More recently—well, I have not ceased to doubt his affection for you—I believe he would gladly even die for you—but I have become less sure of the character of that affection.'

Essa gave a gasp that had a quality of real pain. 'Again you strike in the gold, Simon. You cause me to wonder whether I shall even need to expose to you my principal problem. Do you not know it already?'

'I think so. You have fallen quite out of love with Avran; and, as for Robin, you have never had for him anything more than the love of a daughter for her father. On the other hand, you have plunged deeply into love with my brother Richard.'

She gazed ceilingward and gestured helplessly with her hands. 'Indeed, Simon, all your arrows are finding their targets this night!'

I followed my stream of thought a little further. 'That, of course, was why you decided *not* to travel to Lyonesse after Avran and me; and it was why you chanced the hazards of going to Avakalim—to try to bring to Warrentown, certainly in defence of the city but also in defence of Richard, as mighty an army as could possibly be assembled. But why did you permit Robin to tread the same path?'

Her cheeks suddenly flamed. 'Because I was afraid, Simon—because I was afraid! I needed someone with me upon whom I might rely!'

'Even with Rakhamu to protect you?'

She relaxed and laughed. 'Yes, even with Rakhamu! And that was well—for, as you know, after driving off our ambushers, Rakhamu went away into the mountains to live out his own life. I was glad of that; he was becoming too large, and too potentially dangerous, to remain my companion for much longer. *Much* more dangerous than Sir Robert!'

I laughed in response, then said more soberly; 'I believe I understand your other problems also. However, this time, I think it more proper that you should voice them.'

She leapt to her feet and paced up and down, speaking as much to herself as me. 'Yes, you are quite right, I do love Richard: enough to desire passionately to be accepted as his wife, enough to wish to bear him children. I think I knew that, from the very moment of our first brief meeting in Kesbados.'

'What it is, to be tall and blond and handsome, and valiant withal!' I spoke teasingly, to try to restore Essa to calm. 'How much better than being small, and dark, and easily overlooked!'

My device worked admirably. She turned about and laughed, then perched herself again on her stool. 'Yet small, dark men can be valiant also, Simon—and even very attractive! Well, my first problem is to learn whether your brother would so much as consider taking me to wife.'

'As to that, you need have no doubt,' I said dryly. 'Surely you have noticed that, when in your presence, Richard has eyes for no-one else!'

She blushed and then laughed again, very gently. 'Yes, I must confess I had noticed! But would he wish to have as wife a woman whom he believes to be several *letzalei*, several centuries old—however young in appearance? My principal problem is that I owe my status and power to this belief by the Safaddnese that I am a creature from their past, returned to them after long imprisonment. Their trust in the legend has enabled me to achieve much that is good for Safaddné. If they knew the truth, those achievements might be overturned in a day. That is something I dare not—*dare* not—risk, Simon! Even my own future happiness matters less.'

'That is courageous of you.' I spoke seriously now. 'Yet there is something else that I perceive, and that I suspect you have also perceived. If you do retain your status and do marry Richard, now that he has attained such high rank—well, it will greatly facilitate the future union of Avakalim with Lyonesse.'

'Indeed it will. So, Simon, what should I do?'

I had made up my mind. 'Richard will have to learn the truth, that much is clear; and, maybe, my father also. Fortunately, they are men eminently capable of keeping their own counsel.'

'Yet how shall they be told?' Her voice sounded almost despairing. 'I cannot approach them privately—you know that.'

'Why then, I must do it for you, Princess! The task should prove simple enough.'

Essa smiled at me radiantly, then she leapt to her feet with the smoothness and grace of a bird taking flight. For a while she whirled round that small chamber in so swift and light a dance of happiness that the straws on the floor were scarcely disturbed. When she came to me and hugged me, once more I saw tears in her eyes.

'Avran was right, Simon. You are the truest of friends.'

There is little more to be told; and that is well, for it is time this part of my chronicle was drawn to a close. It was easy for me to talk privately to Richard; and, as I expected, what I told him caused him unbounded delight. Once again I found myself hugged, but my brother's hug was so rib-cracking that I felt sore for days afterward!

After that, the secret was broken to our father, who was hugely amused and quite delighted. He had early recognized that Richard had given his heart to Essa and, believing the legend, had been sorely troubled thereby. Now that he knew the truth, father proved an enthusiastic guide for Richard through the elaborate maze of rules that govern Safaddnese courtships. The finding of a path was made easier by the enthusiasm of Sir Arthur Thurlstone and the sympathetic instruction of letzudirar Balahir, whom I had liked from the beginning and came thereby to like even more.

Nevertheless, the arranging of the betrothal took several weeks, during which much else happened. Some Pavonarans were sent back to their own realm, to carry tidings of the overwhelming disaster that had overtaken their enemies and to arrange a peace. They did not go gladly, for the bright prospect of returning to their homes was overshadowed by the necessity to report what they considered a deep disgrace to Pavonara. Indeed, some pleaded so fervently to remain in Lyonesse that, rather to my surprise, Sir John Warren took them into his service.

The Lyonessans considered it certain that their proposals for peace would be accepted. A key component was that the Pavonarans remaining in captivity would be permitted to go to the Ulkurin, and, after burying the other Pavonaran dead, to take back their monarch's body to his capital, Seriadda, for entombment among his ancestors — a ritual quite as important to the Pavonarans as to the Safaddnese.

Indeed, there came swift word from Pavonara of the acceptance of the terms of peace — a peace designed to last for a whole letzal. However, the Lyonessans had good reason to distrust their neighbours over the mountains. The refortifying of Warrentown and the better guarding of the Lyonessan frontier were proceeded with immediately, regardless of those Pavonaran promises.

Then, with spring greening the meadowlands and the first flowers blooming on the mountain slopes, all of us journeyed to high-turreted Maradiela, for a meeting of letzaharei, letzudirarai and letzumaharei to decide finally the question of Lyonesse—or rather, the details of the new relationship between that realm and Safaddné, for its right to exist had been proved in battle.

At that meeting, a new Kingdom of Lyonesse was brought formally into being. It was to consist of three realms. Avakalim and Brelinderim would each retain much of their existing religious and administrative structure, with three rulers of equal stature, religious, military, and executive (letzudirar, letzahar and letzumahar) responsible for day-to-day decisions and a governing council to draft laws and determine policies. Predictably, Lyonesse itself became an earldom, to be ruled as before by Sir John Warren, but with its own governing council that would be headed by my father Sir William.

It was further agreed that, in all three realms, any person should have the right of choice whether to worship the Nine Gods or the One—a remarkable achievement, when one recalled the violence of past animosities. When he learned of this, Avran was sure that the Safaddnese religion would pass soon into oblivion. However, though as impressed as he by this ruling, I was less sure of its outcome; for I knew the worship of heathen gods to be still persisting in England, even under the ban of the Church and even after many centuries.

Avran had by then accepted that Essa was not for him. That he was heartstricken, I knew; but he was keeping himself so busy that few others can have perceived it, engaging in discussions of the history of the northern lands, limning maps and making copious notes. Yet he was avoiding both Essa and Richard. Nor did my brother find much time for me in those days. That was understandable, since he was busy with the formulation of new laws and policies, while naturally preferring to pass his few leisure hours in the company of his affianced wife.

Most of those laws and policies do not merit mention here; and indeed, of many I never learned details. A few, though, did interest me enough to be remembered. Surprising to me, but surpassingly sensible, was the decision that the new realm of King Arthur I of the House of Thurlstone-Esekh would have not one capital, but three—Maradiela, Tasbered, and Warrentown—and that King Arthur would be crowned successively in all three cities. However, that would not happen till the beginning of the next Safaddnese year, on three dates between 21st November, that year's first day, and 31st December, the last day of the first Safaddnese month, the month of Horulgavar. The new king and his train faced much winter travelling! In the meantime, a palace was to be built for King Arthur in a situation midway between the new capitals. The likeliest site seemed to be near Daryllsford on the River Berelind, just above its confluence with the Lemmeshind; but that question was still to be decided.

On the penultimate day of that momentous meeting of letzaharei, the betrothal of Princess Hiludessa of Avakalim to Richard Branthwaite of Lyonesse was proclaimed. It was announced that the marriage would take place according to Safaddnese ceremonial, in the castle of Maradiela on the second day of July. That is an auspicious date for weddings, in the view of the Safaddnese, for it is in the middle of the month of Radaionesu, god of fruitfulness. Five days afterward, Hiludessa and Richard would be wedded again according to Christian ceremonials, in Warrentown. Thenceforward, marriages solemnized under either rite would be acceptable in all parts of Lyonesse.

Naturally enough, this tiding caused much rejoicing, generating a mighty celebration during which all eyes—including my own—were on that couple, though their own eyes were only for each other. While that celebration was at its height, however, I was surprised to be summoned away by an urgent messenger.

When I entered the tower room to which I had been taken, I received another surprise; for there were Sir Robert Randwulf, indreletzahular of Safaddné and dakhletelar of Ayan, and Avran Estantesec, indreslef of Sandastre and also dakhletelar of Ayan, both of whom should surely have been at the feast! Moreover, both of them appeared profoundly glum.

It was not hard to me to guess the reason for their leaving the celebration or for their mood; yet I pretended I had not done so.

'Why, whatever are you doing here, Robin and Avran? I had thought you'd be in the great hall, busy toasting my brother and his future bride!'

Avran eyed me bleakly, but Robin smiled in a rather embarrassed fashion.

'Aye, and so, no doubt, we should be, for surely we both wish them well. Yet we felt an urgent need to discuss plans with you, Simon. This gathering is to end tomorrow. The letzaharei and their warriors will return to their letzestrei and we, along with Sir William and Sir John, have been bidden to ride back to Warrentown.'

I eyed my friend in puzzlement. 'You tell me only what I know.'

'So I do; so I do! Yet, bethink you, Simon; why should we direct our steps northward again, when our true path lies southward? It would merely cost us sixty leagues of unnecessary riding and the time of many days. Would it not be better for us to remain here in Maradiela, planning and preparing for our own journey; or, mayhap, to travel with the new King to Tasbered?'

I collapsed onto a stool and found that I was rubbing my brow and cheeks in sheer astonishment.

'But . . . but, do you not desire to stay and witness the two marriages? Do you not wish also to participate in the three coronations? We have been promised duties of honour.'

'Oh come, Simon!' Robin was smiling patiently at me, as might a tutor encouraging some slow-witted pupil to strive to comprehend a lesson. 'Surely you do not desire to pass another winter in these mountains? To stay for the coronations is wholly out of the question—surely you must appreciate that?'

'Yes, I suppose I do. But—the weddings?'

'Even to stay for the weddings might be dangerous, if we wish to traverse the mountains before evil weather closes in. Yes, I know, the snow does not come till October or later. However, they tell me that here, as in England, August is often a month of heavy rain and bad travelling conditions, while certainly we dare not chance delaying our departure till September.'

'But—my father and my brother; I'd hoped to spend much more time with them!' This was almost a wail of anguish.

Avran spoke for the first time. 'And Ilven? Sixteen full months are past already, since we set forth from Sandarro. Even if we were to leave here tomorrow, we could scarce hope to be back before next year's beginning. Do you not wish to return again to the arms of your own betrothed wife?'

'Yes, of course I do! You know that, Avran. Yet—well, my father had spoken of ships coming to Warrentown from Bristol. Could we not plan to sail on one of those ships?'

Avran winced. 'You know well my views on sea travel, friend! Well, I suppose I *might* contemplate taking ship, if need pressed; but where will those ships be going? Not to Sandarro, for sure; nor indeed have I heard of their voyaging to any other Rockalese ports, but only to England. Moreover, for my part, I wish the Princess well but—no, I cannot find in my heart any desire to witness her marriage to another.'

So evidently disconsolate was he, my companion of so many weary leagues, that I reviewed my own concerns and found that they did me small credit. Moreover, I had seen a reflection of Avran's distress in Robin's face. These were my friends, who had risked their lives repeatedly in enabling me to fulfil my own desire by finding again my father and brother. It was time, now, for me to reciprocate. I spoke remorsefully.

'My sincerest apologies, Avran my friend; I have not been thinking clearly. Well, then, shall we adopt your second suggestion, Robin— that we travel to Tasbered with the King? Mayhap my father might accompany us, for I believe I can persuade him to bend his steps that way. And from Tasbered we can strike southward. That will furnish us with a fresh path, for personally I am not eager to re-tread the old one.'

Avran drew himself together and shook himself, like a dog emerging from a cold river; then he gave me a smile such as I had not seen on his face in many days. Robin was smiling also.

'Indeed, Simon, I find that my feet are itching to tread new paths; life here is becoming altogether too placid! I consider your suggestion to be an excellent one. What think you, Avran? You agree? Very well, then!'

I rose. 'Please excuse me, friends. I must return to the celebration—and perhaps, later, you'll join it also?'

I had made my commitment; there could be no retreating from it. When I left the chamber, that fact was troubling me; but it did not do so for long. Why, this meant that soon I would be returning toward Sandarro and Ilven—Ilven! Suddenly my thoughts were singing.

Glossary of Rockalese Words

All Rockalese words are defined when first used in this account. However, for the convenience of any reader who finds them hard to remember, they are brought together here for ready reference. Although most words herein are from the Safaddnese language (Saf.), some are used also from Reschorese (Resch.), while a few words from Sandastrian (Sand.), the language most familiar to Avran and Simon, are cited in comparison. Though some gods of the Safaddnese pantheon gain no direct mention herein, the names of all are listed, for completeness's sake.

A   **acha** (*pl.* **achiei**), *n.* temple (Saf.)

    aghar (*pl.* **agharen**), *n.* robber, thief (Resch.)

    akla, *pron.* what (used interrogatively only: cf. Resch. **akha**) (Saf.)

    aliite (*pl.* **aliiteyen**), *n.* thanks, thankfulness (Resch.: Saf.)

    ameral (*pl.* **ameralen**), *n.* small, long-bodied and short-legged carnivore of the high moors and mountains of northern Rockall; pelt grey with black spots in summer, white with black spots (cf. ermine) in winter, when it is much sought for its fur (Resch.: Saf.)

    ang, *suff.* man of (cf. Resch. *eng*) (Saf.)

    asdiesh (**asdyesh**), *adv., n.* yes (cf. Resch. **asda**) (Saf.)

    ast, *suff.* belonging to a place (Saf.)

    asunal (*pl.* **asunalar**), *n.* lake (Resch.: Saf.)

    azhular, *v.* to rescue, save (Saf.)

B   **balahir** (*pl.* **balahiriei**), *n.* strong breeze (Saf.)

    batavinar, *v.* to startle, astonish (Resch.)

    baz, *adv.* here (Resch.: Sand.)

    bazan, *adv.* here (cf. Sand.: Resch. **baz**) (Saf.)

    Beladnen, *n.* or *adj.* pertaining to, or a member of, the southernmost of the three principal **Veledreven** tribes: resident in the south-eastern region of the Northern Mountains, between the Chaluwand and Warringflow (Perringvane) Rivers (Resch.: Sand.)

    branath (*pl.* **branathen**), *n.* sabre-toothed carnivore of the Northern Mountains; fur honey-brown, with darker brown streaks, in summer, creamy white, with grey-brown streaks, in winter; size and build like a tiger; solitary and ferocious (Resch.)

    branzhat (*pl.* **branzhaten**), *n.* branath, *q.v.* (Saf.)

D   **dakheslevat** (*pl.* **dakheslevatei**), *n.* realm: applied to a kingdom, a principality or a **letzestre**, but not to an earldom or other smaller feoffdom (Saf.)

dakhletel (*pl.* **dakhletelei**), *n.* unit of 810 soldiers (Saf.)

dakhletelar (*pl.* **dakhletelarei**), *n.* the commander of a **dakhletel**: there can be no more than nine such commanders in the army of any **letzestre** (Saf.)

dakhletzavat (*pl.* **dakhletzavatei**), *n.* the Council of Nine—three soldiers, three artisans and three priests—governing a **letzestre** (Saf.)

dakhletzel (*pl.* **dakhletzelei**), *n.* period of 99 years (Saf.)

dakhletzelkrayet (*pl.* **dakhletzelkrayetai**), *n.* religious festival of nine days at the beginning of each 999-year period; the greatest of Safaddnese festivals (Saf.)

dakhmen (*pl.* **dakhmeyen**), *n.* a ruler, usually a king (Resch.: Saf.)

dakhmenat (*pl.* **dakhmenatei**), *n.* kingdom (Resch.: Saf.)

Daltharimbar, *n.* god of the winds in the Safaddnese nonarchy of deities: the particular god of Darega (Saf.) His **letzental**, of 41 days, is from 31st August to 10th October of our calendar.

dalu, *pron.* or *adj.* that; used to indicate a person or thing (Resch.: Saf.)

darazar, *v.* to mistake, be in error (Resch.: Saf.)

daruman, *adv.* greatly, enormously (Resch.: Saf.)

datsemar, *v.* to travel a definite path; go in a particular direction (Resch.: Saf.)

devletel (*pl.* **devletelei**), *n.* a unit of two **letelei**, i.e. 18 soldiers (Saf.)

devletelar (*pl.* **devletelarei**), *n.* the officer in charge of a **devletel** (Saf.)

dirar (*pl.* **dirarei**), n. priest (Saf.)

dlaluhanzar (*pl.* **dlaluhanzarei**), *n.* a unit of ninety **letelei**, i.e. 810 soldiers (Saf.)

dratseyar, *v.* to think, consider, ponder (cf. Resch. **dratsehar**) (Saf.)

duvai (*pl.* **duvaien**), *n.* child (Saf.)

E   **Edaénar**, *n.* god of the sea in the Safaddnese nonarchy of deities: the particular god of Vasanderim (Saf.) His **letzental**, of 40 days, runs from 11th February to 22nd March of our calendar.

efredat, *n.* brown spirit, much like brandy but with a smokey taste, distilled from cadarand nuts (Resch.: Saf.)

ehekh (*pl.* **ehekiyen**), *n.* man (cf. Resch. **eyek**) (Saf.) N.B. Not used, in the plural form, of men and women together, for which see **estref**)

ekzar, *v.* to exist, be (Saf.)

eslef (*pl.* **eslevei**), *n.* prince (Resch.: used rarely in Saf.)

eslevat (*pl.* **eslevatai**), *n.* principality (Resch.: used rarely in Saf.)

estref (*pl.* **estrevei**), *n.* person, citizen (Resch.)

evrekhar, *n.* shining coppery-red metal [orichalcum of the ancients] (cf. Sand. **evragar**) (Saf.)

evyé, *adv.* or *conj.* why (Resch.: Saf.)

F falquen (*pl.* falqueyen), *n.* fugitive (Resch.)

faruzlaf (*pl.* faruzlavai), *n.* noble rank, equiv. to count or earl (Resch.: Saf., but a title only of foreigners in the latter language)

ferekh (*pl.* ferekhar), *n.* hill, mountain (Resch.: Saf.)

fereyek (*pl.* fereyekar), *n.* an isolated, very high mountain (Resch.: Saf.)

G Gadarran, *n.* or *adj.* pertaining to, or a member of, the most central of the three principal Veledreven tribes; resident on the eastern flank of the Northern Mountains (Resch.: Saf.)

galatar, *v.* to conduct, bring (a person) (Resch.: Saf.)

galiiletelar, *n.* the title of **Horulgavar**, leader of the Safaddnese nonarchy of deities (Saf.)

Gamvalessdar, *n.* god of animals in the Safaddnese nonarchy of deities; the particular god of Omega (Saf.) His **letzental**, of 41 days, runs from 2nd May to 11th June of our calendar.

gazhalkrayet (*pl.* gazhalkrayetai), *n.* religious festival held on the odd day between each five-year period in the Safaddnese cycle of years (Saf.)

gherek (*pl.* gherekelei), *n.* falcon of the Northern Mountains; size large; plumage cerulean blue above, creamy white beneath; wings acutely pointed, tail long. Considered to signify good fortune (Saf.)

ghorotel (*pl.* ghorotelei), *n.* companion, associate (Resch.: Saf.)

gradakh (*pl.* gradakhar), *n.* a violent storm (Saf.)

H Halrathhantor *n.* god of the rains and of terrestrial waters in the Safaddnese nonarchy of deities; the particular god of Ayan (Saf.) His **letzental**, of 41 days, runs from 23rd March to 1st May of our calendar.

hanzar (*pl.* hanzarei), *n.* messenger (Saf.)

hir, *adj.* strong (Resch.: Saf.)

Horulgavar, *n.* leader (**galiiletelar**) of the gods and god of the Earth in the Safaddnese nonarchy of deities; the particular god of Aracundra (Saf.) His **letzental**, of 41 days, begins the Safaddnese year, running from 21st November to 31st December of our calendar.

I igia, *conj.* and (cf. Sand. iga: Resch. igha) (Saf.)

ilai, *pron.* our (cf. Resch. ilal) (Saf.)

indreletzahular, *n.* 'rescuer of the princess': unique honorific title granted to Sir Robert Randwulf (Saf.)

indreletzar (*pl.* indreletzarei), *n.* princess: title applied to the unmarried daughter of a **letzahar** (Saf.)

K khadutar, *v.* to receive tidings or information (Saf.)

kre, *pron.* she (Resch.: Saf.)

ksasaskever (*pl.* ksasaskevren), *n.* venomous snake of the Northern Mountains, with grey skin mottled with small black marks in a variable and irregular pattern; sometimes used in divination by priests (Saf.)

L   **lakulet** (*pl.* **lakuletai**), *n.* ninety-nine persons (Saf.)

lakuletzel (*pl.* **lakuletzelei**), *n.* period of 99 years (Saf.)

lakuletzelkrayet (*pl.* **lakuletzelkrayetai**), *n.* religious festival of nine days at the beginning of each 99-year period (Saf.)

laskatal, *n.* one thousand (Saf.)

laskatalad, *n.* many thousands; an infinite number (Saf.)

latletelar (*pl.* **latletelarei**), *n.* a commander of nine **letelei** i.e. 81 soldiers (Saf.)

letel (*pl.* **letelei**), *n.* a squad of nine soldiers, the basic unit of the Safaddnese army (Saf.)

letelar (*pl.* **letelarei**), *n.* a soldier leading a **letel** (Saf.)

letkran (*pl.* **letkranen**), *n.* one of nine divisions of the hours of night, each of uniform duration but varying with the seasons (Saf.) Each **letkran** is considered under the control of a particular Safaddnese deity.

letpra (*pl.* **letpraien**), *n.* one of nine divisions of the hours of daylight, each of uniform duration but varying with the season (Saf.) Each **letpra** is considered under the control of a particular Safaddnese deity.

letzahar (*pl.* **letzaharei**), *n.* the elected ruler of a **letzestre**; may be a soldier, an artisan or (in Paladra, always) a priest (Saf.)

letzal (*pl.* **letzalei**), *n.* period of nine years (Saf.)

letzelkrayet (*pl.* **letzelkrayetai**), *n.* religious festival lasting nine days at the beginning of each **letzal** (Saf.)

letzental (*pl.* **letzantalai**), *n.* one of the nine divisions of the year, being either of 40 or 41 days' duration (Saf.)

letzesahar (*pl.* **letzesaharei**), *n.* the wife of a **letzahar** (Saf.)

letzestre (*pl.* **letzestrei**), *n.* 'ninth-realm'—one of the nine divisions of Safaddné (Saf.)

letzudirar (*pl.* **letzudirarei**), *n.* high priest of a **letzestre** (Saf.)

letzuletelar (*pl.* **letzuletelarei**), *n.* commander of the armies of a **letzestre** (Saf.)

letzumahar (*pl.* **letzumaharei**), *n.* leader of the artisan class of a **letzestre** (Saf.)

lindel, *adj.* principal, main (Resch.: Saf.)

lokassiar, *n.* to see (cf. Resch. **lokhassar**) (Saf.)

M   **mahar** (*pl.* **maharei**), *n. lit.* artisan or craftsman: but applied to all workers other than soldiers and priests (Saf.)

mel, *pron.* me; myself (Resch.: Saf.)

Mesnakech, *n.* god of enchantment, sorcery and evil in the Safaddnese nonarchy of deities; the particular god of Paladra (Saf.) His **letzental**, of 41 days, ends the Safaddnese year, running from 11th October to 20th November.

N **navalir,** *adj.* courteous; kind (Resch.: Saf.)

navalirlinar, *v.* to be kind (cf. Resch. **navalirlar**) (Saf.)

nuszudirar (*pl.* **nuszudirarei**), *n.* priest of second rank in a **letzestre** (Saf.)

O **Oburnassian,** *adj.* or *n.* pertaining to, or a member of, the larger of the two major racial groups of the Northern Mountains, usu. stocky, brachycephalic to mesocephalic, brown-haired and brown-eyed (Resch.: Saf.)

P **padim** (*pl.* **padmen**), *n.* dwelling; home (Resch.: Saf.)

padmai, *adv.* homeward (Resch.: Saf.)

Petamedru, *n.* god of the moon and the stars in the Safaddnese nonarchy of deities; the particular god of Avakalim (Saf.) His **letzental**, of 40 days, runs from 1st January to 10th February of our calendar.

praduvai (*pl.* **praduveyen**), *n.* 'day-child', whose birthday places him or her under the governance of a particular god in the Safaddnese nonarchy of deities (Saf.)

pran (*pl.* **pranen**), *n.* day (Resch.: Saf.)

prasal (*pl.* **prasalen**) *n.* goat-like herbivore of the high Northern Mountains, with a shaggy, coarse coat and a single horn curving upward and forward from its brow, dividing into a T-shape at its tip. Horns prized as drinking cups (Saf.)

Q **quetelu** (*pl.* **quetelain**), *n.* horse-like herbivore with single long, spiralling brow-horn; cloven-hoofed, otherwise cf. unicorn; pelage black (cf. Sand.: Resch. **xalihu**) (Saf.)

R **rad,** *prep.* to, into (Resch.: Saf.)

Radaionesu, *n.* god of fertility and healing in the Safaddnese nonarchy of deities; the particular god of Brelinderim (Saf.) His **letzental**, of 40 days, runs from 12th June to 21st July of our calendar.

rafenu (*pl.* **rafneyen**), *n.* antelope-like forest herbivore having two nasal and two brow horns; nasal horns directed outward, brow horns five-tined with three foremost tines curving and moderately long, two rear tines shorter and straight; pelage walnut-brown, flecked with creamy spots; used as a mount and capable of simple telepathic exchanges with its rider (Resch.)

rakhamu (*pl.* **rakhameyen**), *n.* holy warrior (Saf.: archaic)

Reschorese, *adj.* or *n.* 1. pertaining to, or a member of, the large **Oburnassian** tribe occupying the central southern region of the Northern Mountains; 2. the language of that region; 3. pertaining to, or a citizen of, the Kingdom of Reschora.

S **Sachakkan,** *adj.* or *n.* pertaining to, or a member of, the smallest of the three **Oburnassian** tribes, occupying the extreme southeast region of the Northern Mountains and adjacent plains between the Warringflow (Perringvane) and Green Rivers (Resch.: Saf.)

Safaddné, *n.* the nine Safaddnese **letzestrei** (Saf.)

Safaddnese, *adj.* or *n.* 1. pertaining to, or a member of, the formerly large **Oburnassian** tribe occupying the northwestern, northern and north central region of the Northern Mountains; 2. the language of that region (Resch.: Saf.)

Seledden, *adj.* or *n.* pertaining to, or a member of, the northernmost of the three **Veledreven** tribes, occupying the extreme northeast region of the Northern Mountains and the island of Aetselor (Resch.: Saf.)

sesleltas (*pl.* **sesleltasai**) *n.* a broad-leaved plant growing in deep marshes in the Northern Mountains. Its leaves, thick and fleshy with very prominent veins, are dried and cured to make **seslelteven** (Saf.)

sesleltef (*pl.* **seslelteven**), *n.* 'snow-shoes' made from the dried and cured, leathery leaves of the **sesleltas** (Saf.)

sevdru (*pl.* **sevdreven**), *n.* antelope-like herbivore having two forwardly-directed nasal horns and two brow horns, branching twice symmetrically in Y-fashion so that each horn has four tines; pelage grey, with white underparts and central white line down neck and back; used as a mount and capable of simple telepathic exchanges with its rider (Sand.)

stalusar, *v.* to listen (Resch.: Saf.)

T **taman,** *n.* truth (cf. Sand. **talum;** Resch. **talma**) N.B. never used in a plural form, all truth being considered one. (Saf.)

taron (*pl.* **taronen**), *n.* fish-eating sea-bird of Rockall's northern shores; plumage white with flight feathers edged in yellow; body short and chunky; neck short; bill long; bill and feet greenish-black (Saf.)

taslutar, *v.* to answer, respond (Saf.)

tavarar, *v.* to travel, move (Resch.: Saf.)

tazlantil (*pl.* **tazlantenar**), *n.* a 'rootless one'; a second-class citizen of Safaddné. May be 1. a man or woman taken in childhood by **Safaddnese** rulers, brought up by them and sent away to serve them in a place other than his or her own birthplace; 2. the child of two **tazlantenar**; 3. orig. the child of a **Safaddnese** father and **tazlantil** mother (later, the child of such a union was accepted as **Safaddnese**); 4. the orphan child of a **tazlantil** father and **Safaddnese** mother, its parents slain as punishment (Resch.: Saf.)

tef (*pl.* **teven**), *n.* leaf (Saf.)

Tera-ushlu, *n.* god of the sun and of dryness in the Safaddnese nonarchy of deities; the particular god of Desume (Saf.) His **letzental,** of 40 days, runs from 22nd July to 30th August of our calendar. (Saf.)

trasalyei!, *v.* hail! (cf. Resch. **trasalé!**) (Saf.)

U **udirar** (*pl.* **udirarei**), *n.* high priest (Saf.)

ul, *pref.* without, lacking (Saf.)

umahar (*pl.* **umaharei**), *n.* leading artisan or craftsman: see also **mahar** (Saf.)

ushazar, *v.* to praise (Resch.: Saf.)

uvudu (*pl.* **uvudain**), *n.* herbivore of Northern Mountains; very sheep-like, but hornless and having three hooves on each foot; fleece dark in colour; gregarious and sometimes domesticated; wool and skin used extensively for clothing (Resch.: Saf.)

V **vaz**, *adv.* here (Resch.: Saf.)

vazatié, *n.* greeting, welcome (lit. 'We're pleased to receive you'; cf. Sand. **bazatié**) (Resch.: Saf.)

vekhletel (*pl.* **vekhletelei**), *n.* a squad of three **letelei** i.e. 27 men (Saf.)

Veledreven, *adj.* or *n.* pertaining to, or a member of, the smaller of the two major racial groups of the Northern Mountains, inhabiting their eastern regions; usu. rather tall, dolichocephalic to mesocephalic, fair-skinned and with green or pale blue eyes; albinos not infrequent (Resch.: Saf.)

veludu (*pl.* **veludain**), *n.* antelope-like herbivore of Northern Mountains, rather short-legged, having three pairs of horns; short, sharp nasal horns, brow-horns of moderate length and unbranched, and horns at back of head dividing symmetrically into two tines, one directed forward, one upward; pelage dull grey in summer, with irregular lateral streaks of white and brown, but turning wholly white in winter; used as a mount and capable of simple telepathic interchanges with its rider, but less intelligent and less speedy on flat ground that a **rafenu** or **sevdru** (Resch.: Saf.)

vidukhar, *v.* to watch (Resch.: Saf.)

viré, *pron.* you (cf. Sand. **vre**) (Resch.: Saf.)

X **xakath** (*pl.* **xakathei**), *n.* short-legged, very broad-headed carnivore of Northern Mountains; nostrils flaring; eyes on top of skull and large; central ridge of bony plates down back; hide greyish tan with dark longitudinal streaks in summer, turning white with grey streaks in winter; four rows of differentiated pointed teeth, the outer two in use, with lateral tooth replacement by whole row. Gregarious, congregating in large numbers in late autumn or early spring for southward or northward migration; but hunting packs usu. do not exceed two score members in summer and are often smaller in mid to late winter (Resch.: Saf.)

Y **yildrih** (*pl.* **yildrihen**), *n.* broad, flat-bottomed boats propelled by two or more oarsmen; used by the boat people of the Mentone, Aramassa and Atelone river systems (Resch.)

Z **zahar** (*pl.* **zaharei**), *n.* lord (Resch.)

zahuar, *v.* to rescue (Saf.)

zakhatil (*pl.* **zakhatilnen**), *n.* stranger, foreigner (cf. Resch. **zakhafin**) (Saf.)

zestre (*pl.* **zestrei**), *n.* lordship, realm (Saf.)

zha, *pron.* they (cf. Sand.: Resch. za) (Saf.)

zhada (*pl.* zhaden), *n.* all, the whole (Saf.)

zhadis, *adj.* whole, complete (Saf.)

zhatar, *v.* to rule (Saf.)